"A brilliant and nasty piece of joyful ambiguity that I loved deeply. What a marvelous and unexpected bunch of female characters, in particular. With this one, William Boyle vaults into the big time, or he damn sure should." —Joe R. Lansdale, author of the Hap & Leonard series

"It's the women who make this novel such a great read. They are glorious and mad, vulnerable, so human, and very, very funny." —Roddy Doyle, author of *The Commitments*, *The Van*, *Paddy Clarke Ha Ha Ha*, *The Woman Who Walked Into Doors*, and *Smile*

"*A Friend Is a Gift You Give Yourself* is a thunderous locomotive of a novel, driven by remarkable characters and sparkling dialogue. A treat for fans of neo-noir, it's brimming with dark wit and piercing insight. Highly recommended." —Stuart Neville, national bestselling author

"One thing to appreciate about William Boyle's process is that, not unlike the late, great Charles Willeford, he takes his time, he doesn't rush the reader. This is a significant trait, more important than it sounds, the method of a confident writer. He builds his characters patiently, allowing them to adjust to one another, not merely throw lines to titillate the reader. In *A Friend Is a Gift You Give Yourself*, Wolfie Wolfstein is as comfortably intact a creature as any crime writer of recent vintage has put together. I gleefully anticipate the coming of a movie or better yet a TV series in her name." —Barry Gifford, author of *Sailor & Lula: The Complete Novels* and *The Cuban Club*

"Although William Boyle's new novel is clearly a love letter to his Brooklyn roots, (New York being one of the more prominently featured players in the book) the real 'Gift' here is his prose. The writing is so casual and honest that as a reader, you have no idea how much you have invested in these characters until it's too late to turn back. Your heart starts to race and you forget about the time. By the midway point of the book, I was rooting out loud for these

characters. The balance Boyle achieved of warmth between friends and the darkness that comes calling for them is nothing short of brilliant. I also love books with strong female leads, and with *A Friend*, you get three of them, moved along by dialogue that is second only to the master himself, Elmore Leonard. Hellova story. Hellova cast. Hellova writer."
—Brian Panowich, author of *Like Lions* and *Bull Mountain*

"Heartfelt, evocative, and bursting with indelible characters, William Boyle's *A Friend Is a Gift You Give Yourself* is not only an unpredictable and off-the-wall noir, but a meditation on the true meaning of friendship and family. Boyle has created another potent jolt of can't-miss New York crime fiction."
—Alex Segura, author of the Anthony Award-nominated Pete Fernandez Miami Mystery series

"As wildly funny and sweet as it is frenetic and harrowing, William Boyle's *A Friend Is a Gift You Give Yourself* is full of dark splendor. And the three wondrous and resilient women at its center are so richly etched, so powerfully voiced, you'll find yourself wanting to pull up to the dinner table with them, grab a glass, and tuck in. Imagine Martin Scorsese and David O. Russell collaborating with Gena Rowlands and Ellen Burstyn and making magic."
—Megan Abbott, author of *You Will Know Me* and *The Fever*

"Yowza, did I just maybe read a future crime fiction classic? Possibly. It has all the right elements. Great characters—two ex-porn stars, a 15-year-old girl, and a psycho with a sledgehammer—dialogue that tickles the ear, and a sense of place so vivid I thought I was reading in 3D. And the plot! I'm not going to say anything other than 500,000 dollars in a briefcase and a frisky octogenarian are involved. My only regret? I read the book way too fast, just couldn't stop turning the pages. Oh well, there are worse things in life."
—Pete Mock, McIntyre's Fine Books

A FRIEND
IS A GIFT
YOU GIVE
YOURSELF

ALSO BY WILLIAM BOYLE

THE LONELY WITNESS

GRAVESEND

A FRIEND IS A GIFT YOU GIVE YOURSELF

A NOVEL

WILLIAM BOYLE

NEW YORK LONDON

A FRIEND IS A GIFT YOU GIVE YOURSELF

Pegasus Crime is an imprint of
Pegasus Books, Ltd.
148 West 37th Street, 13th Floor
New York, NY 10018

First Pegasus Books hardcover edition March 2019

Interior design by Sabrina Plomitallo-González, Pegasus Books

ISBN: 978-1-64313-058-3

10 9 8 7 6 5 4 3 2 1

Printed in the United States of America
Distributed by W. W. Norton & Company, Inc.

For the libraries and video stores where I spent my childhood.

Remember, no matter what, it's better to be a live dog than a dead lion.
—Motel philosopher in Jonathan Demme's *Something Wild*
(screenplay by E. Max Frye)

Let the people know I am not dead.
—Lisa De Leeuw, in an interview with Richard Pacheco

We walked around looking for ghosts.
—Conor McPherson, *The Good Thief*

A FRIEND
IS A GIFT
YOU GIVE
YOURSELF

Dear Wolfie,

You hanging in there? House good? How's the Bronx treating you?

Monroe is a piece of shit right now. I need cigarettes. I usually keep a carton in the freezer, but I forgot to stock up, and I don't feel like going out. My mother's on the ropes. Eighty-nine yesterday and she can barely see or hear. We celebrated her birthday with some Hostess cupcakes I bought at the gas station up the street. She tells me about all the dead people who come over for parties that don't exist. Freaks me out.

She sees these little kids. Says they're sleeping on the couch. Says they won't eat. She cooks for them. "Cooks" is a strong word. She makes them butter sandwiches, mayonnaise sandwiches. The other day, I go out to ShopRite for two fucking minutes, I come home, and she's buttered all these pieces of paper and left them around the house. Just regular pieces of paper, no sliced bread, and she's slathered all this margarine on there, saying, "The kids must be hungry."

I tried going to church, you believe that shit? You picture me in church? I got worried, thinking I take Communion, the fucking host goes up in flames in my hand and the priest gets one of those crazy, I'm-in-the-presence-of-a-demon faces. I don't know why I went. My mother, she has these moments of clarity, and they're always about church. Usually this biddy brings her Communion in the morning once a week, but I got the notion church might be a break. A snooze, that's all it was. Found myself thinking of that girl-on-girl scene we did in that deconsecrated church in the Valley. I was a nun, you were a Jayne Mansfield knockoff. I'm looking at this stained-glass Jesus behind the altar, thinking of that. What a fucking life.

You know what I found the other day? A stack of your pictures in a green envelope full of tic-tac-toe games we must've played one bored afternoon. Not L.A. stuff. Your marks down in Florida, that's what the pictures are of. Like four or five of that one, Bobby. He was a sad case, and I almost feel sorry for him. He looks like someone drowned a sack of his beloved rabbits in all these pictures.

I also found my Stevie Nicks stub from the White Winged Dove Tour. Best night of our lives. If I had the opportunity to live one day over and over—like that movie Groundhog Day—it'd be that one. Everything was perfect. Me and you getting lunch at Rhonda's, our nails done after, hair done, drinks at Frolic Room, the show, later in Mac's limo with the champagne. And I'll tell you what: I really remember the stars that night. I close my eyes, I can still see the sky I was looking up at through Mac's moonroof. Magic forever.

Come visit me, huh?

Best bad love,

Mo

RENA

After Sunday morning Mass and her regular coffee date with her friend Jeanne at McDonald's, Rena Ruggiero is back on her block, Bay Thirty-Fifth Street. So strange to be from a block, to feel at home on only *your* block while all the others, even the ones directly surrounding you, feel so foreign. Her whole life spent on this block. Growing up in the house, staying through her time at Brooklyn College, and then moving into the upstairs apartment with Vic when they got married. And when her parents died, taking over the whole place. It was big for three people. Even bigger for one. Sixty-eight years the house has been in her family, bought eight years before she was born.

She stands out front now, as she often does, and considers the house's flaws. It needs new siding. That was a project Vic had been in the process of setting up before he was killed. Probably needs a new roof, too. The porch sags. Posts and railings need to be scraped and painted, a lot of the wood rotten. The windows are old. Too much cold seeps in. She could sell it—the

Chinese are buying up houses in the neighborhood like crazy—but selling seems like such a hassle.

And the stoop. She still sees Vic slumped there, as he was on that awful day nine years before. She remembers the exact way the blood pooled on the steps. She looks hard enough, she can still see spots where it has browned the cement forever. Poor Vic. Probably watching the pigeons on the roof of the apartment building across the street, Zippo the landlord guiding his kit in formation with a big black flag. And then Little Sal approaching with his gun raised.

Rena had been inside at the stove, frying veal cutlets. She heard the shot, figured it for a car backfiring, maybe some dumb kids with an M-80. She didn't come out until she heard screaming and sirens and tires screeching. Walking out of the kitchen, down the hallway, the way she remembers it, was all in slo-mo. She wasn't thinking something had happened to Vic. He was just sitting there; he wasn't off at work. The fear had always lingered in her, but it wasn't there just then. They had a ballgame to listen to, cutlets to eat. Little Sal was long gone when she made it to Vic.

Rena remembers how she crouched over him in the ambulance on the way to the hospital, crying, holding her rosary. Vic, who was in a bad business but had a soft voice and thoughtful brown eyes. His associates called him Gentle Vic. He'd raked it in for the Brancaccios. A huge earner. What had gone wrong had nothing to do with his work, just a beef with a punk, a kid named Little Sal trying to make a name for himself by knocking off a made guy. Shot Vic as he sipped on espresso, squash flowers from Francesca up the block in a ziplock bag on the step next to him.

Everyone knows about Vic, what he did, how he died, but no one talks to her about it in specifics. No one asks her what it's like to see your husband bleeding to death. Or what it's like to hose dried blood off your front stoop after burying the only man you've ever loved. The Brancaccios took care of her after the fact, paid for the funeral, gave her some money, but no one comes around anymore. She was never very tight with any of the other wives.

Rena goes inside and turns off the alarm. The alarm was Vic's idea, after some break-ins on the block back in the early nineties. He was gone a lot and wanted her to feel safe. She takes off her coat and puts on water for tea and then decides she doesn't want tea and shuts the burner. The phone is right next to the stove, an old yellow rotary mounted to the wall. A picture of her parents is encased in the plastic center of the dial. They're smiling. It's their thirtieth-anniversary dinner. They're younger in the picture than she is now.

Her friend Jeanne had to go and bring up Adrienne over coffee at McDonald's. Adrienne is Rena's daughter, who lives over in the Bronx. Rena hasn't seen her since Vic's funeral. Hasn't seen her granddaughter, Lucia, either. Lucia's fifteen now; she was six the last time Rena held her, in tears, standing in front of Vic's casket.

Rena wasn't happy when she found out—in the middle of everything else—all the details about Adrienne and Richie Schiavano, Vic's right-hand man, and she let it be known. Turned out they'd been an on-again, off-again thing since Adrienne was in high school. A kid, that's what Adrienne was when they started up. This all came out at the funeral. Rena was floored by the news. She couldn't believe it had gone on behind her back, behind Vic's back. She couldn't believe that Richie would disrespect their family like that. She couldn't believe that Adrienne was such a *puttana*. Sure, she had bigger things to worry about, but she channeled much of her anger toward Adrienne. A natural reaction. Still, Adrienne holds this grudge against her for speaking up about the relationship with Richie. Rena was just concerned with the order of things, that's all, what's right and not right in the eyes of God and everyone. She remains concerned.

But it goes back longer than that, too. Adrienne was always either embarrassed by her mother or hating her for something. Not right. Rena's more than a little sick in her heart over all of it, especially Lucia being caught in the crosshairs. High school age now and she doesn't even have a relationship with her grandma. Shame.

Rena picks up the phone and dials Adrienne. She's written hundreds of letters over the years, tried calling thousands of times.

One ring. Adrienne picks up. Rena hasn't heard her voice since the last time she tried calling a couple of months back. "Yeah?" Adrienne says, sounding sleepy.

"Adrienne? It's Mommy."

Click. Adrienne slamming the phone down without hesitation.

Rena hangs up and just stands there. She takes a few deep breaths. She'd prefer not to cry. She thinks about a horrible article from the *Daily News* she read the day before, about a man hacked to death with a machete on the D train. A machete. Thinking about it keeps the tears back. What kind of person thinks this way?

The doorbell rings. She wonders who it could be on a Sunday. Or any day, really. Maybe those *Watchtower* people. Or a real estate agent trying to get her to sell the house again. Sundays don't really matter anymore. Not what they used to be. Like everything else.

She goes into the hallway and sees a bulky figure through the tattered curtain on the window in the door. "Who's there?" she calls out, refusing to get too close.

Sound of throat-clearing. A man. "It's Enzio!"

She moves closer and pushes back the curtain to look outside. Her neighbor Enzio is standing there wearing a Members Only jacket, his hair slicked back, blowing his big nose with a white handkerchief. He's holding flowers in his free hand—daisies, her favorite. This is no coincidence. Over coffee, Jeanne had been hounding her to get a boyfriend again, saying she was only sixty and far from dead. All the eligible bachelors in the neighborhood had come up. Enzio from the corner was one. Eighty, if he's a day. He washes his beautiful old car with no shirt on in his driveway. He wears his shorts high, the button often undone over his belly. He calls her *baby* and *honey* and *dollface* when she passes his house. He's got the skeeviest smile.

"It's Enzio," he says again, softer this time. He tucks his handkerchief into his pocket.

"What do you want?" Rena asks.

"Just to talk."

"What's with the flowers?"

"Come on, open up, huh?"

She hesitates but makes a move toward the lock. She's what, gonna be afraid of a sad old man like Enzio? All he does is wash that car and read the racing forms in a booth at Mamma Mia across the street. A widower. But a different kind of widower. His wife, Maria, is fifteen years gone. Long as Rena knew her, Maria was a shut-in, wore a housedress and watched TV all day, doped on meds. Whatever the problem was, Rena was pretty sure it was made up. The whole neighborhood knew that Enzio ran around on Maria. Could've been that Vic had a goomar or two over the years, but he kept it quiet if he did, showed Rena respect. Still, everyone forgave Enzio his indiscretions. A wife like that, gone in the head, someone who'd totally cashed in her chips—well, a man needed a little excitement. Rena had always heard the gossip and didn't give it much thought. Disgraceful on his part, sure, but a wife had certain duties.

Enzio had a few out-in-the-open girlfriends over the years. Jody from the bank was one. Jody wasn't her real name. She was Russian. Pretty. It didn't last. Enzio was loaded but cheap. Jody found a guy who took her to Atlantic City every weekend and wasn't afraid to spend. Now Enzio is after Rena. The world in all its strangeness. She pulls the door open.

Enzio pushes the flowers at her. "Daisies," he says. "Your favorite."

She accepts them, but instead of hugging them to her chest, she lets them dangle from her closed fist. "You know that how?"

"A little angel told me, dollface." He smiles his terrible smile. She feels like she's never seen it this close before. His teeth are glommed up with food. His lips wormy. He's missed spots shaving around his mouth.

"Jeanne's a pain in my ass sometimes."

"Your friend has your best interests in mind. She knows I'm a good guy, a good catch. All these years, we're dancing around each other, and now here we are. Vic gone, Maria gone. Last two standing." He puts out his hands. "Don't get me wrong. I respect Vic. *Respected* him. Everyone did. 'God bless Vic Ruggiero,' I always said. Gentle Vic. Hero of the neighborhood. Can I come in or what?"

She steps aside and waves him in. "Come on, I guess."

He walks into the kitchen and takes off his jacket and folds it over a kitchen chair. They stand across from each other.

"You know me a long time," Enzio says. "You know I'm nice. You know I'll treat you nice."

"I bet you treated all the girls you ran around on Maria with real nice."

"Past is past, you know? The way I behaved was in direct correlation to Maria forsaking her wifely duties. The marital bed was cold. Ice-cold. And a man gets heated up. Besides, who we kidding over here? I got one foot in the grave. I'm trying to find someone for company. A nice dinner at Vincenzo's. Maybe a movie." He pauses, looks around. "You gonna offer me anything?"

"What do you want?"

"Coffee? Maybe a cookie."

"I've got instant coffee and Entenmann's."

"That's no way to live."

"It's not how I live. It's what I happen to have right now."

Enzio puts up his hands. Always with the hands up. "Okay, okay. Take it easy. Come over to my place. I've got good espresso and cookies from Villabate."

Rena finds a pitcher in a cabinet over the sink, fills it with water, and puts in the flowers. "Thanks," she says. "For these, I mean."

"See, I'm a nice guy. I'm not scared to buy flowers."

"They're pretty."

"See." He moves closer. "Come over to my place for coffee. I don't bite."

Rena touches the flowers and wonders where he got them. Probably the florist up on the corner. Vic always bought her daisies there after they fought. She wonders if Enzio ever saw Vic coming up the block with the flowers. Enzio and Vic rarely talked. Vic wasn't the chatty type, and Enzio knew better than to try to get deep. When they did talk out by the fence, Enzio passing on his way home from Eighty-Sixth Street, it was about garbage pick-up or someone parking illegally in a driveway or the Yankees. Strange how you could live on the same block as someone forever and barely know him beyond small encounters and through-the-grapevine gossip.

"I don't drink espresso," Rena says, forever remembering it as Vic's last drink. "It makes my heart race."

"A little won't kill you. Have an adventure."

"Drinking espresso's an adventure?"

"I have wine. Maybe we can share a little wine. Homemade. From Larry around the corner. You know Larry? Nino and Rose's son. He makes the good stuff."

"I don't drink wine."

"At all?"

"Not really. I used to have a glass at dinner when Vic and I would go to Atlantic City."

"Pretend you're in Atlantic City. Loosen up a little. Nothing better than a blast of good homemade wine."

Rena sits down at the table and puts her head in her hands.

"I upset you?" Enzio says.

"I don't know," Rena says.

"You don't know if I upset you?"

"That's what I said."

"If I said something wrong, I didn't mean to—"

"It's okay."

He comes over and rubs her shoulders.

"Please stop," she says.

"It's no good?" he says.

"I don't like it. I don't like being touched."

"At all?"

"No's no, okay?"

He takes his hands off her and lets out a big, gusty sigh.

Rena tenses up.

"You're a tough nut," he says. "You don't want any companionship? I'm just trying to be a nice guy here."

"Okay, okay," Rena says.

"*Okay?* What's *okay* got to do with it? I'm lonely. You're not lonely? We could be lonely together. Watch a movie. Drink some wine. Eat some cookies."

"Enough with the wine and cookies."

"A goddamn tough nut." He sits down across from her. "You want me to leave?"

"I don't care what you do."

"I'm not leaving unless you come with me, how's that?" He laces his fingers together and cracks his knuckles. It's loud, a tiny thundering, like stepping on Bubble Wrap. "Maybe I'll tell you a story? That's what I'll do. You know Eddie Giangrande? He was involved in that Fulton Market heist back in the seventies. He lives over on Twenty-Fifth Avenue. You know him, right? Sure you do. His wife's Madeleine. Vic must've crossed paths with him.

"Eddie, he's a big guy. Two-eighty, two-ninety. And he's a happy-go-lucky sort. Every time you see him, huge smile from here to here. Molars showing. Sure, why not? He made out big time with that heist. Never got collared either. Don't ask about the details, by the way. I know—I know a lot—but I'm sworn to secrecy." He mimes locking his mouth and throwing away the key. "Still, Eddie—with all he's got, I mean, what more's he want, right?—gets in with these Russians. The Godorsky brothers. They cross him; he crosses them. Again, the details aren't important. The short of it is he winds up out at Dead Horse Bay with a gun to the back of his head, the

Godorsky brothers telling him to make his peace with God. Don't repeat this story, by the way. This is for your ears only. I know you have experience keeping quiet with sensitive information."

Rena nods. "I won't tell anyone."

Enzio continues: "Good, thanks. So, Eddie, he thinks about Madeleine, he thinks about his kids, he thinks maybe he's gonna piss himself and then his brains'll be splattered on the beach, the end. But instead of pissing himself or begging for his life, he starts laughing. Like a goddamn clown. Just hardy-fucking-har. Excuse me. Just hardy-har-har, you know? Maniac stuff. The Godorskys are taken aback. They've never seen this. Eddie laughs harder. The Godorskys start arguing in Russian. They think maybe he's got something on them they don't know about. They turn on each other. Gun's off the back of Eddie's head. Now the one brother is pointing the gun at the other brother. The other brother takes out a gun and points it at the one with original gun. Then *bam*. They shoot each other. Just like that. Eddie gets up and looks around and the Godorskys are on their backs, choking on blood. Eddie laughs some more and then steals their car and goes home."

"What's the point of that story?" Rena asks.

"Laugh a little, that's what."

And she does laugh. Russian mobsters shooting each other like that. Jesus, Mary, and Saint Joseph. What a tale.

"There you go," Enzio says. "You've got a nice laugh. All these years, I've never heard you laugh, you know that?"

She's still laughing. Now she can't stop. She's looking across at Enzio, this old man who just told this ridiculous story, and she's noticing his elbows on the table, his flabby chin, hair under his nose and around his ears that he's also missed shaving, earlobes that dangle like melted coins, a little burst of blood vessels on his forehead.

"Okay, okay," Enzio says.

"I'm sorry," she says, trying to catch her breath. "I can't stop. I'm gonna pee my pants."

"Don't piss your pants."

"I can't—"

"Christ, what's so funny?"

She gasps. Tries to settle herself. Her laughter finally sputters to a stop. "Sorry. Just the whole thing." She waves her hands in front of her as if swatting away gnats. "I'm done, I swear."

"You're laughing at me?" Enzio asks.

"Not at all," Rena says.

"I'm no fool."

"I know. I mean, you wanted me to laugh, right?"

"Not like that."

She gets up. "I need some water. You want some water?"

"I don't like water."

Rena goes over to the sink and runs the tap, passing her hand through the stream to make sure it's cold enough. She takes a glass from the dish drain, fills it, and slurps down the water, her back to Enzio. "You're mad?" she asks. She doesn't particularly care if he is—he's just a neighbor to her anyway—but she feels bad for laughing at him. She feels bad he knows she was laughing at him. She wishes Vic was still alive for a lot of reasons, but mostly, right now, so she wouldn't have to deal with Enzio.

"I'm fine," he says, picking at his ear.

She runs more water into her glass and downs it. "I'll come with you to your house," she says, and she's not even sure why she says it. Maybe she knows it's the only way the tension will die.

"Yeah? Wine and cookies?"

"One glass. Maybe a cookie."

Enzio claps his hands together. "That's a start."

Rena places her glass in the sink slowly, hoping if she takes long enough Enzio will go away and she won't have to go with him on this, this . . . what else to call it but a *date*?

"You won't be sorry," Enzio says, grabbing his jacket. "I'm a gentleman."

"Famous last words," Rena says.

Enzio's house is just a few doors down, a two-family brick job. Enzio no longer rents out the downstairs. He tried about fifteen years ago and got into a bad situation with a bunch of gypsies. A Christmas wreath still hangs on the front door of the upstairs apartment, which is where he lives. An Italian flag dangles from a pole rigged on the ledge of a third-floor window. The flag is weather-bitten, ragged. The Virgin Mary in the front yard has a chipped nose. Next to her is a flattened garden that died with Maria. Enzio's near-mint 1962 Chevy Impala, driven sparingly, is under a blue tarp in the driveway.

They climb the short staircase up to the second-floor entrance. Enzio leaves his white Filas on a mat outside and asks Rena to take off her shoes.

"Really?" she says.

"I care about the carpets."

She nudges her feet out of her white Keds and kicks them onto the mat next to Enzio's sneakers. All these years, she's never been in his house. Not once. Not for coffee with Maria. Not anything.

It's exactly what she imagines. Totally from the past: green shag rug that's still in decent shape, plastic on the sofa. Elaborate vases. Paintings of vineyards and posters of Jesus on the walls. There's a heavy glass cigar ashtray on a coffee table covered in lace doilies and the smell of bad cologne in the air. The only thing out of place is the big-screen TV in the living room.

"You like the TV?" Enzio says, noticing her noticing it.

"It's big," she says.

"Sixty inches. Picture's great. Like having the movies in your house."

"I don't get these big TVs. Give me a little TV. That's fine. Why do I need to feel like I'm in a theater?"

"I'll show you the picture after. You'll be impressed."

Rena follows him into the kitchen. She takes a seat at the table. It's Formica, the top patterned with white and gold boomerangs. A saltshaker stands alone in the middle of the table, a hulking ring of keys snaked around it. She looks over at the refrigerator. No pictures, no magnets. Dirty dishes are toppled in the sink. Empty pizza boxes are stacked on top of the dish drain.

Enzio motions at the boxes and says, "The bachelor's life." He digs around under the sink and comes out with a dusty magnum of wine. He strips away the seal, humming, and uses a corkscrew key to yank the cork. He fills a couple of juice glasses, their flowered sides laced with smeary fingerprints, and gives one to her.

"Thanks," Rena says, lifting the glass up to her nose and taking a whiff.

"Larry does a great job with this," Enzio says. "He makes it down in his basement. I used to make it like that, but I got lazy. He's devoted." He comes over and sits across from her at the table, reaching out to clink her glass. "*Salute.*"

Rena doesn't clink back. She sips the wine. It's fruity and heavy.

"The good stuff, right?" Enzio says.

"Not bad," she says.

"Not bad, my ass." He takes a long slug. "You want a cookie? What kind? Savoiardi? You're a savoiardi girl, I can tell."

"I'm good."

"Come on, have a cookie." He gets up and opens the refrigerator. The white box of cookies is on the top shelf, wrapped carefully in a plastic Pastosa bag. Keeping cookies in the refrigerator was a big no-no for Vic.

"I'm good."

"You sure? I'm having one." He peels back the plastic, opens the box, and takes out a seeded cookie. He munches on it, cupping his palm under his mouth to catch the crumbs. "I'm lonely eating this alone. Have one."

"I'd appreciate it if you'd quit with the cookies. I want one, you'll be the first to know."

"To each his own." He turns and goes back into the living room. Starts fiddling around with the TV. The screen bleeps on. Bleeps? She's not sure of the word for whatever TVs do now when they turn on. Not bleeps, exactly; more futuristic than that. A big bubble opens up in the middle and then little dreamy rainbow raindrops flood the blackness.

"What are you doing?" Rena says from the kitchen.

"Enough with the slow dancing," Enzio says. "I'm putting something on for you."

"I'm gonna be impressed by your big TV?"

The screen is snow now.

And then it's not.

And then there are bodies. Smooth bodies, tangled, two men and a woman. She's blond and fake with silly boobs. The men are hairless, muscly in all the wrong ways, barbed-wire tattoos on their arms. Rena doesn't want to think about what they're doing, all of them involved like that.

"What is this?" she asks, standing up.

"My favorite kind of movie."

"Uh-uh. Nope." She shakes her arms and puts up her hands, as if she's just touched something skeevy, maybe a dead mouse in a trap. She keeps her eyes away from the screen, not wanting to catch another glimpse of the bodies. It's the first time she's ever seen pornography. Vic, if he ever whacked off, must've done it to old *Life* spreads of Sophia Loren, because Rena never found any dirty stuff in the house. Not even a *Playboy*.

"You don't like it?" Enzio says.

"No, I don't like it, sicko. I'm leaving." She's in the living room now, everything swirling, focused on making it to the front door without any unnecessary Enzio contact. It's weird to be walking around his house in her socks.

"Don't leave. Let's watch. You've lived your whole life like a prude; let it go."

Rena stops. "You're calling me a prude? You don't know me."

"I know you." Enzio's closer to her now, almost at arm's reach. "Loosen up, huh?"

"Fuck you, okay? You like that? You like me talking like that?"

Enzio puts up his hands. She can see the action on the screen behind his head. He says, "It's a nice movie. Nothing too crazy. I've got the wine—"

"Nice movie?"

"It's nothing strange."

"It's strange to me, okay?"

"I've got Viagra. We can have some fun."

"Excuse me?"

"Viagra."

"You're gonna take a Viagra and then we're gonna what? Watch this movie and have sex?"

Enzio shrugs. "Make love, yeah. I can satisfy you."

Rena's not sure if she should laugh again or continue storming out. What those bodies are doing now! Like some horrible painting of hell. He's really thinking she's going to go along with this? Crawl onto the couch and let him go to town? "I don't think so, Enzio," she says, so shocked that her voice feels full of restraint.

He moves toward her and puts his hand on her arm. "Think about it. You're gonna go back to your quiet house? We've got entertainment here. We could have real fun."

"Get your hand off me, please."

"I got this Viagra," he says. He pulls his hand away from her arm, reaches into his pants pocket, and fishes out a small blue pill. He pops it into his mouth and swallows it dry. "Don't you want to touch me? Don't you want to be touched?"

"I told you, I don't like being touched."

He's getting closer again, reaching for her.

She sidesteps him and picks up the heavy glass ashtray from the coffee table, holding it up in front of her chest with both hands. "Touch me again, I'll hit you with this."

"Rena."

"I'm serious."

"You'd hit me?"

And then he's smiling and his hand is on her waist. She can feel how rough and warm it is through her shirt.

"I'm about ready for some love," he says. "Aren't you?"

She lifts the ashtray over her head and then thwacks him across the head with it, hard as she can. A raw-meat sound comes with the impact. And there's a little spray of blood. He makes a noise, a small, prolonged one, like a balloon deflating. He spins and collapses toward the coffee table, his head slamming the edge on his way down. He crumples to the floor.

"Jesus Christ," Rena says to no one. "I told him not to touch me."

She drops the ashtray, blood mapping its bottom.

She looks at the ceiling. Closes her eyes.

Three, four minutes pass like that. A lifetime.

She squats next to Enzio. She looks closely at his back to see if he's breathing. Like the first six months with Adrienne. Watching the rise and fall of her baby's breathing. Paranoia and parenting so intertwined. But this is something different.

He's still breathing, but it's slow.

She thinks of a woman she saw on Bay Thirty-Fourth Street once. Just pushing her shopping cart along and then her feet went out from under her and she fell sideways, hitting her head against the sharp point of an old iron fence. Blood then, too. And slow, pained breaths.

The worst part is Enzio has wood from the Viagra. It's tenting up his pants.

The shininess of the movie draws Rena's attention back to the screen. Moans getting louder. Mechanical pounding. She watches to keep her eyes away from Enzio. She thinks maybe when she looks back at him next, he'll be sitting up, knuckling the blood from his brow, ready to apologize.

What's happening on the screen now mystifies her. They're moving like the oily wrestlers Vic used to love to watch.

Back to Enzio. More blood, pooling around his head on the green shag rug. Clotting darkly. The thick threads pimpled red.

"Jesus Christ," she says again.

She stands up and walks over to the TV and feels around on the side of it for a power button. She hits the volume controls first, and the noises from the movie get louder. She's not shaking. She feels like she should be shaking. She punches a couple of other buttons and finally powers down the TV, the nightmarish final image—the woman on all fours over one man, while the other drills her from behind—sputtering away.

Oppressively quiet now. She swears she can hear the blood leaking from Enzio.

Calling 911 doesn't occur to her.

She goes back to the kitchen and sits at the table. The wine Enzio poured for her is still there. As if it would be gone somehow. Dust specks float on the surface. She downs the rest and pushes the glass away. It's close to the edge. She pauses, but then thinks, *What the hell?* and pushes it farther. The glass falls from the table and shatters on the kitchen floor, a mess of splintery shards. She gets lost staring at the boomerangs in the Formica. She thinks of her house, of this house, of this block, this neighborhood, and decides she should just leave.

She doesn't have a car anymore. She sold Vic's Chrysler Imperial after he died and hasn't needed one. But Enzio's keys are right there in front of her.

If Enzio's not dead, he won't come after her. He'll be thinking she's still connected through Vic. All she's got to do is get on the horn. And it's true. Tell Vic's old crew this creep tried to rape her, he'll probably wind up being dismembered and buried somewhere out in Jersey.

And if he's dead—she's not checking, no way—she didn't mean to kill him. It was an accident. Hitting that table on the way down did the real damage. A man can't just put his hands on a woman like that. Self-defense, pure and simple. If he hadn't turned on that dirty movie and popped that pill and then touched her. What he said, to boot. She's not sorry. He's a dirty old man, but that's no excuse.

Those keys.

She can just get in the Impala and drive to the Bronx. Drive to Adrienne and Lucia. Come to them out of desperation. They won't be able to refuse her. Maybe something good can come of this.

Outside, the key glistens in her hand as she slips her shoes back on. It took some doing, sorting through the other keys on the ring, but the one for the Impala showed itself to her. She and Vic had an Impala back in the early days of their marriage—it was the car they drove to the Catskills for their honeymoon—and she recognized it immediately. A small key with a slot in it. Silver.

She pulls the tarp off the car, folds it as neatly as she can, and stuffs it in the garbage can chained to the front fence.

She wonders if anyone is watching her.

She looks up at the windows in the apartment building across the street. People move behind drawn shades, caught up in their own lives, as they should be. A bus on Bath Avenue wheezes to a stop. Some kids jump around outside the deli on the corner. Otherwise, Sunday quiet reigns.

No one is noticing her.

She stares at the car. It's been a while since she's seen it out from under the tarp. Crayon black and shiny. Rosary beads hanging from the rearview mirror.

Rena remembers how, on summer Saturdays, Enzio used to get in the car, start it up, back up to the edge of the driveway, and just sit there listening to WCBS for about thirty minutes while sunning the hood. Sometimes he'd check the oil and wipe the dipstick on a crusty rag he kept in his back pocket. He doesn't do that anymore.

She opens the driver's-side door and gets in behind the wheel. Red interior. The car smells like gas and grease and vinyl. She runs her hand over the dashboard, which Enzio cleans with expensive wet wipes that he buys at a crammed-to-the-gills automotive store on Benson Avenue. She adjusts the mirrors and starts the car. Shifting it into reverse, she lulls it out of the driveway, careful not to clip the nearby telephone pole.

At the end of the block, she turns left and heads for the Belt Parkway toward Long Island. From there, she knows she'll get on the Cross Island Parkway and then take the Throgs Neck Bridge. The car has a glowing radio. She searches the stations and settles for Lite FM.

WOLFSTEIN

SILVER BEACH, THE BRONX

Wolfstein is sitting in her yard on the paint-chipped bench next to the birdbath, smoking her last Marlboro 100 and drinking a Bud Light. Her neighbor from down the street, Freddie Frawley, wearing Yankees gear from head to toe, walks by out in the street with his St. Bernard. He waves at her.

"Wave all you want, Freddie," Wolfstein says. "Just don't let your dog shit in my yard again. The mound I cleaned up the other day, it was like a garden hose."

"That couldn't have been Freddie," Freddie says.

"Who names a dog after himself?"

"Freddie Junior—what's wrong with that?"

"Watch he doesn't shit in my yard again, okay?"

"Look, he's not shitting in your yard. You're a witness."

"*Now* he's not shitting in my yard. I go inside, who knows?"

Freddie heads away up Beech Place, shaking his head.

Wolfstein stares at her rosebushes. Looking good. She saw that kid from around the block, Billy Farrell, come onto her lawn and pick one for his little girlfriend the day before. She's got a harelip, the girlfriend. Goes to Preston. Let Billy have it. Fucking romance, sure, she'll sacrifice a rose for that.

Two years Wolfstein has been in Silver Beach. She likes it. They don't know her history. No one asked, and it's a long shot that anyone would ever guess she starred in skin flicks all those years ago. The house belongs to her friend Mo Phelan, so the co-op board doesn't give her any shit. Mo's upstate in Monroe with her sick mom. Anything's upstate when you're from the city, but it's only really sixty miles. Ma's stubborn, won't leave her place up there. Otherwise, Mo might be down in the Bronx with Wolfstein. She sees Mo only every once in a while these days. Mo, who she owes everything to. Mo, who helped her navigate San Fernando Valley. Mo, who saved her when she was on the ropes in her late thirties. Mo, who set her up in Florida after Los Angeles spit her out. Mo, who was instrumental in creating the hustle that sustained her, that still sustains her.

Wolfstein grew up not too far away, in Riverdale. Silver Beach is different. Irish Riviera and all. Last name like hers, they give her that second look, but she mostly keeps to herself, and no one really bothers her.

Across the street, there's yelling. That Adrienne giving it to her daughter again. Her voice like a garbage can being dragged across a sidewalk. Who knows what she's yelling about? The poor daughter, Lucia, about fourteen or fifteen, comes storming out the front door and looks across at Wolfstein, open-mouthed.

Wolfstein tries to see herself through the girl's eyes: red macramé top, her gold bra showing beneath it, sleek blue gym shorts from the eighties that still fit her, dyed brown hair. A weirdo. Some kind of messed-up queen, maybe. Not *really* an old lady, but old to a kid.

And Lucia, she's a sorry sight in a tattered Guns N' Roses T-shirt and denim cut-offs, red Chucks with socks that don't match. She takes a lollipop out of her pocket, unwraps it, and jams it between her teeth.

Wolfstein motions for Lucia to come over.

The girl looks over her shoulder and then back at Wolfstein like, *Me?*

Wolfstein nods.

The girl looks behind her, as if to make sure her mom's not watching, and then comes chugging over.

Wolfstein butts out her cigarette on the bench.

"Hey, can I bum a cigarette?" Lucia asks.

"How old are you?" Wolfstein says.

"Fifteen."

"That's a big no, kid. Sorry. Anyhow, that was my last. What are you and your old lady always at war about?"

Lucia shrugs.

"She's got a shrill-ass voice," Wolfstein says.

"Tell me about it," Lucia says, clicking the lollipop around.

"We've been neighbors a while now and we've never even talked. You know my name?"

"Wolf-something?"

"Wolfstein. What's your mother say about me?"

Lucia hesitates.

"Tell me."

"I don't want to say what she said."

"Diplomatic. I get it. We had a little shitstorm about parking back when I first moved in, me and your old lady. I don't even have a car, so I'm not sure why I got so hot. It was just the principle of it. Her boyfriend—your dad, maybe?—he was always blocking my driveway."

"That's Richie," Lucia says.

"Not your dad, then?"

"I never met my dad."

"Tough break. But, honestly, dads are wild cards. Mine was a lazy ball-chunk. Wasn't there my whole childhood, but he came sniffing around in my twenties and thirties when I was raking in the big bucks." Wolfstein pauses. "You want to come into my joint for a drink?"

"A beer?"

"I'm not gonna give you a beer, no way. How about a ginger ale?"

"I guess."

Wolfstein stands up and works out the kink in her right leg. It's been there for a while, this kink, a little locked-in tremble that pulses with pain. She runs her hands over her thigh, as if locating where it hurts.

Lucia watches her.

"You like Guns N' Roses?" Wolfstein says, pointing at Lucia's shirt.

"I don't know."

"You don't know if you like Guns N' Roses? What's with the shirt?"

Lucia chomps down on her lollipop until it shatters in her mouth. She stuffs the paper stick in her pocket and crunches the candy. "It was Adrienne's," she says.

"You're gonna have no teeth by the time you're twenty," Wolfstein says.

"I don't care about my teeth," Lucia says.

"You don't care about your teeth?"

"Why should I?"

"You get teeth troubles, kid, watch your ass is all I'm saying. Everything bad starts with teeth troubles."

Another shrug.

Wolfstein guides Lucia into the house through the side door and gets her settled on the orange counter stool in the kitchen. Lucia spins around, her legs flailing, torn between wanting to be a kid and not wanting to be a kid.

"You fall and bust your head, that's on me, so quit it, huh?" Wolfstein says.

Lucia stops spinning and looks around: at the vintage dinette set, the buttercup yellow retro refrigerator, the dried roses hanging from the ceiling. And then she looks out into the living room. Sofa. Funky lamp. Hardwood floors. Looming wall mirror with gold scrollwork. Pictures on the wall—classy ones. Wolfstein and Hammie Fields at an awards banquet. A behind-the-scenes still with Crystal Desire, where they both have perms and are wearing silver robes. Sitting on a chaise lounge in a red-striped one-piece in Malibu—a B-roll shot from a *Leg Work* spread that was way too tasteful to use. And her prized possession: a framed picture of when she and Mo met

Stevie Nicks backstage at the Wilshire Ebell Theatre on the White Winged Dove Tour. What a time it was.

"Your place is pretty cool," Lucia says.

"It's my friend Mo's house," Wolfstein says. "I've taken it over the last couple of years, while Mo tends to her mom up in Monroe."

"What are those pictures from?" Lucia asks.

"My past life." Wolfstein opens the fridge and grabs the kid a pony bottle of ginger ale that she keeps around only as a mixer. She cracks another Bud Light for herself.

Lucia accepts the ginger ale and the cap twists off with a hiss. "What were you?"

"In my past life?"

Lucia nods.

"I was a goddess," Wolfstein says.

Lucia's clearly not sure what to make of that. "That's not here, is it?"

"I lived in Los Angeles a long time."

"Were you in movies?"

"I was."

"Awesome."

"I did some work I was proud of, but it wasn't all fun." Wolfstein leans on the counter, gives Lucia the once-over. "You're a scrawny kid, anybody ever tell you that? Your mother feed you anything over there?"

"I eat a lot of popcorn and bagels and pizza. I like to eat."

"I once knew a girl called Hunny. H-U-N-N-Y. Sweetheart. But a terrible eater. I couldn't get her to try anything green. A salad, even. I'd say to her, 'Hunny, you need something green, you're gonna croak.' She'd eat chips and drink Diet Cokes and that was about it. Pills, too, but you don't need to know about that. One day, she up and dies. No kidding. I says to myself, 'You see where not trying things gets you? Spread the word. Teach the children.'"

Lucia looks disinterested.

Wolfstein continues: "Eat healthier is what I'm saying. You hungry now? I made a salad. Chickpeas and arugula with a balsamic vinaigrette. Say the word."

"I should go." Lucia hops off the stool and somehow nearly falls on her face, hits the floor with her knees. Wolfstein was clumsy as a teen, too. She remembers a yard in Nyack, where her mother dumped her with her aunt as a kid. Must've been a friend's yard, because they lived in a squalid apartment. She remembers a fall in this yard, a sweet, disastrous slamming to her knees. Bricks thickly scraping away the skin there. Blood. Burning. Just a dumb fall by a dumb girl. Pigtails. Teeth not yet fixed. Everyone calling her *Woof*stein. The girl whose yard it must've been hosing her down after the fall, saying, "Look at all that dumb girl blood."

Lucia's not hurt like that, but she stays on her knees. Wolfstein scurries over and helps her up. "Shit, I'm fine," Lucia says, brushing her away.

"I'm sorry I made you feel bad about eating," Wolfstein says.

Lucia stands up and looks at the floor.

"You come over whenever you want," Wolfstein says. "I'll keep a few ginger ales around for you. Eventually, we get to be pals, you come of age, I'll pass you a smoke."

Lucia nods. Then she turns and walks out the front door.

An hour later, Wolfstein is hunched over the bar at Charlie's Inn on Harding, drinking cold Bud Light on draft in a frosted mug. What she's looking for when she comes out now is a good time, that's it. No strings. In Florida, the hustle occupied her fully. Made her some serious dough, but it was draining. Out of habit, she scans the place for a guy she hasn't seen around. In Florida, she hunted for a certain brand of well-heeled sucker.

Two regulars sit to the left of her—Sharkey and O'Brien, like some bantering duo from a crappy cop show, paging through a shared *Daily News*. Sharkey's a fishing guide out at City Island. O'Brien's an actual retired cop who now slings knock-off designer purses on Fifth Avenue a few days a week. Behind the bar, Garvey, in his white shirt and black tie with a sham-rock pin, a black towel draped neatly over his shoulder, stalks around with a glass of club soda. Charlie's has been in the neighborhood forever, the word being that it started in the thirties as a traditional Viennese restaurant and beer garden. Square-shaped bar. Low wood-paneled ceilings. Smell of potato pancakes and Wiener schnitzel and sauerbraten from the kitchen. Like everywhere else, you can't smoke inside anymore, but the ghost of seventy years of it lives in the walls.

"You see this, where Tropical Storm Alberto's about to hit Florida," O'Brien says.

"You've gotta do like Cuban Nick," Sharkey says. "Down there in the winter, up here in the summer."

"I couldn't live down there."

Garvey gets into it now: "I knew a guy lived down there. Key West. Cooter, his name was. This big fucking hurricane comes through. He wakes up in Miami, no shit."

"You're saying the hurricane picked him up and deposited him in Miami?" Sharkey asks.

"Not a scratch on the guy."

They all laugh.

Wolfstein doesn't bring up Florida in this new life, just as she doesn't bring up Los Angeles and her movies. Nor, of course, does she bring up the dark lost years between Florida and Los Angeles.

Fort Myers Beach is where she lived in Florida, where the hustle gave her purpose. Or repurposed her. Mo was the one who suggested it, who sensed that she had grifter blood. Wolfstein's method: make them love you. Old guys in their sixties, seventies, eighties, just babes in the fucking woods. Down there, they were all nutted on Viagra, too. She gave them a fun time. Moved in, wore their slippers, their robes, demonstrated her wild healing skills. Their stories were always the same: widowers, divorcés, single lads who'd worked for the city, some city, and lived with Mama too long.

Dancing like they'd never known. Refreshed. Red-cheeked. In love. Envisioning a wedding on the beach, reception at the Cottage or Moose Lodge, conch fritters and beer.

And then the hustle kicked in: she was in deep shit, needed dough for an old debt, to square some trouble from her past life. They were always loaded, so they always paid. She never got greedy, never pushed for more than fifteen or twenty grand. Twenty-five, tops. Enough to keep the chains moving. Just an embarrassment for them, not their life savings. The trick was making them disappear afterward. Wouldn't have been worth it if she had to leave town, even if she knew she'd have to eventually. And it was pretty damn easy. She got a guy she knew, Ben Risk—his real name, a cardsharp—to play the tough bastard from her past life, the one threatening her existence. The mark would pay him in person. Ben held a gun to the mark's head, made him crap his undies, told him to get out of town or else. The mark did. Every time. Without hesitation. There were other beaches, other *Golden Girl* pussy. They never called. Never looked back. A lesson, that's what she was to them.

Nine years it lasted. Eighteen marks over that time. Once she surpassed three hundred grand in prize money, she decided it was time to call it quits. Mo had the Silver Beach house and her mother in Monroe, so Wolfstein figured she'd go back to the Bronx and live easy. Her cash is in a fireproof battery bag behind the air vent in her bedroom.

Before turning to the hustle for a living, she did a satellite radio show for four years, *The Naughty List*. Mostly truckers listened. Former adult movie stars spoke in hushed tones about their sex lives. She was famous with men of a certain age. Out in L.A.—the Valley—she made pornos in the seventies and early eighties. She'd been down in Times Square before that, briefly turning tricks before getting lined up with her first movie. All of it pre-AIDS crisis.

She was known for her all-American body. Luscious Lacey, they called her. Cindy in *Corn-fed Cheerleaders* was her most well-known role. Also had substantial parts in *Swallowed Hole* and *Suzy's Last Night on the Planet*.

Famous enema scene in that last one. Better than Desireé Cousteau's in *Pretty Peaches*, you ask her. Sixty-four movies over a ten-year stretch.

She doesn't talk about it. No one recognizes her anymore; it'd take an awfully good eye. She was only ever known as Luscious Lacey, which is why she likes to be called solely by her last name now. No one's ever at the house to see the memorabilia, this kid Lucia being the recent exception; it's just for Wolfstein. At sixty-one, she looks good, no work done even, but the girl she was is gone, way gone. A lot of tough years between retiring from the movies and getting picked up for the radio show. Eighteen, exactly, full of junk, coke. Stripping at sad clubs off sad highways. More truckers. Gaining thirty-five pounds: Wolfstein the Whale. Losing it with diet pills that made her shaky as hell. Her voice gone husky from smoking. More pills. Rehab. Reconnecting with her father, the fucker big-bellied with a goatee and a wife he found at the bowling alley on dollar-shot night. A dozen bad boyfriends, Pete Hightower worst of all. Her father dying of cancer. Her mother back in the mix suddenly, the mother who left her when she was seven with her crazy-religious Aunt Karen in Nyack. No money left from the movies. Always on the ropes. Until Florida. Until the hustle.

"Wolfstein, another?" Garvey asks.

She downs what's left of her beer and nods.

He takes her glass and pulls a fresh draft, lopping off the head with a foam scraper. He puts it back in front of her. "Guy was in looking for you earlier."

"For me?"

"Yep."

"Who?" Wolfstein asks, at a loss as to who it could be.

"Never seen him. Didn't give a name." He slings the black towel down on the bar and wipes up. "Got a joke for you."

"No more jokes," Wolfstein says. "They never make sense."

Garvey turns to Sharkey and O'Brien. "My jokes make sense?"

Sharkey says, "Not so much."

O'Brien nods. "I wouldn't really call your jokes *jokes*, per se."

"Fuck you, fellas. I could go on stage with my material and slay."

"Slay, huh?" O'Brien says.

"I'm gonna tell my joke. Two priests and a rabbit walk into a bar."

"A rabbit or a rabbi?"

"Two priests and a rabbit, I said. They walk into a bar." Garvey stops.

"That's it?" Wolfstein says.

"That's just how it starts," Garvey says. "I'm trying to remember the rest."

"Let me guess," Sharkey cuts in. "The rabbit blows both priests, and then they play pool."

"What?" Garvey asks.

"Well, that's the typical modus operandi for one of your jokes. Always with the priests getting blown by animals. Horse last time, I think."

"Yeah, it was a horse," O'Brien says.

"The rabbit doesn't blow the priests," Garvey explains. "What happens, the bartender comes over, puts down some coasters, says, 'What can I get you three?' First priest says, 'O'Doul's, please,' Second priest says, 'Rye. Neat.' Rabbit says, 'All your register money. This is a stickup.' 'Jesus Christ,' the first priest says, 'not again. This is why I quit drinking.'"

No laughter.

"Worst yet," Wolfstein says.

"Come on, it's funny," Garvey says. "Priest's done with seeing rabbits rob bars."

O'Brien bunches up a napkin and throws it at Garvey. Sharkey boos.

"You guys don't know jokes," Garvey says.

Wolfstein gives up on Charlie's after twenty more minutes. Garvey's jokes deteriorate even further, if that's possible. Sharkey and O'Brien are huddled together, reading box scores. A young guy, bagpiper, just back from a funeral, looms over the jukebox in his kilt, depositing quarters and playing sad-as-shit Irish tunes.

She enjoys the walk back to Silver Beach. At home, she fixes a drink and sits at the kitchen counter. Vodka on the rocks, a little club soda and lime. She thinks about calling Mo. She needs to, soon. Mo's lonely up in Monroe with her dying mother. Last letter Wolfstein got from her said she was losing her mind a little. A woman like her, used to action, and now all she's doing is wiping her mother's chin and changing her diapers and shopping for Ensure and canned peaches at the ShopRite. Plus, Mo's the only one she can talk to about certain things.

When Wolfstein was raking it in from the hustle, Mo had her own con going. Real estate thing. Wolfstein never fully understood it, but Mo was good. No shock there. Be it balling on-screen, talking sexy on the radio, or finagling money from wealthy landowners, she was the best at whatever she did.

A rapping on the door.

Christ—who's this?

She opens up. On the other side of the screen door is Lucia's mother in a pink tracksuit, the zipper open halfway down her chest. Her hair's a little greasy. She's not as much of a looker with no makeup on. But pretty brown eyes and nice teeth. Who the hell's Wolfstein kidding? She's a hot dish.

"Help you?" Wolfstein asks.

"You had my daughter over here before?" Adrienne says, scratching her cheek with her long nails. A nervous gesture or an intimidating one? Maybe showing Wolfstein her claws.

"Just introduced myself to her, that's all. Two years I've lived across the street, and we've never even talked."

"Stay away from my daughter, please."

"Listen. Your name's Adrienne, right? You want to come in for a drink? I just poured myself one." She rattles around the vodka and ice. Some slops over the rim of her glass onto the webbing of her hand. She sucks it off.

"I don't want a drink," Adrienne says.

"Well, there's your problem right there."

"You give my daughter alcohol?"

"Of course not! What do you think I am? Kid's underage, right? Jesus Christ."

"Good."

"Come in. Have something. Club soda and lime. Cool down."

Adrienne scrunches her face. "Just stay away from my kid."

"Hold on one second," Wolfstein says, pushing open the screen and stepping outside, close to Adrienne. "Whatever our beef was—over blocking the driveway, whatever—it's behind me. Here's the thing: I felt bad for Lucia. I hear you yelling at her, I think, *Be nice to the kid. She needs it.* That's all. She's sweet. Already damaged, I can tell, from being around so much toxicity. Try being a better mother, okay?"

"You've got some nerve talking to me like that."

"I got plenty of nerve, that's true."

Adrienne turns to go. Over her shoulder, she says, "Just keep away from my daughter." Then she's walking across the street, clutching the front of her tracksuit. The zipper's what, broken, she lets her tits half hang out like that?

Wolfstein wants to call out, say one last thing, but she takes an ice cube in her mouth, goes back inside, puts in a VHS of one of her old movies—*Trashy Dreams* with Herschel Stone and Valerie Sugar—and cranks the volume.

Wolfstein jolts awake as the movie ends, vodka spilled in her lap. Dazed. Last scroll of credits on the TV and then nothing but fuzz.

Some noise outside. A car pulling up to the curb. A car door whining open. Someone cursing. A woman.

Wolfstein goes over to the window, peeks out. The wetness in her lap is bothering her. Her mouth is fish-tank scummy. What she sees first is the car, a '62 Chevy Impala, a black, sleek two-door. "Hoo boy," she says, taking it in.

Then a woman pops up from behind Wolfstein's rosebushes, having retrieved a dropped key from the ground. She's Wolfstein's age, maybe a little younger, and wearing a long white cotton shirt and black Capri pants and white Keds. She's pretty, if a little morose-looking.

Wolfstein slips out of her vodka-wet shorts, never taking her eyes off the woman. Standing there in her undies, peeping on a stranger; what a sight. She laughs. But she's not about to stop. Broad's got her fascinated. Who is she?

Wolfstein watches as she walks up to Adrienne and Lucia's door and rings the bell. What time is it? Still pretty early. Four, maybe. The woman rings again, then leans her head against the door, nervous. A minute passes. No answer. Knocking lightly now. And then the door clambers open, Adrienne behind the screen. She starts yelling at the woman, same way she yells at the kid. At first, Wolfstein can only hear it muffled through glass. She cracks the window.

Adrienne says: "What are you even doing? You call, I hang up. Now you're just gonna fucking show your face here?"

"I'm in trouble, A," the woman says. "I need your help."

Adrienne shakes her head, bites her lower lip, her face wire-tense.

Wolfstein wants some vodka, some popcorn to go along with the spectacle, but she's afraid to leave and miss anything.

The woman's crying now, saying, "My own daughter treats me like this. What'd I ever do? I've gotta sleep in the car?"

So she's Adrienne's mom, Lucia's grandma.

Adrienne says, "Come on. Go home. You've lost your fucking mind, showing up here like this."

The door closes in Grandma's face, and she trudges back to the Impala, trying hard to collect herself.

Wolfstein pushes the window up farther, calls out in a whisper-yell, "Hey, Grandma. Over here."

Grandma stops in her tracks.

Wolfstein says, "Across the street."

Grandma looks over, sees Wolfstein in the open window, makes a motion like, *You talking to me?*

"Yeah, you," Wolfstein says.

And soon Grandma's at her door and Wolfstein's opening up and inviting her in, still wearing only her undies, the smell of vodka heavy in the air. Big-time hesitation on Grandma's face. She looks around, notices a couple of pictures on the wall: Wolfstein glammed up on the set of *Hard Waitresses*; goofing with Ginny McRae poolside at one of Mac Dingle's famous parties.

"Sorry I'm in my underpants," Wolfstein says.

"It's okay?" Grandma says, making it a question.

"I'm Lacey Wolfstein. Call me Wolfstein; all my pals do." She comes over and extends her hand.

Grandma shakes it. "Rena Ruggiero."

"Looks like you can use a drink."

"I'm okay."

"You're okay, you sure? I've got a lot of vodka, some beer floating around. Whiskey. You like whiskey? Coffee or tea?"

"I'm okay. Maybe a glass of water."

"Water it is." Wolfstein goes into the kitchen and turns on the tap, lets the water get cold. She puts a couple ice cubes in a tumbler and fills the glass, bringing it back out to Rena.

Rena takes a sip. "Thank you."

"Of course. You gotta take a squirt or anything, feel free to use the can. I just cleaned in there yesterday."

Rena nods.

"Have a seat."

Rena moves over to the sofa, a curbside rescue. Uncomfortable as hell. Wolfstein never sits there. She opts for her usual: the recliner, already kicked into relax mode. It's the color of pink-champagne vomit.

"I really appreciate you giving me a minute to get my head together," Rena says. "I'm assuming you heard everything."

"Your daughter's a bitch," Wolfstein says. "Had a run-in with her myself earlier."

"I don't know where I went wrong."

"Just happens sometimes. Nothing you did or didn't do, I'm sure. I've got every reason to be like that—hard-ass upbringing, bad decisions, blah blah blah—and I'm not."

Rena drinks some more water.

"Your granddaughter's an okay kid, though," Wolfstein says. "Talked to her for the first time today, which is why, in turn, your daughter was not happy with me. Two years I live here. I hear the kid getting yelled at, I call her over, thinking she could use a friend. 'Don't talk to my daughter,' your daughter says to me. I feel bad for the kid, I really do."

Rena looks defeated.

"So, where do you live?" Wolfstein says.

"Brooklyn," Rena says.

"Tell me about the car. It's beautiful."

"Old Impala. I don't really know anything about cars. A friend let me borrow it."

"Let you borrow it? A car like that?"

"Long story." Rena disappears inside herself.

Wolfstein's touched a nerve, easy to tell. She lets it go. They sit there in silence for a few minutes, Rena bringing the water glass up to her lips every few seconds and sipping.

"I guess I should go put some pants on," Wolfstein finally says.

Rena half-smiles.

"You're welcome to hang out here if you don't feel like driving back to Brooklyn yet," Wolfstein says. "You're worked up. That's how people get in accidents. Hell, I've got the sofa and some extra pillows, you feel like crashing. You do that, you go across and try again in the morning when everyone's fresh, you want to."

"You don't even know me."

"I know your daughter's being unreasonable."

Rena sets down her water glass on the coffee table next to a perilously stacked pile of Wolfstein's crossword puzzle books. "I'll stay a little while and try to figure out a plan," she says, standing. "Thank you so much."

Wolfstein goes up to her bedroom and puts on her vintage Wranglers. Not vintage like she bought them in some shop but vintage like she's had them since 1980. They didn't fit for a short stretch, but now they're as comfortable as ever.

The way the day's gone, Wolfstein's happy to have company, happy to be able to stick it to Adrienne, happy to be able to help, genuinely happy about that, and also kind of desperate to find out more about the Impala.

LUCIA

Lucia is standing outside Uncle Pat's Deli on Harding, right near St. Frances de Chantal. She's drinking an orange juice and eating a buttered bagel, hoping to shake down someone for a smoke since she couldn't score one from her neighbor. A girl comes out of the deli, tapping a pack of Camel Lights against her palm. Latina. Tattoos. A few years older than Lucia.

"Can I hit you up for a cigarette?" Lucia says.

The girl shrugs and hands her one.

"Thanks," Lucia says. "Got a light?"

The girl passes her a red Bic. Lucia puts her bagel back in the brown bag it came in and sets it down on the sidewalk along with her orange juice. She lights the cigarette and exhales.

"I started smoking around your age," the girl says, grabbing the Bic back and lighting up one of her own.

"That's cool," Lucia says, not sure what else to say.

Just then, this group of nuns in habits roller-skates by out in the street.

She can't believe it. Like something from a dream. They're in a V, like a formation of birds. Lucia's mouth is open, the cigarette just hanging there, spit-stuck to her bottom lip. They're graceful on their skates, these nuns. She and the girl ogle the nuns together as they go looping onto Hollywood Avenue, headed for the convent there.

"Crazy shit," the girl says.

"Thanks for the smoke," Lucia says, picking up her things and walking away up Harding, flicking the cigarette at the side of a passing bus.

On Pennyfield, she gets catcalled by an ugly high school boy wearing an A-Rod shirt. She gives him the finger. She started doing that in sixth grade, and it always feels like a powerful thing to have in her arsenal. She hops a drooping chain linked between white posts and cuts onto Beech.

When she gets home, she notices that her neighbor's not outside anymore. Wolfstein. That was a weird encounter. Or maybe what's weird is that they haven't talked before. She imagines that people used to talk to their neighbors a lot more. She wishes Wolfstein would've given her a beer.

An actress. Lucia's not sure she buys that. Why would an actress be living in the Bronx like this? Don't actresses live in Hollywood and have houses on hills all made out of glass where they dance in front of their windows in sexy red robes even when they're old? That's how she pictures it. She was an actress, she'd ride around in a limo. She was an actress, she'd have cute guys bringing her beers on platters. *Oh, yes, Joseph, thank you, that's just the right amount of cold*. Is that the way she'd say it? *Amount of cold* sounds wrong.

She's had a couple of beers. Once at a picnic down by SUNY Maritime, this kid from her class took her over behind a parked car and passed her a Coors Light. It was really cold but didn't taste like anything. The other time was at Alfie's Place over on the Cross Bronx. Big Paulie from Skyville, Adrienne's boyfriend for a minute, he was so happy the Yankees won, he bought everyone beers, including her. No one said anything because they were all drunk. She can't even remember why she was there. Some dumb event. Big Paulie and Adrienne were so wasted they made Lucia drive them home to Silver Beach. Big Paulie told her what to do. She was thrilled to be behind the wheel, sitting on a stack of newspapers, listening intently to his commands.

Back in the house, her mom's in the kitchen, talking on her cell phone, wearing that hideous pink tracksuit she got last Christmas from whoever she was dating at the time. No shirt or bra on underneath it, the zipper half-open over her boobs. Seeing her mom's boobs, even just in a low-cut blouse, has always been a source of anxiety. She remembers being at Alfie's and the Clipper, Adrienne pressing them on the bar, pushing them up, making eyes for free drinks.

Lucia wonders who Adrienne's talking to now. She's got that new maybe-boyfriend, Marco. And Richie's always in the picture, somehow. Richie's not her dad, but he's the closest thing she's ever known. Her real dad, Adrienne won't talk about. Lucia wishes she knew something about him, anything. She's dug around in Adrienne's papers, looking for a name, at least. He's not even on her birth certificate; the father part's just blank. She has no memories of him. He was gone before she could remember him. If she had a name, maybe she could find him. She wants to know what he looks like, what his voice is like, why he's never come for her. She's afraid he's dead. He could be, and she'd never even know. She doesn't like to imagine him dead, without ever having had a shot at being his daughter.

Richie's come and gone over the years. He was the one who hooked them up with this house in Silver Beach. He stays back in Brooklyn, where he works, but he knew Adrienne wanted out of the old neighborhood. And Silver Beach—well, it's the city, the far reaches of the Bronx, but it feels like something out of a movie. Trees, views, wooden street signs. You had to know someone to get a house here. It's a co-op situation—way she understands it, the house is owned and the land is rented. Richie knows everybody. A firefighter who owed him a ton of money got her and her mom set up here. This was years ago. She doesn't really remember living anywhere else, even though they were in a few apartments scattered around the boroughs during her early years. Staten Island. Queens.

Watching her mom yap into the phone, Lucia wishes she had one. A phone. All the kids in her grade are getting them. She'd call some number where you can just talk to a stranger for hours.

Adrienne flips the phone shut.

"Who was that?" Lucia asks.

"Kids shouldn't ask their mothers who they're talking to on the phone," Adrienne says, puckering her lips.

Lucia feels that seething hate she can feel only for her mother. Her mother has always taken pleasure in being mean, and that meanness has seeped into Lucia's blood. She pictures Adrienne hanging from a meat hook like in *The Texas Chainsaw Massacre*. She gives her the finger.

Adrienne gives her the finger back. "I don't want you talking to that bitch across the street," she says.

"Why?" Lucia asks.

"What'd she want?"

"Nothing. She gave me a drink."

"She gave you a beer?"

"A ginger ale."

"Now I've gotta go have a talk with her."

"Don't, okay?"

"What she said to me back when she moved in, I remember correctly, was, 'Your boyfriend parks in my driveway again, I'm gonna slash his tires.' I said, 'You know who you're talking to? You know who I am? You know who my father was? You know who Richie Schiavano is?' And now she's meddling with my daughter."

"I'm going to my room," Lucia says.

The house is a mess. Crumpled clothes hurled on the steps. Damp towels piled in the upstairs hallway. Lucia can hear the water running in the bathroom sink, and she goes in and twists the knob as hard as she can to make it stop. A hamper overflows with more clothes and towels in the corner. The mirror is dotted with fingerprints and toothpaste splatter. The shower stall is grimy. Two broken bars of soap have congealed near the drain. Lucia sits on the toilet and opens the window. It's warm out, but there's a nice breeze. Still a few hours away from getting dark. Lucia loves the summer because it gets dark so late. She doesn't understand why the winter is the way it is, sometimes dark by four thirty. She's read about how there are places, like in Alaska, where it stays dark all the time. That sounds horrible.

She can see Wolfstein's from where she is. She's thinking of how she jumped off that stool in her kitchen like a little kid. She wishes she hadn't done that.

When her mother goes storming out of the house, she's not surprised. Adrienne's not shy. Butt your nose into her life, and she'll come out swinging. That's what happened with Grandma Rena, as far as Lucia knows. Said something Adrienne didn't like and she was cut off. No holidays. No birthdays. No calls. Nothing. Lucia remembers making struffoli with Grandma Rena at Christmas. She remembers waiting in long lines at bakeries with her. She remembers her smile. She knows that Grandma Rena tries calling and sends cards, but Adrienne hangs up on her and rips up the cards even though they're sometimes addressed to Lucia and probably have cash in them. *Cash.*

Adrienne rushes across to Wolfstein's, her head tilted up. In her tracksuit, she's a pink blur. When she gets up on Wolfstein's front stoop, she cracks her knuckles, her long crimson nails flashing like knives.

Lucia wants to call out to her, but she doesn't. She just watches. Adrienne pounds on the door. Wolfstein opens up. Angry words pass between them. Lucia closes the window, afraid to see something she doesn't want to see. She's not sure what Adrienne's capable of.

Used to be, back when Lucia was little, Adrienne would thwack her with a wooden spoon when she wasn't listening. Five times over the years, Adrienne's slapped her. She'd say, "I'm gonna slap the shit out of you," and then she'd do it. Lucia remembers each time perfectly. Two of the times, Adrienne broke a nail and got even angrier.

She swears that if she ever has a kid, she won't hit her. Or him. She doesn't really think about having kids, though. She doesn't imagine wanting boys or girls. Other girls in her grade talk about it. Pass notes. Play games. *You're gonna have a baby with Vinny. A boy. Black hair.* Ugh. Teenagers dreaming of wanting kids; she doesn't get it.

It hasn't been easy, growing up with Adrienne. It's made her heart hard. She can feel it in there, like concrete. All those nights Adrienne left her alone in this apartment or that apartment, thinking she was asleep, while she went out to a bar or out to Richie's car or wherever. Six or seven years old, being alone like that night after night, it wrecked her. She's jealous of kids with sweet mothers, nice mothers who just fold clothes and make big dinners and spit on their thumbs to clean guck off their kid's face; it sucks Lucia got dealt this angry bitch from the bottom of the deck.

But she's learned a lot over the years, knowing she can depend only on herself. She's learned how to be tough, how to survive. She stopped crying at some point, and she started dreaming of escape.

When she was about eleven, she started keeping a spiral notebook where she'd copy down information about houses she liked in the real estate section of whatever newspaper was around. Some of the houses were in the city; some were in the suburbs. Didn't matter. The joy was in imagining a house of her own, a place away from the burden of Adrienne.

Still, whatever's happening between Adrienne and Wolfstein now, Lucia's sure Wolfstein can take care of herself.

In her room, Lucia sits on the bed, dirty yellow sheets braided around her, stuffed bears tossed to the floor. She's got a Derek Jeter poster on the wall. Yankees ticket stubs taped to her mirror. A boombox on the nightstand with a broken CD player. She never takes care of her CDs anyway. She's only got a few she bought at Best Buy: Mariah Carey's *The Emancipation of Mimi*, Destiny's Child's *#1s*, and Mary J. Blige's *The Breakthrough*. That last one she actually stole, on a dare from her friend Jessica Ruiz. Put it under her shirt and just walked right out of the store.

She can hear a plane in the sky. They're always loud and low over Throggs Neck, headed to nearby LaGuardia in Queens.

The front door slams, and she assumes her mom is back inside. Meaning nothing too bad happened with Wolfstein, just Adrienne firing a warning shot.

So much of Lucia's time in her room is spent just staring at the ceiling, glancing at the Jeter poster, or occasionally riffling through her CDs and reading the liner notes. Sometimes she considers her stuffed bears as the gallery of embarrassments that they are. She tried to throw them out when she was twelve, but Adrienne rescued them from the garbage and set them back on her bed. "I spent a lot of money on these fucking bears," she'd said.

When she hears the door downstairs again, she wonders if Adrienne's going back out or if someone else is coming in. Marco, maybe? Last time he came in like this, at nightfall, half-loaded, Lucia had to listen to them have sex on the couch. The radio couldn't drown it out. Marco was grunty. Adrienne sounded ridiculous, like she was amazed by some dumb guy in a funny hat making balloon animals on the street.

But it's not Marco. She can hear a voice now, one she recognizes immediately. Other than Adrienne's, it's the voice she knows best in the world: Richie's. She gets up and leaves the room, creeping down the hallway to the top of the stairs.

"Baby," Richie says to Adrienne in the kitchen, "it's so good to see you." She tries to remember the last time Richie was here. Maybe six months ago. Begging. Making promises.

"You can't just charge in here," Adrienne says.

"Didn't I get you this place? Didn't I set you up nice?"

"How long you gonna play that card?"

"One call, I could've gotten you the boot whenever."

"Now you're threatening me? That's how you want to start this?"

Richie's voice goes hushed. "Listen, I'm sorry. I lost my patience."

"Get off me," Adrienne says.

Lucia edges down a couple of steps and sees them tangled together by the dishwasher, Richie's hands inside Adrienne's now fully unzipped jacket. Richie's wearing a striped mesh pony shirt that clings to him, rumpled chinos, and gladiator sandals. He hasn't shaved in days. His hair—what's left of it—is puffed up. His big forehead glistens with sweat. He's licking his lips.

"This is all I wanted," he says. "These right here, these are what I dream about."

"Get your hands off me." Adrienne's calm for someone being fondled like fruit at a market.

"You don't like that? You don't like my hands on you? You used to love these hands." He pulls away and holds up his beefy hands. "These hands right here, they used to work magic on you."

Adrienne zips up her jacket. This time all the way. "What do you want, Richie?"

"'Oh, Richie! I love your big hands on me. Oh, Richie!'" Richie says, doing his best girly voice. "That was you. I'd put my hands on your tits and you'd melt."

"Yeah? Tell me more, Romeo."

"Come on, you don't remember it?" He's close to her again, brushing back her hair, whispering against her neck. "Tell me you don't remember it."

"You're looking for a piece, that's why you're here? I've got a boyfriend."

"I know all about Marco. Where you find these bums? You know what your old man used to say to me?"

"Don't talk to me about Vic."

"Vic, he'd be sitting in repose—in a barber chair or at Caccio's with an espresso—and he'd say, 'My daughter, she's got the worst taste in guys. Put five good ones in front of her, she'll pick the pants-shitter.'" Richie laughs, nuzzling her neck.

Lucia wonders if that's in reference to her father, if he was a pants-shitter. She's asked Richie about her father a few times over the years, but he's always brushed her off, said she was an immaculate conception and he was like Joseph and *just don't you fucking worry about it.*

Adrienne picks up the thread: "And Vic didn't even know about our thing. He didn't know you popped my cherry at fifteen."

"You were a beautiful girl," Richie says. "You *are* a beautiful girl."

"I'm not a girl anymore. I'm getting old."

"You still got the body of a girl." His hands are on her hips now. "You drive me crazy, A."

"What do you want, Richie?"

"I've got plans." Richie steps back and goes over to the counter. A loaf of Arthur Avenue bread—fresh that morning—pokes up from the wicker basket there. Richie rips off the heel and starts gnawing on it.

"What'd you do, come in your pants?" Adrienne asks.

Lucia winces.

"I didn't come in my pants, sweetheart," Richie says. "I'm trying to keep my head here. I'm telling you I've got plans. I want you to be part of them. You and Lucia."

"What are you saying?"

"I'm saying opportunity is knocking. I'm saying I've come to an impasse. I've been taken advantage of one too many times. Passed over one too many times. You look down your nose at Richie Schiavano for long enough, Richie Schiavano's gonna get to thinking. And Sonny and Crea, they don't think I know, but I know."

"Richie, what are you talking about?"

"I'm talking, sweetheart, about making a move. There's a sit-down today. Nick Minervino and Ice House Johnny are delivering half a rock to Sonny Brancaccio. Nick feels Sonny's owed over the Bay Ridge situation, and he's aiming to square things before there's a war between the families. An honorable move, but I'm owed, too, the way Crea, that fucking psycho, has treated me. I'm sick of it, A. Getting cut out like this. Vic always said in his later years that everything was falling apart. He'd seen what we've become now, I don't even know what he'd think. Chaos. Guys playing video games all day. Crea's nephew robs a bus full of kids in Canarsie. Catholic kids at camp. Takes their lunch money and their watches. No class left. No one like Vic.

"So what I'm gonna do, I'm gonna infiltrate this sit-down, and I'm gonna get what's mine. And I've got my suspicions about Sonny's involvement with Little Sal's hit on Vic. Crea was behind that on some level, I'm sure." Richie puts a last hunk of Italian bread in his mouth and chews it noisily.

"You're crazy," Adrienne says.

Richie goes over and puts his hands on Adrienne's cheeks, squeezing. "I'm gonna run away. Go somewhere good. Bring my camera, take some pictures. I got a Nikon F5 35 millimeter from Scrummy's nephew. He stole it from this guy in Williamsburg. Sells shit on eBay, this guy. Has a whole apartment full of cameras and record players and typewriters. Maybe the fucking Canadian wilderness is where I want to go, who knows? Take some pictures, that's my goal. I already got my bags packed. They're in the trunk of the Caddy. I want you to come with me. You and Lucia. Be a family. What do you say to that?"

"You're gonna knock off these guys by yourself?" Adrienne asks. "How you think that's gonna turn out?"

"They're a mess, A. Like I said, this isn't the world Vic knew. You blow on these guys hard enough, they fall over. Except for Crea. He's fucking nuts with that sledgehammer he carries around, and he'll be on my tail, but I can run faster. He's a psycho, but he's not blessed in the brains department."

Silence for a minute or so after that, Richie just stroking Adrienne's cheeks with his thumbs.

Lucia leans back against the wall, wondering whether her mother's really considering this. Going on the run, living like crooks. What Richie's talking about, Lucia's heard rumblings of. The Brancaccios. Papa Vic's work. Richie's work. But she's never heard it laid out so explicitly. The motherfucking *mob*.

Adrienne breaks the silence: "The Canadian wilderness?"

"I'm just spitballing here," Richie says. "New Mexico, maybe? Get some nice rugs. Live in a hut. Italy? Book passage on a ship like they used to do. Michael Corleone. I got cousins. In Naples, they'll welcome us with open arms. You got ideas, let's hear them. What's important, to me, is being with you. I did a lot of soul-searching the last few weeks. What I came up with is you're the one. Always have been. I've loved you since you were fourteen." He kisses her nose.

"I love you, too, Richie."

Lucia's heart is racing now. What if Richie scoops them up and they *do* take off for parts unknown? What if he's pursued by goombahs with guns and they all get shot to shit, buried out in a swamp? She doesn't want to die like that.

"You gotta think about it," Richie says. "That's fine. I get it. Big decision. You've got a life here. You says to me on multiple occasions over the years, however, that you're sick of the Bronx, sick of Brooklyn, sick of New York. Am I right?"

Adrienne nods. "You could've given me a little bit more time here."

"I know, I'm sorry. But this is a shot. This is the way it's playing out." His hands are off her face and moving down her body. He's kissing her neck again. She's backing up against the counter. He's taking off his shirt. He's unzipping her jacket. She's sitting up on the counter now, tugging at the button on his pants. Her jacket is off.

Lucia backs just far enough down the hall that she can't see them anymore. Gross. So gross.

The kissing noises are loud. Richie sounds like this pet guinea pig she used to have. Thing used to keep her up nights, the way it'd rustle through the paper bedding in the cage.

Now Adrienne's letting out soft little moans.

Lucia puts her head in her hands.

Then the sound of their bodies thwacking together rockets up the stairs. Richie's grunting. Adrienne's low moans are getting louder.

Lucia closes her eyes so there's no chance she'll see anything, even by accident. Hearing is bad enough.

It's over fast. Richie finishes with a hoot. "I was so backed up for you, A," he says.

Lucia returns to the edge of the stairs where she can see them again. Richie is pulling up his pants. Adrienne, having barely broken a sweat, is back in her tracksuit already. She's fixing her hair, adjusting her boobs.

"I'll be back later," Richie says, putting his shirt back on. "Around nine. I'll have a lot of dough with me. You wanna do this, be ready. How's that sound? We could have a good life. A good new life. You tell the kid I said hey, okay?" He kisses her, and then he's gone. Adrienne stands in the kitchen, leaning against the counter, chewing the polish from her long thumbnail.

Lucia gets up and goes back to her room, shutting the door quietly behind her. She sits on the floor next to her stuffed bears, picking one up. It's torn and frayed, eyeless, a little red hat drooping off the side of its head. It was a gift from Grandma Rena and Papa Vic when she was maybe four. Papa Vic died when she was six. She doesn't remember him. She fingers the little notches where black thread was once sewn in the shape of eyes. This bear she'd named Giancarlo after a boy in her pre-K class.

A knock on her door. Before she can say anything, Adrienne opens up and enters.

"What do you want?" Lucia asks.

Adrienne snaps back: "What'd you hear?"

"I heard how gross you are."

"That's not gross. That's how adults show their love for each other. Besides, you shouldn't be listening."

"You love Richie again?"

"I've always loved Richie." Adrienne sits on the bed. "You heard what he said? His proposition?"

Lucia nods.

"What do you think?"

Lucia doesn't say anything.

Adrienne stares at the Jeter poster. "Jeter was DH yesterday. 0 for 5. Still batting .332. Mussina took the loss. I love Mussina. I had a poster on my wall, it'd be Mussina. He's the hottest."

Lucia looks away from Adrienne, thumbing the bear's eyeholes harder, until her fingers have torn through to cotton.

Adrienne gets up and walks out of the room.

Lucia feels as if she's on an elevator, going down fast. Happened to her once at a building in the city. The buttons didn't work. She was alone and touching the door, hoping the elevator would slow and it would open between floors and she could just crawl to safety without being chopped in half or something. The alarm wouldn't work either. It was a tall building. More than twenty floors. She can't remember why she was there. That's what this feeling is like, a dropping in her gut. Weird thing is, she doesn't remember stopping and getting out, which she must have done because she's here and alive and didn't bite it at the bottom of a desolate elevator shaft. All she remembers is the relentless falling.

A little later, having barely moved, Lucia goes downstairs for a piece of leftover pizza. She finds Adrienne packing a bag and doesn't say anything. She turns on the Yankees in the living room. It's a replay of yesterday's game. Lucia eats her pizza cold. It's a piece of the Napolitana pie they got two nights ago from Patricia's on Tremont. Her favorite. Sausage and broccoli rabe. She eats it over her hand.

When there's another knock on the door, she assumes it'll be Richie again. Except, well, Richie came right in last time. When Adrienne opens up, it's Grandma Rena. From where Lucia's sitting on the couch in the corner, she can see Grandma Rena, but Grandma Rena can't see her. Adrienne goes from calm to angry in less than a second. Before Lucia can even get up and show her grandmother that she's there, that *she* at least would like to see her, Adrienne slams the door in her face.

"You believe this?" Adrienne says. "My mother just showing up like this now?"

Lucia puts the crust of her pizza on the arm of the couch and moves for the door. "I want to see her."

"Don't go out there," Adrienne says.

"Why? What'd she ever do to you?"

"Don't worry what she did."

Lucia's thinking Grandma Rena might just be her way out of this. "She never did anything to me. I want to see her."

"You're eighteen, you wanna go see her, that's up to you. For now, I'm your boss. And you listen to your boss."

"I can't wait to be eighteen."

"It's not as good as it sounds."

"You're packing. Are we gonna go with Richie?"

"Get that pizza crust off the arm of the couch," Adrienne says. "And, yeah, we're going with Richie, so go pack."

"We're leaving for good?"

"Why not? We've got nothing here."

Lucia picks up the crust and carries it into the kitchen, dumping it in the trash. She goes over to the front window and starts to push the curtain open, hoping for a glimpse of Grandma Rena out in the street.

Adrienne storms over and forcibly clamps the curtain shut. "Get away from the fucking window," Adrienne says.

"I hate you," Lucia says.

Adrienne laughs. "Join the club."

Lucia goes back upstairs. The bathroom gives her a better view of the street anyway. She sees a nice old car parked out front, gleaming under a streetlamp that's on even though it's still light out. And she sees Grandma Rena going into Wolfstein's.

RENA

Rena pees in the stranger's bathroom. Nice woman, sure, but strange. Lacey Wolfstein. Strange name for a strange stranger.

Adrienne.

It makes her sick to think about Adrienne.

And Lucia. Right across the street like that. So close. Rena's the girl's flesh-and-blood grandmother. She should be snuggled on the couch with her, catching up, pretending not to care about what happened with Enzio.

Instead, here she is.

The drive over was slow. So much traffic by JFK. Enzio's Impala floated. People looked at her, an automatic class act in a car like that. She nodded to indicate the car was hers and wasn't she lucky, her hands tight on the wheel, straining not to break character. It was easy to feel like what had happened back at Enzio's hadn't happened at all. The ashtray, the blood, none of that could be real. She was headed, she thought, for reconciliation, for a safe haven. Where else to run if not to family? She'd imagined telling Adrienne about Enzio. What he'd tried to do. What she'd done in response. She'd played it many different ways in her head. Now what?

When she gets back downstairs, Wolfstein's sitting on a stool at the kitchen counter, drinking a beer. Rena takes in her outfit. Bra showing under her shirt like that. Jeans that look like something a college girl would wear.

"Sure you don't want one?" Wolfstein asks.

Rena says, "No, thank you."

"Feeling a little better?"

"I don't know."

"You're torn up. It's understandable."

"You have kids? Grandkids?"

Wolfstein puts down her mug and belly-laughs, the laugh turning into a cough. "Me? No, no, hell no." She settles down. "My mother split when I was seven, you know? Off to an artist's commune or some bullshit. Left me with her whacko sister, who'd paddle me when I used a teaspoon instead of a tablespoon to eat my Corn Flakes, no kidding. I saw all the ways I could fuck up as a mother, and I cut it off at the pass. Plus, you know, my line of work."

"Your line of work?"

"Actress."

"Oh, you were an actress. I met Geena Davis once. They were filming *Angie* in the neighborhood. What were you in?"

Wolfstein smiles again. "Nothing you would've seen, I'd venture to guess."

"The soaps?"

"Something like that. What'd you do for work?"

"I was home with Adrienne. After my husband died, I thought about getting back into accounting, which is what I went to college for."

"You're a widow?"

Rena nods. She returns to the sofa. "Vic, my husband's name was. He shouldn't have died."

"I'm sorry. What happened?"

Rena ignores the question, something she's accustomed to. "Adrienne and I had a falling-out at the funeral. It's been all downhill since."

"Your own daughter making a scene at her old man's funeral? Not nice." Wolfstein slugs down the last of her beer and wipes her mouth with the back of her hand. She continues: "I was watching this talk show the other day. I can't remember the one exactly, one that's on in the afternoon, you know, and they were talking about this very thing. Adrienne's behavior towards you—they were saying this on the show, basically—is a sort of violence. I mean, she's not punching you, kicking you, throwing things at you, but it's not that far off. Emotional violence, they were saying. I like those afternoon talk shows. I learn a lot."

Emotional violence. Rena thinking that sounds about right. The victim of some unforeseen rage from Adrienne. What'd Rena ever do but try to be kind, be helpful, be a good mom? Adrienne never got dragged into her old man's affairs. It was a separate world.

The phone rings in the kitchen.

Rena's thoughts start running wild. It's the cops. They found Enzio, tracked her here, and are calling to tell Wolfstein she's harboring a dangerous fugitive. It's Enzio, back from the dead, or maybe never dead at all, on the hunt for his Impala.

"Now who the hell is this?" Wolfstein says, picking up. An old red rotary on the wall with a cord. Just like Rena's, except for the color.

Rena can tell from Wolfstein's face that there's silence on the other end.

"You got two seconds," Wolfstein says into the phone.

Rena counts it out. *One, two.* Wolfstein's true to her word. She slams down the handset. "Heavy breather," Wolfstein says. "Haven't gotten one of those in a long time."

The phone rings again.

Wolfstein's fast to it. "Listen, pal," she says.

This time there's talking on the other end.

"How'd you get this number?" she asks.

Wolfstein has her back to Rena, the cord twisted around her body. She's holding the handset close to her ear, listening intently, whispering *uh-huh*s. She takes a deep breath when the person on the other end stops and then starts talking: "Bobby, listen. I know you're upset. I get it. It was all on the level, I'm telling you. You really helped me out. Saved my skin. I'll be forever grateful. Bobby, I'm just, you know, I'm really thankful you helped me. I felt that way, too." She seems to lose track of what she's saying.

More from Bobby on the other end. Louder this time.

"You're a nice guy, Bobby, I know you are," Wolfstein says. "Don't talk like that."

The line goes dead.

Wolfstein hangs up the phone with a gentle touch, setting the handset in its cradle as if it's something sharp.

"You okay?" Rena asks.

"Shit," Wolfstein says. "Everything's fine. Just a crazy ex."

"He threatened you?"

"'I love you, I'm gonna off myself,' that kind of thing. It's been a while. No idea how he found me. What's he gonna do, blow his brains out on my doorstep? I'm not worried. I screwed him over, and he's just getting some stuff off his chest."

"You wanna call the cops or someone?"

Wolfstein shakes her head. "Bobby's not a bad guy. Sad sack. I hurt him a little too much, I guess. He's got the teensiest little pecker; that's what I mainly remember about him. Like a hazelnut."

Rena's not sure what to make of this. She sits up properly, hands on her knees. She's no prude, but she's also got no desire to think about Wolfstein's ex's privates. Her mind flashes to the movie that Enzio put on—she can't help it. Those smooth male parts like something new in a sleek suburban kitchen, like one of those bullet blenders. All she's known in life is Vic's rig, which always reminded her of a sock puppet, kind of sad and imperfect and cute. One time, they lost power in the house and she had to go down to the cellar in the dark and fondle along the wall until she thumbed on the light switch; it had reminded her of touching Vic.

Thinking like this. Disgusting.

Wolfstein homes in on a bottle of Absolut on the counter and unscrews the cap. "Bobby fucking Murray," she says, taking a slug and shaking her head. "From Woodlawn, I remember correctly. I knew him in Florida."

"You don't mind me asking, what happened?" Not like Rena to pry, but there's an easiness, a looseness, to conversation with Wolfstein.

"Maybe we're on the road to being good friends, or maybe we'll never see each other again after today," Wolfstein says. "Either way, I'm feeling like I can confide in you. You really want to know?"

"If you want to tell me. No pressure."

More vodka for Wolfstein. "You're not too worn out?"

"Not at all."

"Okay, first things first: the movies I was in were skin flicks. Back in the seventies and eighties. Pre-AIDs. Not like now. The men were all hairy, and the women didn't have phony knockers, you know? Real-deal stuff. The balling was mostly fun. I was celebrated for my rack."

"You were in dirty movies?" Rena says, again thinking of Enzio and what he'd put on. Those bodies and the way they thrusted, the noises that happened, squishings and poundings, the strange dialogue. Used to be a XXX theater in her neighborhood. She can't remember the real name. Porno Palace, people called it. She remembers passing it on Bath Avenue, the marquee with its red letters, the vibe of the place. Skeevy men in overcoats—a cliché, but a reality—stumbled in and out of the front doors. The floor was probably greased with semen. She remembers seeing ads for the theater in the newspapers with show times, names of movies, and being so glad Vic wasn't the type of guy escaping there for relief with all the old nasties from that home on Cropsey, men who wiggled their hands in their pants when they were just out walking. Forget what probably went on in that theater. Some kind of hell. Rena wonders if Wolfstein's movies were shown there.

"You're judging me," Wolfstein says.

"Not at all," Rena says.

"I can tell."

"It's just . . . different."

"Anyhow, it's only the beginning of the story. I did movies for a while, into my late thirties. The scene changed. Diseases were becoming more of a thing. I bailed. No one tried to convince me otherwise. After that, I hit a rough patch. Drugs, bad boyfriends, stripping in dives, failed rehab stints, getting mixed up with my folks again, everything generally going down the shitter. I woke up one morning somewhere in Yuma, Arizona. A trailer park. With this guy. He'd overdosed on the toilet. I'd puked in my sleep, miraculously hadn't choked to death. I made a decision right then. Got the hell out of there and went to Florida to get right."

"The guy was dead and you left him?" Rena says.

"Hell yeah, I left the fucker. I didn't even know his name. You ever been to Yuma, Arizona? Guy's probably still there, rotting away. No one gave a shit about him, least of all me."

"And you don't feel bad?"

"Not about that. I feel bad about the time I stole fifty bucks from a fortune-teller. I feel bad about the time back in Hollywood when I slept with Hunny's fiancé—Hunny was a good pal of mine back in those days. I feel bad about shoplifting from that health food store on Santa Monica Boulevard for five years straight. Sister, I've got a lot of regrets, big and small. That worthless junkie's not one of them."

"Why Florida?"

"Florida because I had a pal who'd moved there, Mo. We'd been in a few movies together. She helped me straighten out. I owe her everything. No time at all, I was doing this radio show with her. Thriving. Not making much dough, but getting healthy and getting my head clear. Got to where I could go to karaoke night and do 'Rhiannon' and get the old guys lining up. Wheels started spinning. Mo's wheels first; that's the way she operated."

"Spinning how?" Rena says.

"Thinking how there was an abundance of these rich old bastards down there. In their boat shoes and shitty polo shirts. Widowers, divorcés, whatever, living large. Hunting broads, mostly. They liked me, I liked them. So I took advantage of the situation."

Rena tries to process what Wolfstein is saying. She'll admit she doesn't quite understand. She'll admit she's shocked by some of these revelations. Dirty movies and drugs—she wouldn't have expected that. Wolfstein's a little flashier than her, sure, but she's around the same age, and you wouldn't know she was different, that she had this dark history, just to look at her.

But who's Rena to think about dark histories, anyway? Married to Gentle Vic Ruggiero. She knew some of what he'd done, had heard rumors of other things. She's wondering if you can just decide what's good-bad and what's bad-bad. Why should porno be scuzzier than being a wiseguy? Rena has closed her eyes to certain things, made judgments about the world and other people that aren't fair. Meanwhile, she's been subject to judgment herself. Mob wife. Catholic goody-two-shoes. Hypocrite.

"Maybe I should stop talking," Wolfstein says.

"Don't," Rena says.

And so Wolfstein continues. How she hustled men out of dough for going on a decade. Her intricate system. How it never backfired, all those times it was smooth sailing. How she retreated here to the Bronx, to Mo's old house, when she had enough saved to live on for a long time. But now, she's confessing, an unexpected wrinkle. Bobby Murray, one of the easiest marks of all, is back. Bobby Murray, he just wants her to love him for real the way she fake-loved him.

When she's done, Rena swallows big and asks the most obvious question: "So, what's gonna happen?"

"I don't know," Wolfstein says. "This only happened one other time. This guy, Christopher, he came back to Fort Myers and found me. Threatened me a little. I gave him his dough back and he left. It was a different situation."

"Bobby's on his way?"

"He might be here already. Someone was at the bar looking for me earlier." She pauses. "You think I'm a bad person?"

"I don't think bad people think about whether they're bad or not."

"That's a nice thing to say. Thanks."

"I used to tell Vic that, too. He used to worry about his soul. Not often, but sometimes."

"Your husband had some skeletons in his closet?"

"Vic was a gangster."

"Holy shit. Really? You seem so on the straight and narrow."

"I am. I always was. Maybe I should've been crooked myself. He did what he did. That was the world he knew, and he operated well in it. It was easy not to think about, beyond being worried that someone would off him one day."

"That's what happened?"

Rena nods. "Nine years ago. Shot on our front stoop by Little Sal Lavignani. Vic didn't cross anyone, didn't screw up. Little Sal was just making a move. That's the story."

"Jesus."

"I did something bad, too," Rena says, almost choking on the words.

"You? What'd you do?"

Silence from Rena.

"It's got to do with the car, doesn't it?" Wolfstein gets that slumberparty look, claps her hands together. She rushes over and sits next to Rena. "Tell me."

"I don't know," Rena says.

"I've got this book of quotes in my bathroom," Wolfstein says. "You probably couldn't see it. Big white book next to the stacks of toilet paper. Thousands of quotes. My favorite is 'A friend is a gift you give yourself.' That's from Robert Louis Stevenson. We're meant-to-be pals, Rena, I can feel it. You want to talk, I'm here for you."

"What I did, it's really bad."

"Worse than all the shit I just told you?"

Tears rimming Rena's eyes now. The weight of what she's done, really done, crashing against her heart. Not some fever-dream fantasy. The dirty old bastard, how he made her react. Pushing and pushing. No should've just been no.

"You want me to guess?" Wolfstein asks.

Rena blurts it out: "I think I might've killed someone."

Wolfstein doesn't look shocked at all. "I bet he deserved it."

"How'd you know it was a he?"

"Sweetie, I'm looking at you. If you killed someone, it was because he was trying to hurt you. *He.* I don't suspect it was a woman trying to hurt you. Not the way it goes, generally."

"He was so persistent," Rena says. "My neighbor Enzio. Old guy. Older than me. Wouldn't take no for an answer. He put his hands on me." Looking at her lap, crying a little harder. *Don't cry, Rena.* "I picked up this glass ashtray he had and thumped him in the head with it. His head hit the table on the way down. God help me, there was so much blood. So, so much." She pauses. "I just left. Took his car and didn't look back."

Wolfstein laughs. "You're my goddamn hero," she says.

They talk a while longer, Wolfstein making Rena feel as if not only has she not done the wrong thing, but she's done the exact *right* thing. Forget stealing the Impala and running away to the Bronx. Those things might look bad, but it's all understandable. And who's to say Enzio would even be discovered any time soon? Could be a week, a month, longer. Lonely old bastards die alone in their hovels all the time, Wolfstein was saying, and no one finds them until the stink reaches the street.

The main thrust of her argument: Don't feel bad. Be proud. Enzio got what he deserved.

Rena has calmed down.

"I think fate brought us together," Wolfstein says. "We can help each other. You want to go for a little walk?"

Rena nods. "Sure," she says.

They walk up the street, passing Adrienne's house. No one is watching from the windows that she can see. "I want to try again," Rena says.

"Of course you do," Wolfstein says. "Let's cool off a little and then you try again on the way back. I'll come with you, if you want."

"Yeah?"

"Sure. You deserve to see your granddaughter."

They walk over to Indian Trail. It's beautiful. Wolfstein tells her about the neighborhood, about Mo Phelan's roots there. Rena can't believe it's the Bronx. A barge passes out on the river. She can see down to a private beach. She notices the wooden street signs. Well-tended lawns. A bike overturned on the path. Squirrels darting in front of them. It feels more like Nantucket or Maine than New York City. Not that Rena's ever been to those places. She's seen them in movies. She nods as Wolfstein talks.

Her mind drifts back to Adrienne. She's nervous about going back. Look at her, fearing Adrienne. A mother shouldn't be twisted up about how her daughter's going to react to seeing her. Just *seeing* her. Her confidence is fading.

Rena's own mother was a saint. Chased her with a broom handle as a kid every now and again, and a bit overprotective, sure, but Rena always helped her when she could, let her know she was loved, went out of her way to please her. That's what good daughters do. Maybe it's just time to consider that Adrienne's not a good daughter and never will be. There's no plan of action for this kind of thing. No blueprint. Some daughters just turn rotten, Rena guesses. She can try to heal the rift, but if it doesn't take, then what? Lucia's most important. She's got to try to forge some bond with Lucia. Maybe this is her last chance.

She thinks back to Adrienne at Lucia's age. String bean legs, baggy sweaters, weirdly into hockey. Rangers this, Rangers that. Hiding in her room. One of their first epic fights on her birthday. A party at the Knights of Columbus, family, a buffet from Russo's, a DJ, Vic's associates bringing envelopes stuffed with cash as gifts, Richie Schiavano giving her two large in a shoe box. The wives of the other guys helping with the gravy and meatballs on the stove. She was never very close to any of them. She saw in them what she didn't want to be. Adrienne sat miserable at a table in the corner, picking apart the ribbon at the end of a balloon hovering up against the cork-paneled ceiling.

"All your dad and I did to get this party together and you're just gonna sulk?" Rena said.

"This is such bullshit," Adrienne said.

Rena, pushing harder, said: "Go talk to your cousins. They want to spend time with you. They came from upstate just to see you."

"Rockland County's not upstate," Adrienne said.

"Come on, A. Get it together." The gentle touch. A teenager, hormonal, Rena trying to understand.

"Fuck you," Adrienne said, staring daggers.

Rena wasn't about to cause a scene, so she walked outside and got some air. To avoid her cousins who were smoking on the corner by the bus stop shelter, she headed up the block and leaned against a fence post and cried. She felt like she'd been punched in the chest. Something collapsed that day. Or maybe it'd been a string of small collapses that she just hadn't noticed.

Adrienne strayed. The rest of high school was a whirlwind of missed curfews and broken promises. Things had gotten going with Richie around then, she found out much later. Rena never tried to understand her, she supposes now. She knew that Adrienne knew about Vic. Hard not to. She wondered how much, but she never asked. They never talked about Vic's work, the things he must've seen and done on a daily basis. Rena knew that was tough for Adrienne, but other kids they'd known lived with it and turned out fine. Chazz Caruso's son became a lawyer. Ralphie Baruncelli's daughter was a ballet dancer. Rena wasn't sure why Adrienne got wrecked by it or absorbed by it or whatever it was that happened. Not easy, she knew, but you come from where you come from.

Now she's thinking of Adrienne at six, jumping rope in the yard. Her smile. Little pearly teeth. That rainbow shirt she always wore. The fine down on her arms. Her sneakers thudding against the concrete. The weeds growing up between the cracks in the concrete: green, vivid. Her yard once *their* yard.

"Lost in thought?" Wolfstein says.

"A little, I guess," Rena says. "I don't know what to say to Adrienne."

"Say, 'Have you no heart, you ungrateful shit?'" Wolfstein grins big.

"I don't know," Rena says. "Maybe that's the right approach. Be a tough guy."

"I've got a little Ruger purse gun, you want it. No bullets. Just wave it around."

Rena knows this is a joke, but she doesn't like guns. Vic had a drawer full of them. Little Sal wiped the one he'd shot Vic with clean and threw it in the yard next to her basil. Richie Schiavano used it on Little Sal two days later, shooting him in the face as he got his head shaved at a barbershop near Most Precious Blood. That report came down to her from the top and was confirmed quickly in the newspapers, though Richie was never fingered by the Six-Two. Palms were greased.

"I think I'll pass on that," Rena says. "But maybe I need to be more assertive. Maybe that's always been my problem. Too soft. Too nice. I let Adrienne walk all over me."

"Different situation with my mother," Wolfstein says. "She was the rotten apple. Came crawling back years later. People said forgive her, you can't get closure until you forgive her. I was scared. Scared of her because she deserted me. But I tried. I was in AA at the time, and I was trying to do the right thing. Turns out she just wanted to take advantage of me. Thought I had dough, didn't know I'd blown it all. I cut her loose. She just wasn't any good."

"I'm sorry."

"Some people just aren't good, you know? No matter what you do or don't do. It's not your fault, is what I'm saying."

Rena nods. "I'm hoping Adrienne and I can work it out."

"You need that purse gun, you let me know."

They come to a little park called the Green Grass that looks out at the Throgs Neck Bridge and the Whitestone Bridge, the Manhattan skyline off in the distance. A small 9/11 memorial has little American flags planted all around it. NEVER FORGET is etched into the stone.

"A lot of firefighters from the neighborhood," Wolfstein says. "First responders. I'm not gonna give you the whole spiel. I was in Florida when it happened. People came here and watched the smoke trail."

"Terrible," Rena says.

"Truly," Wolfstein says. "But everybody's got a story. The people, the ones that lost loved ones, that's their story. Their lives are ruined. They don't want to talk about it. Everyone else wants to fucking yap about it. 'I knew a guy who knew a guy.' No one can let a tragedy be a tragedy anymore without claiming some part of it."

"That's true."

"I'm glad for all the firefighters around here, I'll tell you that. I fucking hate fires. Joint I lived in, in Laurel Canyon back in '78, went up in flames while I was passed out half-sauced. Still have nightmares about it. I keep an escape ladder tucked under my bed. I smell smoke, I'm out my bedroom window in less than ten seconds. The trick is not drinking too much. You drink too much, you don't wake up until the fire's right on top of you. My friend Georgina, she was in that fire with me. Zonked on dope. I had to pull her out. Almost got us both killed."

"I remember the church burning down in my neighborhood," Rena says. "This was around the time I was finishing up at Brooklyn College. St. Mary's, my church my whole life. I was just there this morning, matter of fact. The pastor back then, Father Reilly, he was a good guy. I remember I was walking home from getting pizza with my friend Ginny, we see the smoke coming up over the train tracks. We went over and stood there, watched the place just crumble. This is the church I was baptized in, my parents were married there, you know? Father Reilly's leaning against the wall of the bank on the corner, saying, 'We'll rebuild, we'll rebuild.' The place isn't even gone yet, he's talking about rebuilding. It wasn't that different from 9/11. For me, you know? Heartbreaking.

"They did rebuild, though. Took three years of going to Mass in the school auditorium, but they got it done. Vic and I got hitched in the new church not long after. I think about that fire all the time. I'm just sitting there in a pew, rosary beads in my hand, I'm thinking, 'The church that was here burned down.'"

"Terrorist attacks and fires, what a world," Wolfstein says, shaking her head. "You ready to go give it another shot with Adrienne?"

"I am, I think," Rena says.

Rena stares up at the sky, too bright, too blue, making her feel as if she's set to fail. A murderous stillness in the air. The world seeming slack, unpretty. Wolfstein is at her side. She's about to raise her hand to knock when the door swings open.

Adrienne's standing there. "You're back?" she says. Still with that savage look. The dream of the girl she was. If she looked like Vic, as people had always said, it was the Vic Rena hadn't seen much of, the one who broke arms and smashed heads for a living.

"Of course," Rena says. "I'm not giving up on you and Lucia. Never."

Adrienne twists her feet on the threshold, avoids Rena's gaze, looking at the Impala. "Is that Enzio from the corner's car?"

"He let me borrow it."

"He's your boyfriend?"

"He's not my boyfriend, no." Pause, deep breath. "Can I see Lucia?"

Adrienne looks at Wolfstein. "The fuck are you doing with my mom?"

"I'm her muscle," Wolfstein says.

"Her muscle. That's good." Adrienne half-smiles.

A thundering of feet on the stairs in the house. Lucia comes rushing up

behind Adrienne and tries to force her way past her. Rena on the verge of
surprise-crying, somewhere between sadness and joy. Her girls. That blood
feeling. Vic's face flashing in Lucia's. Lucia has something of him in her
eyes, her nose, even that soft chin. Young Vic in the Catskills on their honeymoon, that same tenderness. Rena looking at her own thin, bony hands
now, shaky with the possibility that the moment will end.

"Get back inside," Adrienne says.

Lucia lights up. "Grandma Rena!"

Rena thrusts out her arms, wanting so badly to wrap Lucia up in a hug.
"Oh, my sweetie."

"Adrienne's trying to make us leave." Lucia's voice is harried, anxious.
"Her and Richie. They're taking me away. I don't know where. Can I come
with you?"

"Shut up and get back inside," Adrienne says. "And don't call me Adrienne. Call me Mommy, huh?"

"Don't talk to my granddaughter like that." Rena reaches out for Lucia.

"Or what?" Adrienne says.

"Maybe I'll step in," Wolfstein says.

Adrienne laughs. Lucia is still trying to get past her, so Adrienne pushes
her back into the house, and she lands hard on her bottom. "Stay the fuck
out of our lives," Adrienne says to Rena, slamming the door shut in their
faces.

They go back to Wolfstein's house to regroup, Rena shaken up, Wolfstein
trying to comfort her. When Wolfstein pushes the door in, they're stopped
in their tracks by the lanky old man sitting at the counter in the kitchen.
He's got carrot-colored skin. Hair dyed coal black. Floppy, long-lobed
ears. He's wearing a cheap Hawaiian shirt with parrots on it, and there's a
hard-shelled eyeglass case protruding from the gaping breast pocket. He's
got a cigarette going, lodged between his lips, and he's blowing smoke at
the ceiling. He looks like an actor—Rena can't remember the guy's name.

The one who was in the movie she likes with that redhead—what's it called? She's upset about Adrienne. She's not thinking clearly. She's not thinking it's the guy who called. And then she turns to Wolfstein, who looks more taken aback than frightened.

Wolfstein screws up her face, throws the house keys on the table, and says, "Hey there, Bobby." Playing it cool.

"Lacey," Bobby says, drawing deep on the cigarette. Thick Bronx accent, he's got. "Who's your friend?"

"This is Rena."

Rena waves.

"That your Impala out there?" Bobby asks.

"Sort of," Rena says.

Bobby stubs out the cigarette on the counter. "Sounds like there's an interesting story behind that *sort of*." He reaches into his pants pocket and takes out a small gun.

Rena's chest clenches up.

"Dug around a little and found your piece," Bobby says. He tries to spin it on his finger and fumbles it onto the counter.

"I don't have any bullets for that," Wolfstein says.

He picks it up, aims it at his head, and pulls the trigger on an empty chamber. "Well, shit," he says, and tosses the purse gun in the general direction of the garbage can, missing wide. He reaches back into his pocket and takes out an envelope. "Also found this on top of the fridge," he says, pulling a folded piece of paper out of the envelope. "Letter from a pal of yours named Mo where she talks about your marks down in Florida. 'That one, Bobby,' she writes, 'he was a sad case, and I almost feel sorry for him.' I mean, I came to know all of that elsewhere, but it still hurts to see it laid out like this, Lacey." He stuffs the letter back in the envelope and tosses it on the counter.

"Bobby, get it together," Wolfstein says.

Now Bobby's leaning over on his stool, digging around down near his ankle. Rena sees that he's wearing an ankle holster and he's unfastening another palm-size gun, this one pearl-handled. He brings it up and presses it to his temple. "Guess I'll have to use this instead of yours."

"Come on," Wolfstein says, hands raised. "Don't do this. Don't be dumb."

"You broke my heart," Bobby says, and he starts bawling.

"Bobby, stop. I'll give you your money back. That's what this is really about, right?"

"It's not just about the money!" Bobby says. And then he takes the gun away from his head and aims it at Wolfstein.

RICHIE

BACK IN BENSONHURST

Caccio's Social Club is on Eighteenth Avenue and Seventy-Eighth Street. Richie walks in. It's been a while since he's been here, but it was a regular haunt in his days with Vic. Since Sonny got bumped up and spends so much of his time hulking at a table in the far corner, Richie comes less often. Kaplan is behind the bar, working the gleaming espresso machine. The same tattered tinsel shimmers on the walls. A framed and signed picture of Joe DiMaggio is propped over the register. Five card tables are set up with folding chairs. Richie's left the MAC-10 he got off Freddie Touch in Williamsburg in the trunk of his Caddy, the silencer on it made special by Wheelchair Jim Strazella. Richie's thought through this plan. He can see how it all might backfire, but he's not prepared for it to. He just wishes Crea was set to be here.

Ice House Johnny and Nick Minervino are sitting at a table in the corner, a sleek black briefcase on the floor between their feet. No sign of Sonny in the joint.

Richie greets Kaplan.

"Been a while," Kaplan says.

Kaplan: the guy's gotta be forty-five, but he looks sixty-five. Richie trusts him. Whatever happens here, Richie knows Kaplan will keep it close to his vest. He's fireproof. Vic always used to say, "Kaplan's got his priorities straight." Richie likes that he's not making a big scene, that he's acting like it's still routine for Richie to be there, knowing likely that the air is cold between him and Sonny. He's heard the rumblings all these years, Sonny and Crea with everything to gain from Little Sal's move on Vic.

"Do me a favor," Richie says, picking up a toothpick from the dispenser on the bar and playing it between his fingers.

"Anything," Kaplan says.

Richie leans in. "Leave the back door open for me in a bit."

Kaplan nods. He seems to know what this means.

Richie goes over to the table. Johnny stands first. Richie kisses him. Nick's next. As soon as he pulls back, Nick says, "Fuck you doing here, Richie?"

"Been a while, that's how you greet me?" Richie says.

"Nice day, huh?" Nick smiles. "Good weather. You see the new Vietnamese joint they put in where DiBella's Bakery was?"

"How's Crea?" Richie asks.

"Crea's Crea. You know Sonny's on his way, I take it?"

"I know everything."

"And you're feeling, what, excluded?"

Kaplan brings over three espressos with lemon for the rim and sugar cubes. That's what they have. You don't like it, you fuck off. One time, Richie was in here with Jackie Epifanio's son, and the fucking guy orders decaf and asks for cream. You would've thought the guy sniffed someone's daughter's underpants, the shit they gave him. They threw him out in the rain like garbage. Jackie was there, too. He was all for it. "Little sissy with his decaf," Richie remembers Jackie saying. "I'm sorry for that, fellas. Kid's gotta learn. Thank you." He *thanked* them. Unbelievable.

Richie rubs the rim of his cup with lemon and gives Kaplan a high sign.

"You looking to make waves here?" Nick asks him.

Richie settles back onto his chair, puffs out his cheeks, looks up at the wood plank ceiling. "What *am* I looking for? That's a good question."

"Just tell me if I'm gonna have trouble or not. I'm not feeling very enthusiastic about life today, you know? My daughter's got mono, you believe that? All the shit I do for her, she goes and gets mono. That's from kissing, right? I mean, who the fuck is she kissing so much, that's what I'd like to know."

Ice House Johnny interjects: "I don't know, Nick. Tragic."

"Mono's not tragic, you chooch," Nick says to Johnny. "Take it easy. I just want to know if she's whoring around. Thirteen years old, she is. I thought I had a little more time. I just got her a new bike last year. You go that fast from bikes to making time?"

"Thirteen's not that young nowadays," Johnny says.

"Listen to fucking Yogi Berra over here." Nick laughs, sips his espresso. "I can always count on Johnny to cheer me up. That's one of the powers of someone with limited capacities."

"You're making fun of me," Johnny says.

"He's making fun of you," Richie says.

"It occurs to me, Richie," Nick says, "that maybe you're the wrong person to talk to about this. Didn't you start up with Adrienne when she was, like, in eighth grade? Vic, God bless him, I'm glad he never knew. How is she? You still see her?"

"Don't talk to me about Adrienne, okay?" Richie says.

"Touched a nerve, I'm sorry." Nick's fingers curl up like a goddamn limey as he tilts back the espresso cup again.

Sonny Brancaccio enters the club. Three hundred pounds. Short getting shorter, it seems. Sweating. His oversize suit jacket is draped halfway down his thigh, yellow tie undone around his neck. Wiping his bald head with a handkerchief. Big rings on his fat fingers. The peppery splatter of moles on his neck. Knotty lump of scar tissue on his earlobe where Mad Dog Rizzo took a bite out of him back in '88. Ralphie Baruncelli and Chazz Caruso are at Sonny's side, both lumbering oafs.

Kaplan gets Sonny's special red chair and pulls it up to the table next to Richie. Nick and Johnny stand and kiss him. Richie kisses him. Ralphie and Chazz get kisses, too. Everyone settles down after all the kissing.

"Richie, now why the fuck are you here?" Sonny asks. "I didn't say for you to be here. I didn't say squat to you about this meeting, far as I remember."

"You didn't, no," Richie says.

"To what do we owe the honor of your presence, then?"

"I'm tired, Sonny."

"You're tired, go take a nap, huh?"

Everyone erupts into laughter.

"This guy's tired," Sonny says, taking out his wallet and holding up a hundred-dollar bill. "Ralphie, Chazz, go across the street to the dollar store and buy Richie a pillow and one of them little sleep masks, how about that? Then we'll set him up on a pallet in the back, so he can get some beauty sleep."

More laughter.

Sonny withdraws the hundred and stuffs it into his jacket pocket.

"That's funny, Sonny," Richie says. "*Funny. Sonny.* Look at that. I'm a poet."

Sonny doesn't seem amused anymore.

Kaplan brings him over a double espresso and a plate of seeded cookies and then disappears to the back.

Sonny dunks a cookie in his coffee and munches on it. "I can only assume," he says to Richie, "that your intent, for whatever purpose, is to fuck with me today. And, if I can be frank, it seems as if you've been leaning toward fucking with me for quite a while. This, I don't like at all."

Richie drinks from his cup even though it's empty. He's surprised it's empty. He shows it to everyone. "Empty," he says, pointing to the gravelly residue at the bottom. "You remember Sally Boy Provenzano?" he says.

"You're asking me do I remember Sally Boy Provenzano?" Sonny says.

"Of course he remembers Sally Boy," Ralphie Baruncelli says. "Fuck is this? You wearing a wire?"

"You go rat on us?" Chazz says.

Sonny motions to Ralphie and Chazz. "Check him, maybe."

"You can check me all you want," Richie says. "You ain't gonna find a wire or even a piece. All you're gonna find is a heart that's changed."

"What's this whack-a-doodle talking about?" Nick says.

"Let me tell you the story of Sally Boy Provenzano," Richie says.

"I got time for this?" Sonny lets out a big heaving sigh. "I know the story, assclam."

"'Assclam'?" Ice House Johnny says, and Nick nudges him again.

"Sally Boy Provenzano got tired," Richie says. "He got tired of getting taken for granted. He got tired of getting looked past when big scores came down the pike. He got tired of betrayals, guys like Gentle Vic clipped by nobodies so people could move up. He got tired of psychos like Crea with no fucking code. Sally Boy was loyal for a long time—"

Sonny finishes for him: "And then one day he wasn't." He sucks on his upper lip. "You know what happened to Sally Boy, correct? He ripped off close to a rock and got clipped by Cosimo the Fig in Maryland at a rest stop. This is a threat? You gonna make a move here, Richie? You're gonna announce it like this?" Sonny struggles to stand up. His feet are little. He's angry. He picks up another cookie, jawing it to a paste as he continues talking, crumbs raining down on his lapels: "All I did for you since Vic kicked the bucket, you're gonna come in and threaten me at the club? This is gratitude?"

"There's an order to things," Nick says. "You got a beef with Sonny, you gotta consult over your head. What we're doing here, we're trying to square a beef, that's it."

"A beef?" Richie says. "Well, I got a beef with Crea, too. How come only Sonny's issues get addressed?"

"Are you hot with us, or are you hot with Sonny?" Nick says, genuinely confused.

"I'm hot with everyone," Richie says.

Sonny slams his hands on the table, the espresso cups rattling on their saucers, the rest of the seeded cookies knocked from the plate in a wild scatter. "Well, you better cool the fuck down, Richie, before I have Ralphie and Chazz take you downstairs and put your head in the ammonia bucket."

Richie's not scared. He feels wired. Alive. He's thinking about Adrienne. He shot so fast with her in the kitchen, that's how nuts she makes him. He can't wait for another go, maybe in a motel on the road. Get the kid a separate room and put something on pay-per-view for her. He just stares at Sonny.

"Why you looking at me like a goddamn Christmas decoration?" Sonny says.

"I got a proposition," Richie says.

"You got a proposition for me?"

"For all of you." Richie waves his hand around the table. "How about I take that briefcase on the floor between Nick and Johnny and just walk right out of here? And you, Sonny, and Crea's crew representatives here, everyone just considers it as a peace offering *to me*."

"You just ride off into the sunset with the dough?"

"That's the tentative plan. Of course, I've gotta factor in other possibilities."

"You gotta factor in my balls." Sonny laughs. The table shakes with his laughter. Nick and Johnny start laughing. Ralphie and Chazz follow suit. "This guy's *got* to be fucking with me."

"Hey, you're right, Sonny," Richie says. "It's just a goof. I got wind of this here sit-down and thought I'd bust your balls a little."

"This fucking guy," Nick says. "You had me very perturbed, Richie. Very perturbed. The insinuations you were making."

"Yeah, I really didn't want to have to kill you," Ralphie says. "I always liked you because you gave me that Mickey Mantle card the one time."

"That was a valuable card," Richie says.

"You're still a friend?" Nick asks.

"Of course."

"I don't know if you've got to go on meds or what," Sonny says, "but your goof was a stupid idea. You had me going, but you don't want to get me going, do you? Sally Boy Provenzano—what were you thinking? Just saying that guy's name is enough to get you clipped."

"I know, I know," Richie says. "I'm sorry. My sense of humor's all fucked up these days."

"Your head's shot to shit maybe. The wiring up there. Too much stress, anxiety, I know how it goes. Go to the Russians and get a little action, huh? Start thinking straight."

"That's a good idea. I am feeling a little nerved up." Richie gets up and walks around the table, stopping to kiss them all. "Gentlemen, I apologize for my immaturity," he says.

"Sick fuck," he hears Sonny say, as he heads for the door.

Outside, he goes over to his white '82 Cadillac Eldorado hardtop coupe, parked at a hydrant, and he gets in under the wheel, keying the ignition and letting the car idle. He opens the glove compartment and takes out a De Nobili Toscani cigar he's got waiting there. He fires it up using the car lighter and puffs away with the window open, scanning the radio for something good. Hendrix. Springsteen. He settles for Yes on 104.3. He watches the club.

After a few minutes, he pulls away from the curb and drives around the corner, backing into the narrow alley that comes up behind the club. The alley has a high fence on both sides and is shielded by trees from the neighboring houses.

He stubs out the cigar in the coin-scattered ashtray. He pops the trunk and leaves the car running. He gets out and leans into the trunk. He's got a pair of heavy-duty work boots there on top of his packed bags. He changes into them, leaving his sandals in their place. He takes a look at the new

Nikon F5 he scored from Scrummy's nephew. He can't wait to use it. He imagines a life of roadside motels, eating burgers at drive-in joints, shooting old neon signs and faces behind steering wheels.

The other thing in the trunk—the most prominent thing—is the MAC-10 with its special Wheelchair Jim Strazella silencer. Fucking Strazella has that magic touch. Vic's favorite guy. The thing whispers. He picks it up and holds it across his chest. It's the same gun that Butch kills Vincent Vega with in *Pulp Fiction* is why he likes it. He saw that movie five times in two weeks at the Loew's Oriental on Eighty-Sixth Street the year it came out. Classic. What was that, '94?

He's got a New York Rangers ski mask next to the gun, but he decides not to wear it. Fuck's the point? Might as well let them see his face. He leaves the trunk popped.

The back door of the club is covered in green graffiti. Kaplan's left it unlocked and wedged open. Good. Kaplan's lack of hesitation in helping him is further proof that wrongs need to be righted here. Forget Richie's private beef, his frustration with and ambivalence toward the family these days. Sonny and Crea most likely giving Little Sal their blessing to off Vic was a breach of protocol. The oath used to mean something. To hear Vic talk about it, *that* was poetry. The outfit merely overrun with no-good punks now.

Richie kicks past an overturned poker machine and scurries down a dark hallway lined with boxes. When he comes to the dark curtain, he takes a deep breath. He thinks of the dogfights he used to go to with Vic out at Floyd Bennett Field. This one pit bull, Erasmus, he was a killer. Richie channels him now. Clenches his neck. Pushes back the curtain with his free hand and leads with the MAC-10 in the other. Kaplan seems to have disappeared for good, which makes him happy.

Sonny, Ralphie, Chazz, Nick, and Johnny—they're sitting ducks. The MAC-10's spitting bullets before they can even move. And none of them are even armed—regulations of the sit-down.

It's a scene out of a gangster movie. Bodies jolt. Espresso cups shatter. The walls are painted with holes. Sonny, Nick, and Johnny slump over the table. Ralphie and Chazz have been blown off their feet.

Richie takes it in. A masterpiece. Blood in bolts on the floor. The drab quiet of the place. Spilled coffee leaking off the edge of the table. Last gurgling breaths. Sonny saying Richie's name twice before falling silent.

Seeing things like this, *doing* things like this, no matter how many times, Richie can't help thinking it's not real, it's a movie, the bodies aren't real bodies, the blood is fake blood. But it's real and this one's different, because it's the end of this life for him.

He goes over and grabs the briefcase where it's flopped over on the floor between Johnny and Nick, blood-streaked. He cleans it off with some paper napkins from the table and snaps open the lid. The money's there. Half a rock is what he heard, and half a rock is what it looks like. He slams the top closed, struggling with the safety lock. Then he takes the last cookie on Sonny's plate, the only one the fat fuck hasn't ravaged, and eats it in one big bite as he walks back to the Caddy and places the MAC-10 and the suitcase in the trunk with his other bags. He gets back under the wheel, lights the remaining half of his De Nobili, and drives calmly out of the alley as if he's just left his grandmother's house on some Sunday long ago.

WOLFSTEIN

"When I was a kid," Bobby Murray says, still holding the gun on Wolfstein, "I stole some money from my mother's dresser drawer. You know what she did? Some mothers, they come after you with a wooden spoon back then. Not my mother. My mother comes after me with a tire iron. Had me put my hands on the table. Smashed them. I was in casts, both hands, I forget how long. Different day and age. Doctors didn't give a shit. Rotten kid deserved it, stealing like that. I couldn't eat. Had to suck everything up through a straw. Couldn't write. Couldn't hold my wang to take a proper leak. Pissed all over the floor. But I learned my lesson."

"Bobby," Wolfstein says.

"'Bobby,'" he says, mimicking her. "I didn't want no trouble in Florida. I had plenty of trouble in my life. I wanted to have some fun. Pop some Viagra, dabble around in the sack a little with someone appreciates a good time. I worked sanitation my whole life. Had a little dough saved. Figured

I had a few years of living it up down there before I was too feeble for screwing or anything else." Now he's looking at Rena, telling her the story, explaining his side. "And then Lacey comes along."

"I thought you had a decent heart," Wolfstein says.

"Oh, I got a decent heart. Doesn't mean I'm gonna let you stomp all over me, you know? I'm no chump, that's for sure."

"Can I say something?" Rena asks.

"Maybe you should stay out of it," Wolfstein says, feeling semi-bad that Rena's been dragged into this but glad it's not just her and Bobby in the house. Also, Bobby's probably figuring Rena for just some neighborhood biddie, not realizing she's a wiseguy's widow.

"Let her say what she's gonna say," Bobby says, keeping the gun on Wolfstein.

"Put the gun down, huh?" Rena says. "This is just a misunderstanding, that's all."

"I'll get your money for you, okay?" Wolfstein says.

"The money's a secondary concern," Bobby says.

"What then?"

Bobby puts the gun back to his own head. "I'm gonna off myself, I swear." He's crying now.

"What can I do to stop that from happening?" Wolfstein asks.

"Marry me," Bobby says.

The first night Wolfstein met Bobby in Fort Myers, they'd gone back to the condo he was subleasing in Cane Palm. Nice place. Coffee table stacked with paperbacks, clean windows, big-screen TV, stereo system, leather sofa, fake flowers on the table. They were drunk. She remembers that he was humming—what was it? A Sinatra song? His refrigerator contained low-fat plain yogurt, prunes, and leftover mahi-mahi from some bar or other. On the counter was a shaker full of salt substitute. He talked about his mother then, too. How she was only fourteen years older than him. Crazy, right?

The sex was disappointingly long, as it often was when the mark popped a Viagra. He'd fallen down, bare-assed, swatting at a fly.

She's trying to remember something personal they talked about, something she can use to disarm him a little.

"I remember you said your sister lives in Connecticut," Wolfstein says suddenly, scrambling for anything.

"Come on," Bobby says. "You're gonna try this game with me? I know the score."

"I'm just making small talk."

"Quit it."

"Your sister's name was what—Marsha?"

"Never mind my sister."

"She still a gun nut? I remember you saying she liked classical music, too."

"This is her piece. She doesn't know I took it." Bobby shakes his head and thumps his free hand against his chest. "Never mind my fucking sister, okay? I'm gonna blow my brains out in your living room if you don't marry me!"

"Marry you right now?"

"Agree to marry me, I mean. Lacey, I was never so happy as I was with you. I've been miserable since I left Florida. Two years, I been trying to find you. I didn't even know your last name. I had to hire this private investigator out of Yonkers, Quinlan, and he finally tracked you down."

"Bobby," Wolfstein says, "listen to me. I took you for fifteen grand, from what I remember. I got that much right upstairs. Let me give it to you and then we'll part ways, okay? I'm not gonna marry you, because I'm not marrying anybody."

"Go get the money," Bobby says, wiping tears from his cheeks with his gun hand.

"Now you're using your head," Wolfstein says. "You just put the gun down and sit tight a second."

"Okay, okay." He sets the gun on the counter.

Wolfstein goes up to her bedroom, locking the door behind her. She's ambivalent about leaving Bobby alone with Rena, but this is her only shot to shake him. She stands on the bed. The vent is in the center of the wall above the bed. It's big, with a steel cover kept in place by six screws. She keeps the screws half-tightened so she can just undo them with her fingers and push the cover up. The fireproof battery bag fits snugly in the duct. She yanks it out and drops it on the bed. She unzips it. The money is wrapped in plastic. She counts out fifteen large. She hopes Bobby doesn't come knocking. She works fast. She closes the bag and puts it back in the duct, replacing the cover. She gathers the money in her hand and wraps it with a hair tie she finds in the top drawer of her dresser. One hundred and fifty hundred-dollar bills. The pile doesn't look that substantial.

She goes downstairs and offers it to Bobby. "We're square," she says.

"This was never just about the money," Bobby says.

"Take it. And let's be done here."

Bobby pockets the money. "I appreciate the gesture."

"It's time to go. We've got a lot going on right now."

"You and your pal here?"

"Right."

"How about a quick celebratory drink?"

"Celebrating what?"

"Your effort to make right by me."

"Stop."

"You owe me a drink, I'd say. All I'm asking. One drink and then I'm out of your hair."

"Fine," Wolfstein says. Then to Rena: "Would you like something?"

"Thanks, I'm good," Rena says, sitting back on the sofa, her head in her hands.

Wolfstein fills a pint glass with ice and then pours vodka with a heavy hand. She squeezes lime juice in until it clouds the vodka, the way Bobby likes. She brings it over to him, and he takes a belt.

"That's a good idea?" Rena says.

"He needs to stay calm," Wolfstein says.

"I shouldn't have aimed the gun at you; I'm sorry," Bobby says, slurping more vodka. "I just have this deep love for you, Lacey. I never felt like that before. My old gal, Myrna, the broad I went with for years before Florida, I never felt like that once. I know you were just hustling me. I had Quinlan track you down. He found out some stuff. I was just a mark, like your friend said. But I don't believe you were faking it all."

"I like you," Wolfstein says. "But, listen, there's no future or anything here. I've squared things with the dough, and that's as far as I'm going to go."

Smacking his hands together, Bobby says, "Can't pull a gun on a broad and expect fireworks after that."

"I also think there'd be some trust issues, me having ripped you off."

"Maybe, yeah. I just think there's still a connection." Another long pull from his glass, draining what's left.

"That was a lot of vodka," Wolfstein says.

"Turns out I was thirsty. I'm feeling a little looser."

There's no shaking Bobby. He talks Wolfstein into another drink and tries to dance with Rena, pulling her up from the couch. "There's no music," she says. Wolfstein's losing patience.

He starts singing "Mack the Knife," twisting Rena's arm.

"Aw, leave her alone, Bobby," Wolfstein says.

Rena escapes his grasp and heads up to the bathroom, whispering something about needing to freshen up.

"I chased her away," Bobby says.

"You're loaded."

"I'm feeling good. Sue me. Turns out I really needed a drink. And I got this dough burning a hole in my pocket. You want to go to the casino with me?"

"It's time to take off. You want me to call a car service? That's how you got over here, car service?"

"Not yet, come on. Let's shoot the shit a little. Let's play rummy."

"You sick in the head?"

He comes over and tries to dance with her, sloshing some of his vodka onto the floor, singing: "Oh, the shark has such pretty teeth, babe. And he shows them pearly whites." Fading to a whisper, forgetting the words. His voice becomes something of a sludgy hum. "I'll give you a hundred bucks for your time," he says.

"You're gonna give me a hundred bucks from the money I just gave you?"

"Sure, yeah. I'm so lonely."

"I don't think so."

The shove catches her off guard, and she topples back against the wall. Bobby, flustered, steps back and runs his hands through his hair, exhaling. He's managed not to drop or spill any more of his vodka. He downs the rest of it. Wolfstein's seen a lot, but she's never seen someone chug vodka like beer. She leans back on her hands and gets up slowly, remains poised.

"I'm just so goddamn lonely," Bobby says again.

Rena comes back as Wolfstein is dusting herself off. "What happened?" she asks.

Bobby looks at the floor. "I shouldn't've pushed her."

"You pushed her?"

"I just wanted to dance a little. Have some fun." He goes over to the counter and pours three belts of vodka into his glass, no ice or lime even this time. He drinks it in two big gulps.

"I don't want you puking in here," Wolfstein says.

He shakes his shoulders, lit up from the inside, his face a mask of fluctuations: regretful, boozy, proud. "Listen. You shouldn't ever push no broad. I was frustrated. I'm sorry, Lacey." He pours another half-glass of vodka and drinks it. "You could've just cut the rug with me, you know?" He motions to the bare wood floor. "So to speak."

"My pal Rena over here already took out a bum like you for this sort of behavior," Wolfstein says. "Be careful."

"I'll give you five hundred bucks for your trouble. No shit." He sits on the stool and takes out the stack of money Wolfstein just gave him. "Money's no problem." He peels off a few hundreds and fans them out on the counter over the scattered condensation rings left by his vodka glass. He puts his head down on the money and, almost immediately, starts snoring.

"He just passed out?" Rena says.

"Looks like it," Wolfstein says. "Some piece of work, this fuck."

Bobby stays passed out. Wolfstein pulls the money out from under him, sticky wet from the condensation, and puts the bills back into the hair-tie-banded stack. She stuffs the fifteen grand back in his pocket. Rena is sitting on the sofa, every once in a while crossing to the window to check Adrienne's house.

"What are we gonna do with him?" Rena asks on a pass back to the sofa.

"Let him sleep it off," Wolfstein says. "He'll wake up and skedaddle, I bet."

Rena sits, nodding.

A knock on the back door.

Wolfstein jumps to attention. "Now who the hell is this?" she says.

Opening up, she's somehow not surprised to see Lucia standing there, wearing a tattered Yankees cap with a curved bill, twisting her sneakered foot into the spongy welcome mat, holding a small blue suitcase covered in silver hologram stickers against her chest. "Can I come in?" Lucia asks.

"Kid?" Wolfstein says. "Of course. Come in."

Rena notices her then and rushes over. "Oh, Lucia, what are you doing here?"

"Running away," Lucia says.

"Your mom doesn't know you're here?"

Lucia shakes her head. "I hate her." She pauses. "I know we don't know each other that well, but I think I want to stay with you from now on."

Wolfstein's got Rena pegged as a commonsense kind of dame, the kind who'll put her hand on her granddaughter's shoulder right now and explain all the reasons why that's a bad idea, the main one being they're right across the street, and chances are good that Adrienne will come sniffing over here soon. Another one being that she's on the lam from what she did in Brooklyn and it's probably not a good idea to drag Lucia into that.

It doesn't happen that way.

"We'll get to know each other better," Rena says, hugging Lucia. "You shouldn't talk like that about your mother, but it's easy to see it's a bad situation over there. I'd love if you stayed with me."

"That's a good idea?" Wolfstein asks.

"We'll get out of your hair right now—"

"I'm not saying that."

"Adrienne's leaving anyway," Lucia says. "Running away with Richie. He's stealing a bunch of money and then they're taking off." She pauses, considers Bobby. "Who's that guy?"

"He's no one," Wolfstein says. "Say again about your old lady and this Richie?"

"They want me to go, but no way I'm going with them," Lucia says.

"Richie's stealing money from who?" Rena asks.

"The people he works for," Lucia says.

"You know about this how?"

"I heard them. And Adrienne told me to get packed. He's probably on his way back soon. She's going nuts over there now, tearing the house apart."

"You're not using your head here, Rena," Wolfstein says. "You're already on the run from one thing. You want to add this?"

"We'll get in the car now," Rena says. "Don't worry. This is an opportunity. An opportunity to give the two of us the relationship we deserve. We deserve a life together. My daughter's clearly not fit to care for Lucia. And she's putting her in more danger than I'll be putting her in."

"That could be true, but I don't see how it's the right move."

"Let's go, Lucia," Rena says. "Let's hurry. Thank you for everything, Wolfstein."

"Hold on a sec," Wolfstein says. "Just hold on."

ENZIO

This day and age, you get anybody's address off the internet. Where else this *zoccola* gonna run to but her daughter in the Bronx? Enzio used to know the kid, Adrienne, from around the neighborhood. Hot-to-trot little number.

He still can't get over the fact Rena bashed him in the head and stole his Impala. Better not be a scratch on the goddamn thing. Or a stray pussy hair on the front seat. Him just being nice, trying to get a little fun started. Broad in her sixties like Rena, however the fuck old she is, nobody's lining up. Him thinking she'll take what she can get at this point. He could've paid for it with some Russian bird, easy, no stress, but he thought he'd go for the romance angle. Vic's wife deserved a little respect. Not anymore.

To take the Impala was the lowest of the low.

Truth is, he would've let the attack go, bloody gash and all.

But the fucking car.

So he's on the subway, the D into the city first, where he switched for the Pelham Bay Park–bound 6, the train he's on now, his head wrapped in bandages, wearing fresh chinos and a red-and-black bowling shirt, having had to throw out the clothes that'd been bloodied up by the incident with Rena. Crawling to the phone, eyes closed, feeling the blubbering buzz of his head wounds, unwieldy boner from the Viagra he'd popped, that'd all been a big pain. They gave him stitches at Maimonides. Twenty. He told them it was a fall. They said it's lucky you didn't kill yourself, your age. He laughed and said he's always been a lucky son of a bitch.

Guy across from him is reading a pocket Bible. Sure, Enzio likes the Bible. He listens at church. He used to take collections, wear his best purple jacket, go around with the basket at St. Mary's, wave it in people's faces, but you read the Bible on the subway like it's the new James Patterson? What bullshit. He wants to nudge the guy in the gut, tell him take a break. Only possible point could be letting everybody know you're a goddamn Bible-thumper.

The guy notices him noticing the Bible. Smooth chin on this guy. Captain America shirt. Olive skin. That cologne he's wearing—what is that? Flowery smell. Maybe he's a poof, using the Bible to cover it up.

"You okay?" the guy says, closing his Bible, a frilly ribbon marking his page. "Your head?"

"Fine," Enzio says, shuffling closer to the window.

"You have an accident?"

"Little fall, that's it."

"I'm John."

"What're we, pals here?" Enzio says.

"I'm just trying to start a conversation," John says. "We go through our lives afraid to talk to people, especially in a city like this. What are we afraid of?"

"Whatever you're selling, bud, shove it up your twat."

"I love New York," John says. "Who talks like that? So, so great. I'm from Texas originally."

"Why don't you go back to Texas and leave me alone?"

"You read the Bible, sir?"

"Here we go."

"It's got everything," John says. "Blood, sex, death, redemption, you name it."

Enzio purses his lips. "You're saying what about the Bible?" Not that Enzio's read the thing all the way through. Mostly he's heard it from the altar. Readings. Bits in homilies from Father Ricciardi, Monsignor Stankus, and Father Reilly all those years ago. But he's not sure if this John's saying something he should be offended about. Maybe he's reading the Bible as a joke. That case, Enzio should give him a hard time.

"I'm just saying it's got everything you could want in a book."

"Okay, fine," Enzio says.

"I've got an extra copy here in my bag. Would you like it?"

"I got plenty of Bibles. I look like a guy wants for Bibles? What's your scam?"

"No scam, sir. Just spreading the Good Word."

"I will tear you a new asshole, John, if you don't leave me alone."

Enzio puts his elbows on his knees, staring hard at the floor. John gets off at the next stop, Grand Central. Let him go try to push his phony Bibles on some tourists.

After finding out where Rena's daughter lived in the Bronx, Enzio called his old pal from the neighborhood, Harry Guttuso, who'd just recently moved over to his sister Nancy's joint in Bronxville to be closer to Empire City Casino at Yonkers Raceway, which was opening soon and was going to save guys like Harry the trouble of taking a bus down to Atlantic City a few days a week. They stayed in touch, him and Harry, though Enzio wasn't generally big on keeping in touch once people moved outside of about a ten-block radius. A lot of hours they spent talking and playing cards at Mama Zucco's on Bath Avenue, and Harry really made the effort to stay in touch. Called every couple of weeks. Invited him over to Bronxville. He was good that way. When Enzio called and said he was coming up to the Bronx, Harry said he and his nephew would drive over from Bronxville and pick him up at the station.

Enzio gets off at the Westchester Square/East Tremont Avenue stop. Stinky and crowded. Bronx-stinky. No Brooklyn smells.

Down at street level, he looks around for Harry. Big schnoz, surefire identifying marker. Been six months or so. Could be Harry's gained a shit ton of weight living with Nancy, her pushing spaghetti and meatballs and chicken cutlets on him seven nights a week.

He sees him finally, over by a coffee stand, young kid at his side. Kid's maybe eighteen or nineteen, wearing tight jeans, tight T-shirt, got a sloppy beard needs trimming. Hungover, that's how the kid looks. Harry looks pretty much the same as he's always looked. Schnoz like an eggplant. Wiry arms. Shirt with palm trees on it, notepad in the breast pocket. Cargo shorts. Loafers.

Harry smiles, trudges toward Enzio, the kid staying nearby. "What happened to your head?" Harry asks.

"Little fall," Enzio says.

Harry throws his arms around Enzio, kisses him on the cheek. "Jesus."

"I know, I know. A real dolt."

"I took a fall in the shower last week. Almost broke my dick off."

"Getting old's no good."

"You can say that again. This here's my nephew Lou." Harry pulls Lou over, Lou reluctant, embarrassed. "Lou, meet Enzio."

"This is what, Nancy's kid?" Enzio asks.

Harry, nodding: "Looks like her, right?"

"A little bit, yeah. Around the eyes." Enzio puts out his hand. The kid shakes, limp-wristed. "What're you supposed to be with that beard?"

"Just too lazy to shave," Lou says.

"Too lazy to shave. Get a load of this kid."

Walking across the street and past a joint called National Diner, Enzio's thrown off by the fact that it's dusk. He's not out in the world much these days at dark or near dark. If he goes out, he's usually home by the end of the afternoon at the latest, bowl of Cheez Doodles in his lap, nice little porno on his big-screen TV. He gets tired of watching titties bounce, maybe he puts on *Scarface*. Pacino, what an actor.

"You got a broad over here or something?" Harry asks.

"Something."

Lou lags behind them.

"Kid, you got shit in your drawers?" Enzio says to Lou, laughing. To Harry: "What's wrong with your nephew, he got shit in his pants?"

"He's a slow walker," Harry says.

"Slow everything. Beard's weighing him down. You tell him he looks like a goddamn terrorist? Way things are in this world nowadays, you tell him his goal should be to look American?"

"Ah," Harry says, waving Enzio off, "I leave the kid alone, let him live his life. I'm parked just up here on Ferris."

Enzio shakes his head. "Listen, I need to, can I borrow your car?"

Harry: "I can do you one better. Lou's between jobs. He can drive you around, you need it. You don't know around here."

"Not necessary."

"Trust me. Especially night. We don't want you getting in an accident in unfamiliar territory."

Enzio tosses it around in his head. His objective being get to Adrienne's and get the Impala back; he's not really anticipating any hitches in that plan. But say the car's not there. Or, worse, say the car is beat up. What then? He goes apeshit, it gonna be okay to have this Lou around? "Okay, if you're sure it's no problem."

"Lou," Harry says, calling over his shoulder, "it's no problem you drive Enzio around a little, right?"

"Happy to," Lou says.

"Might be I need to go somewhere right now," Enzio says.

"Whatever you need," Harry says. "You gonna stay with us in Bronxville the night? Nancy's got the guest room set up. You don't need to worry about getting back to Brooklyn."

"It all works out, maybe." Enzio pauses. "I'm here for my car is what it is. I *don't* like to drive in the dark."

"The Impala?"

"Long story, but it wound up over here, I think, and I gotta get it back."

"Someone stole it?"

"Pretty much."

"How's someone pretty much steal a car?" Harry motions to an electric blue Nissan Maxima wedged between an SUV plastered with Yankees stickers and a graffitied white van of indiscriminate purpose. "This is us right here."

Enzio gets in the back. Harry does a slow dip into the passenger seat, pulling his legs in one by one, groaning as he settles roughly against the leather. Lou finally dribbles over, opens the driver's door, and plops under the wheel.

"Lou does all the driving," Harry says.

"That's nice," Enzio says.

"You were saying how someone pretty much stole your Impala."

Lou pulls out of the space, tapping the front bumper of the van, and then they're moving fast up the block.

"You remember Vic's wife?" Enzio asks.

"Gentle Vic Ruggiero?" Harry says. "Course. Rena. Real straight shooter."

"I'll come clean with you. I was trying to get her into the sack. Lot of years we live near each other. Vic's gone a while, I'm thinking maybe she's backed up, never another guy in her life I know of. Her friend Jeanne tells me I got a shot. What the hell? I'm always looking for a piece. Rena's nice for her age, too. I should've just gone to Coney, gotten me a Russian streetwalker, as per the usual. But, no, I go and get ambitious."

They turn onto Westchester Avenue, Lou rolling down the window and letting in the noise from outside. Harry turns around. "Christ, man. You put the make on Rena Ruggiero? Vic's crew finds out, then what?"

"Far as I can tell, she's pretty cut off from them. Always was, really."

"Here, get on the Hutch right here," Harry says to Lou, motioning frantically at the on-ramp, and they speed onto the Hutchinson Parkway, almost sideswiping a minivan.

Enzio's not sure where they're going, but he doesn't ask. Harry already said Lou would drive him around.

"So what happens?" Harry asks Enzio.

"I bring Rena over to my place. I give her some wine. I put on a skin flick."

"You put on a dirty movie?"

"That's right."

"Thinking this'll get her all hot and bothered?"

"That's right, yeah."

Harry laughs a raucous-old-man laugh. "Let it never be said that you know what the fairer sex desires. Who does that as an icebreaker?"

"I'm thinking, you know, it's been a while. She sees that action, she wants to screw."

"Vic's gonna come back from the dead and hunt you down, my friend. What happens next?"

"I pop a Viagra, try to get close."

Harry spits out a long, rumbling breath. "You put your hands on her?"

"Not in a rough way. I'm being a gentleman, for the most part. I'm trying to coax this desire out of her, that's all."

"Let me guess. She up and smacks the shit out of you."

"She grabs this fucking glass ashtray, used to belong to Maria. It was her old man's, for his stogies, you know? Thing's heavy like a couple of bricks. She clocks me with this ashtray. I go down, zonked."

Harry laughing again. "KO?"

"Fucking KO."

"Rena's got a little Mike Tyson in her, how about that shit?"

"I wake up. Blood everywhere. Head's killing me."

"You got a chubby from the Viagra?"

"Mean one."

Harry's laugh becoming a cough, leaning forward, straining against the seatbelt. He taps Lou. "You hearing this? You're not laughing? Enzio wakes up with a boner, covered in blood. Old broad bopped him one with an ashtray. That'll teach you about consent."

Lou nods.

"I make it over to the phone," Enzio says. "Call nine-one-one. Ambulance shows up. They take me out on a stretcher. I'm so cloudy I don't even notice."

"Notice what?" Harry says.

"The fucking Impala's gone. They take me to Maimonides, I get twenty stitches. Doctors look me over, I'm otherwise okay. I get a car service home. That's when I notice. I get out of the car-service car, I see an empty driveway, my tarp balled up in the garbage. I'm thinking, at that point, it's just a regular theft. Some kid from the Marlboro Projects taking it out for a joyride on the Belt or something. I'm about to call it in to the cops, it occurs to me: *Fucking Rena.* My key's gone. Just the Impala key. Missing from my big ring. I go over, check her house, she's nowhere to be found. I know she's got this daughter over in the Bronx. I'm guessing she thinks she killed me, so she stole my car and went on the lam."

"You gotta be shitting me," Harry says.

"I shit you not."

"Well, my friend, you are in an unenviable position, I'd say."

"I want the Impala back, that's it."

"What happens it's not where you think it is?"

Lou chimes in: "Or it's messed up?"

"Cross that bridge when we get to it," Enzio says.

Enzio's antsy to get to Adrienne's, but Harry wants to be dropped at Nancy's in Bronxville. He tells Enzio Lou will take him to look for the Impala. Lou saying, "Yeah, right on."

Fifteen minutes to Nancy's, a little brick joint with flowers in the yard, red shutters, a DirecTV dish, and a heavy-duty mailbox. The suburbs, that's what it looks like. Harry struggles out when they pull up to the curb, asking Enzio if he's hungry, maybe he wants to come in and eat something first, Nancy's got some Arthur Avenue Italian bread and can defrost some gravy. Enzio says he'd rather find the car first, it's tap-dancing on his nerves not knowing where it is or even if it's in one piece.

Harry says, "I don't gotta warn you, do I, it looks like Vic's crew is involved at all, I'd like my nephew out of there?"

"They're not around. It's a restrained situation. No danger for the kid."

"Some of the beefs you had back in the neighborhood, you could be a little reckless."

"I could be a hothead, yeah."

"I'd say treat Rena with kid gloves, you can. This is a widow. This is Vic Ruggiero's widow."

"I know, I know. I got blinders on for the Impala right now."

"Understandable."

Harry disappears inside.

"You want to ride up here?" Lou says.

"I'll stay in the back," Enzio says. "How long to get there?"

"You got an address?"

Enzio digs around in his bag, finds the address where he scribbled it on last week's church bulletin. He shows it to Lou.

"Silver Beach. Probably take us twenty minutes to get back. We weren't far when you got off the train." Lou pulls away.

"So, what's your story? You just drive your uncle around all day?"

"I'm an artist."

"An *artist*, huh?"

"I do comics."

"That's art?"

"You don't think it is?"

"Superheroes, all that silly shit?"

"I don't do that kind of stuff. I write and illustrate stories about regular people. Barflies, clerks in grocery stores, jockeys, a lot of kinds of people."

"Sounds boring."

"People living isn't boring."

"You draw big jugs, anything like that, maybe you're talking my language. I see the appeal there."

Silence as Lou negotiates them through traffic back to the Hutch. Enzio staring out the window, tapping the glass. Red lights swamping the road.

"Tell me about your car," Lou says.

"It's a 1962 Chevy Impala two-door. Black paint a mile deep. Red interior. Red vinyl seats with cloth inserts and carpet that's got black flecks. Under the hood's a 5.3-liter LS 2 with less than a thousand miles since rebuild. Champion three-row radiator fed by a Holley 600 carburetor. Freshly rebuilt Muncie four-speed manual transmission. Rear axle houses a set of 3.36 gears. Borgeson power steering. Power front disc brakes. New polyurethane bushing between the body and in the control arms. Radial tires. Aluminum alloy wheels. You know cars at all? Long time I've had this car. A lot of dough I've put into it. Got a guy who works on it special over on Avenue X."

"I don't know shit about cars," Lou says.

"You don't know shit about cars, why'd you ask?" Enzio says.

Lou shrugs. "You ever think how amazing the world is? Three hours ago, I'm jerking off with this hand." He takes his right hand off the steering wheel and holds it up. "Now I've got it on the wheel, driving you around. A couple more hours, I'll be eating pretzels with it while I watch the rerun of last week's *Sopranos* finale. Not really a finale, but you know. The end of part one of this last season. Anyhow, that's amazing, isn't it? Same hand. You'd think maybe we should have different hands for different things. Like: *Oh shit, it's time to put on my jerking-off hand or driving hand or eating hand.*"

"What the fuck are you talking about?"

"Guys with hooks for hands, how you think they jerk off? Just rub against stuff?"

"Why you got me thinking about guys with hook hands? What is this?"

"I'm just saying."

"You're just saying?"

Lou shrugs, and they drive on in silence.

When they pull up to Adrienne's house, Enzio is relieved to see that the Impala is parked out front. Undamaged. He lets out a breath. "Thank Christ," he says.

"What?" Lou says.

"We pull up, it's just here, was the best-case scenario. That's come to pass, and I'm relieved."

"You want me to stay?" Lou says. "In case there's any issues?"

"Nah. Car's here. I'm gonna get the key and go."

"You don't want to follow me back to Bronxville? You told Uncle Harry you might stay the night."

"Same shit, I drive to Bronxville or back to Brooklyn. I don't like driving in the dark, but I've got to do it, I might as well just go home."

"Okay. You got Uncle Harry's number, you need it. Just let us know."

"Thanks for the ride," Enzio says, pushing out his door and then closing it behind him.

Lou gives him a salute through the window. The Maxima screeches away.

Enzio walks around the Impala, looking for little nicks and scratches and dents in the glow of the streetlamp it's parked under. Nothing he can see. He tries the handle. Locked.

It's just dark out, the sky still showing a bit of purple on the horizon. It's nice out here in this part of the Bronx. Different. Feels a little like a beach town or some shit. He takes in the houses around him. A goddamn quality tricycle on one lawn. Enzio wonders why anyone needs such a nice tricycle. How long's a kid gonna use it? And then to leave it outside like that. Fancy.

He approaches the house. No bulb on over the front door. He rings the bell, the button crackling a little when he pushes it. He wonders if maybe he should've brought a weapon. Not a piece—he's never liked carrying a piece. But maybe a bat, something like that. He needs to get a little mean, a little confrontational, it's good to have something to swing around.

Door pops open, and there's the daughter. Must be the daughter. Even prettier than he remembers. Nice brown eyes, like the girls he went to school with. And she's got these long nails. Sexy. He imagines them scratching up his back as he throws a mean lay on her. A little bit of Brooklyn left in her, but she's got some Bronx swagger now. That's sexy, too. Behind her, he can see the living room's a mess. Clothes strewn on the couch. A couple of boxes overflowing with junk.

"Jesus Christ," she says, looking him up and down, really lingering on the bandages. "Enzio from the corner?"

"That's my car out there," Enzio says. "Where's your mother?"

"I recognized it."

"Recognized what?"

"Your car. You're what—dating Rena now? She says no. Says you let her borrow the car. I'm thinking you don't just let someone borrow a car like that unless you're fucking."

"I'm not dating Rena, believe me." He looks over her shoulder. "And I'm definitely not making time with her. She in there?"

"She's not here. I didn't want to see her. I don't know why the car's still here. She was hanging out with the lady across the street earlier. Maybe she's over there."

Enzio turns and looks at the house opposite them. "I want this to be easy," he says.

Adrienne, dismissive: "I've got nothing to do with this."

Enzio biting his tongue.

"Good luck finding Rena," she says, trying to shut the door on him.

He stops it with his foot. "I'm not done talking to you."

Adrienne sighs. "Whatever's going on, I've got nothing to do with it."

Enzio looks over her shoulder again, not believing that Rena's not in there. "But she's been here and maybe she's coming back." He moves forward. "I remember you from the neighborhood. Your old man, I had a lot of respect for him obviously."

"Don't talk to me about Vic."

"Far as your mother, I was just trying to be nice. She clocked the shit out of me and stole my Impala."

"Rena did that to you?" Adrienne says, pointing at his head. She laughs. "What'd you do to make Rena go nuts?"

"Don't worry what I did. She was out of line."

"Well, great to see you, but it's time for you to fuck off." Adrienne succeeds in forcing the door closed, Enzio getting his foot out of there before it gets rammed against the jamb.

Enzio walks back to the Impala and tries the handle again. Still locked, as if it would've miraculously opened itself. He looks at the house across the street, tries to get a sense of whether Rena's in there.

A big car turns the corner and pulls up behind his Impala. It's a white '82 Cadillac Eldorado. Enzio soaks it in. A beaut. His buddy Phil Gambole used to have one just like it, except brown.

The Caddy purrs to a stop.

When the guy behind the wheel gets out, Enzio's taken aback. It's Richie Schiavano, Gentle Vic Ruggiero's onetime right-hand man. Richie's admiring the Impala, maybe remembering it. They only ever talked a handful of times, a *Hey, how's it going* here and there.

"I know this car," Richie says, looking up at Enzio. "I know you."

"Richie, how's it going?" Enzio says.

"Vic's neighbor, right? Fuck you doing here?"

"Let's just say there's been a little issue. It's under control now."

"Issue, huh?"

Adrienne comes out of the house. Harried. Looking all around.

"I'm here, sweet thing," Richie says. "You ready for a new adventure?"

"Where's my daughter?" Adrienne says. To Enzio: "You see my daughter come out?"

"She what, left?" Richie asks.

"I thought she was upstairs packing," Adrienne says. "I go up, she's nowhere to be seen. You believe this shit?"

"Maybe she's with Rena?" Enzio says.

"Rena's here?" Richie says.

"I need this like I need a hole in my head," Adrienne says.

Richie: "We gotta scoot."

Adrienne: "I know we've gotta scoot. I didn't anticipate this shit."

"Crea gets wind of this fast, he knows to look here for me. I wish he'd been at Caccio's so I could've just taken care of him, too. Lu got a friend she'd run over to their house?"

"Maybe she's with Rena?" Enzio asks again.

Richie's confused. "Fuck's Rena doing here?"

"You said maybe Rena's across the street?"

Richie to Enzio: "What's your business with Rena?"

"She stole my car. I just want the key back, that's all, and I'll be on my way."

"Rena stole your car?"

"That's what I said."

"That can't be the whole story."

Enzio ignores Richie and slug-shuffles in the direction of the house across the street, picking a rose from a well-tended, overflowing bush as he passes it. He hears the trunk of the Caddy open and slam shut behind him, hears Richie telling Adrienne, "I did it, I got the dough," and then they're bickering, but he doesn't look back. He climbs the front stoop of the neighbor's joint, using the railing for leverage. Standing before the door, he knocks as hard as he can, clutching the rose in his fist, careful not to get pricked by its thorns.

RENA

Rena is glad that she allowed herself to be drawn back in by Wolfstein's words. *Hold on a sec. Just hold on.* She's sitting on the couch, Lucia next to her, and thinking about what to do. She takes off with Lucia, what exactly happens? Where will they even go? Not back to her house in Brooklyn. Will Richie and Adrienne pursue her? How much does Adrienne really care about Lucia? And what about Enzio? Is he dead? If he's still kicking, how far will he go to get the Impala back? Maybe she should just leave it where it is and catch a Greyhound. Her head's spinning with questions. She can't believe where the day started and where it's gone, and there's that Bobby Murray just passed out at the kitchen counter to make everything that much stranger.

"Life's a wild card," Wolfstein says, touching the bouquet of dried roses that hangs from her ceiling. "That's one thing I've learned. I knew this girl Yum Yum out in L.A. Real sweetheart. She was on the lam from something. I never figured out what. But I'll never forget, the last time I saw her, she says to me, 'Wolfie, what's it all for? All that ever happens is I get my heart broken.' And that really stayed with me. Everything we do, every decision we make, we're just trying not to get our hearts broken, right? My thinking is you can't live in fear of heartbreak. Sometimes you've gotta face it head on."

"That's true," Rena says.

"I can't tell you what to do," Wolfstein says. "I can just suggest you not be rash about your decision. Adrienne comes over, what happens?"

"I'm not going with her," Lucia says.

"What do *you* want to do, sweetie?" Rena asks her.

"I don't know. Tell me something about Papa Vic. What did he like?"

"I'll talk about Papa Vic until I'm blue in the face, that's what you want. He would've been so proud of you. Especially with that Yankees cap on." Rena breaks the tension with a wink.

Lucia half-smiles. The way she's sitting, though, Rena can see just how much aggression and worry she carries in her body. Slouch to her shoulders. Legs goose-pimply and quivering. She picks up one of Wolfstein's cross-word puzzle books from the coffee table and thumbs through it anxiously.

Some commotion out on the street now. Voices whisper-yelling. Night all of a sudden, Rena sees through the blinds, a purplish gloom burying the neighborhood. A trunk slams. Footsteps. And then a loud knocking at the door.

"Guessing that's your daughter," Wolfstein says in a huff.

"We should've just gone, maybe," Rena says.

"I'm not going with her and Richie," Lucia says again.

"I know."

Wolfstein goes over and opens the door, ready to duke it out with Adrienne.

But it's not Adrienne.

Enzio stands there. Anger coloring his cheeks. His head bandaged. A rose in his hand. He looks past Wolfstein at Rena on the couch. She can't believe it's him. She's more surprised than shocked or scared.

"You're alive?" she says. "How'd you find me?"

"You're gonna go where but your daughter's?" Enzio says. "You don't like daisies, how about a rose?" He underhands the rose in her direction, and it falls at her feet.

"I'm sorry I hit you," Rena says, "but you shouldn't—"

"This is the guy?" Wolfstein says to Rena. And then to Enzio, getting in his face: "You shouldn't touch a woman who says don't touch her."

"Where's the key to my car?" Enzio asks, one hand stroking his bandages, ignoring Wolfstein.

"I'll give you the key," Rena says. "Just go."

Richie and Adrienne come trudging up the walkway behind Enzio. "Where's my daughter?" Adrienne asks, pushing past Enzio.

"Rena, what are you doing here?" Richie says.

"I'm not going with you two," Lucia says.

Adrienne: "The hell you're not."

Rena: "Adrienne."

Adrienne puts up her hand. "Don't you fucking speak to me."

Enzio clears his throat. "Where's the key, you crazy old bitch?"

Rena takes the key out of her pocket and throws it at Enzio. It bounces off his shoulder, clanking to the floor.

"Now you're throwing keys at me!" He trembles into a lean, struggles to pick up the flat key. "These miles you put on my car. There should be hell to pay for this behavior. Be happy I'm a forgiving guy."

"You can shove your *hell to pay* up your ass," Rena says. "What you did, you're lucky I don't have you killed."

Richie puffs up. "This stugatz did something to you, Rena?"

Adrienne shoulders against him. "Stay out of it. Let's get Lucia and go."

"He tried to rape me," Rena says.

"You tried to *what* her?" Richie says to Enzio.

"The lady doesn't know what she's saying." Enzio is still unable to grasp the key. "She's trying to pin this on me. All I was after was a good time. No disrespect was meant. What she did, now, that's another story. Wallops me with an ashtray, steals my Impala."

"This is Vic Ruggiero's wife!"

"I don't need to be defended by a bum who started sleeping with my daughter when she was fourteen," Rena says.

Lucia looks shell-shocked, pulling her cap even lower over her eyes.

"Now, Rena. She was fifteen when we slept together the first time. I got a code." Richie pauses. "How do you even know that?"

"You've got a code?" Rena asks.

Richie turns to Adrienne: "She knows all of everything about when we started?"

Bobby lifts his head from the counter and tries to shake out of his drunkenness. "What's going on here? Now we got a party?"

"Bobby," Wolfstein says, "please go back to sleep."

"'Go back to sleep,' you're gonna say to me?" Bobby straightens out in his chair. His hair is wild. He smacks his lips. "Listen. All these people, whoever they are, I don't care about them. Let me ask you something again real quick, Lacey." He gets off the stool, smoothing down his shirt, running his fingers through his hair, a facial expression like he's chewing something tough turning into a sudden smile. "Lacey, Lacey, bear with me here. Interesting day, I know. Let me just say, I really think we got something here."

"Jesus Christ."

"Let me just say, we're a good pair, we are. I see big things for us. Now, I don't have a ring or anything, but why don't you marry me?"

"Bobby, you got a cigarette? I'm dying for a cigarette."

Bobby fishes around and comes out with what's left of his pack. He hands one to Wolfstein, lighting it for her.

"Thanks," she says. "You're funny, Bobby, I'll give you that. A funny guy." Liotta to Pesci in *Goodfellas* coming out in her voice a little. Impossible to say those words and not say them that way.

"Now, Lacey, this isn't very nice. I'm no clown. Come on, honey. I want to marry you. You gonna marry me or what? I'll take you to Vegas."

"Goddamnit," Enzio says, frustrated, his face close to the floor, trying to use a penny he's fished out of his pocket to flip the key so he can grab it.

Lucia laughs a little. Amped up. Thrown off by the spectacle around her. "He's really having a hard time with that key."

"Shut that little turd up!"

"Don't you dare talk to my granddaughter like that," Rena says.

Enzio finally gets a grip on the key and lets out a sigh of relief. As he's rising back to a standing position, he fumbles it, and it clatters to the floor.

Richie busts out laughing.

Adrienne, showing her claws, says, "Lucia, let's go *right now*."

Enzio pinches the key up between his fingers, gazes at it as if he's holding some long-sought glowing treasure, and then drops it again.

"Too goddamn good," Richie says, shaking his head.

Enzio succeeds in picking up the key on his next try, standing now, grasping the key in his closed fist like it's a do-or-die pill he can't lose.

"I had time, I'd break your neck," Richie says to Enzio. "Putting the moves on Vic Ruggiero's old lady like that."

"Richie, Lucia, *now*," Adrienne says.

Richie looks over at Wolfstein and seems to really focus in on her for the first time. "Where I know you from?"

Wolfstein shrugs.

Richie's eyes dart around the room, taking in the pictures on the wall. "Holy shit. Luscious Lacey? You've gotta be kidding me. *Suzy's Last Night on the Planet* was my jam. What was that, 1982? Such a sick year." He raises his right hand and extends his stubby little thumb, nail chewed to the quick. "*Corn-fed Cheerleaders*." Next is his pointer. "*Swallowed Hole*." Then his other three fingers shoot up all at once. All raw, all low-bitten. "*Swedish Catastrophe, Sex Barge, Trashy Dreams*. Classics, the whole bunch. What am I missing?"

"You're missing a lot," Wolfstein says, dropping the butt of her smoke into an empty Bud Light bottle.

Adrienne exhales. "You were in what, porno movies?" she asks Wolfstein. And then back to Richie: "And you used to what, whack off to them? I'm so skeeved out."

"*Charity Box*," Richie says, throwing up his left hand and starting anew with that thumb.

"Not a lot of people saw that one," Wolfstein says.

Left pointer. "*Nuns Not Guns*."

"That was fun."

Richie's searching the ceiling. "Help me out."

"I don't think so. We're not in a very good situation here."

"Give me one more. I'm seeing you and, like, a guy in a spacesuit."

"*Alien Seduction*."

"That was wild."

"Directed by Tony Cardinale. He was a genius in a lot of ways. A sicko, but a genius."

Adrienne tugs at Richie's arm. "Not a good situation, like the lady said. Let's go."

Richie shakes out of it. "Yeah, right. Crea."

Enzio starts to take notice of the pictures on the walls now. "Luscious Lacey?" he says. "I know your movies."

"Oh, I'm sure you do," Rena says.

Bobby's back on his feet, shaking his head like a shaggy dog. "You were in skin flicks? That's wonderful. I flat-out admire you, Lacey. All the shit you navigated. Movies like that, conning guys like me. That takes guts and brains. I ain't kidding. I say *you're* a genius.

"You won't marry me, huh? Sweetheart, I'd take care of you. That dough you stole—and returned, thank you very much—was just a drop in the bucket. I'll take you on carriage rides around Central Park. We'll get a room at the Waldorf, you want. I'll take you on a cruise. Norwegian Dawn. That big ship passes under the Verrazano. You seen that one? They'll treat you like a queen. Buffet, manicures, shows. We'll go to Atlantic City three times a week, you want. I get comped rooms. They give me front-row tickets to any show I want. Who do you like? You wanna go see that Jerry Seinfeld do his stand-up? There's a funny guy.

"One thing. In these movies, you didn't take it up the dirt track, did you?" He's back over at the counter. No one's listening to him. Least of all Wolfstein. He picks up the gun, which Rena had all but forgotten about, and starts waving it around. "I've got a piece here, people!" he says.

"Who is this guy?" Richie asks.

"He's nobody," Wolfstein says.

"I'm nobody, huh?" Bobby's pissed. "I'm getting awful tired of being called nobody. My name's Bobby Murray, and I'm in love with Lacey Wolfstein. Even though she ripped me off for fifteen grand and broke my heart. I'm willing to put that behind me."

"Well, Bobby Murray." Richie steps forward. "I'd put that gun down if I was you."

"Richie, who cares?" Adrienne says. "Let him shoot himself, my mother, Wolfstein, whatever. Just put my daughter under your arm and let's go!"

"Fuck you!" Lucia shouts.

Bobby's hand is fish-flop wild. Everyone ducks as he arcs the gun from floor to ceiling and then lasers it from left to right. "I'm telling you, I'm not messing around here. I gotta yank the trigger to get what I want, I'll do it."

"Bobby, calm down," Wolfstein says.

Richie puts up his hand, a flat stop sign. "Hold the phone, old-timer. You got a full house. Women, a kid. And, to be honest, you don't look like you know how to handle that piece. What's your beef? Who you want to kill?"

Adrienne: "Don't get in the middle of this."

Bobby: "I don't know."

Richie: "You don't know, right? So put the piece down and try proposing marriage another way, okay? How's that sound? Reboot the situation."

Bobby turns the gun on Richie, his feeble hand doing a zonky-hard DT tremble. "Maybe I want to kill you?"

Richie laughs. "I'd definitely think that over. You know who I am?"

"I give a shit who you are?"

"How about we go out to the street? I got my piece in the Caddy. We can have a duel. Ten paces. All that."

A pulsing silence fills the room for a moment. Bobby's keeping the gun on Richie but looking at Wolfstein. Wolfstein's looking at Rena and Lucia. Richie's looking at Bobby. Adrienne wears the expression of someone who wants and expects something to be over and is deeply disappointed to find that it's not. Lucia is excited and confused, like this is Shakespeare happening in front of her. Rena, she's not sure what to do with her eyes.

Adrienne prods Richie. "You're gonna get yourself shot by this nobody when you're this close to getting free?"

"You're right, A," Richie says. To Bobby, hands up: "Listen, fucko, you just lucked out. I've got a bright future ahead of me, and I'm not gonna louse it up on account of some no-count piece-of-shit old man. God bless. Good luck with Luscious Lacey. Luscious Lacey, thanks for the memories. I was gonna say, 'Thanks for the mammaries,' but I bet you get that one all the time." He moves toward Lucia, his car key out in his hand now, motioning at her blue suitcase. "This your bag, kid? Don't make me carry you like an insane asylum patient, okay?"

"I said she's not going anywhere right now," Rena says.

"Rena, all due respect, you don't just swoop in and call the shots with your daughter's kid. You remember Crea, right? You heard Vic tell plenty of stories about Crea. With the hammer and the eyebrows? What I did, no doubt Crea's hunting my ass. Believe me, you want us out of here before Crea shows."

"Put your hands back up!" Bobby says.

"I'm trying to do right by you, guy," Richie says. "Don't fuck with me. That's sound advice, and it cost you nothing."

Bobby, without hesitation, steadying his arm with his other hand, squeezes off a shot.

The bullet goes wide and hits Adrienne, standing by the doorway, right in the neck.

A gasp rips from Rena. She can't believe this is happening. Everything's slo-mo. She looks away from Adrienne—her daughter, her only daughter—and she wraps Lucia up in her arms, trying to block her eyes. Lucia struggles away, crushing underfoot the rose that Enzio threw.

"Mommy?" Lucia says.

Adrienne is holding her neck. She has this tragic look on her face, something like the time she had pneumonia in fifth grade, frail as garlic paper, convinced she was dying. She shrivels to the ground, blood seeming to swarm from her neck like a blur of red moths, her hands in the flow like she's trying to choke it to a stop. Those long nails of hers, that's what Rena focuses on. Gurgling noises sputter from Adrienne's mouth.

"Call an ambulance!" Rena says, a bolt of pain roaring through her whole body. Her toes thrumming with pain. The backs of her eyes. Her bones burning with it.

"What did you do, Bobby?" Wolfstein says, making a move for the phone on the wall.

Enzio slips out the front door, headed for the Impala, shuffling along as fast as he can, holding the seat of his pants as he goes.

Richie, shocked, drops his car key on the floor in front of Lucia and jumps forward, falling to his knees and taking Adrienne in his arms, "Baby, no," he says. "Baby, you'll be okay. Baby, I got my new Nikon. I'm gonna take your picture at the best roadside diner we find. I'm gonna get you a milk shake. Vanilla. We're gonna see new places. Baby."

Adrienne coughs up blood, her eyelashes fluttering. She always had the prettiest eyelashes. When she was a girl, strangers would come up to Rena, women, and say, "I'd kill for your daughter's eyelashes." When she was a girl.

Bobby puts his hands in his hair and lets out a big breath. "Jesus Christ," he says. "I never even fired this thing. Not ever. I told him put his hands back up. I told him. No one takes me serious."

Richie looks up at Bobby. "How I'm gonna kill you," he says, tears in his eyes, "it's gonna hurt, and it's gonna take a long time, you degenerate fuck." Spit flying from his mouth. Sobbing. He's trying to get his arms under Adrienne to pick her up. Blood everywhere. "I'm gonna get you to a hospital, A. I'm gonna get the best doctor to fix you up. I've got all this dough in the trunk, and I'll throw it at these docs. They'll fix you up fast."

Rena is stroking Lucia's hair furiously. Lucia pulls away, disgusted. Rena calls out again: "Get an ambulance here, Wolfstein!"

Wolfstein is at the phone already, pulling the nine on the rotary dial and waiting for it to come back.

"Jesus Christ almighty," Bobby says. "I didn't mean to shoot the broad. I didn't mean to shoot her. What'd I do?"

When the new man enters the house, no one other than Rena seems to notice. Not even Richie. The man is squat, wearing a blue velour tracksuit, his gray hair slicked back with gel, his eyes registering twisted glee, as if he's overjoyed to stumble onto a scene like this. Dark creases in his forehead. Arched eyebrows. Patches of hair on his ears. He's carrying a big sledge-hammer across his chest. It takes Rena a second to fully recognize him. Crea. So much older-seeming now.

Rena wipes tears from her cheeks—her daughter, her only daughter bleeding out there right in front of her—and points at Crea, but she can't find a voice to say anything. She looks back at Wolfstein, who is talking to an operator. But then Crea approaches her and rips the handset from her grip, yanking the curly cord from the jack. He smashes the housing of the phone with his hammer, Wolfstein putting her hands over her face as pieces of the shell shatter.

When Crea's done, what's left of the phone hangs from a frayed wire. All eyes are on him now. "Kaplan was reluctant to give you up at first, Richie," Crea says. "But then he folded like a cheap chair. They always do when I bring out the hammer. I ever tell you how I got started with the hammer? I was just looking for, like, a trademark. Tried a lot of things. Hammer just seemed right. Anyhow, you're wondering how I found you in this house, I bet. It's like you fucks left a trail of bread crumbs over here." Crea walks back over to Richie and Adrienne. "Fuck happened? Who shot the twist?"

Richie turns to him, still sobbing, snot webbing down from his nose. "Crea, listen. A's dying here. Let me get her to a hospital. Please. Me and you, we'll get straight."

Crea smiles. "Get straight, that's good." He raises the sledgehammer up over his head. He looks over at Rena. He recognizes her, of course. He knows Adrienne is her daughter. He knows Adrienne is Vic's daughter.

"Crea, come on," Richie says.

The way Richie's sitting with Adrienne in his arms, it's the way you hold dying people in war movies. Rena's trying to think a step ahead, trying to protect Lucia from what's about to happen. Whatever Richie did, he's gonna get his head knocked into next week. And then what? What will Crea do with them? How will they get Adrienne help?

Crea smiles even bigger. His eyes are smiling. His whole face. "I ever tell you it was me killed Vic, not Little Sal?" he says. "Now how about I put Vic's bitch daughter out of her misery like an old racehorse?" He waves the hammer over Adrienne and then presses the head down hard against her throat.

Richie tries to get his arms out from under her, scrambling to reach for the handle of the hammer. Adrienne's making a low, flat dying noise. The fight she's got left isn't enough. What Crea's doing, he's doing for kicks. Rena's world goes dark.

LUCIA

Not every day your mother gets shot and choked out with a hammer right in front of you. Truth is, Lucia has daydreamed about this very thing. Or some variation. Wished for it, even, in the name of being free. But now she's not sure what to feel. She doesn't feel much of anything, really. She wonders if that makes her a psycho. She's not crying or puking or anything, just full of a sort of cold hollowness. Her mother's pain doesn't echo through her. She doesn't want to hold her hand or hear her say all the things she never said.

Grandma Rena's passed out on the sofa next to her. She went down like she was struck by a shock wave. Grandma Rena probably believes in God. Lucia doesn't. No way. Sunday always makes her feel like she believes in God even less, if there's any lower to go than not at all. And now this is what Sunday will always mean. The day her mother was killed.

Richie's wailing, on his knees, pushing Adrienne from his lap. "She's fucking dead," he says.

Lucia notices her mother's disgusting nails as her body tumbles away from Richie. She's always hated how long they are. She doesn't remember what color they were painted today. Now they're bright with blood.

Hammer Dude's laughing. Sick laughter. Did she hear him right? Did he say he was the one who killed Papa Vic? He's holding the sledgehammer across his chest again. Ready to strike. Ready to punch the hammer through Richie's chest now. Maybe Lucia wouldn't mind seeing that, either.

The old guy, the one who shot Adrienne, he's leaning over the kitchen counter, moaning. About to hurl, seems like. His gun—where's his gun? Lucia can't see it. "All I wanted," the guy is saying into the counter, blubbering, "all I wanted was to get hitched to Lacey."

"Bobby, shut the fuck up *right now*," Wolfstein says.

"I'm gonna kill you, Crea," Richie says, rising to his feet, his shirt striped with her mother's blood.

"With your bare hands?" Hammer Dude says.

Wolfstein rushes over to Lucia. "Grab your grandmother's feet. I'll get under her arms."

Lucia doesn't register what Wolfstein's saying for a sec. She looks down and sees Richie's car key on the floor. She plucks it up and stuffs it in the pocket of her cut-offs. She's thinking about escape. She's thinking of all the money Richie just said he has in his trunk. She knows Crea's here for that money, and she knows they'll need to get away from him first. But money means freedom. Money means a new life. Money means maybe finding her father. She needs to, she can drive. She remembers everything Big Paulie taught her. She thinks she remembers.

"We're gonna carry her upstairs to the bedroom," Wolfstein says.

"And then what?" Lucia asks.

"I don't know *and then what*. Can you carry your end?"

"I think so."

They pick up Grandma Rena and head for the staircase. Lucia's struck by how feather-light her grandmother is.

Crea doesn't pay them any mind. He's focused on Richie, ready to slam him in the jaw with the hammer.

Richie growls and lunges past Crea, going for Bobby's gun on the counter.

Crea takes a gusty swing and whiffs, knocking over Wolfstein's weird lamp and smashing one of her pictures on the wall, opening up a hole in the sheetrock. The hammer gets stuck, and Crea struggles to yank it out.

Richie's got Bobby's gun.

Bobby's mumbling, his head down. "Just shoot me," he says to Richie. "You've got the piece now. Just end it for me."

Crea clobbers Bobby in the back with the hammer. Bobby yelps like a dog slammed up against the grille of a fast-moving truck.

Richie, all nerves now, drops the gun.

Crea thwacks Bobby again. This time for the hell of it. Bobby's noises go feral, a deranged man giving birth to a new kind of pain, his body twisting.

Wolfstein is leading the way upstairs, Rena's limp body clunking against the steps, Lucia trying to keep her raised up and steady. "Jesus Christ," Wolfstein says. "You okay, kid?"

Lucia gulps and nods. She should feel shattered by the violence, by the noises. She should feel afraid. It's one thing that Adrienne's gone. Another thing that Crea's coming upstairs for them as soon as he's done with Richie. But she doesn't feel any of that. Maybe she is a psycho. Psychos must feel at home and alive in moments like this. She wonders—if she makes it out of this—if she'll be fucked up for life. Probably she's already been fucked up for life anyway, with her bloodline.

Rena's eyes open as they move down the hallway, Lucia finally letting her feet fall to the carpet. Her skin is green, and she's biting down on her breath hard like she's holding in puke. Lucia wonders what she's seeing and what she's thinking. Like, is she staring at the smudgy ceiling, feeling maybe it was all just some horrible dream?

"Rena, sweetie, how you doing?" Wolfstein whispers.

"I don't know," Rena says.

More crashing sounds from downstairs. They get in the bedroom, propping Rena on the bed. Wolfstein locks the door behind them.

"What are we gonna do?" Lucia asks.

"Is this all real?" Rena says.

"Sorry to say it is," Wolfstein says, trying to push her dresser in front of the door. "Help with this, kid, huh?"

Lucia goes over and helps. The dresser totally blocks the door.

"All that crazy fuck's got is a hammer," Wolfstein says. "We shelter in place, maybe we get out of this. The cops show, we're in the clear. Anyway, maybe he's finished when he gets done with the boyfriend."

"I think we should run," Lucia says. "Look"—taking the key from her pocket—"I got Richie's key. We can take his car. You want to deal with cops?"

"I avoid them when I can," Wolfstein says. "Rena?"

"Vic always told me, you got an option to keep the police out of it, you take it," Rena says. Stern. Focused suddenly. Less green.

"Both of you, I'm looking at you with serious eyes now. That's your mother down there," Wolfstein says, pointing to Lucia, "and your daughter," tilting her finger at Rena. "Honor-wise, I don't want you to have any regrets. We leave her behind, we leave her behind."

"She's dead," Lucia says.

"Rena?" Wolfstein says.

Rena nods. "What that bastard Crea did to my daughter, I want blood for that. And Vic. He said he killed Vic, didn't he? Jesus. We get out of here, it gives me time to process it all. Make a plan."

"Fine," Wolfstein says. "I don't give a shit about the house. That bastard smashed the only picture that was extra special to me. But I've gotta retrieve my dough, and we've gotta go to my pal Mo's straight from here and warn her about possible fallout. This is her joint. I'm sure the cops will be up in Monroe looking for her by tomorrow morning. Could be a good place to hide out and collect ourselves for the night, anyhow."

"Okay," Rena says.

"What money?" Lucia asks.

Wolfstein stands on the bed next to Rena and yanks the half-tightened screws from the vent cover in the center of the wall. She pulls out a square-shaped black bag and throws it on the bed. "This dough. My nest egg."

"How we gonna get out of the house?" Rena says.

"Out the window," Wolfstein says, getting down and dropping to her knees. Talking Lucia through it now: "I lived in a house in L.A. once that had a real bad fire. Since then, the joint I'm in doesn't have a proper fire escape, I carry around this ladder." She reaches under the bed and pulls out a compact ladder. "I attach it to the window, it drops down about fourteen feet." She stands and then goes over to the window, pushing up the screen. She latches the top part onto the sill and deploys the ladder. "It holds a thousand pounds. We go down in quick succession and make a break for Richie's car. Sound good?"

"I'll drive," Lucia says.

"I'll drive," Wolfstein says. "You two gotta be shaken up bad. And we get pulled over, we don't need a fifteen-year-old behind the wheel. Kid, you go first."

Wolfstein throws the bag out the window. It lands with a thud in the yard. Lucia turns her Yankees cap backward on her head and spiders down the ladder fast. She thinks about her suitcase, left behind on the living room floor, and realizes how little she cares about its contents. There are other Best Buys. Plenty more CDs to steal. She hates the clothes she has. Her toothbrush is so old. She wants an electric one. Only thing she really cares about losing is the tubed-up Jeter poster she managed to fit in there and those sorta-precious Yankees ticket stubs.

Rena's next. She's slow on the ladder. Unsure. She slips on one rung and almost flops down. Wolfstein is fast behind her, though she complains about a pain in her leg.

Soon they're all standing in the yard. Wolfstein's holding her bag of money like a football, shaking out her right leg. They look around. Across the street, The Guy Who Couldn't Pick Up His Key—Enzio is his name, Lucia remembers—is on his knees at the side of the beautiful old car Rena stole, searching underneath it for something, his reach limited. He seems nerved up. He's oofing and aahing, his old-man sounds echoing through the neighborhood. The hood of the car is glinting under the overhead streetlamp.

"Shit, the other one's still here," Wolfstein says. She nudges Rena. "Tell me this dummy dropped his key again."

"Looks like it," Rena says.

As they pass the car, Enzio draws back and looks up at them in horror. "My key," he says, mostly focusing on Lucia. "I dropped it, and it went under the car. Help me get it, please. I don't want to get killed."

Lucia ignores him. So does Rena. Wolfstein laughs a little.

"Please help me," he says. When he realizes no help is coming, he's back on his knees and elbows, reaching around under the car, groaning.

Lucia rushes to open the driver's-side door of Richie's car. She gets in, scooching over to the middle of the big front seat. Bench seat, it's called. She likes these old cars, how you can sit three people in the front. The kind of car where no one wears seat belts, either. She leans over and unlocks the passenger side. Rena climbs in and puts her left arm around her. Wolfstein gets under the wheel and throws her bag in the back. Lucia passes her the key, and she starts the car, a sweet rumble.

Lucia looks over in the direction of Wolfstein's house. Both Wolfstein and Rena seem to be stubbornly keeping their gazes away from it. Another car is parked out front. It's black and long, almost like a hearse, with tinted windows. A Mets flag hangs from the antenna. Probably Hammer Dude's car. Beyond that, the front door of the house is open. Richie and Hammer Dude are wrestling in the living room, right in front of Wolfstein's recliner. The hammer's gone. She doesn't see the gun. The men roll out of the threshold, and then they're gone from her line of vision.

She can't see her mother's body, but she knows it's there. Richie said she was dead, but Lucia wonders if she really is and, if she is, what that means, exactly. Is she seeing anything? Feeling anything? Lucia doesn't believe in God, so she guesses she doesn't believe in an afterlife, but she hopes that Adrienne and Papa Vic get to at least smoke a cigarette together or something. She doesn't even know if Papa Vic smoked, and her mom smoked only rarely, but that's something she'd want: one last smoke before it all went dark forever.

She makes a quick scan of the rest of the block now, expecting to see some curious neighbors outside, anxious about what's going on at Wolfstein's, but there's nobody yet. Maybe someone's peeping from behind a curtain. That's the way city people are. When the cops show, they'll gather like gossips out in the street, but when danger's still present, they're nowhere to be found.

Wolfstein pulls a quick three-point turn and then drives away up the block, lights still off. Lucia looks back and sees the old man shaking his fist at them.

Wolfstein negotiates the car through Silver Beach with its limited-access roads and then makes a left onto Pennyfield Avenue, hopping onto the Throgs Neck Expressway from there. Wolfstein flips on the lights. No one says anything. Rena looks as if she's totally passed through terror into anger. It's hot in the car. The windows are down. Lucia's ears are filled with the buzz of other cars whipping by. She doesn't know for sure where they're going—she's never really been beyond the edges of the city except for a couple of trips to Jersey, knows only these five boroughs—but she's glad not to be headed wherever with Richie and her mom. Or her former mom, whatever. Wolfstein said Monroe, and Lucia's pretty sure that's north, that soon they'll be out of the city, that probably there's no going back.

Lucia breaks the silence. "You were in porno movies?" she says to Wolfstein.

Wolfstein, hands loose on the wheel, says, "We've gotta get some cigarettes."

WOLFSTEIN

Of all the things she had to leave behind at the Silver Beach house, Wolfstein's only really bummed about the Stevie Nicks picture. That whackjob mobster with the hammer had to go and smash the hell out of it. Otherwise, she would've made an effort to grab it. Like Mo had said in her letter, that was the night of their lives, one to remember forever.

Now her eyes are steady on the road. Rena's in shock. Lucia's clammed up. They're in the middle lane on the Cross Bronx Expressway. She hasn't driven in a while, since Florida, maybe, but it's old hat. From here, they'll cross the George Washington Bridge and get on the Palisades. Without traffic and without any other hitches, it shouldn't take them but an hour to get to Mo's.

Wolfstein's admiring the Eldorado. Adrienne's boyfriend—or whatever he was, probably dead meat now—has kept it pretty immaculate. She could run her finger along the dash, she bets, and she wouldn't swipe up any dust. She knows cars. Admires them. Especially from the seventies and eighties. She got fascinated with them back in Los Angeles. Hard not to. You look around, there are all these beautiful cars eating up the landscape. Convertibles. Sleek machines. Big boats with chrome bumpers you could see the history of the world in. She liked nothing more than driving around L.A. and taking in the cars. She owned a couple of good ones when she was there, a Challenger and a Thunderbird, both sold when she hit the skids. Mo had a Trans Am once. The big shots in the industry she knew, they had ridiculous cars: Lamborghinis, DeLoreans. She still, most of all, appreciated a nice Caddy like this. The way you could throw your arm across the back of the bench seat and just cruise. Cars now, they're made like shit. Plastic. Toys. Built for safety, her ass. You drive around in a little Civic and a truck hits you, you get crunched up like an accordion. This Eldorado, it could take a licking. A tank, that's what it is.

She should be thinking more about Adrienne and Bobby and the whole nightmare scene back at the house, but she's not. Her hands are clattery on the wheel. She's got nervous energy. Her bones feel like hot glass. She's licking the back of her teeth.

Instead, her mind wanders to a call she got on her radio show this one summer night about a year into her run. It was particularly hot in the studio that night, the AC busted and a box fan humming in her face, and she was particularly breathy. The driver was a trucker who called himself Dr. Twatwaffle. The name got her giggly. He was flirty in mostly inoffensive ways. A lot of the callers, they were truckers and they weren't very nice or sweet, and they stayed on the line only long enough to shoot a load. But Dr. Twatwaffle, despite his alias, was sincere. And what he said to her, after complimenting her voice and her movies, was the truth. He either let it slip or he was just comfortable enough to reveal something about himself. He said, "I'm so scared. Since my divorce, I don't know what to do." Her response, one of the smartest things she's ever said in her estimation, was: "Just say *fuck it*, sweetie. Keep pushing forward."

And that's what she's trying to do now, she guesses. It's always been her nature.

In the rearview, she sees a car zooming up on their tail. Hard at first to make out in the cluttering grind of the Cross Bronx, cars ripping by on both sides with precise madness, but then it's easy to tell that it's the Impala that Rena showed up in. It stands out, the road lights reflected in its hood. Richie's behind the wheel now. She can see that as they get closer, nearly kissing bumpers. She can't figure how they could've caught up so fast. She should've been going faster, getting out of the city at ninety, smoke spinning up from the wheels.

"Shit," she says to Rena and Lucia, or maybe just to the night, "they're behind us."

Rena, shaken from her stillness, turns and looks out the back window. "Richie made it out? And Enzio's with him?"

Lucia turns now, too, fully on her knees, chin pressed against the back of the seat. "Where's Hammer Dude?"

"Maybe Richie killed him," Rena says.

"I doubt it."

Wolfstein speeds up, swerving into the next lane.

"Are we in a chase?" Lucia asks.

"I guess," Wolfstein says.

"Richie wants the car and the money."

"My money?"

"The money he stole. It's in the trunk. Didn't you hear him say that? Plus, he really, really loves this car."

The traffic is getting thicker. Wolfstein is switching lanes at a rapid clip. Richie's staying with her, elbowing the horn, motioning for them to get off at an exit. Rena rolls up her window. He gets next to them on the right, his window down, and screams, "That's my fucking car!" Enzio's slouched in the passenger seat, shell-shocked by the way Richie's jolting the Impala around, his cheeks ruddy, his mouth drooping open.

Richie gets so close to them, Wolfstein pulls the wheel left to keep from getting sideswiped.

"Open the window!" Richie calls out.

Lucia leans across Rena and cranks down the window. "Fuck you, Richie! Your money's my money now!" she says. Determination in her voice. A hard edge.

Richie scrunches up his face, confused, maybe a little wrecked by hearing that from Lucia. His face saying, *You were like a daughter to me.*

It occurs to Wolfstein they're not even going that fast anymore. Down to forty-five, but it feels much faster with the boxed-in tension of the Cross Bronx. All the other cars. The walls and overpasses. She's trying to get the needle over fifty, but the lanes are swelling and slowing up, and there's just no way to shake the Impala.

Richie's back behind them. Wolfstein makes another quick lane switch, and then he's a full lane over, two car lengths removed. Some breathing room.

"How we gonna lose them?" Rena asks.

"We're not," Wolfstein says. "Not until we get across the bridge at least."

Richie's riding the horn now.

Closer to the bridge, Wolfstein slips the car into a gap ahead of a big wobbly van with graffiti-covered windows and no hubcaps. The van blocks out Richie totally.

"It's like I picked up that ashtray," Rena says, "and then the world fell apart. I didn't do that, my daughter would be alive."

"Hey now," Wolfstein says. "Don't you think like that. Don't you talk like that. Does no good."

"I'm keeping Richie's money," Lucia says. That hard-edged voice again. "He got my mother killed. I deserve that money."

"Okay, kid," Wolfstein says. "You and Grandma Rena'll figure it out when we get to Mo's. Let's just get there in one piece, huh?"

"I don't pick up that ashtray, nothing goes wrong." Rena's stuck in that line of thinking. "Richie and Adrienne are riding off into the sunset."

"Probably doesn't happen like that."

Lucia: "And what about me? I wasn't going anywhere with them."

The Impala cuts out from behind the van and comes up on their left again, Richie hitting the horn in short spastic burps.

Lucia reaches across Wolfstein and flips Richie off.

"You're a goddamn firecracker, kid," Wolfstein says.

Rena's muttering under her breath.

Wolfstein catches a quick glimpse in the rearview mirror of another familiar car behind the Impala, the one that had been parked outside her joint when they took off, a black Lincoln Town Car, probably a '95 or '96, Mets flag looped on the antenna. It's bathed in bright highway light. Richie doesn't see it, she can tell that much. "Shit," she says.

"What?" Rena says.

"The other guy."

Rena twists her body around. "Crea? Where?"

"The car behind the Impala."

Rena, at the top of her lungs, starts howling. "You fucking monster!" she says, as if Crea can hear her across lanes and through the heavy hum of traffic. She's crying. "My baby girl, what you did to her! Vic!" She pounds her hands against the roof of the Eldorado, tinny thwacks echoing through the car.

Wolfstein sees two things simultaneously in the side-view mirror: Richie's horror at Rena's treatment of his car and Crea swigging from a bottle of green Listerine and spitting it out his open window.

"Grandma," Lucia says, but that seems to be all she can think of.

"That monster," Rena says, her voice settling down to a whimper.

They pass underneath or through something—it's not quite a tunnel, but it feels like a tunnel, Wolfstein a little loopy, disoriented—and the lights are sooty, a bootsuck gloom ricocheting against the walls. They come out on the bridge in the center-left lane. Orange cones in the road. Lights swishing everywhere from cars. The lights on the bridge, rising in the air. An enormous American flag hanging from the high part at the center of the bridge, moving in the wind like a dress over a sewer grate, making Wolfstein think of Marilyn Monroe. She's always loved Marilyn. Ate up every book there was to be had. Likes to think of her on a bed wearing nothing, swirled up in white sheets.

Lights down on the water. Lights of the city behind them. Wolfstein's planning a move. Make it look like she's staying to the left, headed on 95 into the deep hustling veins of Jersey and then cutting quickly off the exit for the Palisades, losing Richie and Crea and on the path to Mo. Seems easy enough.

But it's not easy, of course. The Impala's nuzzling them. And the Town Car looms majestically on Richie's tail, no longer a secret to him.

Wolfstein moves left, no signal. They're lined up like a funeral: Eldorado, Impala, Town Car.

"What are you doing?" Rena asks.

"Trying to shake them," Wolfstein says.

"Like this?"

Wolfstein looks over her right shoulder, the center lane thick with steady-flowing traffic. She hopes it's not a tell. She needs to lose both cars. "I'm gonna make a last-second move for the Palisades," she says.

"Across three lanes? You'll get us killed."

"I sure hope not."

The flag is over them, its wild flapping loud enough to sound like a big engine. The Palisades exit is in sight.

Lucia and Rena are both looking over their shoulders, trying to figure a way Wolfstein can possibly pull this off. There's just no let-up in the center lanes. It's an arcade game. She'll have to fit between fast-moving cars and hope Richie and Crea are totally boxed out. Wolfstein will be amazed if she can pull it off, but it's their only hope, as far as she can tell. Getting tracked close onto the Palisades would mean being royally fucked. No shaking them then on that dark two-lane parkway with long stretches between exits—it'll be easier to be driven off the road, to be shouldered into a rest stop lot or off into the trees.

She's thinking about Marilyn again. Seeing her sweetly stretched on the hood of the Eldorado. Now's the time. *Swerve, Wolfstein. Make it count. Get free.*

RICHIE

Richie's on the floor, dazed. His hands are painted with blood. Adrienne's blood. He sees her splayed out across from him. He scrambles to his knees and looks all around. The whole thing with Crea is a blur. He gets a flash of them tangled up, tumbling across the room. He thinks maybe he got the hammer away from Crea. He did. For a minute, at least. Crea pulled a piece from under his jacket. His Sig Sauer P220. Richie swung with the hammer. Missed. Crea fired. Missed. They butted heads like fucking goats or rams or whatever. Crea laughed at him, shook it off.

Richie tries to shake out of it. Sirens off in the distance. Crea and his hammer are gone now. Richie's bet is that he's right outside, somewhere in the shadows, waiting to pounce. He just doesn't want to be in the house when the cops show. That's Crea's way. And who knows where Lucia, Rena, and Luscious Lacey are. Maybe in a neighbor's house on the horn with a police dispatcher. Or out on Pennyfield trying to wave down a blue-and-white.

He gets to his feet, goes to the open door, knowing he has to move fast. He looks out at the street. His Eldorado's gone. Jesus Christ. That means the MAC-10 and the dough and the camera are gone, too.

But there's dumb old Enzio on his knees in a cone of light from the overhead streetlamp, reaching around under the Impala, his bandages making him look like some kind of an escaped shock-therapy patient.

Richie goes back into the house, scans the walls, the refrigerator, looking for a sign, for anything. He's desperate. They went where? They took his money where? Back to Brooklyn? Rena wouldn't. Not with Crea in the mix.

Fucking Crea. Richie wishes now more than ever that Crea had been there at Caccio's for the massacre.

Richie kicks past the body of the old wiry bastard who shot Adrienne, noticing a letter on the counter where the guy had been sitting before he crumpled to the floor, bashed to death by Crea. He gets a whiff of vodka from a nearby glass. He paws at the edge of the envelope. Must be something, that's why it's sitting out. The envelope has a return address up in Monroe. He takes out the letter and reads it fast. He's thinking maybe this Mo is Luscious Lacey's best pal, and they'll head up to her place to hide out. Only bet, right now. On the floor is the guy's piece, the one Richie had for a minute before he lost it. He picks it up and checks the chamber. Two bullets. He tucks it in his waistband and feels it against his skin. Not cold or warm. Just there. Foreign.

Monroe. He's been there. To the diner once. And for some dealings with a Hasidic Jew in Kiryas Joel regarding a jewel thing back in '02.

He puts the letter back in the envelope and stuffs it in his pants pocket. Sirens sound closer but still not too close. He goes over and stands by Adrienne. He leans down on one knee and kisses her, tastes her blood on his lips. He feels her hips, her legs, touches the fragile tips of her long nails. He wishes they were in a bed somewhere. This world. This business. You don't cry, that he knows. You cry, it's over.

He's seeing Adrienne in high school. The way she crossed her legs. Put on lip gloss. Made jokes that went nowhere. Always wanted him to take her to MSG to watch the Rangers. Girl like her, a hockey fan. His mother liked Adrienne. The true test. Adrienne would help roll the braciole, wear an old apron that belonged to his grandmother. She made good gravy herself. Made her own dough for pizza, too. So pretty, his A. Special thing like that comes along once in a lifetime. No matter what went wrong between them, she was always there to lean on, to come back to.

He's got to move. He palms some of Adrienne's blood from his lips, rises back to a standing position, and walks out of the house.

Richie closes in on Enzio, his boots thumping the pavement, the neighborhood full of haunted quiet. He drops to his knees and elbows Enzio out of the way. He reaches far under the car, farther than Enzio possibly could, and feels around for the key. He comes out with it and stands back up.

"You got it! God bless."

"Where's Crea?"

"Split in his Town Car about five minutes ago. The sirens are getting closer."

"I know, I know."

Richie opens the driver's-side door of the Impala and gets in under the wheel.

"What are you doing?" Enzio asks, putting a hand on the doorframe.

"I'm going after what's mine." Richie jerks the door closed, knocking Enzio off balance, rolling down the window. He starts the car. The engine hums.

"I didn't try to rape Rena," Enzio says. Pause. "Let me come with you."

"Why would I let you do that?"

"Please. Come on. I gotta watch over her." His hand on the roof of the Impala. Tears in his pissy old eyes. "She's all I got."

"Fine. You know what? Get in. Hurry up. I need a human shield when Crea shows—and he *is* showing again, I can assure you of that—you're it, pal."

Enzio goes around to the passenger side and gets in the car.

Richie ratchets them away from the curb. They zoom side streets until they catch the Expressway off Pennyfield, moving away from the sirens.

"Take it easy," Enzio says, his head in his hands. "Please."

Cop lights whirling in the dark by St. Raymond's Cemetery. Backup upon backup. Calls coming in. Neighbors a hush until the scene's clear. Service road beyond the Expressway fence lit red and blue. Richie feels reckless, but he's driving steady and fast. He's still tasting Adrienne's blood on his lips.

"You said Crea's coming back?" Enzio asks. "How you know that for sure?"

"Crea likes games," Richie says, spitting out the window.

Richie is visiting Adrienne in his memory. He's talking to who she was. The kid she was. The woman. He's kissing her outside of Our Lady of Angels in Bay Ridge. They're about to go in to watch his pal Bruno Bonnano get hitched to some little bow-legged nurse. He's watching her read box scores in the *Daily News* at his kitchen table in her nightie. The way she pushes her hair over her ear. Her good teeth. Always those good teeth. "Take care of your teeth like A does," Vic used to say. He's watching her after their first breakup. Tracking her. She's on Twentieth Avenue, getting an espresso and a little box of rainbow cookies at Licenzo's. He's watching through the frosted script on the window. He's looking over the stacks of Italian bread. He's thinking she looks like Annabella Sciorra. *Jungle Fever*. Funny he never thought that before. Now they've broken up, he sees it in her eyes. Maybe she's got her hair different. He's seeing her on the beach in Coney Island. He's seeing her in the shower, trimming her bush, getting ready for the beach. He's seeing her taking the host on her tongue at St. Mary's. He's seeing her waiting for what used to be the B train. He's seeing her all the ways he's ever seen her. Those first days. Kissing in his car on Shore Road. She's so goddamn young. Hiding it from Vic. Her hands on him. His hands on her. Memory like a movie.

One night—this is when she was over in Queens, after the third or fourth time they split—he went to see her after he'd killed Mikey the Goon over at Deno's Bus Stop. He was shaken up by it. The Goon was only eighteen. But the orders had come down. Vic made him believe he was doing God's work. But he was still rattled. Kid like that, how could he not be? Sure, the Goon fucked up, Richie knew that better than anybody, but you gotta make a kid learn. What happened that night at Adrienne's place, he's seeing it now. Lucia was maybe four, asleep in the other room. Him and Adrienne, they fucked on the floor with that Hitchcock movie *The Birds* on the TV in the background. All those birds. Wild. He's seeing it now, her on top of him, wearing a Yankees T-shirt with a ripped collar, the way she's moving, saying his name, not caring if they wake up little Lu, and then Crea's hammer is coming right at her, smashing her face like glass.

Everywhere Richie looks, there's Crea. Cars next to him are filled with grinning Creas. Creas crawling on overpasses, over fences. Hovering in the back windows of buses and vans and ambulettes.

Crea saying back there, Richie's remembering now, that *he* killed Vic. Richie thinking how fast untruths spread. No one saw Little Sal, not even Rena. It was Crea all along. And it was Richie had to do the hit on Little Sal over it.

Richie's keeping his eyes peeled for the Eldorado. Trying to keep focused on that. Afraid that the real Crea will roll up out of nowhere, open fire on him like he did to Ozzie Gigante on the Belt Parkway. Ozzie turned to splatter inside his Escalade, went peeling off into the Fort Hamilton military base fence. One time he and Ozzie had gotten a tour of Monument Park at Yankee Stadium together. Ozzie was tight with Joe Kelly, who had a big in there. It was a good day. Arthur Avenue afterward. Crea clipped him three months later.

"You know they're headed this way how?" Enzio asks.

"I want to talk to you, I'll let you know," Richie says.

Enzio puts his hands up like *whoa, whoa.*

In and out of lanes. Needle pushing eighty. Enzio's clutching his gut, moaning in misery for the stress Richie's putting on his poor Impala.

"Your car's a beaut," Richie says, shifting gears. "I'm a good driver. I'm the best driver. We find them, you get it back. Just like that."

Could be Richie's wrong, though. That Monroe letter's pure guesswork. Say they don't find Rena and Lu. Say it's not as easy as Monroe. Say they're headed in any other direction. Luscious Lacey with a million other connections. A hotel upstate. Atlantic City. Vegas. California or Florida or Panda Puss, Tennessee.

"You don't find them, what happens to me and my car?" Enzio asks, as if reading his mind. And then, as if on command, Richie spots the Eldorado up ahead. He can tell because it's his. That shape. How the brake lights hit the road. The tight rectangle of his perfect back window. Sturdy roof. Tires steady and high. It makes him heartsick seeing it. He can't believe he's managed to catch up to them so quickly. "It's there, it's there," he says aloud.

"Where?"

"There." Pointing hard over the dash.

"I don't see it."

"You're blind then."

"What now?"

"Now I get my car back by any means necessary. You don't want your Impala fucked up, you better pray my Eldorado goes unharmed."

Looked good for a second there. Richie had them in sight, and he honestly thought they'd just pull over and let him have his car and money back.

But then the jagged pursuit. Lucia yelling at him out the window. Something unlocking in those pretty eyes of hers. The desire for all that dough, probably. She has the same eyes as Adrienne.

Lucia. He'd slip her twenties all the time when she was a little kid. Fold them into rings and put them on her thumbs the way his uncles used to do for him. She'd blow it all on baseball cards and Swedish Fish and whatever else kids spend money on. Memories of Lucia flooding in: Cookies she liked. Those pistachio-roll ones—what are they called? Lard bread, too. Kid could eat her weight in lard bread. Taking her for pizza at Spumoni Gardens or Lenny's. "Take me to the circus," she said to him when she was eight, and what'd he do? Front row at Ringling Brothers. Limo into the city, popcorn, peanuts, cotton candy, the whole nine. They laughed at all the big heaps of elephant shit together, guys scooping it up with shovels. Now look at her. The same age Adrienne was when he first made it with her. All that's happened, and she's got dollar signs in her eyes.

And Crea's back on his tail, too. Must've followed them out of Silver Beach. Probably hiding in the shadows the whole time and staying far enough behind not to be seen. Games. Swishing Listerine, the psycho. Probably not wanting to just blow Richie away. Wouldn't be enough for Crea. At this point, Richie guesses, what Crea is after is getting him tied up in a warehouse, breaking his legs with the hammer, jolting him with electricity, doing some *Lethal Weapon*–type torture.

On the bridge now. In a line. She's up to something, Luscious Lacey. Crazy that he used to crank it to her. That rack for the ages. She's gonna, what? Break right for the Palisades, try to shake them? Or maybe she wants him to think that and then she floors it, shoots straight onto 95. You can't just fool a smart guy like him. And give Crea, the psycho, some credit. They didn't want to continue this, they shouldn't have dragged his Eldorado—and, by extension, his score—into it. Take an express bus right on Tremont and go to Penn Station, Grand Central, the Port Authority, whatever the fuck. Now they're all in line for more trouble, more heartache.

When the Eldorado makes its abrupt move for the Palisades exit, Richie is boxed in by a van. The driver of the van has a neck like a fat preacher. He's got a phone book on a chain hanging from his ceiling. He's motioning wildly with his hands, flipping Richie off, bonking the horn. Richie's cursing. Crea's Town Car taps the Impala. Enzio moans, the minor collision sending shivers through him. "No," he says, restrained. "No, no, no. Richie. Please, no."

"Take it easy," Richie says. "We're losing them."

In the rearview, he sees Crea laughing.

It happens like one of those little red flip books he had as a kid. Luca Cicotte used to supply the junior high boys with them. You'd thumb through it. Little pencil drawing of a stripper onstage going down to her G-string and pasties. Last page is her, knees touching, knockers finally fully exposed, smiling wide. Luca had an uncle worked in Times Square kept him in shit like that. Luca was a big hit in the school. Back then, tits weren't everywhere. The way the car—*his* fucking car—moves reminds him of that book, the fast action, zippy like he's seeing it through a whirring fan blade.

And then the van boxes them in, the fat-necked preacher guy looking right at Richie and howling, spit splattering his window.

The women are off the exit, spinning into the dark of the Palisades. Richie rides the horn. He knows another way to the Palisades up ahead, but he's gonna lose ground. Maybe lose them for good if they take one of the first exits. No assurance that they're actually headed to Monroe. That's just a gamble, after all.

Crea's next to him in the Town Car suddenly, shrugging, holding up the hammer and miming beating his head in.

"Oh, Jesus fucking Christ," Enzio says, noticing Crea. "Just let me out and take the car. I've thought twice. I got what, a few years left, if I'm lucky? My heart don't need this. Let me out. I don't care where."

"Pipe down, huh?" Richie says. "I'm thinking here." He's trying to see his plan like a map in front of him, what exactly he has to do to get back on track without getting totally lost up Jersey's godforsaken ass. He's learned, on several occasions, you get lost up Jersey's ass, you're screwed dead to rights. So much signage. So many potential bad turns. So many smoke-stacks and billboards and barbed-wire fences. And so much land that looks barren, piled with car parts and rubble. You get into that part of Jersey, you're in a puzzle.

"What are we gonna do?" Enzio asks.

"You're gonna shut up, that's what," Richie says.

What Richie finds himself thinking about just then, his hands clutched tight on the wheel of the Impala, is enemies. Is Lucia his enemy, and is he hers? He doesn't want it to be like that. He always wanted to be a dad to her. Or at least an uncle. The kind of guy slips her a few bucks and puts a smile on her face. Crea's his enemy, he knows that with rock-solid certainty. Enemies infect your blood, he knows that, too. The Goon wasn't an enemy. Sonny Brancaccio, he was. Plenty of enemies, whatever they're made of. Plenty of almost-enemies.

See, you blink, God's made the world worse. Jersey looms, potential for evil everywhere. You're one dick fiddle away from being lost or dead or spaced on a highway to Shitsville. He can feel the money in the trunk of his Eldorado getting farther and farther away. He can feel Crea's hammer on his knees. And this old wimp next to him, huddled like a dog he's taking to be put down, making him even more raw-nerved. There's no moon. His feet are cold. Night like this, his feet are cold, you believe that?

He's thinking of summer sin. Him and Adrienne in his car on Shore Road. Almost lost in the pleasantness of that memory. *Adrienne, Adrienne.* His confused brain saying her name over and over and over again, hurling it *Rocky*-style against the vast emptiness. "It's not spelled like that Adrian," she'd say every time he did his best Rocky Balboa.

Crea's nudging him again. Enzio's horrified. Crea's following close behind as he gets off at the first exit up ahead, Richie not even looking at the sign, not even sure if it will lead him into a tangle of tolls and roads going in the wrong direction, hoping only that it's a key to the secondary route he's remembering.

Fuck Jersey. Fuck lost. Crea wants to butt heads again, let him come.

RENA

Rest stop off the Thruway, the Eldorado still running. They're parked away from the main lot, to the side of the squat building where the shops and fast food joints are. Rena's feeling unhinged. Lucia keeps looking out at the traffic to see if they've really shaken Richie and Crea. Wolfstein's over at the pay phone, calling her friend Mo.

It was a good idea on Wolfstein's part to get off the Palisades onto the Thruway. Both roads go to Monroe. They had to figure Richie would try to pick them back up on the Palisades, not knowing where they were headed, and it wouldn't be that hard for him to escape 95 and recover their trail. As for Crea, he's not following them. Yet. He doesn't know they have the money. He's following Richie.

They should ditch the Eldorado; that's all Richie wants. Well, not all.

The money Lucia mentioned. What Rena's thinking is she'll use some of the money to pay someone to kill Crea. Who, though? Not Richie, clearly. Would anyone in Vic's crew do it? Maybe, probably, she'd have to steer clear of whoever's left. Vic went to that guy Freddie Touch to deal with some outside issues here and there, she knew that much. She'd met Freddie at Torregrossa and Sons when he came around to pay his respects at Vic's wake. Reach out to him, maybe.

Her head's spinning. Watching Wolfstein on the pay phone in the lights of the car, her good posture, standing firm even through this madness that Rena's brought into her life. Then again, there was Bobby. That's probably weighing on Wolfstein, with what he did. Rena looks over at Lucia now and tries to feign a smile.

"Maybe we should ditch her," Lucia says, taking off her Yankees cap and tossing it on the dash.

"What? Who?" Rena asks, as if shaking into consciousness.

"Wolfstein. For her safety, I mean."

"You're saying what? All her money's in the car. She trusts us. She's been good to me."

"It was her boyfriend that shot Adrienne. I'm not . . . Grandma . . . We could leave her money, I don't care. We've got more." Lucia perks up. "Come look. The trunk's full of Richie's money. Who knows how much? We could go anywhere."

"I'm thinking about your mother right now, that's it. And Papa Vic."

Rena looks out and watches as Wolfstein hangs up the phone. Wolfstein makes a motion that she's going inside for a second. Rena nods.

"Come look," Lucia says. "Let's see how much is there."

"I don't care about the money. I mean, I care about it, of course. I'm gonna use some of it to get Crea."

"That's a waste."

"With what he did . . ."

"She was dead already. That old guy shot her by accident."

"Lucia."

"She was."

"That's your mother. And it's more than that. What I know now."

"I'm going to look in the trunk." Lucia scooches over and pushes the driver's-side door out. She forgets to pop the trunk and then comes back and looks for the release. It takes her a minute to find it. "Come look with me."

Rena feels cold about this money. But she gets out anyway. She wants to please Lucia. "Okay," she says, climbing out of the car. "I'll take a look."

They stand in front of the trunk, and Lucia shoves open the lid. What they see they see together, but it makes Rena feel even colder. Machine gun, camera, luggage, briefcase, ski mask, sandals. Lucia looks all around to make sure they're not being watched and then leans into the gaping trunk. She snaps open the briefcase, and her eyes go wicked.

"Jesus Christ," she says, thumbing through bills. "How much is here?"

"A lot," Rena says, and then she reaches over Lucia and slams the briefcase closed. "And please don't take the Lord's name in vain."

"How much is a lot?"

Rena ignores Lucia and zips open Richie's luggage, withdrawing a neatly folded Van Heusen dress shirt. Blue with polka dots and a starchy white collar. She shakes out the shirt, with its size-eighteen neck, unbuttoning it like a pro. She spreads it out over the gun the way she used to spread out Vic's shirts on the bed for funerals or weddings or Mass. The gun's bulky outline shows under the shirt. "We can't just have that out in the open."

"Have you ever seen that much money? I'm sure you have with Papa Vic." Lucia's peppered up, bouncing on her heels, almost smiling. Hard to understand with all that's gone on, all that's going on.

"I'm closing the trunk," Rena says, but she's slow to actually do it.

"And that gun!"

Rena shushes her. Now it's her turn to look around. People milling by their cars in the main lot with crinkly bags from Sbarro and steaming cups of Starbucks coffee. Not many people. It's late. You get the feeling—this time of night—that anyone in a lot like this is caught up in something sketchy. Like the middle-aged Wall Street–type in sunglasses leaning against his car.

Probably coming home from a tryst at a hotel with a girl half his age. And the short junkman in overalls with the bushy eyebrows, what's he doing? Cleaning up after something? Big buckets in his truck. You live the life Rena's lived, married to the man she was married to, you know there's a dark story behind everything. You know someone might be watching, even if it seems like they're not. She finally shoulders the trunk closed.

"We could clean up with that thing," Lucia says. "Take out Crea and Richie if they find us. The both of them. Bam. Just like that. Then we don't need to pay for it."

"What's gotten into you?"

Wolfstein comes up behind them with a pack of Marlboro 100s and a handful of sad oatmeal-raisin granola bars. "Nutrition," she says. "Anyone have to take a squirt? Bathrooms are pretty clean."

"I'm okay," Rena says.

"News was on in there. Saw a quick something, one of those between-commercial segments. Some anchor in a red dress with Silver Beach in a little box behind her. Cop lights flashing. Couldn't really hear what she was saying."

Rena looks down at the pavement. A squashed soda cup to the right of her feet. Flattened green gum. Specks of yellow paint. Exhaust from the Eldorado puffing away around her ankles.

"Eat something," Wolfstein says, palming the granola bar into Rena's hand.

"Thanks," Rena says, stuffing it in her pocket. "Maybe later. My stomach's uneasy."

"I can imagine." Wolfstein turns to Lucia. "How about you, kid?"

Lucia says sure and scarfs down one of the bars, looking away from Wolfstein at the cars thrumming by on the Thruway.

"Did you talk to your friend?" Rena asks.

"I did. Figured I'd give her a little heads-up. She's excited. I mean, she sounded pretty drunk, but she's excited. She loves when things get wild." Wolfstein tears the cellophane off the Marlboro 100s, rips away the silver foil, and pops one between her lips. She lights it with a little purple Bic she must've gotten inside, too.

"Can I have one?" Lucia asks.

"Kid," Wolfstein says. "Don't put me in this position."

Rena: "You are *not* smoking."

"You can't tell me what to do," Lucia snaps back.

"The hell I can't."

"I'll smoke if I want."

Wolfstein takes a deep drag and blows the smoke away from Rena and Lucia. "Kid, clam up, would you? Listen to your grandma. You haven't crossed that line yet. You're eighteen, you call the shots."

"I don't have to listen to lectures from some lady who was in porno movies."

"A firecracker, like I said." Wolfstein exhales dramatically, goes out of her way to make it look extra good to Lucia.

"The money and the smoking," Rena says to Lucia, shaking her head. "What am I gonna do with you?"

"Nothing." Lucia twists her feet so they're pointed in. "I don't care. I'm a bitch."

"You're upset; it's understandable," Wolfstein says.

"I want one of those cigarettes," Lucia says.

"A bitch?" Rena scrunches her eyes, tries to process the word. Again: "A bitch?" She wonders if Wolfstein's thinking, *Just like her mother.*

Wolfstein stomps out her cigarette. "We should go," she says. They get in the car, Lucia in the back seat now, to be closer to the heat of the money in the trunk likely, Rena turning around to look at her as they merge into the flow of traffic on the Thruway.

They get off at Exit 16 for Harriman and Central Valley. Rena remembers this road, this exit. After a toll, they're on Route 17, which runs to Monticello, where Vic took her to the track a few times because he had a horse he was maybe going in on. The horse's name was Bright Fancy. This was when it was just a racetrack, before the racino part opened. One time, driving up to the track, she saw an old hobo sitting on a fence near the entrance. It was early in the morning. The sky was purpled with clouds. The hobo had a big white beard and generous eyes and a walking stick, and she started thinking up a story for him. Freight-hopping. Scratching monikers on the sides of train cars. Sleeping in the woods and eating beans over a campfire. Her whole idea of hobos shaped by what little she'd seen in movies. Maybe he wasn't even a hobo.

Route 17 is also the way to the Catskills, where she and Vic went on their honeymoon back in '68. Gershwin's. A beautiful resort. Comedians. Horseback riding. Drinking by the pool. They had a cottage. The walls were so red, freshly painted and tacky to the touch. Vic had gotten her about six bouquets of daisies and scattered them around the room in empty wine bottles. They stayed in bed late every morning, had coffee brought to them. They drank the coffee out of china cups on fragile saucers that looked as if they were from another century. She and Vic had matching silk robes. He'd bought her the most beautiful bathing suit she'd ever owned at Martin's on Fulton Street, a blue Jantzen with white piping trim. She'd turned heads the whole time, as Vic said. Lived in it. Shaved her legs every night in the old cast-iron tub while a candle burned on the windowsill. Best two weeks of her life. Quiet, peaceful, idyllic. Away from the madness of Brooklyn. Away from the stress of Vic's work.

Except now, she's remembering, Crea was there. A teenager at the time. Not *there*-there, but staying up the road at a dive motel. He'd show up once a day and give Vic a rundown, relay any messages that needed relaying. Even then, as a kid, he had this psycho arch to his eyebrows.

Rena and Vic went back to Gershwin's in '88 for their twentieth anniversary, no Crea or anyone else accompanying them this time, but Vic got pulled away for a job after two days. He felt bad making her leave early, so she stayed and sat by the pool, playing solitaire, making friends with a lady named Adelaide from Poughkeepsie. The bathing suit she had this time was nothing special. At night, she ate dinner with Adelaide and her husband, Ron, and then went back to her room and watched old movies or read a Danielle Steele. Adrienne was staying with the sitter back home, Ralphie Baruncelli's sister, and Rena felt guilty about that, but it was nice to have the time to herself. She remembers her feet in the grass over by the tennis courts. She remembers relaxing on a float in the pool. She remembers sneaking away to go to church in Callicoon and being amazed by the smallness of the church and the smallness of the congregation. She put fifty bucks in the offertory basket and felt especially holy, tried not to think about what Vic was off doing.

Another thing she remembers from that visit is how far downhill Gershwin's had gone. The walls were cracked. Dust everywhere. Leaves and gristle in the pool. Sad dining room. A stage where no one sang or told jokes. Decrepit chaise lounges. Cottages with broken shutters and ancient roof shingles. She remembers thinking about time a lot. She remembers thinking about her body and the resort and how everything melted away. She didn't shave in the bathtub with a candle going. There wasn't a bathtub anymore. Just a small shower stall with a frosted-glass door edged with mold. She would've given anything to be back at Gershwin's in '68 in her Jantzen, nothing but the future and possibility in front of her.

Last she'd heard, Gershwin's closed down in '04. She'd seen some pictures on the computer of the abandoned main house, a drained pool full of mud and cinder blocks, rusted chairs, ivy eating up the beautiful old sign, a collapsed stage, graffiti on the cottages, and broken and boarded windows. Tragic.

Rena watches the dark out the window as they come over a rise, and Wolfstein flips on her right blinker. The blinker lights the road red behind them. Wolfstein keeps it on even though the exit isn't for a mile. Finally, she slows down and takes the first Monroe exit, keeping left and then making another quick left at a green light. She bears right at a dark Mobil and then comes out on a main stretch across from a brightly lit diner.

Monroe is a suburb, probably once considered the country to city types. Two lakes stretch off to the left. More like scummy little ponds, really, but the centerpiece of the downtown. There's a park with a renovated Korean War airplane stationed beside the slides and swings across from the close end of the nearer lake. Rena sees two girls in hoodies sitting on the swings. Across the street is a plaza with a bagel shop, a dollar store, a Chinese buffet, and a Dunkin' Donuts. The squat, eerie feeling of a suburb settles over her. High school kids in running cars sit outside the still-open diner smoking cigarettes and conspiring on cell phones. Rena is glad she doesn't have a phone. She's glad Lucia doesn't have one.

Wolfstein, who has been silent for a while, says, "Mo can be a bit overwhelming, especially when she's loaded, but you're gonna like her." Then, looking over at Rena this time: "She's gonna be happy to help."

⌐

Mo's house is back in a community called Little Lakes, past a Burger King with a craggy parking lot and a Chase bank and an unnamed ice cream shop featuring three wooden bears painted in patriotic colors propped against the front window. It's a split-level with some Christmas decorations still on the lawn: toppled reindeer, a dirty Santa, an elf hanging from a tangle of extension cords. Houses loom close on both sides and there's another huddle of houses right across the narrow street, all dark and dreary-looking. The community must have been built in the sixties or seventies. Two nearby roads dead-end in pitch-black cul-de-sacs. Mo's house, however, is alive with light as the Eldorado pulls into the driveway. The flowered curtains are open. Music is pumping. A woman who must be Mo dances her way past the bay window wearing only a purple bra, jangly beads around her neck, and sequined gym shorts. Her dyed red hair is piled high on her head.

"That's Mo?" Rena asks.

"In the flesh," Wolfstein says. "I wonder what she's celebrating. Maybe just Sunday winding down."

"Doesn't she have a sick mom?"

"Deep sleeper."

"We're going in there?" Lucia asks. "We should just keep driving."

Rena: "And go where?"

"Anywhere. Canada."

"We've gotta at least fill Mo in a little more," Wolfstein says. "And we can lay low. Rest. Get our bearings before we take off in the morning. Mo's full of good ideas."

They climb out of the car, Wolfstein grabbing her black bag. Lucia goes around and pops the trunk and gets the briefcase with Richie's money, saying to Rena, "I'm not letting it out of my sight."

Rena's not sure how to respond, Lucia only seeming to have eyes for the money. Maybe it's shock.

"You look in there yet?" Wolfstein asks Rena and Lucia.

Lucia tucks her chin into her chest, doesn't answer Wolfstein.

"That much?" Wolfstein says.

Mo's at the door as they walk up the stoop. "Welcome, welcome, welcome," she says, guiding them inside to the ground floor landing. She's wearing lots of makeup and crimson lipstick, like she's been having some kind of glamour night, and her bra is lacy and expensive-looking. She's got a big smile. Her teeth are yellow. Rena focuses on a stray whisker protruding from her neck. Mo was in movies with Wolfstein is mainly what Rena remembers Wolfstein telling her, so her mind goes to the two of them doing the kinds of things she saw briefly on the screen at Enzio's.

Wolfstein embraces Mo and laughs. "You having a party?"

"Let me go turn the music down." Mo points at Rena and Lucia, as if putting a freeze on actually meeting them. She jogs up the few steps to the top level. In the kitchen, she powers down her little boombox, Rena unable to place what she'd been listening to.

Mo says, "Shit, sorry, I hadn't heard that song in forever. 'Thunder and Lightning.' Last time, I remember, I was in a supermarket in Salinas, coked up, just wandering the aisles with an open box of Fruit Loops. I went straight to a bar afterward and looked for it on the jukebox, but they didn't have it. That would have been the eighties. Song was a hit back in the summer of '72. Chi Coltrane, she's the singer." Mo starts singing. "*Oooh, what a good thing I've got,*" that's the part she's belting out. "*Oh, it's such a good thing I've got! Oh, thunder and lightning, ooohooo! I tell you it's frightening, oh yeah! Thunder and lightning, ooohooo! Thunder and lightning, I tell you it's frightening, oh yeah!*"

"We're in a bit of a bind here, Mo," Wolfstein says.

Mo picks up a bottle of wine and takes a long slug. "Nothing you could tell me could bring me down. Mama croaked two days ago, Wolfie. I'm free. That's why I'm tying one on. Been a nonstop boozefest since I left the hospital. I had Joe Petrovic from the Captain's Table here last night, otherwise I would've called to tell you the news." She places the wine back on the counter and puts out her hands, showing her palms. Rena sees that *Get trash bags* is written in black magic marker on her right palm. "You've got cigarettes, right?" Mo continues. "Tell me you've got cigarettes. Otherwise you're driving me over to the Shell near ShopRite."

"I've got smokes," Wolfstein says.

"I'm sorry about your mother," Rena says.

Mo waves her off. "Shit happens. She was ancient. Had dementia. Point is, I can breathe easy a little for the first time since I moved in with her. No more changing her diapers. No more wiping her ass. No more making her Cream of Wheat. No more cleaning up the coffee and creamer that she spills everywhere. No more talking through a megaphone because she can't hear me and she won't put in her hearing aid. No shit, I actually did that. No more listening to her talk about how there's dead people everywhere. I mean, I know she was hallucinating or dreaming, but it freaks you out at a certain point." Mo pauses. "I'm sorry," she says, coming back down to Rena,

Lucia, and Wolfstein on the landing and extending her hand to Rena. "I'm Mo Phelan. Me and Wolfie go way, way back."

"Rena Ruggiero," Rena says, shaking Mo's hand. "And this is my grand-daughter, Lucia."

Mo turns her gaze to Lucia. "How old are you?"

"Fifteen," Lucia says.

"You've got this kind of heavy feeling you're giving off." Mo puts her hands over Lucia's head as if she's checking for strings or ruffling her aura.

"What's happened isn't good," Wolfstein says.

"Well, come on in," Mo says, strutting back upstairs, motioning for them to follow. "Tell Mo all about it."

Wolfstein does all the talking at first. They're sitting in the living room on plastic-covered sofas under paintings Mo's mother made before the dementia kicked in. Some fruit. A jar of dill pickles. Fields and farmers. Waterfalls. Wolfstein walks Mo through meeting Rena and explains what Rena was running from. Enzio. The ashtray. She gets to Adrienne, Lucia, Richie, and how the whole mess got set up. She backtracks to cover the Bobby problem. Dumb Bobby with his dumb piece. Crea the madman showing up after Adrienne got shot. What he did. His Vic history. Then the chase on the GWB.

Mo's eyes grow wider every time the story takes a turn. She's smoking cigarette after cigarette from Wolfstein's pack. Lucia tries to sneak one, but Rena puts a stop to it. Lucia snaps at her again.

When Wolfstein's done talking, Mo exhales and drops the smoking filter between her fingers into the empty wine bottle at her feet. "Well, that sure as shit sobered me up a little. So you think the cops'll come sniffing around up here?"

"I'd wager they will," Wolfstein says. "Only a matter of time before one of the neighbors tells them you're the owner."

"And Bobby—I remember that little shit. You said he had out a letter I sent you. How do we know these other guys were chasing you didn't see it and get my address from the envelope?"

Wolfstein puts her hand over her mouth. "We don't. Bobby left it on the counter."

"So they're maybe headed here right now?"

"It's a long shot but a possibility, I guess."

Lucia jumps to her feet and goes to the window, carrying the briefcase. "Let's just go now," she says.

"Hold on a sec," Wolfstein says.

"I'm going to get the gun, at least."

"What gun?"

"In the trunk."

"I can't tell if I like this kid or if she scares me," Mo says.

"Who does the gun belong to?" Wolfstein asks.

Rena: "It's Richie's. When we went in the trunk, it was there with the money."

Lucia: "I'm not afraid."

Wolfstein: "What kind of gun?"

Lucia shrugs.

Rena tilts her head and looks under a coffee table holding a gaudy swan lamp and some large-print puzzle books. She notices a bundled diaper. She starts to think about Mo's mother and feels ashamed that Mo seems happy the old woman is dead and that she's only really concerned with freedom. Freedom is a strange thing. You get it, you don't always need it or want it to last. Like her time at Gershwin's. Nice as it was, by the last couple of days, she was climbing the walls. "A machine gun," she finally says.

Wolfstein laughs. Mo does, too, as she lights another of Wolfstein's Marlboro 100s.

"I don't think any of this is funny," Rena says.

"It's not, sweetie," Wolfstein says, lighting her own cigarette now.

"It's definitely not," Mo says in a scratchy voice. "But it's fucking exciting."

The last word trailing off in a cough, Rena trying not to watch but watching anyway as the tops of Mo's old, wrinkled boobs rumble as she talks and laughs and smokes. Her skin is leathery and about as dark as pale Irish skin gets, as if she took the sun in Florida as often as humanly possible, probably sitting topless on a beach chair with one of those aluminum foil reflectors under her chin. Rena is astounded that Mo hasn't gone to put a top on yet, no matter what their situation is. And the wild beads she's wearing around her neck—which look as if they were bought at some parking lot market in the East Village thirty years before—only accentuate the boob shimmying.

"So what are we gonna do?" Wolfstein asks.

"Well, the way I understand it," Mo says, crossing her legs, "you guys are pretty much clean. I mean"—she aims her cigarette at Rena—"this one clocked an old perv with an ashtray, and you, Wolfie—well, you've got your Florida history that might catch up with you, but I just don't see how it will if Bobby got clipped. Of course, it's a shame about—What was her name? Adrienne? Truly a shame. But it's a good thing you're not running from the cops. You're running from these other psychos. If you can avoid them, when the cops finally find you, all you've gotta do is say, 'Look, these are the bad guys you're looking for. We were hiding from them.' Right?"

"So, we hide. Worst-case scenario is they have my address and they're on their way here. We could get in the car and just drive like the kid suggests, but the cops could also be on the way here. Let those two parties figure it out, is what I'm saying. All we've gotta do is stay out of sight. Simple: we go next door."

"What's next door?" Rena asks.

"Next door's vacant." Mo jerks a thumb in the direction of the dark, dreary house on their left. "Couple lived there got a divorce a couple of months ago. All these two did was scream at each other. Wife took off to Paradise Island with her hedge-fund boyfriend, husband is balling the Slovenian skank who bartends at Doc Carlisle's and living with her now. House is up in the air. I don't know why, exactly, but it's empty. The husband—Goose, they call him—left a key with me, asked me to let in the gas guy. We pull your stolen car in their garage, leave the house lights off, and just huddle up in the downstairs. If these psychos ever get to my joint, they see I'm not there, they think you picked me up and we split for parts unknown. In the morning, the cops show."

"What if we sabotage them?" Lucia says. "Like rig your door with explosives."

"You watch too many movies, kid. One: Where we gonna get explosives? Two: I don't necessarily want to blow up my mom's house even though it smells like old-lady diapers." Mo drops her cigarette in the wine bottle and turns to Wolfstein and Rena: "What do you say?"

Wolfstein nods to Rena. "I told you she was full of good ideas."

Moving next door does seem like something of a solution to Rena. Mo gathers up her boombox, some cassettes, a laptop with a bulky charger cord, two more magnum bottles of wine, a flashlight, a box of Saltines, and throws it all in a canvas ShopRite bag with a handle that's about to snap. She takes off her beads and finally puts on a top, a T-shirt that reads GOOD GIRLS GO TO HEAVEN, BAD GIRLS GO BACKSTAGE, and then she leads Rena and Lucia downstairs through sliding glass doors into the backyard, illuminating their path with the flashlight, while Wolfstein goes to move the Eldorado. Lucia is still clutching the briefcase with Richie's money.

From what Rena can see, Mo's backyard—or, more accurately, her mother's backyard—is full of ceramic birdbaths, marble gnome statues, bubble stakes, and overturned patio furniture dirtied with puddle residue. Rena almost stomps a citronella candle in a metal bucket. They tread lightly across the grass in the dark, hopping a small chain of bushes into the yard that belongs to the divorced neighbors. An aboveground pool sits covered in a sad tarp weighted down by rainwater. Aside from a grimy soccer ball and some battered barbells on the back patio, Rena doesn't see much of anything.

Mo unlocks the back door on the ground level, and they enter the dark, cool house into what must've been a sort of family room, given its shape and size. Rena can easily picture a comfortable sofa and a shelf full of photo albums, wedding photos on the wall, and a flat-screen TV where a couple could watch cable on a Friday night to avoid conversation. She walks carefully behind Mo, following the dancing flashlight, holding onto Lucia's shoulder.

"Is there electricity at all?" Rena asks.

"I don't think it got cut," Mo says. "I hope not. We've gotta open that garage door for Wolfie."

This house, like Mo's, is a split-level. It's devoid of furniture and life. It feels like the kind of place where a tragedy unfolded. Rena believes in ghosts. She believes that unhappy spirits can linger in a place. It's not that. Not exactly. More a reflection of the quality of the lives that were lived in the house. How the stress of the husband and the wife leaked into the structure. Maybe Rena's just projecting that feeling, but it seems real enough. Toxicity. Dankness.

They fumble down a blue hallway. Mo's light shines briefly on an open electrical panel. A door at the end of the hall leads them to the garage, which seems even emptier and draftier. They can hear the Eldorado idling outside. Mo finds a switch and punches on a small overhead light, and then she presses the heel of her hand against another button and the door rises with a groan. Rena notices a pink umbrella stroller hanging from a nail on the wall and wonders if the divorced couple had a child or children. Stupid to ask. Doesn't matter. Maybe the child died. Maybe that accounts for the bad feeling in the air.

Wolfstein backs in the Eldorado slowly. It feels swollen and alive in the small garage. Wolfstein shuts off the lights and then the engine. Mo hits the button again. The door reverses track, grinding shut.

"Jesus, was somebody murdered in this joint?" Wolfstein asks, getting out of the car with her bag of dough.

"You feel that, right?" Mo says.

"Like a brick in the face."

Rena: "What is that?"

"Bad energy," Mo explains. "Those unhappy bastards cultivated the shit out of it."

"This couple, did they have a child?"

"Nope. Don't know what that stroller's all about."

Back to being led by Mo's flashlight. Back down the blue hallway. They decide to hide in a small room at the far end of the ground level. Mo plops down her canvas bag in the far corner. Wolfstein does the same with her bag. Lucia won't let go of hers. Since the room has no windows, Mo turns on the light. It's a typical suburban setup, with a ceiling fan swirling over four energy-saving bulbs in cased white glass. Only one of the bulbs works. The room remains pretty dim. The walls are dotted with nail holes and dusty outlines where frames used to be. The floor is bare except for a pile of dirt swept up and abandoned. In the pile is a torn tampon wrapper.

"One of us can go upstairs and keep watch, if we want," Mo says, "but I think we're better off just staying put."

"We're just gonna sit here?" Lucia says, dropping to the floor and sitting with her legs crossed.

"Don't worry." Mo digs around in her canvas bag. "I brought along some distractions. Kid, you wanna see pictures of me and Granny Wolfstein from our heyday?"

"Don't call me Granny," Wolfstein snaps back.

"I don't think that's appropriate," Rena says.

"Don't worry. I'll only show her the tasteful ones. Artful, even." Mo takes out her laptop and flips it open, powering it up. She clicks around on the keyboard and then sets the laptop in front of Lucia. "This is from *White Apples* magazine. Summer of '77. The Buxom Belles issue."

Wolfstein smiles. "Jesus, Mo, come on."

"She loves it," Mo says to Rena. "She wants everyone to see what a knockout she was."

"I'm *still* a knockout," Wolfstein says.

"Hey, knockout, give me another cigarette, huh?"

"Shit, I left them in the car." Wolfstein shuffles out of the room, heading back to the garage.

Rena, curious, sits next to Lucia and leans in to see. *Luscious Lacey and Maureen Swallows* is looped in pink curlicue script at the top of the screen. And, below that, there they are, earlier versions of Wolfstein and Mo, posed together on a tiger rug, touching hands, as if they're mirror images of each other, in electric blue baby doll lingerie. Butts in the air. Hair feathered and blown out, Mo's more candy apple red than the burgundy it is now and Wolfstein's somewhere between sable and nutmeg. Makeup muted. Wearing choker necklaces, mood rings, and blue star sapphire bracelets.

"You're Maureen Swallows?" Lucia asks Mo.

"Hell of a stage name, right?"

Wolfstein comes back in with the Marlboro 100s. Wolfstein and Mo light cigarettes. Rena coughs into her hand.

"Hot numbers," Mo says. "That's what we were. You get old enough, kid, see a movie called *Tumbling Wives*. Our finest work, in my opinion."

"Not my favorite," Wolfstein says.

"Here we go again." Mo blows smoke at Wolfstein.

"It's your best performance, I'll give you that," Wolfstein says.

"Marty Savage was a stone fox." Mo turns to Rena and Lucia. "We called him Pecker Tracks. Everyone called him that. He was like Jackson Pollock flinging paint."

"Gross," Lucia says.

"He'd just splatter his batter everywhere. One time, it was a misfire obviously, it kind of cometed up to his mustache somehow and it looked like he had all these beads of candle wax hanging there." Mo's laughing. "It was a miracle. I mean, people see the Virgin Mary in their soup, that's great, but I saw Marty Savage shoot"—Mo mimes an upward hose blast with her free hand—"like a geyser into his own mustache."

Rena's a little lost, not exactly sure what Mo's even saying right now.

"That's really gross," Lucia says, shaking her head.

"Kid, you don't know gross. Gross was Valerie Sugar queefing 'God Bless America' behind the scenes on *Ambrosia*. Gross was Willa Starch cramming a whole package of raw hot dogs up her cooch and shooting them out one by one. Gross was Stump Lady going to town on Herschel Stone while she gobbled up pickled eggs."

"Stop . . . I think," Rena says.

"I know, I know," Mo says. "*That's* all gross. Pecker Tracks was an artist."

Wolfstein laughs behind her cigarette, swatting the smoke out of her eyes. "Mo's a character. I'm telling you, the first time we met, the stars aligned. Like me and you, Rena. We clicked."

"I looked up from underneath grunting Marty Savage and could tell Wolfie was a like-minded individual," Mo says. "The Bronx connection helped. We went out for Italian and talked all night."

Rena's trying to imagine what Wolfstein could possibly see in her that's anything like what she saw and still sees in Mo.

"I've got more pictures," Mo says, "but we'll hold off on those for now. I run this little website. Got a following among the old Golden Age crowd. You want to hear Wolfstein's voice from our radio show?" Digging around in the bag again. Coming out with a cassette labeled *The Naughty List*.

Wolfstein protests.

"Just a sec. Just to let them hear your voice."

"I'm sorry," Wolfstein says to Rena.

Mo takes the tape out of its case and pops it in the boombox. Presses play. Wolfstein's talking in hushed tones through the dust-specked speakers about what a sweaty night it is and how she hopes her listeners are feeling good.

"Okay, enough," Wolfstein says, moving in and slamming the stop button. "All that's happened, it's probably not the time for memory lane."

Truth is, Rena's thankful for some distraction, any distraction, even if she feels a little out of her element.

Wolfstein and Mo simultaneously stub out their cigarettes on the floor, crunching up the filters like tiny accordions. Wolfstein flicks a piece of tobacco from her lip.

"You know what the last thing my mother said to me before she stroked out was?" Mo says.

"What?" Wolfstein says.

"'You want to play rummy?'" Mo smiles. "Far as last words go, I like those. I'd ask you guys if you want to play rummy, but I forgot to bring cards. Did you used to play I'm Going on a Picnic in the car as a kid? Wolfie, I know you probably didn't go on many road trips. I always liked I'm Going on a Picnic. I mean, we didn't go far. The Catskills, Lake Placid once. I always liked that game. 'I'm going on a picnic, and I'm bringing artichokes. I'm bringing alfalfa sprouts. I'm bringing arugula.' I was always good. Top of my head, I could think of ten things for every letter. Not silly things, either. Things you'd really bring on a picnic. I was sincere. I could use more wine. Anybody want wine?"

Lucia squares her shoulders. "I'll have some!"

"Lucia, no," Rena says, like she's telling a dog to get down.

"'I'll have some,' the kid says." Mo yanks out a bottle and unscrews the cap. "Would you get a load of her?"

Lucia shrugs.

Rena takes out the granola bar Wolfstein bought her and opens it. She nibbles it a little before deciding it'll make her sick and setting it aside.

She's thinking about Vic again as she sits there. About this one time in particular. A kid in the neighborhood Vic helped out. Italian kid, of course. Mikey Benvenuto. Mikey beat up this black kid on the basketball courts over on Twenty-Fifth Avenue where there's just a parking lot now. Beat him up bad with an aluminum bat. Vic and his crew were at Angelo's Bakery across the street, just standing outside with espressos and sfogliatelle and racing forms and they saw it happen. Cheered Mikey on. Hustled him back to Vic's house before the cops got there. Rena fixed him a veal cutlet parm hero. Mikey was so happy. He was smiling this big dopey smile, chowing down. Rena was happy to feed him. Vic and his crew, they were laughing with Mikey, saying nasty things about the black kid, saying you've gotta plunk a kid like that in the head to keep the neighborhood the way it is. Rena pieced it all together after a few hours. Next day she found out the kid died. His parents were on the news, heartbroken. A black kid in an Italian neighborhood, killed for the color of his skin. Mikey never got caught. She'd fed him happily. He wound up working for Vic until he got himself bumped off in Atlantic City over a gambling debt. She could never shake that. Vic taking the kid under his wing, laughing with him, congratulating him, protecting him, rewarding him with a job. And her feeding him like he'd worked a long day and needed sustenance. She feels confused. Maybe she's always been confused. What she knows now is she feels so complicit. In everything.

ENZIO

Enzio is pleading his case to Richie as they hurtle along the Palisades, chased by Crea. "There's a pull-off coming up ahead. Just let me out. Please."

"I'm gonna pull over and let you out here?" Richie says. "Then what? Crea lights us both up, that's what. I said pipe down."

Enzio feels sick. He hadn't made a move on Rena, none of this would be happening. He wishes he could play it all in reverse. Get a do-over. Go to Coney Island, score a quick handjob from a Russian with long legs and foul breath, pick up a white pie from Totonno's, and then go home. Watch one of his movies. Eat a slice of pizza over his lap, no paper plate or napkin even. His Impala would still be in the driveway instead of thumping along the Palisades Parkway in the nightmare dark.

As a kid, Enzio hated danger more than anything. He tried never to feel afraid, which was hard when you had an old man like his. A lot of kids he knew had a father who was quick with a belt. With Pop, it was more than that. Pop had come to Brooklyn from Naples in his twenties. Work and booze had made him mean. Enzio remembers, at six, cowering in the corner by the boiler, counting screws that had fallen out of a tool chest near Pop's workbench. He remembers buckets full of wires and a soldering iron that he'd focus on as Pop came rampaging toward him. He never wanted sympathy for having an old man like that, never talked about it. Not even to Maria. One time he got to yapping with this young hooker. Told her more than he'd ever told anybody. She didn't give a shit. What she'd come from in Serbia was a million times worse.

Enzio has many regrets. Maria on her deathbed flashes in his mind. Forget what she did or didn't do for him all those years, there's a lot he should've said. "Get you anything?" being the main one.

Crea disappears from behind them, the inside of the Impala going dark.

"Did he just shut his lights off?" Richie says.

Enzio turns around to look, hoping that Crea's gone, hoping that whatever he's doing affords Enzio the opportunity to get out of the Impala and escape. It's not that his car doesn't matter to him anymore. It's that he's suddenly afraid of death in a way he's never been. He should've anticipated that before he got in the car with Richie. What if there's nothing? What if you get clipped and it all just goes dark? Or, worse, what happens if your body is dead but you can still see yourself and still feel regrets and still feel afraid? What if being dead is nothing but feeling afraid forever? "I don't see him," Enzio says.

"Games," Richie says.

"Pull over. Please."

Another flash of Maria on her deathbed. Her wilting mouth. Her bony body. The color gone from her face. "I'm nothing," she said to him. "I've never been anything. You're worse than nothing."

"I'm something," he said. "We're both something."

"What was it all for?"

"What do you mean?"

"Why did we even live? We weren't happy."

Enzio hadn't answered her. He'd known happiness, just not with her. The Dean Martin hero from Lioni's. A perfect egg cream at Hinsch's. His Impala, of course. Being in the stands when the Dodgers won the Series in '55. A hot dog from Nathan's on the Boardwalk in the summer, just sitting there on a bench, watching the Wonder Wheel and watching the women on the beach and watching all the seagulls swoop down for tossed-away bread. That young Serbian spitting in her palm in this very passenger seat and smiling at him, showing her yellow teeth. Jody from the bank wrapped up in the curtains at the Harbor Motor Inn on Shore Parkway, light from outside streaming across the little green dragon she had tattooed on her back.

The only happiness Maria brought him came when she died. Friends showed up with hulking trays of ziti, loaves of semolina bread, and boxes of cookies. He was kissed on his cheeks by women wearing strong perfume. He liked the feeling of cleaning out Maria's closet, giving away her clothes or throwing them in the trash or taking them to the Knights of Columbus. He liked being called a widower. He liked going to Single, Separated, Widowed, and Divorced group dances at the church. He liked playing cards with other widowers. He had purpose as a widower. He no longer felt like he was capable of bad things.

"Where'd he go?" Richie says, looking over his left shoulder and then over his right, the car swerving with its jerky movements.

Enzio starts to blubber.

"Jesus Christ, shut up."

Enzio's thoughts turn to Crea. He sees Crea stripping him down on an abandoned stretch of road and throwing him in a shallow grave.

"I'll push you out the door," Richie says.

"Just up here," Enzio says. "This pull-off. Please." He wants to walk off into the woods. He wants to be cold in the woods. He wants to come out on the other side of the tall trees and see a house where someone will welcome him with hot coffee and bacon, where someone will change his bandages and see that he is tended to.

A fantasy unfolds before him.

This house he stumbles upon, a nurse lives there. He's always wanted to fall in love with a nurse. When he was at Maimonides earlier, he looked down his young nurse's top and touched her hand as much as he could. She had tired eyes and wore unattractive sneakers. Her scrubs were purple. She needed a mint and more sleep. The nurse who owns this imaginary house at the edge of the woods is in her forties. She's pretty. Her hair is black but a little gray at the roots. It looks like she works and goes to the gym and that's about it. She has an old television because she doesn't watch much, maybe the news. Her scrubs are pink. Her breath smells like bubblegum. "You must be freezing," she says to him when she finds him on her porch.

"I am," he says.

She takes him by the hand and brings him inside. She unwraps his bandages and cleans his head with peroxide and slathers on Neosporin. She applies new bandages. They're softer and better than the ones from the hospital. She does a better job of putting on the bandages. "Who did this to you?" she asks.

"I don't know," he says, and he feels like he's telling the truth.

She makes coffee and puts on the bacon. He asks what time it is. She says late. When she kisses him on the cheek, she kisses him like someone who would never let anything else bad happen to him.

He looks out her front window for Richie and Crea, but they're gone from here, spinning off to another world.

"I'm here," she says.

"What's your name?" he asks.

"Lily."

"I'm happy I found you."

"I'm happy you found me."

Life could be like that, he's convincing himself, if he could only get out of the car. This Impala that he's long felt to be an extension of himself. Maybe, when it comes down to it, the only thing he's ever truly loved. And now, suddenly, he's ready to deny it, to let Richie do with it what he will. Crash it against a tree. Drive it into the river. He feels so separate from it now. He wants the nurse in her house. He wants her to touch him and kiss him and cook for him and tuck him into her soft bed. He's not even thinking about anything dirty.

The pull-off approaches, a dark, twisting road that branches from the parkway. Richie, exasperated, yanks the car sharply to the right at what feels more like an exit than a mere pull-off just as they're about to pass it, Enzio assuming that he doesn't want to give away too soon that he's getting off, hoping to shake Crea if he's ghosting them with his lights cut. It seems to work. Enzio turns and doesn't see a car close behind them. Maybe Crea's fallen far enough behind, though, that they just can't see him, making it seem as if he's no longer on their trail.

The pull-off is way, way more than Richie bargained for, and he's cursing, pounding the wheel. A long two-way road cuts back through trees and opens up into a parking lot with a rest stop and tower viewers looking out over the Hudson. Since it's late, the parking lot is empty except for one car, a cream Ford Explorer with a bumper held on by duct tape and a cracked windshield and clear plastic over the broken back door glass. It's backed into a spot next to a small gravel heap.

Enzio can tell that Richie's troubled by the fact that the only road returning to the parkway is the same road they took in. "I told you not to come with me," Richie says, leaning across him, jerking the handle, and pushing open the passenger door. "Now get the fuck out."

Enzio wipes his eyes and climbs out as quickly as he can, knocking his bandaged head against the doorframe. He tries not to look at the Impala as he takes several steps away from it. Tries to pretend that it's no longer his. He sees glints of light in the dents that Crea has made in the bumper. He thinks of his nurse. She's nowhere. There are no nearby houses. He'll have to stay at the rest stop until morning. Find somewhere warm and hope an old man like him can make it through the night. That's fine. Maybe there's a pay phone somewhere. Maybe he can call Harry, and Harry will send Lou. Enzio would kill to see that dumb fuck Lou about now.

Enzio notices a bench over by a tower viewer. He thinks that he'll just curl up there like a bum. He can't see the river from where he's standing. He wonders if he'll be able to from the edge. He can see cliffs silhouetted against the night. He can see dark, low-hanging clouds, almost purple in their darkness. He can see the lights of the George Washington off to the right. He can see the swampy lights of houses and buildings and whatever else is across the river. All these people going about their normal lives. Sleeping in their beds. Working late. Maybe his nurse is over there.

Richie pulls the door closed with a huff and speeds off, his tires kicking loose gravel against Enzio's legs.

Back at the entrance to the lot, a pair of lights snap on. Crea's Town Car, Enzio can tell. Blocking Richie's path. The Town Car starts moving.

Instead of slowing down, Richie barrels along. The driver's-side window is open. With one hand still on the wheel, Richie leans a little out the window with a small piece in his unsteady hand, firing twice at the Town Car and hitting the front fender once and the passenger-side windshield. The gunshots get sucked up in the valley. The river muffles them. Richie is screaming. Crea is still coming.

Richie cuts the wheel in an attempt to get around the Town Car, but Crea plows into the driver's side of the Impala. This noise is louder. What's happening now is slowed down, the messy tangle of the cars, all that metal, the Town Car pushing the Impala back into a ditch and flipping it. The last thing Enzio notices before he closes his eyes is Crea laughing his ass off.

When Enzio's father died in Victory Memorial, he was at his side, even though the old man didn't want him to be. His father had said to him, "I don't need you here." He stayed anyway. He got his father coffee and ate the hospital food that the old man couldn't eat. Slimy fruit and pale cold cuts and tough bread. A sad carton of orange juice. Enzio was in his forties when his father died. So long ago, but now time seems different, as if there are all these avenues to different moments and everything is one moment. He's trembling. His father's last words to him were "Get the hell out of here, would you?" After he finally left that last night at Victory, his father died alone. The nurses got to him quickly, but he wanted to die alone, and he did. It made Enzio happy to think that this was why his father had said what he'd said. He didn't want his son to watch him die. Enzio is not upset he never had a son or daughter. Never felt like something was missing. Still doesn't. Man is a cancer.

He opens his eyes to smoke trails. He thinks about climbing over the railing, if he can even make his old body do that. He would skid down the enormous rocky hill to the river. He would swim across the river. He would come up on the far shore and his nurse would be waiting for him.

Richie, dazed, is out of the Impala. He's somehow climbed out of the car and up from the ditch and is on his knees next to a green garbage can. The Impala is battered, on its back like roadkill. All the years it was Enzio's baby, he never imagined he'd see it roof-down like this.

Instead of climbing the railing, Enzio makes a move for the Ford Explorer with the clear plastic taped over its rear right-side door glass. He's hoping there's a key inside. He's hoping there's a way out of here. He's mad at himself for not thinking of it sooner. He gets there and rips open the plastic, sticking his hand inside and unlatching the door lock. He climbs in the back seat, feeling overwhelmed by the task of moving up to the front to search for a key or to see if he can rub wires together and make the thing go. He sits there for a moment and catches his breath. He doesn't remember how old he is. He's old, he knows that. His nurse does not exist.

Through the windshield, he sees Crea with his hammer. He's standing over Richie, bringing the hammer down on one of his knees. Richie is howling with pain. The sound of him howling streams into the car through the ripped-open plastic. Enzio doesn't want to hear it. He reaches and unlocks the driver's-side door and then moves up to the front. His breath is fogging the glass. He turns down the sun visor, hoping a key will spill out.

Nothing. He feels around in the cup holders. He opens the glove compart-
ment and the center console. Nothing. Under the dash, he plays with wires.
It's been a long time since he started a car this way. He's not having any luck.
He doesn't remember exactly what to do.

When he looks up, sweat beading his forehead, his bandages soaked
through with sweat, Crea's coming for him.

"I remember you!" Crea calls out, waving the hammer around. "Vic's
neighbor!" It's like he's recognizing him in a crowd, like he hasn't seen him
in years and he's approaching for a hug. Richie is still wailing over by the
cars.

Enzio has evacuated his bowels. The smell is terrific. Maybe he's never
been a man. The darkness in the rearview mirror seems to get darker.

Crea opens the door and pulls him out. Enzio is panting, his hands over
his face, saying, "Please, I've got nothing to do with any of this."

"Did you shit your pants?" Crea asks.

"Please. I'm nothing. I'm just a nobody." Enzio's hands are on Crea's
shoes. "You want money? I'll give you whatever you want. You want me to
kiss your shoes? I'll do whatever you want."

"None of that matters," Crea says.

Enzio thinks maybe Rena killed him with the ashtray and everything
since has just been the road to hell. He looks up at Crea's cheap smile. His
teeth seem razor sharp. Crea brings the hammer down. Maybe Enzio stops
existing. Maybe he's never existed in the first place.

WOLFSTEIN

Wolfstein and Mo are passing the wine back and forth, chain-smoking cigarettes. Lucia is snuggled up against Rena, both of them passed out from exhaustion, the briefcase held tight between Lucia's legs. She looks like a real little kid now, even with the way she's been acting. Fifteen's tough. Especially when your world gets turned upside down.

The wine is cheap stuff, not quite bum wine but not far off. Wolfstein unscrews the cap and takes another swig. "I've gotta clear my head," she says to Mo.

"This will help, I promise."

"I can't believe what we saw back there. I can't believe any of it. A chase, too."

"Freaked you out bad, huh?"

"Mob wife." Wolfstein tilts a thumb at Rena. "I don't know if she ever saw someone get shot before. Maybe she saw a lot of other people get shot. But she shouldn't have it happen to her daughter right in front of her. That fucking Bobby. And the other guy, what he did. My god."

"No shit, she's a mob wife?" Mo asks in a whisper, swatting Wolfstein's leg. "You didn't tell me that."

"I mean, she was. Mob widow, more accurately."

"That's what this is all about?"

"Part of it, anyway."

"Jesus Christ, Wolfie."

Rena opens her eyes. "I'm not really asleep," she says.

"I'm sorry," Wolfstein says.

"It's fine. I understand."

Rena straightens out against the wall, adjusting Lucia's head on her shoulder while simultaneously stretching and yawning. "She looks so peaceful when she's sleeping," Rena says.

"She's a tough kid," Wolfstein says. "It's good to be tough."

"What you were talking about, all those years, I never did see somebody get shot. I found Vic, like I said." Rena turns to Mo. "Vic was my husband. He never ever let anything happen in front of me. I heard of some things, sure. Hard to keep totally removed from that. Some rat got cut up, buried in cement. I don't know, that's different."

"Your daughter," Mo says. "I'm so sorry."

Rena nods into her chest, looking down. "We were, what's the word? Exiled from each other. Not exiled. Disconnected? I can't think of the word." She pauses. "Estranged, is what I mean. Doesn't make it hurt less. I just . . . I hardly knew her anymore."

"Me and Wolfie, we never had kids, thank Christ." Mo shakes her head. "That's not an appropriate thing to say. I'm sorry. I've been drinking for days."

"It's okay. None of this seems real right now."

Wolfstein can't imagine what Rena's going through. She really can't. How torn up and confused she must be. She wants to keep her talking, though. You disappear too far into your own head after something like this, there might be no coming back. You start seeing replays. So Wolfstein turns the conversation away from Adrienne. "I tell you me and Mo knew some mob guys out in Los Angeles? Few guys involved in the industry. This one, Lenny Olivieri, I really liked him. Class act."

"Vic was a class act."

"I'm sure. Lenny, he'd always bring me bread from my favorite bakery. Flowers every now and again. This wasn't a guy trying to get his dick wet. He was just a gentleman. Nice suits. Like De Niro in *Casino*. You ever see that? He'd be wearing suits like that, hair slicked back, always clicking a breath mint around in his mouth. Just nice. With me, anyway."

"Vic liked that movie. *Goodfellas*, too, of course. There's a picture up in the Meats Supreme I always go to on Eighty-Sixth Street, Vic and two of his guys with Scorsese, De Niro, Pesci, and the other one. What's his name? Guy played Paulie. I go in there now, the owner's dead, his kids run it, they don't even know that was my husband. Signed picture. Right there on the wall. I should've stolen it."

"You should've."

"How am I supposed to know what I really want anymore?" Rena says, and then stops herself. "I want to take Lucia with me to Vic's grave. How's that gonna happen? Are we gonna have to run forever? Does she even love me?"

"We need some music," Wolfstein says. "On low, so the kid doesn't wake up. You got anything, Mo?"

Mo takes out a couple of the other cassettes she brought along. "Paul Simon and Peggy Lee," she says.

"No Stevie?"

"My mother hid my Stevie tapes."

Wolfstein laughs. "Peggy Lee."

Mo puts in her Peggy Lee *All-Time Greatest Hits* cassette and presses play. The sound is distorted, a bit too slow, but it'll do. Miss Peggy's singing "I'm a Woman."

Wolfstein had a friend in Florida named Gloria Levene. Got diagnosed with pancreatic cancer one summer, and it took her out fast. Six months.

Wolfstein used to sit with her and listen to tapes like this. On a stereo, though. Gloria always wanted to hear Linda Ronstadt.

"My friend Gloria used to imagine lives for us where we were famous singers," Wolfstein says, tilting back the bottle. "She was sick, and she'd tell these stories like they were real memories. Like we were on the road together, singing our hit songs. I'd go along with her. I'd really start to elaborate. I'd say, 'Remember the time we played with the Rolling Stones?' I'd say, 'Remember the time we played Red Rocks?' That was how we got through it. I'd tell stories about the dresses we wore, how we did our makeup, and Gloria would just be nodding and smiling. We could've had that life. I'm not sure we didn't. I believe there are parallel worlds where things you think and dream like that are absolutely true."

"I remember Gloria," Mo says. "Sweetheart."

No response from Rena. Maybe she's weirded out. Or just tired.

Wolfstein keeps going: "My earliest memory, I'm four or five. Back in Riverdale. Wearing an eyelet twirl dress. Standing in front of a piano. Some guy in glasses is playing. No idea who he is. Greasy hair, bad teeth. His fingers are really plunking down on the keys. The piano sounds off, like this tape. Warped a little. I'm singing. Not a real song. One I'm making up as I go. The thing I most remember is that I was seeing myself from outside myself, like a movie. Like I *was* this girl, but I was watching her, too. Later, when I chewed it over, I got to wondering if that was me seeing another me, you know?" She pauses. "The stories Gloria and I told each other, it seemed like we were making them up, but maybe we were just telling about other lives we lived."

"I think I need to stand up and move around a little," Rena says.

"You okay?" Wolfstein asks.

"A little sick to my stomach."

Rena gets up, moving the briefcase under Lucia's head as a makeshift pillow. Lucia stirs a little but doesn't wake up.

Rena paces back and forth.

"You need to puke, puke anywhere," Mo says. "Who cares?"

"I just need some fresh air."

"That's not a good idea," Wolfstein says.

"I'm just gonna duck my head out the back door a sec." Rena goes out of the room, letting the door crackle shut behind her.

Wolfstein wonders why she bothered talking about Gloria and that childhood memory. Must've added to Rena's unease. She sits there with Mo and the music. An automatic tension comes with tapes. When a song ends, she's wondering if it's the end of the side. No one likes when a side ends. It's a lonely sound, the clatter of the tape stopping, the play button popping back up. Back when tapes were the main way to listen—not a very long window when it comes right down to it, but a prominent one for her—Wolfstein always feared that sound. She liked the act of flipping a tape to the other side but not the sound of a side ending. She remembers wondering if that's what happens when people die. Things just click to a stop and then silence. You'd look behind that little window and see stillness. Nothing left to spin. A heartbreaking sight.

A bar she used to hang out at occasionally in Hollywood, Frolic Room, had this guy who used to come in selling bootleg tapes. She'd be sitting at the bar with Mo or Hunny or someone, and he'd waltz in, all wild strides. Ulmer, his name was. Baggy T-shirts, construction boots, torn jeans. Always smiling, always hustling. She loved him. She loves all the hustlers of the world. To be a hustler is to be free of some agony that regular folks seem to hold on to. Hustlers know the quick demise, failure no stopping force. You have to hustle through failure. She admired hustlers even before she became one. Ulmer, sure, but also pool sharks, girls in the business, anyone with the smarts to hustle hard. She sees a little of that fire in Lucia.

What she's thinking of now, she's thinking of one afternoon in the Frolic Room, Ulmer spreading out some tapes on a little fold-out mat he carried everywhere with him, talking up live shows, mixes, dubs of dubs. The tapes were cheap. Two bucks. Wolfstein always willing to plunk down for one, no matter the quality. Ulmer usually kissing her hand after accepting the cash. This time, though, Ulmer downtrodden, no smile, weepy-eyed. Wolfstein asked, "What's wrong?"

"I don't know," Ulmer said.

"You look really upset," she said.

"I don't know what it is. I just feel everything crashing down on me." A rare glimpse into a hustler's heart, she thought at the time. That fear is there, but you learn to beat it down. Something about that moment, Ulmer just let his guard fall. Maybe something about her telling him it was okay, she wouldn't spill his secret sorrow.

She bought eight tapes from him.

It took her a few days to realize he'd gotten her good. That he'd figured out how to make a true mark of her. Letting his guard fall his most effective hustle against her.

A great lesson.

⌐

"When I hold you in my arms," Wolfstein's aunt Karen used to say, "I can feel all that God has planned for you." Wolfstein, even at ten, scoffed at this on the inside. Aunt Karen had soft skin that glowed with a sullen ripeness. From the right angle, she looked like a pudding-soft banana, one that you needed to use in a recipe for bread or throw away. Wolfstein hated her aunt. This the aunt who she'd been dumped with unwillingly. Who made her stay on her knees and pray every night for ridiculous things. Space on a new ark when a new flood roared upon them. Forgiveness for things she didn't feel bad for. For hateful policies to take hold on God's behalf. The feeling that Wolfstein had in those days could best be expressed as a sort of raging readiness, for something, anything, else. When the opportunity came to leave, she never looked back. She could've never imagined the life she wound up having. Praise be random adventures. Praise be survival. Praise be not having a plan.

She finds herself thinking of her aunt now as she goes out to check on
Rena. Whatever she feels, whatever she sees, whatever horrors she's encountered, she's just glad she had the smarts to break free from Aunt Karen so
young. That's a form of being positive. That's the optimism that's always
hovered over her, even in dark stretches. Talk about parallel lives. She sees a
poor girl trapped in Nyack. She sees a poor girl Bible-battered by a glowy,
bitch-wild aunt. She sees the fat hand of a God she doesn't believe in
crushing her windpipe. She sees this girl still trying to escape.

Her aunt probably died years before. Or maybe she's alive, a bony witch
in some woebegone nursing home, still praying for a long-gone niece who
had no gratitude, who never lived with the right kind of fear.

In the darkness just outside the back door, Wolfstein suddenly swears
she sees Aunt Karen, edging off behind the pool. It takes her a moment to
realize it's just Rena, who looks nothing like her aunt.

Wolfstein says her name as quietly as she can, and Rena doesn't answer.
She goes over. "Rena, you okay?"

Rena falls to her knees and pukes on a patch of leaf-strewn cement beside
the pool. She leans back, wiping the corners of her mouth.

"It's just nerves," Wolfstein says.

Rena retches. Tries to puke again. Nothing comes.

"Take it easy," Wolfstein says, massaging Rena's neck.

Watching Rena try to puke is strangely comforting. Wolfstein knows her
purpose in the moment: help Rena get better. Like with a pilled-up Hunny
or a sick Gloria. Rub her back. Say gentle things. Bring the softness. Wolfstein, usually hard, likes having such a purpose.

"I'm done," Rena says after a few more throaty tries.

"You feel a little better?" Wolfstein asks.

"I think so." Rena stands up, dusts off her knees.

"We've got to get back inside." Wolfstein looks all around, trying to see
beyond the edge of the house. No action over at Mo's as far as she can tell.

"I know. I'm sorry." Rena wipes her mouth again and walks to the back door.

Inside, standing in the dark and closing the door behind them, Wolfstein says, "My aunt Karen was a real bitch."

Rena looks at her, puzzled. "Were you talking about your aunt?"

"Thinking about her. I don't know why. Head's all over the place tonight. I hate her so much, but I'm thankful for her, you know? That kind of hate breeds real resiliency. She made me tough, whether she meant to or not."

They move farther in, standing outside the closed door of the room where Lucia and Mo are. They can hear another Peggy Lee song winding down.

Wolfstein says, "My aunt Karen, I'm not lying now, when I did something she didn't like, she'd make me get down on my knees and say my prayers on a tray of broken glass. No kidding. She had this big silver serving tray. I don't know where the hell she got all the broken glass, but she had quite the collection, apparently. Green glass. Old Mason jars, maybe. My knees would get cut up pretty bad. When I was done, she'd leave me a bottle of hydrogen peroxide, some cotton balls, and bandages. I always said, later on, that's why I was so good at staying on my knees for so long." Winking into the darkness.

"That's terrible," Rena says. "How long did that go on?"

"Until I ran away. You look at my knees close enough, you can still see these little horseshoe scars. They mostly healed okay, but there's some thin cords of tissue. After I first ran away, I was pretty scared. I was a kid still, really. I used to look at myself in the mirror and say, 'There's no time for sorry. There's no time for sorry.' I'd say it fifty times. It became my mantra. And then I'd say, 'Make a move.' I'd only say that once."

"I like that."

"Got me through."

They fall quiet and go back into the room. Lucia is awake and sitting up, hugging the briefcase. "Where'd you go?" she says to Rena.

"I was feeling sick," Rena says.

"Any action out there?" Mo asks.

"Nothing I saw," Wolfstein says. But she's learned that the dark can hide so much.

RICHIE

Richie is on his back in the parking lot, Crea having clubbed him in the knee and then raced off to deal with Enzio. The pain is enormous. He's biting his lower lip. He's looking up at the sky. His head is spinning from being flipped in the Impala. He's trying to straighten out the world. He's afraid to reach down to touch his knee. His body is sore in other places. Broken ribs from the crash. His neck stiff and hard to move, as if he's already wearing a steel brace. Damage to his hip. He can taste blood between his teeth. He guesses this is how it will end. He was stupid. He didn't plan well. He deserves to die in this lot. He's not smart. He's never been smart.

When he turns his head to the left just a little, what he sees is Crea off in the distance going to town on Enzio with the hammer next to the Explorer. It's like he's demolishing an old statue, as if he's sick of looking at this statue and hammering it down to ash piece by piece. First the arms and then the legs and then the body. Enzio's moans are wet and terrible.

Richie tries to roll over onto his side. The piece was thrown away from him on impact, Crea's Town Car lunging for him, the Impala taking that first blow like a stocky, grief-waddled old boxer. If he had the piece back and if he had the two bullets he'd fired so stupidly, he's honestly not sure if he'd try for Crea or if he'd just put himself out of his misery.

Fully on his side now, the pain is worse. He has to try to get to his one good knee. Try not to involve the battered, bad one. And then what? Hobble out on the long exit road to the parkway? Won't be long before he turns around and Crea is there, grinning.

In his mind he's playing stickball in the PS 101 schoolyard. He's holding his trusty stickball bat, the handle crisscrossed with electrical tape. Hank De Simone is getting ready to pitch the Spaldeen. He looks back at the white strike zone chalked on the wall behind him. Hank unloads. Richie swings, cranks it over the far fence. A miraculous homer. He throws his bat down and jumps in place. "The kid does it again!" he says at top volume.

"Luck," Hank says, spitting.

"Luck and power," Richie says.

Hank is his best friend at the moment. This is eighth grade. Him and Hank, they're inseparable. Reading comics. Playing stickball. Stealing magazines. Doing little jobs for Stacks Brancaccio, Sonny's old man, and for Gentle Vic, who was pure class from the start. He's one year away from not talking to Hank ever again. One of the strange things about being a kid is how you just stop being friends with people. Go a different way or cut someone off because they cease being interesting to you. He cut Hank off. Found tougher friends who took him to a nice joint in the city to get his cherry popped and scored him a beginner's piece. Hank was still a kid. He'd see him around now and again, trudging somewhere with a comic book, chewing gum like a dumb horse munches hay, and he'd feel bad for the kid. Now he feels bad for himself. He wishes he'd been a kid more. He wonders about Hank. He probably lives somewhere up here. Trees in the backyard. Treehouse. Got a couple of kids. A wife who says things like, "Hank, you stop that now." Waking up in a few hours, putting on coffee, taking the bus into the city for his job. Monday. Feeling refreshed. Ready to get going.

The Hank memory, which feels so present, dissipates.

Richie is on his hands, using his good leg for leverage, in what seems like some sort of bullshit yoga pose, his ass turned in the air. He knows yoga. Adrienne made him go once. She was into it for about two weeks in the summer of '99. Bronx-style yoga. Place was in a strip mall next to a Barnes & Noble in the Bay Plaza Shopping Center on Baychester Avenue. He farted loud when he bent over, and the whole class laughed. He stormed out. "You fucks are better than a fart?" he'd said. Roomful of women in spandex or whatever looking like he'd just shit a pigeon and smashed it against the glass wall of the studio.

The sound of a train in the distance. Maybe not a train. He's afraid to look over at Crea and Enzio again. Afraid to see Enzio hammered down to dust. Afraid to hear Crea's feet smacking against the pavement, rushing at him with violent energy. Afraid to hear that hammer dragging against the ground. Afraid to bring his eyes up to the level of Crea's eyes. He feels turned inside out, the world on the other side of midnight raw against him. He's a coward. He's always been a coward. He hops forward and crashes to the ground.

"Whoa there, you graceless fuck," Crea calls out.

The pain is worse. His knee feels shattered. Richie leopard crawls now, pulling his pain with him. He's headed for the wreckage of the two cars. He hopes he can crawl under the still-right-side-up Town Car. Hopes he can shelter there, just out of reach. Hopes he can disappear inside the smoke.

"Where you going?" Crea says, getting closer.

Richie thinking if he pretends not to hear Crea's voice, it's not really there.

"You wanna call a cab? We can split it. Fuck it. Let's just take that Explorer. I know what you're thinking. You're thinking, 'What about your Town Car, Crea?' That's not my Town Car. It's identical to my Town Car, but this one's Clyde Finelli's. You think I'd have a Mets flag on my vehicle?" Crea hovering over him now. "You know me better than that. You know my feelings on the Mets. Keith Hernandez, I met that fuck once. Richie, talk to me. Richie, where you going, guy?" Crea leans down over him, pressing his knee hard into Richie's back and letting the hammer clank to the ground.

Richie's crawling is suspended. It's as if he's a mouse pinned down by a mad child.

Crea continues: "Where are your balls now? You got the balls to go into Caccio's and mow down our unarmed friends at a sit-down, where are they now? Say you're a sad fuck."

Richie puts his mouth against the pavement. It tastes of grit and tires and darkness.

"Say you're a sad fuck. Say it."

Richie can smell Crea's minty breath over his shoulder. "I'm a sad fuck," Richie says.

Crea hacks out a laugh. "Indeed. You saw the way I did old Enzio? That was me getting loose, warming up."

"I'm a sad fuck," Richie says again.

Crea cools it with his knee. Stands. Picks up the hammer. "You stay right here, okay? I'm gonna go get the Explorer. It's a piece of shit, but it'll do for now."

Footsteps moving away. Richie starts to crawl forward again. What he thought about Lucia back there on the bridge, he feels sorry about it. Lucia's not his enemy. He wishes he could call her his daughter. He wishes they were on the road—him, Adrienne, and Lucia—with no trouble behind them. Or ahead. He wishes he could buy her a good dinner somewhere. Girl likes to eat. He wishes he could think of her as his real daughter now. Pray for her and ask her to pray for him. Prayer. That's good. He's going to die, and he guesses he's glad she's got the money. If anybody, her. Of course, Crea will go after it. Crea doesn't let things rest. Richie's going to die, yeah, but he's got to take Crea down with him.

When the Explorer pulls up at his heels, he can feel heat emanating from under the chassis. Crea beeps the horn. Richie can hear the electric buzz of a window. "Come on, get up," Crea says, Richie able to tell there's a smile on his face. "Who knows whose car this is? I don't need to kill a stranger for a '95 Ford Explorer. Hotwiring it was a bitch. I used to be good. Fast. Now I'm fumbling under the dash like I'm twelve, trying to unclasp a broad's bra. You know who had a truck like this? Al Burke, that little Irish prick. His mother was always spilling holy water in there. I says to Al, I says, 'Where the fuck's your old lady get all this holy water?' You know what this Mick says to me? 'The priest comes over, he blesses all these jugs of water she's got laying around.' A priest blessing random jugs of Poland Spring, you believe that shit?"

Richie tries to get back to a standing position. He wonders if Crea, still behind the wheel, will run him over for kicks. That's something Crea would do. Like that sick flick *The Toxic Avenger*. What those gym rats do to that skinny twerp on the bike in the beginning. How they run over his head and pop it like a zit.

"Okay," Crea says, opening the door and getting out of the truck. "You need some help. I get it. I'm not gonna kill you, Richie. Don't worry. Not yet. I'm gonna hurt you a little here and there maybe, but I'm not gonna kill you until I get the money back. I got myopic vision for that dough. Beyond that, I got my mind set on revenge. Beyond *that*, I never liked you, and I'll take great pleasure in watching you die. But, first, we get the money." He puts his hands under Richie and lifts, groaning. "I'm sore from the little accident we had. You? Beating Vic's neighbor to death really took it out of me, too." Another laugh.

Crea leads Richie toward the rear right-side door of the Explorer, the glass missing, the plastic that was there ripped away. "You dream about beating people to death when you were a kid?" Crea asks. "I did. Real thing's way more satisfying. I wish I could tell my kid self that."

"I'm not getting in that truck," Richie says.

"The hell you're not," Crea says, opening the door and shoving him in. "You're my navigator."

—

Next thing Richie remembers he's sprawled out on the back seat of the Explorer. They're moving fast. Probably on the Palisades. He thinks he must have lost consciousness for a few minutes. He's cold. Wind whips in through the broken window. The car smells like shit. Crea has the radio on loud. "You Can't Always Get What You Want." He's singing along and pounding the steering wheel.

"Can you lower that?" Richie asks.

"You're awake, Principessa?" Crea says over the music, tilting the rearview mirror so he can see Richie. "What'd you say now?"

"Lower the music." Richie's always had a distaste for this song. It's not that he hates the Stones. He likes them. Saw them four times over the years. It's just one of those songs that's everywhere. Movies, supermarkets, tire shops, sushi joints. Makes him sad as shit. He's gonna die, he doesn't want to hear it. He wants to hear something unique, something you don't hear on the radio every damn day. Hendrix wailing away on "Red House." Or some metal maybe. Adrienne got him into metal a little back in the day. Dio's "Rainbow in the Dark" or Iron Maiden's "Wasted Years" or Motörhead's "Ace of Spades" would be nice.

"Listen to this guy," Crea says. "'Lower the music.' You've got some balls, Richie. It's the Stones. Who doesn't want to hear the Stones?" He turns down the volume. "Now you ruined it."

The pain is still thumping in Richie. He crosses his arms over his chest.

"I'm gonna stop for food and then you're telling me where to go, okay?" Crea says.

"I don't know where they are," Richie says, closing his eyes.

"Don't 'I don't know' me. You know. You fucking know."

Richie drifts away.

⌒

When he wakes up again, the car is heavy with food smells. Sausage, grease, hash browns. Coffee, too. Crea is biting into a sausage, egg, and cheese on a bagel. The melted cheese is dripping onto his jacket. He inhales the sandwich in a few bites. Then he plucks a forkful of hash browns out of a paper bag in his lap and washes it down with coffee. The clock radio reads 2:03. Richie can't believe it.

Crea's looking at him in the rearview mirror again, noticing his eyes are open. "Finally," Crea says. "Sleeping Beauty over here. Thought you were dead. Tried waking you up to no avail. Let a couple of good farts rip. Nothing. Rode the horn for five minutes. Nothing. Went into a gas station and freshened up, bought some more Listerine, you're still snoring away. Got food at this all-night joint. Out like a light. As my old lady used to say, you must've really needed it."

Richie pushes back against the door a little bit. He's not sure how he slept through this shattering pain in his knee. His head feels swimmy. His neck even worse than it was. He wonders if he has a concussion. He was dreaming of hockey, he remembers that. Going to a Rangers game with Adrienne. Standing on the steps outside MSG, Adrienne wearing a long red scarf and a fuzzy wool Rangers hat.

His mouth is so dry, it's tacky. His tongue clicks against his teeth. "Water?" he says.

"You want water?" Crea says.

Richie nods.

Crea throws back a bottle of Aquafina. It bounces off the back of the seat and ricochets down onto the floor. Richie feels around for it. He gets it onto his chest and tries to unscrew the cap. He's weak, and it's hard to even accomplish that. Finally, he pops it off and the water splashes on his shirt. He sits up a little and brings the bottle to his lips, drinking deeply.

"Drink up," Crea says, taking another sloppy bite of hash browns. "You're gonna need it."

"Where are we?" Richie asks.

"Who knows? It's all the same to me up here. Where are they going?"

"I don't know. I lost them on the bridge. You saw. They could be anywhere."

"Bullshit."

"I wouldn't have had to chase them if I knew where they were headed."

"I'm calm, Richie. I'm gonna find them. Might not be tonight. But I'll sniff them out. Kid and a couple of old ladies on the run with all that dough, what're they gonna do? They'll leave a trail. Maybe I *will* have to kill you first. But I'm gonna find them, and I'm gonna get the money back, and I'm gonna kill the girl like I killed her mother. And"—he waves his finger—"*and*, my friend, your Eldorado will be my Eldorado, and I'm gonna drive it all around Brooklyn proudly. Maybe I'll hang your scalp from the antenna. People will know: this is what happens when you betray your friends."

"You were never my friend," Richie says. "Sonny was never my friend."

"That's true," Crea says, slurping some coffee.

Richie puts his hand down in his pocket and slowly removes the letter that's there. He's thinking if he can withdraw it without Crea noticing and slide it under the floor mat or between the driver seat and the center console that the fucking psycho won't ever know of its existence. But if Crea finds it on Richie, that's another story. Say they *did* go to this Mo's house, and Richie's betting they did given their trajectory. Say they're just holing up there, hoping this will all blow over. People do unpredictable, stupid things in times of crisis and catastrophe. He gets the letter out of his pocket. His hand feels twisted and arthritic. He pushes it up his belly and then lets it fall to the floor carpet.

"Fuck you doing back there?" Crea says, his eyebrows arching in the rear-view mirror. "You got something for me?" He reaches over to the passenger seat and picks up his hammer, which—as Richie just now sees—is covered in Adrienne's and Enzio's blood and is propped there at the ready. Crea snatches it up by the handle and then wallops Richie in the stomach as hard as he can one-handed in this confined space.

Richie scrunches up as he receives the blow, the gristly face of the hammer landing square in the meatiest part of his gut.

"What're you hiding from me?" Crea slams the wheel to the right, lurching the Explorer onto the shoulder of whatever road they're on. He reaches over the center console and plucks up the envelope from the floor and takes the letter out and looks it over. "What's this?"

Richie turns on his side, facing away from Crea. He knows the hammer's coming again. He doesn't want to see it.

This time Crea nails him in the arm. Right above his elbow.

Richie flips back over, his eyes closing and then opening again.

Crea laughs, picks between his teeth with a coffee stirrer, and bunches up the foil his sandwich came in. He rolls down his window and tosses the foil ball out onto the road. He reaches into the brown bag and pulls out a handful of hash browns, shoving them into his mouth like he's the one that hasn't eaten in twelve-plus hours. "Shit, I get it." Talking with his mouth full. "This is your lead. This return address on the envelope. You're not a hundred percent, but you think this is where they're headed."

Richie hopes he's wrong. He hopes Lucia and Rena are long gone in a new direction. "Monroe," Crea says, scratching his chin against the handle of the hammer. "That was a president, right? Monroe. You into presidential shit? That clown we got in there now, Dubya"—he speaks in his best Brooklyn-doing-Texas twang—"fucking dumb shit, right? Reminds me of a runt I went to school with. Milty. Put a tomato in his drawers to make it look like he was packing serious meat, you know? You use a cucumber or some bunched-up socks maybe, but a tomato? My friend Tino goes over in class, right in front of Mrs. Pascione, kicks him square in the tomato. Splat. We laughed for months at Milty over that. Reminds me of this Dubya. Monroe, I don't know shit about him. Got a presidential name. Let's go to Monroe, what do you say?"

Richie tunes him out, folding into his pain.

↪

More time gone. He must've passed out again. But he's awake now and staring at the ceiling, the little dome light. Wind is whipping harder through the car. Crea's going fast.

"Tell me a story," he calls back to Richie.

"What?" Richie says.

"You started banging Adrienne when she was fifteen, right? What was her snatch like back then? Must've been snappy like a rubber band."

"Don't talk about her."

"I put her out of her misery, that's all. Tell me a story about that tight fifteen-year-old snatch of hers."

Richie coughs, and his whole body rattles with pain. Especially his ribs. He wants to tell Crea to fuck himself. He wants to defend Adrienne. He's failed at everything. Now he's failing at keeping the beast from Lucia's door.

"We're lost," Crea says. "You believe that shit? I'm driving around like a rookie. No eye for anything. Just spinning the wheels. Where are we? Peek-skill, that sign says. How'd we get here? I shouldn't have crossed that bridge. Bear Mountain Bridge. Thought it sounded good. Sometimes I'm as much of a numbnuts as anyone, I'll tell you. You see those lights over there?" Crea points out the cracked windshield.

Richie, his head crackling with pain, can't see what Crea's pointing at.

"Indian Point. You listen to the Yanks on the radio, they're always doing commercials for it. 'Safe. Secure. Vital.' My balls. That thing goes, it'll take out everything for a hundred miles in every direction. Fucking Chernobyl part deuce."

"Can I ask you something?" Richie asks.

"Why not? I'm feeling generous."

"Why'd you kill Vic?"

"He was in my way. He kept me cooped up. I felt like one of them calves they keep in a box for veal. He didn't trust me. He thought I was an animal."

"You are."

"True enough."

"What happened that day? He knew it was you?"

"Sure. He knew as soon as I pulled up out front."

"Little Sal wasn't even there?"

"He was driving."

"Vic say anything?"

"I had the gun on him. He said, 'Shit or get off the pot.'"

"Sounds like Vic."

"He died noble. Didn't beg. I threw the gun near the basil as a memento. I hadn't really started with the hammer yet. It was very traditional. Now tell me about Adrienne's snatch. What'd she taste like? You seem like a guy likes to eat a broad out. Like a watermelon Jolly Rancher, that's what I imagine. Tell me. I need some entertainment here."

Richie coughs again, the pain tearing through him. Everything goes black again.

Sunlight glare on the windshield. Richie works himself up into a sitting position. They're parked across from Mo Phelan's house. They must've been lost for three or four hours, Crea taking bad turn after bad turn.

Crea is slumped over the wheel now. "I can't believe this piece of shit didn't break down," he says.

"No sign of the Eldorado," Richie says. "They'd be stupid to come here."

"They would be, you're right. But we came all this way, we're sure as hell going in to check."

On the edge of the glare, Richie sees blinds open in an upstairs window of the house next door to Mo's. He sees Lucia for a moment, just standing there, and then she slams the blinds shut again. Stupid fucking kid. She's lucky Crea didn't notice her.

He thinks through his options. What he wants now is to sacrifice himself so Lucia can make it. Seems like the only viable option. He's got to kill Crea. He knows Crea has a piece, but he's not sure where it is. He needs the piece. It's his only chance. Lucia's only chance.

LUCIA

Lucia's thinking about how life isn't fair. All this money sitting here between her legs, and she can't do anything with it. She can't just go live in an expensive hotel and get room service every night. She'd get burgers and steaks and put so much butter on her bread, and she'd drink soda and beer and eat chocolate lava cake and curl up on the bed in bright white sheets and let someone else clean up her mess. She can't go buy a house on a beach somewhere and take a swim and come back and make a sandwich and count her money and smoke cigarettes. Not a beach like Silver Beach. A beach like somewhere you run away to. Quiet. Private. Blue water. Birds. Maybe some shirtless guy running in the surf with his cute dog. But maybe she can at least try to find her father.

Money is strange. She's worried that Grandma Rena will make her do something stupid with it. Not even like pay-someone-to-kill-Crea stupid. Like turn-it-in-to-the-authorities stupid. She's seen that in movies. There's always a person who doesn't want to stumble into a fortune in the wrong way. A person who will insist it's blood money *blah blah blah* and wants absolutely nothing to do with it. Grandma Rena could be that person, despite what she said about not trusting cops. Lucia wonders if there's a bus or train station in this town and if it's a station like in those same movies where they have lockers and you can hide your money in there and then wear the key on a string around your neck and lay low until it's safe to go get it.

Lucia wishes a million things. She wishes she was born in another place and another time. She wishes she'd been born in the subway tunnels. She took a book out of the library once about the Mole People who lived down there and had these little shacks with electricity and they showered in the water that dripped from pipes, and she thought that sounded pretty good. She wishes she'd been born to a mother who was a famous actress and took her to all her movie premieres. She doesn't really even know how she was born. Her mother never told her anything. Victory Memorial Hospital, that's all she knows. She's never seen pictures of herself in swaddling, rosy-cheeked. She wishes she'd been born in Italy. She wishes she'd had a father who tossed a baseball around with her and bought her teddy bears or dolls or anything. She wishes she'd known her father growing up. That she could see his face when she closes her eyes. His face is a big blur. His hands are a blur. His body and the clothes he wears, they're all something she's created in her mind. Richie is just flashes. Something like a father, in that he picked up pizzas from Patricia's and fell asleep on the couch watching the Yankees with his hand down his pants. But never father enough. She hopes he's dead. She hopes the string between him and this money is cut forever. She doesn't care how he died. Or how he dies. Maybe he's dying somewhere now. She doesn't imagine what happened to her mother happening to him and feel sick at all. What she feels is relief.

Lucia looks across at Wolfstein, curled up on the floor next to Mo. They're both asleep. Grandma Rena is asleep, too, leaning back against the wall, her mouth drooping open, looking like a tired old lady on the subway who has slept past her stop. Lucia is amazed that Wolfstein is not more protective of her money. She's just letting it sit there in front of her. The bag's not locked. She could go over and take what she wants and add it to what's in her briefcase.

The porno stuff is so weird. Seeing those pictures. The clothes they were wearing. Their hair. Their young bodies, which still seemed old to her. What those bodies must have done. They probably even kissed each other. More than that.

She stands up and stretches, putting her arms over her head and cracking her back. She exhales and picks up the briefcase and walks out of the room. She slept a little, waking up when Grandma Rena came back in from puking, and then she slept a little more. Her dreams were nothing special. Dreams are stupid. Dreams don't mean shit.

Exploring the house seems like a good idea. She brings the briefcase with her as she leaves the room. She wonders if she should find a vent to hide it in, like the way Wolfstein had it back at her house. It seems like a better solution than a bus station locker. But a briefcase like this probably wouldn't fit in a vent. Unless it was a huge vent.

She closes the door behind her as quietly as she can, hoping not to wake Grandma Rena, Wolfstein, and Mo.

Stairs to the left of her. She takes the steps slow because they're creaky. At the top of the stairs is a carpeted room that smells of mildew. The blinds are closed, but she can tell the light is coming up outside. It must be almost six in the morning. She doesn't remember what day it is. Monday? Monday. She's thirsty. She wonders if it's okay to drink water from the tap in the kitchen or bathroom when she gets there. She wonders if the water will even be on.

She thumbs open the blinds and peers outside. The street is quiet. A red tint to the light of the squat houses across from them. She can see Mo's front yard and driveway and mailbox. No one is parked there. No one is waiting. This is bullshit. The dumb fucks probably killed each other. That's what guys like them do.

She takes off her red Chucks and mismatched socks and rubs her feet in the carpet. It feels kind of gross. She bunches up her socks and stuffs them in her sneakers, leaving them there, and padding barefoot around the top floor. The carpet is full of indentations where there must have been tables and chairs and maybe a china closet.

In the kitchen, the tile floor is cold. A dusty outline in the far corner where a refrigerator once stood. Lucia sets the briefcase on the counter next to the sink and looks through the cabinets and the drawers. Nothing good. Hair ties, scraps of paper with lists on them, gas station receipts, pennies. She runs the cold water in the sink on low so it doesn't make too much noise and drinks straight from the tap. She hasn't even realized how thirsty she is. How dry her mouth is. Her lips have been glued to her teeth. The water is icy and tastes good. She shuts the tap and wipes her mouth with the back of her hand.

Over the stove, she finds a cookbook called *Simply Salads*. She flips through it. A picture of what she guesses to be the couple who once lived here falls out. They're standing in front of a sign that reads MADEIRA BEACH. The woman is in a red bikini and a straw hat. The man is in a Speedo. They both have on big sunglasses. She rips the picture in half and lets it flutter to the floor.

She gazes out the back window. The tarp-covered pool looks disgusting from above. Beyond the pool, at the edge of the yard, is the woods. She hasn't seen trees like that in a while. Just stretching out. Maybe there's something on the other side of them or maybe the woods just keep going. It's hypnotic to watch the morning breeze move the branches.

She opens the briefcase, gazing down at the money. She touches it. It feels perfect. She takes out one banded stack and thumbs through it as slowly as she can. Hundreds only. She smells it. She's seen people do that in movies, too. Everything in movies. The money smells clean and inky and new. Not like the crinkled, musty bills she often has in her pocket when she goes to Uncle Pat's Deli or to grab a slice somewhere. She's never wanted to smell money like this. Part of her wants to taste it, too. Just run her tongue over it the way she used to run her tongue over blankets as a little kid. It was a weird desire she had, licking blankets. She liked the texture. Now she wants to lick money. Not for the texture. Just because it looks so good. And it's hers.

But she doesn't. She pockets the stack she's holding. It's thin enough to fit perfectly in her back pocket. She wants at least that little bit on her. She wants to know it's real. She wants to picture herself spending it. She puts her head down on the open briefcase, ear to the money, and listens. The money sounds perfect, too. Like holding her ear up to a seashell and hearing waves and distance.

She closes the briefcase, snapping it shut, and carries it with her out of the kitchen. She touches a thermostat that's hanging from the wall in front of her, red and green wires dangling around it, and fiddles with the soft gray buttons. Three doors at the end of hallway to her right. She goes ahead to check them out. One opens into a bathroom with a broken toilet and a tub with no shower curtain. The showerhead is fizzy with mold. She checks the drawers of the vanity. Some left-behind mascara. More hair ties. Tampon wrappers.

One of the other rooms, facing out to the street, must have been an office. She's not sure why she's thinking that as she enters. Something about the shape and size. She pictures the husband and the wife sitting in there at a desk, paying bills. More likely, the husband just jerking off to porn while the wife was at the gym. She hates to think of a guy jerking off like that. So sad. She wonders if other women like to think about guys jerking off. She can't imagine that they do. She wonders if Wolfstein and Mo think about all the guys who have jerked off to their movies. Imagine. She rustles her toes in the carpet.

It takes her a second to realize that the slats on the blinds are half-open. She can see out to the street, and the street can see into her. A woman in sweats is walking a dog on a long leash. The dog is a mastiff. The woman is throwing her arms up in the air like those really dramatic walkers Lucia sees sometimes on the promenade at Orchard Beach. Lucia rushes over and flits the wand so the slats slap shut quickly and the room darkens, worried that the woman will look up and see her and wonder if she's a squatter and call the police. Not what they need. Not what she needs.

She turns and walks out. The other room—on the back side of the house, so there's no need to worry about windows and who can see in—must've been the bedroom. The floor is wood, but it looks tacky, like a carpet has been pulled up, and she keeps stepping on little pinchy things. Now she's thinking about the strange, sad couple in this room together. She sees them as she knows them. The woman in a red bikini and straw hat. The man in his Speedo. Both wearing sunglasses. They're arguing. She goes over to the window and looks out at the woods. It's gotten lighter out.

She hears something in the hallway. The trudge of anxious feet. She feels nervous. She's not sure what she'll do if she ducks her head out there and it's Richie or Crea. She doesn't think they could've entered the house so silently, though. Certainly they would've made a ruckus opening the door or called out to announce their presence.

Rena comes in, yawning, her hands behind her head, elbows up in the air. "What are you doing up here?" she asks in a whisper.

"Exploring," Lucia says.

"What time is it?"

"I don't know. A little after six?"

"Jeez."

"Nobody's coming. Let's just go."

"I don't know what to do. I really don't." Rena pauses. "You're sure glued to that money."

Lucia looks down at the briefcase.

"You want to talk?" Rena asks.

"Not now," Lucia says.

"Are you sure?"

"I'm sure."

"Let's go downstairs just to be safe."

"I don't want to go back down. I'm bored just sitting in that room. And I'm hungry. What are we going to eat? You went outside. I want to go outside. There's got to be a gas station around. I just want to get a bagel or something."

"You're right. I've been so worked up I haven't even given much thought to eating and drinking. I tried to take a bite of that granola bar from Wolfstein."

"I just had some water from the sink."

"That's good. Drinking water's the best thing for you."

"There's woods behind the house. I could run into the woods and see where I come out on the other side. I'm sure it'll come out on a road."

"That's not a good idea."

"No one's coming. They don't know where we are."

"Maybe so. Let's just go down and talk to Wolfstein and Mo about our options."

"I don't want to."

"Lucia. Please. I'm trying here."

Lucia walks back into the office room. Rena follows her. Lucia pulls on the string, opening the blinds fully. She's testing Rena this time. She sees that an SUV with a cracked windshield has pulled up in front of Mo's house. She can see into the car. Crea's behind the wheel. She doesn't see Richie. She closes the blinds and backs away from the window.

"What is it?" Rena says.

Lucia lets out a trembling breath. "It's them. Or just him. I only see Crea."

RENA

Rena rushes downstairs, holding onto Lucia's arm, practically dragging her along. "They're out there," she says to Wolfstein and Mo. "At least one of them is. Lucia saw Crea."

"Okay," Mo says. "Let's try to stay calm. No way he knows we're in here. He'll check out my house, see no one's there, and probably come to the conclusion that you picked me up and we split."

"Right," Rena says.

"I give him fifteen minutes. Tops."

"Let me get the gun from the trunk," Lucia says. "I'll go out there and shoot him."

"You've never even held a gun," Wolfstein says.

"How do you know?"

"Look at you."

"It's easy."

"Kid, calm your jets."

"What if he saw me?"

"What do you mean?" Mo asks.

"I was looking out the window when he pulled up. What if he saw me?"
Mo chews on this.

Rena finds herself thinking of where she was the morning before. In
her regular pew over by the tabernacle at St. Mary's. The church she's
attended her whole life, daily since Vic's death. This will be the first day
she's missed in a long time, not including the week she had the flu in '04.
She was sitting there with her rosary beads and collection envelope in her
lap, listening to Father Ricciardi drone on in his homily about surren-
dering to Christ. That's the way, Ricciardi had said in his froggy voice, that
we achieve eternal safety and approval, find forgiveness, make peace with
what haunts us. The gist of his pep talk being that people get redeemed
through restraint, not recklessness. What she thought then—and what
she believes even more fully now—is just how much that's a big line of
bullshit. *There's no time for sorry. Make a move.* Faith isn't about restraint
and obedience. Can't be. It's about force and desire and challenging God.
Making things happen. And, for the first time, she's seen how exactly
that works. Cut your path. Tear down what needs tearing down. Put your
tongue to the rail. You can do bad things and God can still love you. You
can do dirty work that needs doing. One time—this is something she
must've buried way deep—she said something to Vic about a guy who
ogled her, this back in the early days of their marriage, even though the
guy didn't ogle her at all, and Vic smashed his face in with a brick. That
had felt good, she remembers. She's got fight. She's got power. She knows
how to survive.

"The woods behind the house, Mo, where do they go?" she finally says
aloud.

"You walk through about a quarter-mile, and you come out on Lakes
Road," Mo says.

"Where's Lakes Road go?"

"Make a left when you come out, you go right into the village."

"There's a bus station?"

"Sure is. Right near Planet Pizza on Millpond Parkway."

"Here's what we do then: the three of you go through the woods and get to the bus station. I'll stay here and face Crea. This is my fight. What he did to Adrienne and Vic."

"No way," Wolfstein says. "We stick together."

"I dragged you into this," Rena says.

"Rena, no."

"Get out while you can."

"Just for the record, this is the most fun I've had in years," Mo says.

"It's not gonna be fun when Crea finds us."

"We're four. He's one."

"But he's evil."

"You've got the kid now," Wolfstein says. "The kid's your priority. Take Richie's money, and you and Lucia go to the bus station. Buy a ticket to the farthest place you can go. We'll hold down the fort."

"The kid thinks he might've seen her, why don't we all just go?" Mo says. "But we should move fast."

Rena nods. No time to think twice. It *is* her fight, but she likes the idea of sticking together. She likes that there are others to stick together with.

They move out of the small room where they've been holed up. Acting on the assumption that Crea noticed Lucia in the upstairs window is risky. Rena can't help but wonder if Lucia knows for a fact that there's no way he could've seen her and is just trying to get them to leave the house. She can't believe her granddaughter would put them all in harm's way like that. Still, the girl clutches the briefcase hungrily.

"Where are your sneakers?" Rena asks Lucia.

"I forgot them upstairs," Lucia says.

"You're going to go barefoot through the woods? Run up and get them."

"It's okay. I'll be fine."

Just another act of defiance on Lucia's part. They've barely spent time together, and she's already challenging her the way Adrienne used to. Whatever Rena says, Lucia's going to do the opposite. But going without her socks and sneakers is stupid. "I'll go get them," Rena says.

"Forget it," Lucia says. "It's fine. I have tough feet."

Mo opens the back door and they move into the yard, staying low. Wolfstein has her bag. Mo has left behind everything she brought with her. Rena isn't carrying anything, but it feels like she's carrying Lucia, her eyes on the girl's back and bare feet.

The tree line is a short distance away, about fifteen feet beyond the pool. Rena can see now that the woods are not as deep as she'd initially thought. Mo said about a quarter-mile to come out on the other side. Looking hard, Rena can see through the woods some signs of where that road might be, a scatter of white houses on a slope. Lucia's feet crunch against the ground.

They duck around the right side of the pool, using it for cover.

When they hear a voice, they stop moving.

Rena can't quite hear what he's saying, but she recognizes the voice as Crea's. She can hear him moving over by Mo's house. She looks around the edge of the pool and sees him circling the house, carrying his sledgehammer. The sledgehammer looks like a fake Halloween prop, painted with blood. Crea, in his bloodstained blue tracksuit, his usually slicked-back hair wild and messy, looks happy to be where he is. He cups his hand over his eyes and looks in through a ground-level window on the side of Mo's house. "Ladies?" he calls through the glass. "Laaaaaadies? Where are you?"

So maybe he had no idea they were next door after all. Maybe Lucia lied. Rena thinks of the gun in the trunk of the Eldorado. They were stupid not to grab it. Wolfstein, she can tell, is thinking the same thing.

Crea loops around to the back of Mo's house. He picks up a marble gnome and talks to it: "Have you seen the ladies? I'm looking for the ladies. No? You fucking worthless little gnome." He throws the gnome against the house, and it doesn't break. It just falls to the ground with a thud.

Now he's doing De Niro as Max Cady in *Cape Fear*: "'Come out, come out, wherever you are!'" He pauses. "'I am like God, and God like me. I am as large as God. He is as small as I. He cannot above me nor I beneath him be. Silesius, seventeenth century.'" Now he's doing the laugh from the movie theater scene. As if Rena wasn't scared enough. She saw that movie with Vic at the Loew's Oriental when it came out. Must've been '91. Or was it the Marboro? Either way, it scared the hell out of her. She didn't sleep for two nights. Every guy she saw on Eighty-Sixth Street she didn't know could've been Max Cady. Gina Gianfortune's son—Rob Cap, they called him—he had tattoos on his arms and neck, and it'd make her so nervous when she'd see him outside the Chinese market on Twenty-Fifth Avenue.

The fear doesn't seem to be registering in Lucia's eyes. She's focusing only on the woods, her brow pinched in reckless defiance of Rena, of everything that's happening.

"You ladies are in there, aren't you?" Crea says to the house at top volume, seemingly not concerned about waking the neighbors. He presses his ear to the aluminum siding as if he's trying to detect the house's heartbeat or listen to its closest secrets.

When he makes a turn around the far side of Mo's house, they instinctively know that this is their chance to make a break for the woods. The four of them take off simultaneously, Rena lagging behind just a bit to keep an eye on Lucia.

Rena can't remember the last time she ran like this. Maybe in high school. Sprinting around the track during gym class. When Lafayette was still a school where a girl like her could go. Short of breath afterward. Doubled over. Hands on her knees.

The distance to the tree line seems enormous, even though it's so close. Everything is slow and strange. Her eyes are fixed hard on Lucia. It's as if she anticipates the girl tripping before she actually does. A branch in her path, crooked and sharp-looking. Lucia stomps it with her bare right foot mid-stride and tumbles forward, the briefcase ejecting from her grasp. Rena says her name aloud and then puts her hand over her mouth, as if to silence herself. Wolfstein and Mo stop in their tracks.

Rena, on her way to help Lucia up, looks over her shoulder and sees Crea back behind Mo's house. He's noticed them. He's grinning. Holding the hammer like he's about to destroy a wall or drive bolts into concrete. "Ladies!" he says. "You *are* here!"

Lucia stands and dusts herself off. She lifts one foot up and pulls a piece of bark off her heel. Rena's thinking how stupid it was to not take the extra minute to retrieve her shoes. "Lucia," Rena says.

Lucia doesn't even look at her. She locates the briefcase a few feet ahead of her and leaps for it. She snatches it up and then flees into the woods.

"Don't let that kid run away!" Crea says, coming toward them.

Rena feels stuck in place. She looks at Wolfstein and Mo. And then she snaps her head quickly back in Lucia's direction, watching her disappear behind a stand of big trees.

"Go after her," Wolfstein says.

"What about you?" Rena says.

"We'll go for the gun."

Rena takes off after Lucia. Wolfstein and Mo break back for the house. Crea is not moving like he's determined, merely like he's capable of catching whoever he wants, whenever he wants. Rena can't see Lucia in the woods. She's wondering where on earth she could've gone. She hears a door close behind her. Hopefully it's Wolfstein and Mo getting safely back into the neighbor's house. Not many steps down the blue hallway to the garage, to the gun, to the Eldorado. She half-hopes they just hop in the car and drive away. She hears Crea now. He's laughing that *Cape Fear* laugh again.

Rena's trudging through the woods, the earth crackly under her shoes. She's looking for some sign of Lucia, who might have zigged and zagged and shot off in another direction. The road ahead of her is getting closer. Rena wonders if Lucia could already be there somehow. A barefoot girl with what must be close to a half-million dollars. Jesus, Mary, and Saint Joseph. She thinks about a show on sex trafficking she watched one night. Little run-aways disappearing lightning fast from the nation's back roads and bus stations and being sold to men who kept them locked up in basements. Her head going to other horrible places, too. Lucia flattened by a truck on the road. Lucia attacked by an animal.

She feels lost now, even though the road is there. She should go back. She should help Wolfstein and Mo. She should be the one facing down Crea.

She feels light-headed. What was it Mo said? Get out to Lakes Road and make a left and take that straight into the heart of the village? Lucia has to be headed for the bus station. A kid. The world is too big, and her options are too small.

Rena looks around. She wishes Vic would appear from behind a tree. That's what would happen in a movie. She'd need him as her guardian angel, call for his advice, and he'd show up and smile, as if he were late for dinner, tell her she's beautiful, tell her not to worry, call her a name that only he ever called her. Except there is no name like that really. He mostly called her Rena. Sometimes shortened it to Re.

"Help me, Vic," she says aloud.

Only birds chirping. Silence from the trees.

Now she's talking to her dead husband. And the man who killed him is back at that vacant house. She doesn't want to lose Lucia. She wants Crea to pay. She looks up at the sky through a dark net of branches. Bursting blue with traces of pink.

She presses on.

When she comes out of the trees, she crosses a gully and finds herself on the narrow shoulder of the road. Lakes Road, she hopes. No sign to confirm it. She starts walking to the left, hoping to see Lucia up ahead. No such luck. Back in the direction of Mo's house, she hears a burp of sirens. Her nerves raw, she picks up the pace. A few minutes later, a single gunshot followed by a rapid spray of gunfire echoes through the woods. She hopes that it's

Wolfstein and Mo taking out Crea. *We see your hammer, and we raise you a machine gun.* So many hopes. She sticks out her thumb like a hitchhiker. When the first car passes, it swings into the oncoming lane to steer way clear of her. The second car that passes does the same. She thinks she sees Lucia on the other side of the road in the distance, but it's only a mailbox. Her old eyes are playing tricks on her.

WOLFSTEIN

Mo closes and locks the back door behind them. Wolfstein leads the scramble into the dark garage. She keys open the trunk and tells Mo to take out the gun. Mo makes a sound like she's overwhelmed by its presence. "It feels good to feel alive," Mo says, picking it up.

"Take it easy," Wolfstein says.

"Let's go down in a blaze of glory."

Smashes from the other room. Crea likely breaking through the door with his sledgehammer. "Ladies!" he calls.

Wolfstein hits the button to open the garage door. They hop in the car as the door begins its mechanical rattle, Wolfstein under the wheel, her bad leg stiff. She puts her bag on the floor in the back.

"I just pull the trigger until it goes click, right?" Mo asks.

"Something like that," Wolfstein says, starting the car and almost flooding the engine as she anxiously pumps the gas.

Mo has the gun leveled on the entrance to the garage, waiting on Crea to show his face.

As soon as the door is open enough, Wolfstein steps on the gas and they lurch out of the garage. Richie is in front of them, zombie-shuffling up the driveway. He's battered and bruised. Wolfstein swerves around him, the tires going up on the grass.

The obstacle causes Wolfstein to be late cutting the wheel at the end of the driveway, so she zips straight into the mailbox of the house across the street. An old man with a white chinstrap beard is watching from the front stoop, and he cries out as she shatters the post. Wolfstein slams the brakes, and they wrench to a stop on Chinstrap's lawn. She puts the car in reverse and backs out into the street. Straightening out, she sees that Richie is now right next to the car. His gait unsteady, he opens the passenger door and pushes Mo's seat up as she protests, diving into the back and stretching out across the bench.

"Where the hell did you come from?" Mo says to him.

"I've gotta be in my car," he says. "I've gotta die in my car."

Chinstrap calls out from the stoop: "You're gonna pay for my mailbox, Mo!"

Mo holds up the gun. "Mr. Romano, we got a situation over here. I'll get you the best mailbox money can buy."

"No problem here, Mo," he responds, looking suddenly as if he realizes there's a level of danger he couldn't have possibly anticipated. He rushes back into his house and shuts the door.

Wolfstein struggles with the gearshift—it's stuck between gears. She looks over her shoulder at Mo's house, waiting for Crea to show. She figures he's watching from somewhere and isn't coming out yet for a reason.

"He's fucking with you," Richie says. "He's playing games."

A Monroe patrol car pulls up in front of Mo's place just as Wolfstein elbows the gear into drive. The cops bleep their sirens a couple of times as if to tell Wolfstein to stay put. Wolfstein keeps it in drive with her foot on the brake.

Mo puts the gun on the floor and cranks down her window.

"What are you doing?" Wolfstein asks.

"I know these two," Mo says.

"Know them how?"

"We smoke cigarettes at the gas station together a lot."

The cops get out of the car slowly. A man and a woman. Strutting dumbly in their navy blue uniforms. The woman wears sunglasses and has her hair in a bun under her hat. She's pale, freckled, pudgy. The man walks like a duck and has a big round belly that seems to be pressing open his uniform. His bald head is ceramic-smooth. Podunk cops if Wolfstein's ever seen them.

Crea emerges from the garage, hammer in hand. Wolfstein notices that he sees the cops before they see him and that he backs up into the shadows until he's out of sight.

"What's going on here?" the male cop asks. It's not clear who he's talking to.

"Falsetti, Fitzgerald," Mo says, sticking her head out the window. "It's me, Mo. Your cigarette-smoking pal from the Shell."

"Mo?" the woman cop says. Fitzgerald, Wolfstein guesses from the freckles and paper-white skin. "We got a call about a disturbance. What's happening? You knock over that mailbox?"

"We did and we didn't," Mo says.

"What's that mean?"

Wolfstein's figuring they haven't gotten a call from the Bronx yet. Must've been Crea's yelling that drew them here.

"You're looking pretty anxious in there," the man, Falsetti, says.

"You hear my old lady just died?" Mo asks. "That's it. Things are a mess. You can think you're ready, but you're not ready."

Fitzgerald takes off her glasses. "Jesus, I'm sorry, Mo. That's tough. My mother's got Alzheimer's. Similar. It's heartbreaking."

"This right here"—Mo puts her hand on Wolfstein's shoulder—"is my best friend, Lacey. She came to support me."

Falsetti and Fitzgerald come up on either side of the car, Falsetti on the driver's side, Fitzgerald standing over Mo. Mo buckles her knees together in an attempt to keep the gun hidden. "That's nice," Fitzgerald says.

Falsetti motions for Wolfstein to roll down her window. She does. "Whoa!" he says, pointing to Richie in the back. "What do we got here?"

"He's nobody," Mo explains.

"I didn't ask you, Mo," Falsetti says, playing it tough. "I asked your best friend."

Wolfstein could spill about Crea, but she knows that's unwise. He's watching. She does that, he comes out and the cops draw down on him, and the whole thing goes to shit. Best thing for everybody is to keep quiet, let it play out some other way, take it off Mo's block. "That's my cousin," Wolfstein says of Richie, thinking on the fly. "He tied a good one on last night. We're bringing him to ShopRite to get some Pedialyte in him."

"Looks like he got hit by a car." To Richie: "You okay, big fella?"

"Take care of the girl," Richie says.

"What was that?"

"Nothing," Mo says. "He's still drunk. Talking nonsense."

"Lucia," Richie says. "The half a rock goes to her."

"He said 'half a rock'?" Fitzgerald says. "I heard that once on *The Sopranos*. That's a half-mill."

"The guy's dead broke," Wolfstein says. "Look at him. He's dreaming. We're getting him into rehab soon."

Falsetti smiles. Wolfstein sees herself in his glasses. She looks haggard. Heavy bags under her eyes. Cheeks sunken. Pale. Hair frizzy. "Jesus," she says.

"What?"

"Just saw myself in your glasses, that's all."

"You had a tough night, too, huh?"

"Emotional time."

"Nice car. Eldorado, right? You did some damage to your front end."

"I'm heartsick over it."

"You know who that truck belongs to?" Fitzgerald says, pointing to an Explorer that's parked directly across from Mo's. Cracked windshield. Wheels up on the curb. One of the door windows busted out.

"No idea," Mo says.

Falsetti leans into the car and whispers. "You ladies sure you're okay? If you're under duress, just wink."

"Adrienne," Richie says from the back. "I'll take care of Lucia. Don't you worry."

Wolfstein and Mo look at each other. They speak to each other without speaking, a gift. Mo's on the same page as her. They turn to Falsetti. Mo just shrugs. Wolfstein says, "We're good, I swear. Thanks for your concern, Officer."

"Mo, I'm real sorry about your mother," Falsetti says.

"I appreciate that," Mo says. "She's at peace now." A beat. "No more shitting herself, either."

Falsetti and Fitzgerald erupt in laughter. "You're a real character, Mo," Fitzgerald says. "We'll be seeing you over at the Shell. My girlfriend wants me to quit smoking, but I'll keep sneaking them just so I can hang out with you."

Big smile from Mo. "Give Bethany my best."

"Take care of that mailbox when you get the chance," Falsetti says.

"Will do."

Falsetti and Fitzgerald back away from the Eldorado, heading to the patrol car.

Wolfstein looks over at the open garage. Crea emerges, no longer holding the hammer, seeming less powerful somehow at first. He puts a finger over his greasy smile, shushing her. His piece is out, and he's holding it at his waist.

Wolfstein's sudden shouts confuse Falsetti and Fitzgerald. Mo's slow with Richie's gun, pulling it up into her lap, fumbling it as she tries to turn it on Crea. Wolfstein's eyes flash to the note on Mo's hand: *Get trash bags*. Crea's charging down the driveway. He fires at Falsetti, hitting him square in the back. Falsetti crumples to his knees on the pavement, feeling around on his waist for a piece he's probably never had to pull and then flopping forward. Fitzgerald takes cover behind the patrol car. Last Wolfstein sees of her, she's on her radio calling it in and drawing her piece, but she looks shaken. She's calling Falsetti's name. He's groaning.

Mo takes aim at Crea. He's laughing. "Let's see what you've got," he says.

Mo pulls the trigger and unloads in Crea's direction. The bullets all go high, shattering windows in the vacant house. Crea does a little dance like a kid in a schoolyard who's avoided being pegged during a game of Suicide.

Wolfstein steps on it, the tires screeching as she peels away.

Crea fires at the Eldorado, shattering the back window. Mo lets out a yelp. She's drawn the gun in.

Richie, bathed in glass, moaning in agony, says, "I didn't kill him. I couldn't kill him."

In the rearview mirror, Wolfstein sees Crea climbing into the Explorer, starting it, and making a quick three-point turn in Mo's driveway. Fitzgerald rushes after him with her gun drawn, but he doesn't stop, and she doesn't fire. She collapses to her knees in the middle of the street, exasperated and shocked, as he passes out of her reach.

Crea is on their ass in no time. They're headed out of the development a different way than they came in. A buckle of narrow residential streets. Little houses with manicured yards and ugly plastic mailboxes. Having heard the sirens and what they can't imagine could've been gunfire, people are out in their robes consulting with one another, newspapers under their arms, coffee steaming in big-handled mugs. An Eldorado and an Explorer racing through their community is not what they expect.

Wolfstein lets Mo guide her: "Take a right here, a left here, let's see if we can shake him."

Crea's fully staying with them, though.

Wolfstein feels a tug of emotion for the cops, just more people caught in the middle of this fucking crazy-ass thing. Falsetti shot in the back like that. Probably has a family. Probably likes whatever things cops like. She hopes he makes it. Fitzgerald not taking the shot when she had it. Probably worried about the houses full of sleeping people around them. Just wanting to get home to her girlfriend.

Wolfstein's trying not to look back at Crea. She knows he'll just be sitting there behind the wheel, calm, smug as a perfumed dog. She knows he knows they don't have his money. She's assuming that he wants to off them because they're witnesses. She can only keep her fingers crossed that more cops show soon. She can only keep her fingers crossed that Rena and Lucia are okay.

As they're coming to an intersection for Lakes Road, Mo motions fast to go left. Wolfstein takes the turn hard, almost spinning out into a ditch. Crea's masterfully close, almost nudging them again. Lakes Road loops into a curve as they pass an old mill and a couple of stone houses with blue-and-yellow historical markers out front. "That's 17M up at the light," Mo says.

The little lakes of the village are ahead of them. The light they're coming to is red. Two cars are waiting in front of a Dollar General and a pet grooming place for the light to change. "What should we do?" Wolfstein asks.

"Go around the traffic. Go through the light."

"Yeah?"

Mo shrugs. "I guess."

Wolfstein guns it and cuts into the oncoming lane, passing the two cars waiting at the light. No cars are coming toward her, which is good news. She rides the brake a little as she blows through the light and coasts cleanly across the intersection.

Lakes Road continues between the lakes and then crosses Millpond Parkway and becomes the main drag in the village. A couple of pizzerias, a bakery, a hair salon. It's not crowded at this time of the morning. Nothing's open. A scatter of sirens rides the air now. Police responding to Fitzgerald's officer-down call.

"The bus station is right over there," Mo says, motioning toward the north end of Millpond Parkway where a deli doubles as a depot, a Short Line bus idling at the curb.

"We shouldn't be here," Wolfstein says.

"I'm sorry," Mo says. "The police station's right up here. Every other direction goes nowhere." A police cruiser buzzes past them in the other lane just as she says it, rushing to help Falsetti. Fitzgerald must've made Falsetti her priority and forgotten to call in the Explorer's plates. Inexperienced in matters like this. Soon enough.

"The cops are headed to your house."

Richie, in the back, starts mumbling.

"Can you understand him?" Wolfstein says.

He raises his voice. "Let me just die in my car, okay? I just want to die in my car. I'm here. It's okay."

"We'll do what we can, fucko," Mo says.

Wolfstein takes a right on Stage Road and slows to a stop in front of a pub called O'Leary's right next to the justice court. The police station is across the street, bustling with activity. Cops getting in their cars. Cops standing out front, some in uniform and some in plainclothes, troubled eyes scanning the sky, trying to make sense of why chaos might visit them on a normal morning like this.

Crea parks in the spot behind her.

The pub has a banner hanging out front that reads 9/11 NEVER FORGET. THANK YOU FOR YOUR SERVICE CAPTAIN RON KEEGAN. It looks open. Or maybe it never closes. A neon Miller Lite sign is still on in the window.

"What are we doing?" Mo asks.

"I don't know," Wolfstein says.

"He'll kill us where we sit."

Wolfstein reaches into the back and grabs her bag of money, brushing glass shards from it. Richie, ornamented with debris, has dissipated into a heap of silent, confused anguish. His eyes are closed. His mouth is closed. His breathing seems broken. Beneath the glass, he's all blood and bruises and swollenness.

"Get out of the car," Wolfstein says to Mo.

"And?"

"We walk over to the police station."

"I don't know about this."

"Don't take the gun."

"Don't take the gun?" Mo says.

"No."

"Doesn't sound like much of a plan."

"It was your idea. You said, 'The police station's right up here.' You got a better plan? You're usually the one with the plans."

"Keep driving."

"Where?"

"Until we lose him."

"And if we don't?" As Wolfstein's about to open her door, Crea pulls up next to the Eldorado on the driver's side. Close. About three inches between the Explorer and the Eldorado. Wolfstein bites down on a gasp. She's stunned by the move. Mo tilts the gun up, but it seems more in line with Wolfstein than it does with Crea.

Crea reaches across the passenger seat in the Explorer and rolls down the window. "Manual windows in this shitbox," he says. "You believe it?"

Wolfstein and Mo look at him.

"Look, I've only got a second here. These cops"—Crea motions at the small crowd in front of the station—"they're not gonna be too happy they find out I shot that bald fuck. But I've gotta score what I've gotta score before I leave. Where'd they go, Rena and the girl?"

Wolfstein flashes Crea her own wicked grin. "Listen, *sweetie*," she says, nerves extinguished by adrenaline, "me and my pal here, we're gonna get out of this car and walk into that station."

"That so?"

"That's so." She pauses, puts her hand on Mo's knee. "Mo, go ahead and get out."

Mo nods. She opens the passenger door and slips out, leaving Richie's gun behind. Wolfstein, without looking back at Crea, follows Mo, holding on firmly to her bag and then deciding to leave it on the seat. Crea hasn't seen it yet, and she doesn't want him to. He'd mistake it for Richie's haul. Her nest egg up in smoke like that. They stand there in front of the pub, Mo dressed like she's going to the gym, Wolfstein in her Wranglers and red macramé top, an outfit she used to wear out line dancing in Fort Myers. Richie's dying in the back seat of the Eldorado.

"You ladies got balls, I'll give you that," Crea says. "I like you a lot." And then he pulls away up Stage Road.

Whatever cops are still milling about outside the station take notice of Wolfstein and Mo. Lowering their sunglasses to check out this oddball duo who just landed in front of O'Leary's in an Eldorado with a shattered back window. Another off thing about the morning. Wolfstein waves. She feels like a gambler who's just bluffed her way to victory and an even more uncertain future. What an extraordinary world.

"We get out of all this," Wolfstein says to Mo, barely moving her lips, "let's go back to California for a visit."

"Shit, sure," Mo says. "Maybe get some work."

"The *Cocoon* parody the world's been waiting for."

"Time's right for that. A dirty joke twenty years in the making about a movie no one remembers."

"Thanks, Mo. Whatever happens next, thanks a lot for sticking with me. Now let's see if these cops have any smokes." Wolfstein steps into the street, stopping to reach into the Eldorado for her bag. As she does, she looks back at Richie, hoping that he's run out of steam and thinking that he probably has.

When they finally approach the herd of cops a minute later, Wolfstein kicks into hustle mode.

LUCIA

Lucia says she wants a ticket on the next bus going wherever. The big guy behind the counter at the station, wearing a tight T-shirt that reads HEY ASSHOLE MY EYES ARE UP HERE and reading an *X-Men* comic, tells her a Binghamton-bound Short Line is arriving in a few minutes. Prepaid cell phones and calling cards hang on the wall behind him.

She says that's fine and pays with a hundred from the stack of bills she has stuffed in her pocket.

He cringes when he sees it, acts like maybe it's counterfeit. She tells him it's real and to keep the change.

He says, "What's your story?"

She shrugs, takes her ticket, and goes to wait on a bench by the pay phone.

She sits there, briefcase in her lap. She's tired and thirsty. She's never heard of a place called Binghamton. She wonders what's there. Her feet hurt. They're grimy from the woods and the road, bottoms speckled with gravel impressions. She should've just gone back for her sneakers. That was stupid, trying to prove to Grandma Rena that she could do whatever she wanted. The muscles in her legs feel twitchy. The run through the woods hadn't been easy. She was afraid she was lost until she found Lakes Road. Even then, she wasn't sure she was headed in the right direction. When she hit the village and saw the lakes, she stopped in front of a beer distributor and asked a dude pushing boxes around on a dolly where the bus station was. He pointed catty-corner to them. She saw the pizza place Mo mentioned and then noticed the station.

"What happened to your shoes?" the guy asks her, coming out from behind the counter and bringing her a bottle of water.

"They got ruined," she says. "Thanks for the water."

He nods. "You look thirsty. How old are you?"

"Seventeen," she says without hesitation, unscrewing the cap on the bottle and taking a long pull.

"*You* are *seventeen*?" he says.

Her turn to nod. "Yeah, why?"

"No reason." He goes back behind the counter.

Lucia figures it's about a fifty-fifty chance Grandma Rena shows up before she can get on the bus and get the hell out of town. So be it. She just hopes the rest of them don't show. She knows the situation. She doesn't want them dead. She just wants to be alone. Or as alone as possible.

In school, there's a boy named Dom Fischetti who always bothers her to no end. Draws dicks on loose leaf with chalk and then presses the paper against her back, so she's got the outline of a dick on the back of her shirt the whole class. Her friend Liz says it's Dom flirting. Fuck that. She's glad she doesn't have to go back to school. Or church. All these routines people put you through that just don't mean anything. Confession's the worst. Sitting there like in one of those prison booths, making up stories to beer-breathed Father Flaherty on the other side of the screen. "Go ahead, my dear," he'd say. She hated being called *my dear* like that.

One time she said something true to Father Flaherty: "I wish I knew my real father."

"That's no sin," he'd said. And then he told her some kind of parable-sounding thing that didn't make any sense.

All she was saying was she wished she knew her father. Now she's wondering if maybe he lives in Binghamton. Sounds like a place for fathers.

The door opens. A man in jeans and a work shirt and an Irish flat cap comes in. He buys a ticket at the counter for the city and then sits next to her. "I'm Pete," he says.

"Hi," she says.

"A lot of ruckus out there. I wonder what's going on. Sirens and what not. Must've been an accident."

Lucia shrugs.

"I'm going to work in the city. I'm an electrician. I'm working at the Javits Center. Where you going?"

"Nowhere," she says.

"I wish I was going nowhere. Work sucks. I'm sorry I'm bothering you. I'm nosy. My wife tells me I talk to strangers too much. I like to talk to strangers. I've got a daughter about your age. She's a runner. Hey"—he looks down and notices her feet—"where are your shoes? Do you need shoes? I can call my wife and ask her to bring over an old pair of my daughter's. She's away at running camp, my daughter. We have lots of old shoes of hers in the mud room. What size are you?"

"That's nice of you, but I'm fine."

"You sure? Barefoot's no way to be."

"I'm sure."

"To each his own. To each *her* own, I'm sorry."

They sit there in silence for a few minutes. Pete takes out a little notepad from his shirt pocket and starts writing with a golf pencil. "I jot down these ideas I have," he says. "Nothing special. Ideas for inventions sometimes. Ideas for how to make my commute nicer. Like your situation made me think there should be a guy here at the depot selling shoes. Where better? Your shoes get messed up and you're getting on a bus, you're in trouble. Not designer shoes. Just something comfortable and cheap. Good idea, right?"

Lucia nods.

"Eric," he calls out to the guy behind the counter, "you hear my idea? Shoes for sale right here."

"Good one, Pete," Eric says without looking up from his comic.

"I think so."

The Binghamton bus pulls up outside. "I've gotta go," Lucia says, standing up.

Pete says, "I'll always remember meeting you because you gave me this great idea for selling shoes."

The tiles are cold on her feet as she walks from the bench to the door. She pushes the door open and walks out. The sirens Pete mentioned, she hears them now. Sees a police car speeding up Lakes Road. Probably headed to Mo's. She doesn't know what happened. She cares, but she cares more about leaving.

The bus is at the curb in front of her, the driver standing on the sidewalk, opening the luggage compartment. "Binghamton?" he says to her. He's got hairy ears and wears a plain blue ball cap and uniform. He's probably about Grandma Rena's age. Lucia looks at his hands and sees that his wedding ring is secured in place with electrical tape. He's also got a small Celtic knot tattooed on the back of his hand.

"Yep."

"No other bags?"

"Nope." She hands him her ticket.

He looks down at her feet. "Are you okay, kid?"

"I'm seventeen," she says. "I'm walking barefoot for my friend with leukemia. The more miles I walk, the more money I raise." She's not sure where that lie came from, but she thinks it sounded pretty convincing.

"Okay," the driver says, laughing a little. "Good for you."

She looks up at the big bus with its dark windows. She can see some people scattered around. She climbs on, taking a seat in the back behind a lady wearing an NYPD cap, and puts the briefcase on the floor. The lady turns and gives her the once-over. She's obviously not concerned about Lucia's well-being; she just thinks she's up to no good.

Out the window is one of the lakes or ponds or whatever. Early-morning dog-walkers and runners are on the path. Lucia drinks her water, scrunching the bottle after she's done for the noise. She picks off the label. She sees Grandma Rena then, coming from Lakes Road. Grandma Rena crosses the street and disappears out of her view behind the bus. "Fuck," Lucia says. The lady in the cap looks at her now like she's uncivilized. Barefoot and cursing.

Grandma Rena's voice outside carries into the bus. She's talking to the driver. She asks about Lucia, mentioning the briefcase and that she's got no shoes on. The driver says the kid just got on, wants to know if she's a runaway. Grandma Rena says she isn't and asks if she can get on and just talk to her granddaughter for a second. The driver says he's leaving in less than five minutes, she better go in and get a ticket if she wants to get on. She says the girl has her money. The driver says go ahead. Lucia ducks down in her seat.

Grandma Rena boards. "Lucia?" she says, looking at everyone as she passes.

Lucia feels small behind the seat in front of her.

Grandma Rena stands in the aisle next to her. "What are you doing?" she asks.

"Getting away," Lucia says.

"Without me?"

"I don't know."

"Can you give me some money so I can go in and get a ticket?"

Lucia sits up in her seat and digs around in her pocket. "I already gave the guy enough for two tickets," she says. "But here's more." She passes her a hundred. "Can you get me some popcorn while you're in there?"

"I'll be right back," Grandma Rena says, walking up the aisle and off the bus. She pauses to talk to the driver, telling him she'll be right back, please don't leave.

As Grandma Rena's in the station, Lucia weighs her options. Run? Where? Crea is still out there probably. Maybe he's killed Wolfstein and Mo. Maybe he's coming for his money. She wishes the bus would just leave before Grandma Rena gets back, but she'll settle for leaving soon with both of them on board.

Grandma Rena comes back and hands a small bag of popcorn to Lucia. She also has two of the prepaid phones. "Scooch over," she says.

Lucia moves close to the glass, the briefcase clenched between her calves. She tears open the bag of popcorn and eats it all in a minute flat, holding the bag over her open mouth and pouring in whatever's left.

Grandma Rena settles in next to her. She opens the packages the phones come in, hands shaking, and gives one to Lucia. She finds a stubby golf pencil and abandoned racing form stuffed in the pocket of the seatback in front of her and writes down the numbers for both phones twice, tearing off one scrap for herself and one for Lucia. "I thought we needed these. Just in case. I don't really know how they work. They're prepaid."

"Thanks," Lucia says, stuffing the phone and the paper in her pocket. She's glad to finally have a phone, even if it's just a burner. "Are Wolfstein and Mo okay?"

"I'm not sure," Grandma Rena says. "I took off after you through the woods."

"And they stayed behind?"

"They decided to go back into the house. Trying to get"—she lowers her voice—"the thing that was Richie's in the trunk. Maybe they got in the car and drove away."

"There are a lot of sirens."

"I know. I really hope they're okay. I brought this into their lives."

"You knew my real father, right?" Lucia asks.

Grandma Rena turns and looks at her. "Not really. He was out of the picture fast."

"What do you mean?"

"It was a short-term thing. I don't even know if Adrienne ever told him."

This information shocks Lucia. "She didn't tell him about me?"

"I don't know. He wasn't much of anything, from what I remember. Adrienne wanted nothing to do with him."

"You remember his name?"

"Lucia, I can't think right now. Why do you want his name?"

"I don't know."

"Don't you want to stay with me now?"

"I don't know."

Grandma Rena looks up at nothing in particular. "I always tried to do things right. But you can't do things right when everything's built around lies. My whole life's been shaped by violence, even if I never took part. I looked the other way. I heard whispers. I don't want that for you, Lucia."

"My mother was just killed in front of me," Lucia says with a clenched jaw. "You said you wanted Crea taken out."

The lady in the NYPD cap is obviously finding it difficult not to eavesdrop, head turned slightly to them.

"I know. I know. I'm so sorry." Tears in Grandma Rena's eyes. "I'm so, so sorry. I don't know how to say the right thing. I'd like a chance with you. I want to help make your life what it can be. We can do that. What I see for you, what I want for you, is a husband, a yard, some kids on a seesaw. I don't want you to be torn apart."

"What if I want a wife, not a husband?"

"I just want you to be happy. I want you to have a happy life. I don't care about the money. Will you tell me you love me?"

"I barely know you."

Grandma Rena takes a deep breath. "His name was Walt. Your father. 'Not My Fault' Walt, they called him."

"Walt?" Lucia says, eyes scrunched. It sounds like a name a character's called in a cartoon. She didn't know there were Walts in the world. There are. One's her old man.

"Walt Viscuso," Grandma Rena says. "Real lowlife. I don't know how Adrienne ever got tangled up with him. They met at some club, I think. It didn't last long."

"He's still alive?" Lucia says.

"I don't know. I really don't."

The driver is on the bus now. He whooshes the door closed with a lever as he plops down in his seat and then consults his passenger list.

An SUV rolls slowly past the bus on the left. Lucia recognizes it immediately as the one she saw pull up outside Mo's through the blinds. She puts her hand over her face and slouches in her seat. She doesn't look long enough to see Crea behind the wheel.

"What is it?" Grandma Rena asks.

Lucia motions to the truck, exhausted. "It's him again."

The SUV pulls in front of the bus, boxing it in. The driver leans on the horn and then throws his hands in the air. "What the hell's going on here?" he says.

"He knows we're here," Grandma Rena says to Lucia. "How?"

"Probably guessed," Lucia says. "Saw the bus, figured where else would they go."

"I don't believe this."

They watch as Crea gets out of the SUV and stands in front of the bus, seeming to simply consider it. He stretches. She sees a gun in his waistband. It's not big like Richie's, but it looks pretty serious. Are there guns that don't look serious? The one her mother was taken down with looked silly, and it still did what it did. Maybe she needs a gun when she gets where she's going. Binghamton sounds like the kind of place you can score a gun, too. Like she's actually going to make it there. If she does, it's probably going to be without this briefcase full of money. She imagines a scenario where Crea comes on the bus and kills Grandma Rena and takes the briefcase but spares her because she's a kid. That's giving him a lot of credit.

Lucia stands up. As Crea moves closer to the bus, she notices the blood splattered on his tracksuit. It's hard not to see. Other people are out walking their dogs and jogging and enjoying the morning, and here's this killer. "We're trapped," Lucia says.

Adrienne didn't teach Lucia much, but she did teach her to watch out for herself. Maybe Adrienne never realized just how much she emphasized that while Lucia was growing up. You witness something that doesn't concern you, look the other way. Your friends are in trouble, you stay out of it and keep your own record clean. Trouble finds you, put yourself first and get out fast. At any cost.

Lucia can't let Grandma Rena hold her back here. Her life is her first priority. The money is second. Though her life is this money now. What life is even possible without it?

She looks around for an emergency exit. She knows city buses have them in the roof and that the back windows push out. She's never been on a bus like this, its seats reminding her of the casino rugs she'd seen in Atlantic City the two times she'd accompanied Adrienne and Richie there for concerts. She sees an escape hatch in the roof and wonders how she might hoist herself up to it.

"What are we gonna do?" Grandma Rena asks.

Lucia shrugs, as if she's actually waiting for Grandma Rena's decision.

Crea's motioning through the glass for the driver to open up and let him in.

The driver's agitated. He's beeping the horn, saying, "Get the hell out of the way. Come on. We've got a schedule here." He's in drive now, actually inching up on Crea a little.

Lucia stands up on her seat.

"What are you doing?" Grandma Rena says.

Crea sees her over the tops of the seats and smiles. He takes out his gun and points it at the driver. People around the lake are watching with furious concern. Several have taken out their cells and are calling it in. Maybe Crea's lost it. To do this so publicly. Maybe he wants a shootout with the cops. Maybe he's got a death wish. Maybe he thinks he's death-proof.

Lucia half-expects the driver to put the bus back in park, throw up his hands, open the door, and let Crea on board. But this guy—with a Celtic knot tat on his hand and hairy-ass ears—has brass balls to boot. He punches the gas. Crea dances back, almost dropping the gun, but then reaffirms that he's got it and points it harder at the driver. Lucia reaches out to hang onto something but falls into her seat. The bus keeps moving, ramming the rear end of Crea's SUV, forcing it out of the way. Crea is on the side of the bus now. The SUV is being pushed like a sad bumper car. Crea bangs on the side of the bus with his closed fist. The bus clears the SUV out of the way by turning it fully around. The driver's voice booms over the speakers. "Hold on," he says. The bus jerks forward. The passengers clap. They're moving at a normal clip up Millpond Parkway now. Lucia looks out the window and tries to see Crea, but he must be behind the bus.

"Sorry about that inconvenience," the driver says, as if they've just encountered a little splotch of traffic.

"I really can't believe this," Grandma Rena says.

Lucia exhales and checks to make sure the briefcase is still there on the floor. She pictures herself in a fancy hotel with a Jacuzzi. She pictures herself going down to the front desk and getting change for a hundred. And then she finds the vending machines nestled away in a nook by the pool and she buys a 3 Musketeers, a Snickers, and a can of Coke. She goes back to her room and puts on the Yankees and gets in the Jacuzzi and eats her chocolate bars and drinks her Coke and wonders about Walt Viscuso. When she's done eating, she puts on a towel and smokes out the window. Grandma Rena is not in her fantasy. The hotel might be in Binghamton. It might be anywhere.

She's thinking of Pete the electrician now. She can't believe girls have fathers like that. He probably would've missed his bus and gone home to get her his daughter's shoes.

When the SUV zooms up next to them, its battered front end nosing against the side of the bus, Lucia looks down and locks eyes with Crea. Grandma Rena, panicked, stands up in the aisle.

"What does this psycho want?" the lady in the NYPD cap says. "He looks like a two-bit hood."

"Maybe this is a terrorist attack," a college girl wearing a SUNY Binghamton shirt says.

The bus driver is mumbling under his breath, and the sound he's making is coming through the speakers. The road turns a bit. They're headed for the intersection of 17M, which comes out in front of the diner. To the right of them is a park with swings and slides and an old warplane for kids to climb on.

Crea speeds up and cuts in front of the bus, causing the driver to whip the wheel sharply to the right. They go over the curb and through a log fence, slamming into the plane. Smoke rises up between the plane and the bus. Everyone's rattled. Grandma Rena has lurched into the seatback in front of her. Lucia stands on her seat, briefcase in hand, and climbs over the empty seat next to the lady in the NYPD cap. She hops another couple of seats like this until she gets to an empty row and maneuvers into the aisle.

It's taken Grandma Rena a minute to get her bearings, but she finally calls out to Lucia: "Where are you going?"

"Open the door!" Lucia says to the driver.

The driver has a hand on his neck. He's straining to look out the window to see exactly what damage has been done to the front of the bus. "I'm so screwed," he says.

"Open the door!" Lucia says again, stumbling to a stop next to him. She looks back. Grandma Rena is coming after her.

"I'm not. I don't know where that whackjob is."

Lucia saw the lever he pressed to close the door before, and she reaches down and jabs it forward.

"Hey, don't do that," the driver says.

The door opens with a wheeze. She skips down the steps and comes out on the wing of the plane. She looks around for Crea and sees him struggling out of the SUV back by the log fence, where he managed to screech to a stop.

Lucia jumps down off the plane and darts away across the park. She doesn't look back. She's running on grass now, ignoring the pain in her feet. At the far end of the park, beyond a merry-go-round and a teeter-totter, there's a five-foot-tall chain link fence. Beyond that, more trees. She's going to climb over the fence. She expects to hear a gunshot behind her. She wonders what it will feel like if she gets shot in the back. When she gets to the fence, she throws the briefcase over and then follows it. No shots. No looking back.

RENA

The bus crashes into the Korean War plane with a crunch of metal. Rena's first thought is again about how consequences spread out. The town brought that plane to this spot who knows how many years ago. It's a memorial, a shared space for people to meet and play and probably to meditate on sacrifice. And every choice she's made over the last day has led to its near-destruction.

When she slams into the seat in front of her, she wonders if she'll just bolt upright in bed and realize that this has all been some wild, illogical dream. She wants that, and she doesn't. She certainly doesn't want to be back alone in her house, doing dishes, vacuuming dust bunnies out of corners, worrying about what needs to be fixed, ghosting after memories of Vic, waiting for her next lonely walk up to church.

But it's all real. Crea is out there. She looks over at Lucia and doesn't see a girl who's afraid. She sees a girl who wants to survive. She wishes she was seeing a girl who needed her, who wanted to be taken care of. "Oh,

Grandma," she wishes Lucia would say, "what do we do now?" She wishes they could get back to her house somehow and she could cook for Lucia. Baked ziti. Braciole. Sausage and peppers. If Rena could just feed Lucia, she has no doubt the girl would stay with her and that they would be happy, as happy as they could be, like in a fairy tale.

Lucia stands and starts climbing over seats. Rena doesn't register what's going on at first. Then the horror of Lucia running away again hits her full force. She says something aloud, she's not even sure what.

But Lucia opens the door and hops down onto the plane and from there to the ground and she legs it across the park, disappearing over a fence.

Rena drops the prepaid cell phone and then leans over to pick it up, putting it in her pocket. She's lost the little paper with the number for Lucia's phone. She searches all around for it under the seat. She can't even remember if it was just sitting there on her knee. She should've been more careful. She's sweating, choking on a hard breath.

"Everyone, please, remain calm!" the driver says.

Remain calm? How on earth is she supposed to remain calm?

Out the window, Rena sees Crea moving toward the bus. The gun is out. She doesn't think he's noticed Lucia's escape. There's a blue smear of cops behind him. Crea's yelling about the money. He's got a little hitch in his step.

The window muffles the sounds from outside. Crea's voice, the sirens, the cops shouting for him to put the gun down. A female officer leading the charge. She's got both hands on her gun. She's about ten feet behind Crea.

Rena sees that Wolfstein and Mo are in the crowd that's gathered. She didn't get them killed. What a relief. There's that, at least.

Her eyes go back to Crea. He's looking right at her. He lifts the gun. He's going to shoot her through the glass. Maybe it's what needs to be. Maybe heaven. Maybe Adrienne. Maybe Vic. Maybe. Her mind a scatter of maybes.

The female officer's voice fills the moment, muted as it is. "Put the fucking gun down!"

Crea doesn't listen.

She fires and hits Crea in the back. It's a pleasure to watch him fall. Morning light seems to fold over him. Blue edged with pink and purple. Rena notices hills and mountains around them for the first time. She's been totally blind to them. She doesn't know anything about these hills and mountains. She knows they're there now. She's thinking about Vic and Adrienne. She's happy Crea's been shot in the back by a cop. She hopes he's dead. She feels alive.

He is dead. Even though he's not technically dead yet. Rena gets off the bus and knows it almost immediately. The cops are gathered around him. Crea is laughing and choking and gasping for air, and the laughter, sinister and defiant, makes the cops madder. They're in no rush to get an ambulance to him. The officer who shot him is off to the side, her head in her hands.

The driver leads Rena and the other passengers out past the collapsed log fence.

Distracted, Rena forgets to scan the woods beyond the park for Lucia. Where will she go? What will she do? She'll come back. She has to.

A tap on Rena's shoulder. She turns and finds Wolfstein and Mo standing there. They're both smoking cigarettes. Wolfstein has a newspaper folded under her arm and is holding her bag. She hugs Rena. "Where's the kid?" Wolfstein asks.

"I don't know," Rena says, shaking her head. "She ran off again."

"You want to tell someone? Get the cops looking for her?"

"I don't know. I should. But she obviously doesn't want to be with me."

"She doesn't know what she wants."

Three cops come over and talk to them. They're happy because word is that the cop who got shot is going to make it. Rena asks what happened. Wolfstein and Mo tell her about Falsetti and Fitzgerald. They point to the officer who shot Crea and identify her as Fitzgerald. Wolfstein explains how they met these other three cops over at the station when Crea was after them. Wolfstein's handing out cigarettes. One cop offers to share his pint of peach schnapps, and both Wolfstein and Mo take professional nips. An officer in uniform named Gold brings them over to the swing set and tells them to stay put, they're going to need statements, and then he goes off to consult with some plainclothes cops.

They sit there on the swings, not moving. Wolfstein's bag is on the ground at her side, her *Daily News* set on top of it. Rena thinks about Lucia. Wolfstein and Mo finish their cigarettes and butt them out in the sand under their feet. They light two more and ask Rena if she wants one, insisting it'll help. She says no.

"We didn't tell the cops about Lucia and the money," Wolfstein says. "I wanted to leave that decision to you. I mean, they might piece it together. People saw her. She's memorable as hell, barefoot kid with a briefcase."

"I know," Rena says.

"She's her own girl. A tough cookie. That's not a bad thing. It helps in this world to be tough."

"Richie's dead?"

Wolfstein shrugs. "We left him in the Eldorado. He was on the way to dead, I think. The cops say Crea clobbered Enzio at a rest stop off the Palisades. Guy from the Bronx is up here prying around. Detective Pescarelli. He's gonna want to talk to us."

"I'm sure."

"Listen, Rena," Wolfstein says. "There's no saying sorry enough about what happened to Adrienne. Things lined up that way. Bobby. Richie. Crea. Enzio." She shakes her head. "We all make bad decisions. We all make mistakes. Get in messes. Look over there. That bus you were on, how it crashed into that plane."

"That plane's a big fucking deal here," Mo says.

"That bus crashed into that big-deal plane, and they're both still there. Plane's got its wings. The bus is a tank. Maybe it needs, what? A new grille? Some new suspension parts? I don't know. Point is, we're all like that all the time. We're all unfinished wreckage. Whatever's not dead is fixable. You and

Lucia, you're not dead. You've been surrounded by some bad things, that's true. But you've still got life. You're a righteous woman, and I'm your pal."

All the fear and pain in Rena loosens up for a second.

Wolfstein holds up her *Daily News*. "Look at this," she says, flipping to page four. "Skip the article about the Silver Beach fiasco. It's no good. But I read here"—she points hard at an article on the bottom half of the page—"how this eighty-six-year-old woman in Queens tried to knock off a jewelry store. She's been robbing jewelry stores and banks for *sixty fucking years*. She got caught this time. Ninth time she's been caught in her career. She did a five-year stretch in prison once. Another two years here, three years there, six months over here. Persistence, Rena. We never give up. We can't."

The cops are headed over to talk to them. Officer Gold again, and a man she guesses to be Detective Pescarelli from the Bronx. Rena looks up just then at the glare on the windows of the diner across the road. She feels the phone in her pocket and wishes she hadn't lost the other number.

RICHIE

Richie's still got some fight in him. He sputters blood from his lips. He feels the glass on him. He's looking up at the dome light of his Eldorado and then at the back windshield. He's pushing against the seat, trying to tell himself to move his hands, to curl his fingers. He can see himself sitting up. He can see himself climbing into the front and driving off. But he just can't make himself do it. There are voices outside. Women. Men. The breeze. Does the breeze have a voice? He blinks his eyes. He says Adrienne's name. He keeps his eyes closed. Squeezed tight like that, he sees only little neon bolts.

Memories come crashing in. The day he got the car. Driving around with Vic. Leaning over to kiss Adrienne, Lucia in the back seat. Driving his mother to church. Parked on a gravel path at his father's funeral. Going through the carwash on Eighteenth Avenue. The night, no shit, he gave Steven Seagal a ride to Peter Luger. They'd been filming *Out for Justice* in the neighborhood. Seagal had been hooked up with Vic somehow. Vic put Richie on Seagal detail. The big fuck was quiet the whole time in the

Eldorado. It was like having a regular nobody in the passenger seat, little grunts and groans, no sentences. Pulling teeth trying to get a conversation going. The worst thing about Seagal was he thought he was Pesci or De Niro or some shit. Guy was a joke. Which is why Vic, who had stars in his eyes for the *Goodfellas* guys, had pawned Seagal off on Richie.

Women other than Adrienne had been in the car with him, too. Angela Di Pietro was the best of them. Tongue ring. Lots of bracelets. Hair dyed blond. Tattoo of her grandmother on her arm. Richie remembers tracing his finger over her grandmother's face because Angela was always wearing sleeveless blouses. The art was good. She'd had the work done at some famous joint in Queens.

He's amazed that this is what it's really like. Bleeding, close to croaking, he's seeing scenes from his life, remembering faces. Now, he swears, there's even the smell of fresh bread in the car.

He just wants to get up and get behind the wheel one last time. He wants his foot on the gas, his hands on the wheel. He could, he'd drive the thing off a cliff. Go up in flames. Like *Thelma and Louise*, but he's both of them and a dumb-piece-of-shit guy instead of a tough broad. He likes that movie. Susan Sarandon. He's at death's door, now he's thinking of Susan Sarandon. What was that one where she's washing herself with lemons or whatever? Burt Reynolds is watching from his window. Not Burt Reynolds. Burt Lancaster. *Atlantic City*, that's it. Then there was *Pretty Baby*. He remembers she's a whore in that one and she's breastfeeding a baby. Not a bad note to go out on, truth be told. Thinking about Susan Sarandon's knockers. There was that, after all. That was a small joy.

He met Luscious Lacey, right before things went south. Crazy. He remembers his neighborhood video store, that skanky back room with saloon doors where they kept the porno tapes. The room smelled stale. Jizz marks dotted the old carpet; there were old-timers who'd just come in and crank it to the pictures on the covers. He remembers going into that room and coming out with an armful of big boxes. The Russian who owned the video store winking, jabbing a toothpick between his teeth, saying he was in Luscious Lacey's fan club, that he had a signed picture at home.

What would be good, if he could muster the strength to get into the front and drive off, would be to make it to a liquor store. He'd walk in—this wreck of a man no one's expecting—and he'd buy a pint of MD 20/20 like the bums used to do in the liquor store on New Utrecht Avenue where he worked when he was twelve. He swept floors and lifted boxes there. The bums would come in when the sign got flipped and they'd grab their bottles and take them in the alley next to the shop and down them. He never wanted to wind up like that. He wanted nice shoes and a pretty girlfriend and a big car and a gun on his hip. He wanted to be like the Brancaccios. He wanted to be with them. He wanted that gangster strut, grease in his hair, a billfold as fat as a Bible.

A knock on the glass. "You okay, guy?" a voice asks. A mean voice. A cop voice.

It could only ever end badly. You pay for what you've done wrong. Call it justice or karma. Call it whatever the fuck you want to call it.

Richie makes a noise. He's got no words left.

The cop's calling over to whoever he's with, probably other cops. Richie doesn't even know where he is. A town. Some town. How he got here he remembers only vaguely now. Crea. Lucia in that window. Rena. Adrienne.

He finds some inner reserve of strength and rises from the glass. He hurls himself over the bench into the front. He saw this in a movie, he'd be laughing his fucking balls off. He's *Weekend at Bernie's*. He's *Night of the Living Dead*. He lands heavily, sprawled on the front seat.

He wants. He wants, and then he doesn't want anymore. The windshield goes hazy. His head is close to the wheel. He wishes his hands were there. He wishes he was keying the ignition. He closes his eyes and feels a great weight crushing his chest. A gasp fills his lungs. He wonders if he'll become aware when he stops breathing. He licks his lips. His last breath feels like a scream.

LUCIA

A little creek winds its way through the trees. Shafts of sunlight hang all around her. Lucia's not even sure if it's appropriate to call these woods. She can see houses and buildings just twenty feet ahead. She wades through the creek. The water is up to her ankles. It feels good on her sore feet. She hears a gunshot come from Airplane Park. A single shot. On the other side of the creek, another small stretch of trees. And then she's in someone's yard. A riding mower sits covered under a new-looking deck. The house is white and tall. Her feet are in grass again, getting dry. Soft, green grass.

She looks around. She's not sure where to go. She wishes she had a cigarette. She goes around to the front of the house and she's on fresh blacktop. A driveway decorated with a Fisher-Price Tough Trike and a street hockey net. At the end of the driveway, a short road that edges out against a main road, maybe the one they were just on. She walks cautiously to the stop sign and sees, off to the left, the bus and plane joined together, and she sees lights from cop cars and she sees a crowd gathering.

The diner she noticed before is across the street. She runs to it, dodging a slow-moving car, trying as hard as she can not to be noticed. If Grandma Rena's still alive, she's standing there somewhere and looking for her, grabbing strangers by the shoulders and saying, "Have you seen my granddaughter?"

Only two cars in the diner lot. A striped and dented black Camry with Monroe-Woodbury stickers on its back bumper and a red Civic with vanity plates that read ONLY 1 NUN.

Lucia enters the diner, the door clanking behind her.

A waitress standing at the counter gives her a long, confused look. "You okay, sweetie?"

Lucia nods. She sits at a booth in the back, plunking down the briefcase on the seat next to her.

The waitress comes over and hands her a menu. "You sure?"

"I'm fine. Can I have a Coke?"

The waitress sighs and goes to get the soda.

An older woman is sitting a few booths away from Lucia. She's dressed plainly. Probably in her forties. Dark smudges under her eyes. Hair in a bun. A delicate gold cross hanging outside her white blouse. She's got a steaming cup of coffee in front of her and is picking at a plate of cottage cheese and fruit. She locks eyes with Lucia and comes over, bringing her coffee. "You mind if I sit?"

"Why?" Lucia says.

"You look like you could use company."

"I'm fine."

"Big commotion across the street," the woman says.

"I saw."

"I'm Sister Dorothy."

"You're a nun?"

"Sure am."

"That's your car out there with the nun plates?"

"I borrowed it from Sister Rory. I'm driving up to New Paltz to see my mother. She's in a nursing home."

"Nuns have mothers?"

"You're funny." Sister Dorothy sits across from her, slugs some coffee. She's got hard eyes and a sharp jaw. "I'm going to sit."

"Whatever."

The waitress brings Lucia's Coke and asks if she wants anything else. Lucia says she wants a sesame bagel with cream cheese and a chocolate muffin and a piece of apple pie. The waitress seems astonished. Lucia tells her she's really hungry. The waitress says she hates to do this, but she's got to ask if she's got the money to cover it. Lucia flashes a hundred. The waitress walks back to the kitchen and puts in the order.

"Where are your shoes?" Sister Dorothy asks.

"Everyone's so interested in my feet," Lucia says.

"Concerned, that's it."

"I'm fine. My feet are fine. A little wet. I'm walking barefoot for a good cause."

"That so?"

"Raising money for my friend with leukemia."

Sister Dorothy is wearing plain blue slacks. She reaches down into her pocket and comes out with a shiny silver flask and pours whatever's in there into her coffee and says, "Our little secret." She stuffs the flask back in her pocket and mixes in the booze with her pinkie.

Lucia: "You're a drunk? How original."

"You know a lot of drunk nuns?"

"I live in an Irish neighborhood in the Bronx. Every priest and nun I know is a lush."

"'Tis a curse," Sister Dorothy says, putting a sweet lilt of brogue in her voice.

Lucia sucks down half of her Coke. "You're not gonna try to teach me something, right?"

Sister Dorothy puts up her hands. "I just wanted to make sure you were okay, that's all."

"I stopped believing in God years ago."

"How old are you?"

"Fifteen."

Sister Dorothy takes a belt of her booze-spiked coffee. She leans across the table and whispers, "I don't believe in God anymore, either."

"Really? That's cool."

"What's your name?"

"Lucia."

"You know about Saint Lucia of Syracuse? Saint Lucy."

"I don't like being called Lucy."

"I won't call you Lucy."

"I know about her. She's the one with the eyes, right?"

"Right." Sister Dorothy takes another drink. "What are you running from, Lucia?"

Lucia finishes her Coke. She looks anxiously out the window. She can see the bus and the spinning cop lights, but she doesn't see Grandma Rena or Crea in the crowd. She's trying not to look too hard. She's glad the diner windows are frosted. "Who says I'm running?"

"Where's your mother?" Sister Dorothy asks.

"Dead," Lucia says.

"And your father?"

"I'm going to try to find him."

"You're *alone*-alone? There's no one looking for you?"

Lucia thinks of Grandma Rena, out there—*right* out there—looking for her as she sits here talking to Sister Dorothy. She saw a TV show once about a bank robber in Texas who robbed a bank and then went to eat right in the Chili's across the street from the bank. She feels sort of triumphant, the way that bank robber must have felt. "No one," she says.

The waitress brings back her food and takes the Coke glass for a refill.

Lucia chomps a big bite of bagel. When the waitress comes back with her second Coke, she asks for a scoop of vanilla ice cream to go with her pie.

The waitress shakes her head and says, "Okay, kid." She leaves and comes back with a little bowl of vanilla ice cream and Lucia's check.

Lucia takes the hundred she flashed out of her pocket and gives it to the waitress.

"You can just pay on your way out," the waitress says.

"I'll pay now, if it's okay," Lucia says.

"You don't have anything smaller? Your bill's only twelve bucks."

"Sorry, no."

The waitress shrugs and heads over to the register. She comes back quickly with Lucia's change.

Lucia stuffs a ten under the ketchup bottle as a tip and pockets the rest of her change, seventy-something bucks. She puts down her bagel and spoons some vanilla ice cream on top of her apple pie. She picks up her fork and digs in. Chewing, fork poised in the air, she looks at Sister Dorothy and says, "Sister, if I paid you, would you give me a ride somewhere?"

"Where?" Sister Dorothy asks.

"Wherever you're going. New Paltz, you said? That sounds good. I just need to get away for a few days."

"I wouldn't mind making some extra dough," Sister Dorothy says, sitting back.

Lucia smiles, her mouth full of pie. "You're okay, Sister," she says.

⌒

Lucia watches as other cars blur by in the left lane. They're in Sister Rory's red Civic on the Thruway, and Sister Dorothy is driving forty-five, both hands clutched on the wheel, her back straight as a board. The car is immaculate and smells of pine air freshener. The briefcase is lodged between Lucia's calves.

On the way out of the diner parking lot, Lucia caught a quick glimpse of Grandma Rena, Wolfstein, and Mo, but they didn't see her. She's trying not to think of them now. Cops were swarming all around. She didn't see Crea.

"You don't smoke, do you?" Lucia asks.

Sister Dorothy takes her eyes off the road and looks over at her. "You're a real little spitfire, huh?" Her eyes drift back to the road, and she motions with her hand toward Lucia's knees. "They're in the glove compartment there."

Lucia pops open the glove compartment and finds a pack of Parliament Lights next to a sleeve of pine air fresheners and a folded map.

"I'll take one, too," Sister Dorothy adds.

Lucia hands her a cigarette and takes one for herself, tapping the filter against the tip of her finger. A girl in school, Myra, a really troubled girl, she'd sometimes snort cocaine or something from the recessed filter of a Parliament Light. "Lighter?" Lucia asks.

"The car one works." Sister Dorothy reaches down and pushes in the lighter and waits for it to pop. When it does, she lights her cigarette off the glowing coils and then passes it to Lucia.

Lucia lights hers and takes a long drag. It doesn't taste bad. She feels tough. She rolls down the window and blows her smoke outside. She curls her toes against the grainy mat under her cold, dirty feet. "Can you go any faster?" she asks.

"You're really something. I don't like driving, sorry. The faster I go, the less I like it."

"I can drive."

"You've got, what? A learner's permit?"

"Sure."

Sister Dorothy pulls over to the shoulder, leaves the engine running. They get out and switch places. Lucia keeps the briefcase at her side, pressed up against the door. Buses and trucks and SUVs thrum by, rattling the little car. Lucia flicks her cigarette out onto the pavement. Behind the wheel, she already feels free. She pushes the whatsitcalled, the gear, into drive and stomps down on the gas, catapulting them into the right lane just behind a Freihofer's bread truck.

Sister Dorothy's cigarette pops out of her mouth and drops down to her lap. She swats at the cherry, burning hot on her leg. "Take it easy there, kid," she says. "Sister Rory will kill me if I get burn holes in her upholstery." She throws the ruined cigarette out the window, thumps at some more live embers on her thigh with the heel of her hand, then settles down and takes a slug from her flask.

Lucia tries to keep it steady, checking her mirrors, hands firm on the wheel.

"Tell me about your father," Sister Dorothy says.

"What?" Lucia asks, looking over.

"Eyes on the road now."

Lucia's eyes go back to the glittery blacktop, the white lines, the tires of the truck booming along in front of her.

"You mentioned at the diner maybe trying to find your father," Sister Dorothy says. "Can I help?"

"I only have his name. I just learned it."

"So, you're just at the beginning of something here? Barefoot, with a briefcase and your old man's name. What's in the briefcase, you don't mind me asking?"

"Half a million bucks," Lucia says, smiling.

Sister Dorothy busts out laughing. "'Half a million bucks,' she says. Regular spitfire."

Lucia doesn't quite know where she is beyond the fact that they're on the Thruway, headed north. They get off at Exit 18 for New Paltz. It's not a long trip, only about fifty minutes from Mo's town and all Lucia left behind there, and that makes Lucia a little uneasy. There's no way they can track her here, but she'd like to be farther away. Maybe she can just grab a bus to somewhere else. Or maybe—and this is a big maybe—she can steal this car from Sister Dorothy. The fact that it's not actually hers means Lucia wouldn't feel as bad about it. Sister Rory's nobody. Just a person who exists out in the world and pays extra for dumbass vanity plates. Plus, Lucia can leave Sister Dorothy some money, so it wouldn't be stealing at all. Not that she needs to give a shit about being moral.

"How is it?" Sister Dorothy asks.

"How's what?" Lucia replies.

"Driving barefoot. Does it feel weird?"

"A little. I don't know."

"You should get some shoes."

They stop at the tollbooth. The guy inside is wearing an eyepatch and reading a big fat Stephen King book, *The Stand*. Sister Dorothy searches around for the ticket, finds it stuffed behind the driver's-side visor, and then reaches over Lucia to pay. It's not much, a dollar and change. The guy gives Lucia the same once-over she's been getting from everyone she encounters, and he can't even see her feet. He simply seems shocked by her youth. He has questions, and he wants to ask them. Lucia rolls away before he manages to make a coherent sentence.

Sister Dorothy points and tells her to take a left into town. They pass a gas station and supermarkets. The view straight ahead is of mountains and blue sky. Her window still rolled down, the air feels crisper here.

"It's a nice town," Sister Dorothy says.

Lucia nods, almost forgetting to put on the brakes at a red light, coming close to rear-ending a yellow VW Beetle.

"Down by the bus station," Sister Dorothy says, "there's a hostel. You know what a hostel is?"

Lucia shrugs. "Not really. I know the movie."

"What movie?"

"*Hostel*."

"The only movies I like are *Rain Man* and *Beaches*."

"This one's gory."

"Anyhow, a hostel's just a cheap place to stay. You can get a room there, or you can get a bus at the station. We haven't talked about my rate."

"Your rate?"

"How much I charge for rides. Forty bucks fair?"

Lucia shrugs again. "Sure."

They pass through a green light outside of a strip mall with a sign for a movie theater. They pass pizza places and a beer store and pharmacies. They seem to be coming downhill now. Stopped at another red light, off to the left is a deli and off to the right is a dive Indian restaurant. The mountains feel closer. Lucia thinks about how stupid it was to even consider stealing the car. She'd never be able to pull it off.

After a gas station and another deli and a little scattering of other shops, Sister Dorothy points at a big old white house with a weird sculpture on the front lawn. "That's it," she says. "Pull over."

Lucia does that, jolting to a stop right outside the house, tires up on the curb, nearly clipping a fire hydrant.

Sister Dorothy takes a long pull from her flask. "Good luck finding your old man."

Lucia reaches into her pocket and comes out with the folded money from the diner. She peels off two twenties, dropping them into the ashtray. She then pulls the briefcase up into her lap, fearing a scenario where it pops open and her money's everywhere. But that doesn't happen. Lucia gets out, and she's standing on the pavement, clutching the briefcase.

Sister Dorothy scooches into the driver's seat and then leans out the open window and says, "Get some shoes, huh?"

Lucia nods and says thanks. She walks around the back side of the car and steps onto the sidewalk. Sister Dorothy screeches away. Lucia thinks how strange it is how people come and go.

Her father's name is spinning through her head. Walt Viscuso. All these years, he's been a blank page to her. A blank face. Nothing. And now he's a name, letters on the black screen of her mind. *Walt.* Four letters. An ugly name. And *Viscuso*—that should be her last name. Lucia Viscuso. She doesn't like it one bit.

She looks up at the hostel. It looks like the kind of place where college kids live in movies. She imagines mattresses on floors, band posters on walls, people sitting cross-legged and smoking pot out of little glass pipes.

The Trailways bus station is right next door. Three taxis idle in the lot. A long-haired man works on his motorcycle. Three girls wait for a bus, talking.

Lucia's plan is to go to the library to research her old man. And then she's going to buy sneakers and a backpack for the money so she doesn't have to carry it around in a briefcase like some dipshit. And then, maybe, depending on what she finds out about her father, she may or may not buy a ticket at the bus station going north or south, east or west. Or she might come back and go into the hostel and get a room and lay low for a couple of days—but she thinks that might be dangerous. She's not far from Monroe, and if word gets out about her being on the lam, as she imagines it will, they'll know right away who she is and call the cops. So, no, Sister Dorothy, maybe getting a room's not a good idea, as nice as it would be to lie down on a bed and sleep.

She's worried about being out in the open.

She goes into the bus station. A burnt-out hippie in flannel is behind the glass window, reading a paperback. The walls are wood-paneled. A long bench and a pinball machine and a sad plant on a little plastic table are the only things in the lobby.

"You want a ticket somewhere?" the guy says, looking up at her.

"Where's a library?" she asks, ignoring his question.

He stares at her. "You like books?" He holds up his: *Jitterbug Perfume*. Blue, a woman's hand opening a perfume bottle, some kind of smoke rising up. "This is good."

"I just need the library," she says.

He leans over the counter and gives her feet a good look. "You're a runaway, huh? I know you probably don't want to go to the cops. Fuck them, right? There's a shelter in town. Maybe you can go there?"

"I'm not a runaway."

"You're, like, walking barefoot to prove something?"

She doesn't answer.

"The library's up Main Street on the right. You can't miss it."

She says thanks and walks out of the bus station lot back out onto the sidewalk, holding the briefcase against her chest. She heads down Main Street toward the heart of the village. She passes a Thai restaurant and an Italian market and a college bar.

The library's right there on the corner where Main Street bears left a little. A rut of shops and markets. Those pretty mountains on the horizon. She goes into the library, and there's a giant behind the front counter; at least he seems like a giant to her. He's maybe six-five and three hundred pounds with a big mole on his cheek. He's also wearing a flannel and dirty jeans. She asks about the public computers, and he points her to them and tells her how to log in as a guest.

She sits down and puts the briefcase between her legs and does an internet search for Walt Viscuso. She doesn't really like using computers. She should, but she doesn't. She doesn't like them for games or for music or for anything. Whenever she's at a computer, she feels like she's in some dumb version of the future, where people are tapping at unwieldy keyboards and staring at boxy screens.

There are no articles or obituaries about her father, which hopefully means he's not in jail and not dead. She's looking for a phone number or an address. She's trying to think how old he would be. The same age as her mother. The same age as her mother *was*. Adrienne's not that age anymore. Or she'll be forever that age.

She finds only two Walt Viscusos in New York. One in Brooklyn and one in Buffalo. The Buffalo one is listed in his fifties. The Brooklyn guy's thirty-five and makes more sense; he never left. It's got to be him. She can't imagine her luck. He could've been anybody. He could've been someone with a name way more people shared. She finds a pencil and takes out the paper Grandma Rena gave her and writes down what might be her father's number under the other two numbers in Grandma Rena's shaky print.

She looks at the rest of the hits and doesn't see much of value, except for an Our Lady of the Narrows alumni letter indicating that a Walt Viscuso graduated there in '88. Our Lady of the Narrows is a Catholic high school in Bay Ridge. She's heard all about it from Adrienne, who went to its sister school. Makes sense that her old man would've gone there.

On her way out of the library, she asks the giant where she can get sneakers. He tells her there's a shoe store a couple of blocks down. He walks her outside and tells her to make a right here at the library on North Front and then walk past Church and make a left on North Chestnut and the place, whatever it's called, will be right there. He wishes her good luck because, he says, she sure looks like she needs it.

In an alley next to a bakery on North Front, she kneels down and opens the briefcase slightly, yanking a few hundreds through the slat. She looks around to make sure no one's watching and is relieved to see only a gaggle of summer-break college kids, slugging coffee, the girls braless in crop tops and cut-offs, the boys in sandals and cargo shorts and band T-shirts, none of them giving a shit about her.

She walks over to the shoe store and picks out an expensive pair of blue Pumas in her size. The lady working is keeping an eye on her, thinking probably that she's a likely candidate to stuff something under her shirt. But Lucia goes to the register proudly with her Pumas and cash, and the woman acts as if she's being filmed and needs to respond to this weird young girl respectfully.

Lucia pays and puts on the sneakers right there, leaving behind the bulky red box. "Is there a good place to get a backpack?" she asks the woman at the register.

The woman nods back in the direction of Main Street. "There's a rock-climbing place just off the corner. Couple of head shops, too. The vintage place. You might find something in one of those."

Lucia leaves and walks up North Chestnut into the village. After she scores a backpack, her goal will be to call Walt and maybe get a slice or two of pizza.

The store the woman was talking about is called Rock and Snow. Lucia approaches and guesses it's perfect with its big, clear windows, racks of bright clothes, walls full of equipment. They've got to have backpacks. She walks in and asks for the backpacks and is pointed to where they are by a guy in his twenties with a long red beard.

She picks out the one that looks the nicest. It's red nylon with a lot of zippers and a kind of curved mesh part that's probably meant to be good for the back. It's big enough to hold the money. It's expensive, high end, almost three hundred bucks, and Lucia feels like a rock star buying it. Red Beard rings her up, unsmiling, considering her businessman-like briefcase, her bright blue sneakers, her aura of fatigue. He asks if she wants a bag for the backpack, and she shakes him off.

She looks around. She can honestly say she's never given one single thought to rock climbing. She's seen movies. People scaling walls, using ropes and picks and shit, dressed silly.

Back outside, she heads up Main and settles on a little hole-in-the-wall pizza shop called Gourmet. She goes in and looks over the slices behind glass. Lots of specialty pies. She orders two plain slices and an orange soda from the dude behind the counter, pays, and goes over to a booth to wait while her slices heat up. Behind her, there are two narrow doors for the bathrooms, scuzzy, splattered with graffiti.

She opens the door on the right. It smells like piss and bleach. The toilet is dirty. She uses the toilet and then takes the money out of the briefcase, stuffing it in her new backpack and double-checking it to make sure all the zippers are secure. It feels good to have her hands on the money. She feels around in the briefcase to make sure she's not missing anything. She would hate to think that there's a secret compartment she overlooked. Nothing else, as far as she can tell. She props the briefcase behind the garbage can, brown paper towels spilling over the edges, and thinks about the next person who walks in there finding the empty briefcase and wondering how it got there. She slips the straps of the backpack over her shoulders.

The slices and soda are waiting for her when she gets back to the booth. She sits up on the bench, the backpack on. She scarfs down the slices, studying the poetry of the grease stains on the white paper plates.

What will she say to her father? What if he doesn't pick up? What if he's married and his wife answers? Maybe he's got six other kids. Maybe they're terrible, running all around and knocking things over and he's just trying to sit there with a beer and watch something that he likes. Maybe he never even knew that Adrienne was pregnant. That seems like Adrienne: getting knocked up, keeping it quiet. Grandma Rena said he was a lowlife. What's that mean, coming from a mob wife?

She takes out the scrap of paper with the numbers on it and works on memorizing Walt's in case it gets lost. Scraps of paper can float away, rip into nothing, the ink can be washed to a fade in rain or from sweat. But a number can burn itself onto your brain so you never forget it, that much she knows. She still has every number of every apartment and house she and Adrienne have ever lived in rattling around her mind. She doesn't memorize the number for Grandma Rena's prepaid cell, not yet, but maybe she should. She stuffs the paper back in her pocket.

Done with her pizza and soda, she goes up to the counter and orders garlic knots. She is congratulated on her appetite by a fat man in a Knicks jersey who peeks his head out of the kitchen. The dude behind the counter laughs and agrees that she can sure eat. She pays for the garlic knots.

The garlic knots are served on a paper plate with a plastic cup of marinara sauce. She devours them standing up at a slim counter scattered with shakers of crushed red pepper and parmesan cheese. The garlic knots are rubbery and greasy and good. Her stomach feels like a brick. "Hello, is this Walt Viscuso?" she says aloud.

From over by the register, a shout: "Huh?"

"I'm just talking to myself," she explains.

A shrug, a nod, the oven door being opened and whooshed shut, a clattering of pans.

Lucia takes out the phone Grandma Rena bought her and dials Walt's number from memory.

After two rings, someone picks up, but they don't say anything.

"Hello, are you there?" she says into the void.

"Who is this?" a voice shoots back. Raw, scratchy. "Is this Gruffo's kid?"

"Who is this?"

"Who the fuck are *you*? You called me!"

"Is your name Walt Viscuso?"

"What is this, a goof? Did Slam Bam and Chub put you up to this?"

"Walt?"

"Yeah, I'm Walt. And whatever it is"—he's laughing now—"it's not my fucking fault."

"My name's Lucia. I'm your daughter."

Deep silence that seems to last a minute or more. Then the sound of him clicking his tongue against the roof of his mouth.

"My mother was Adrienne Ruggiero."

"*Was?*" Walt asks.

"She died yesterday."

"Aw, fuck." More clicking, some heavy breathing, the sound of a cigarette being lit. "What do you want, kid? I've got a life here. I've got responsibilities."

"I don't know."

"Are you in trouble?"

"Maybe."

"You need money? If there's one fact in this fucked-up world, it's that I'm broke. I'm scratched out. I owe Gilly three hundred bucks. Forget what I owe Slam Bam and Chub. Plus, there's Mackey. He's about to sic his goons on me, no shit. Could be you're talking to a dead man. I'm in the hole with Mackey for twelve grand."

"I have money," she says.

A beat. "You have dough? An inheritance?"

"Yeah."

"How'd she die, your old lady?"

"Cancer."

"Of the titties or brain or what?"

"Ovaries." She'd seen that on an afternoon talk show one time—ovarian cancer—it was a thing, for sure.

"Oof. Tough deal. You know, she didn't give me the time of day after I knocked her up. She was blitzed that night. She came to where I was working at the time, Century 21, wasted, had a purse full of little airplane bottles of gin and vodka and tequila. We went to a show at this club together, the way we sometimes did, and she screamed herself hoarse. She dragged me into the bathroom and we went at it. I'd wanted it to happen as long as I'd known her, but I wasn't ready. I stuck it in for only a minute. She was so far out of my league, I shot that fast. She was disgusted with herself. Right away. She puked on the toilet. Not in it. When she found out she was pregnant, she told me Richie Schiavano would kill me if I ever went near her again. He came around to see me once or twice. I wasn't scared, but I didn't see any percentage in fighting her on it."

"Okay." Lucia is rattled by this image of how she was conceived. A skanky club bathroom. A quick, sad fuck. Adrienne puking afterward.

"But you have your inheritance and you're looking to strike up a relationship with dear old Dad, huh?"

"Can I come see you?"

"Shit, sure. Come on over. Where are you? You need a ride? I'll gas up the old Citation and play chauffeur."

"I'm upstate. I don't need a ride. I'll get there."

He gives her his address. He's on Thirteenth Avenue between Seventy-Fifth and Seventy-Sixth Street in Dyker Heights. His apartment is over a Laundromat and across the street from a lingerie shop that's just a front for a brothel, he tells her. She doesn't think she's ever heard the word *brothel*. He says he's going to clean for her and reminds her to bring some of that inheritance and not to involve Grandma Rena, who he calls a rigid old pain in the ass. She says her grandmother is out of the picture. She lets out a breath and ends the call.

She's not stupid. She heard how his voice changed when she mentioned the money. He probably figures he can make a killing off her, that some of Papa Vic's money will trickle down to him. She lets out a breath. The dream of being on her own is bullshit. And no one will expect her to go back into the city. She's tough—she's proven that. She can get out of trouble if she needs to.

There's a lot of money. She can share some with Walt. She wants to know him. At least a little.

She leaves Gourmet and walks the few blocks back to the bus station. She doesn't intend to get on a bus. Too much of a trail. Instead, she goes over to where the taxis are parked. She comes up on the driver's side of the first one on the left and knocks on the window. The guy behind the wheel is in his twenties with shaggy blond hair and a messy beard and those glasses that turn into sunglasses in the light. He rolls down the window. He's wearing an open flannel with a Nirvana shirt underneath, and he's got a guitar magazine open in his lap. He smiles at her. "Help you?" he asks.

"How much for a ride to the city?" she asks.

He bites his lower lip. "It'll be a lot. You can just catch a bus."

"I don't want to take the bus."

"A hundred bucks."

"That's fine." She opens the back door and gets in, taking off the backpack and holding it in her lap, pulling the belt across it and snapping the buckle shut. She reaches over and closes the door.

"Hold on," the driver says.

"What?"

"I don't mean to be unreasonable, but can I see that you have the money? I can't afford to drive all the way to the city and have you hop out on me at a light or something."

She nods, takes a hundred out of her pocket, one of two she has left there, and passes it up to him. "Keep it," she says.

He holds it up to the windshield to make sure it's not counterfeit, seems convinced, pushes the guitar magazine out of his lap, and starts the car. "Where to?" he says.

"Brooklyn," she says. "I have the address."

He turns around. "I'm Justin."

"I'm Mikaela," she says, and she's not sure where it came from or why she chose that name, but she likes the freedom of being able to name herself. She's always liked that name: Mikaela. Sounds like a girl with a chip on her shoulder, like a girl who can start some shit. She's ready for Walt. She's ready for the future.

WOLFSTEIN

Mo gets chummy with Detective Pescarelli, and they drag Wolfstein and Rena along to O'Leary's for a good dose of questions over early drinks. As they go in, they see Richie being pulled out of the Eldorado and loaded into a coroner's van. Rena puts her hand over her face. Richie must remind her of Adrienne, of where they are and where they've been and all that's different or not-that-different, just new. Panic and anger set in again.

Wolfstein, Mo, and Pescarelli sit down in a booth, while Rena scurries away to the bathroom to wash her face. Wolfstein keeps her bag in her lap.

"She's been through some shit, huh?" Pescarelli says.

"One dirty old man put the moves on her, one dirty old man shot her daughter, and the last dirty old man finished the job," Mo explains. "It's like some fucked-up folktale. Plus, her granddaughter's on the lam."

"It's normal to do this in a bar?" Wolfstein asks.

"Normal for me," Pescarelli says. "I do things how I do 'em. I'm an old-school individual. I get respect. I get breathing room." He sits back. He's sweaty in his corduroy blazer and heavy shirt. He's got a half-beard that makes his face look dirty and bags under his eyes and wiry hairs jutting from his nose and earlobes. He looks like the kind of guy who orders two meat-ball subs for dinner and eats them alone in his car listening to a Mets game.

Wolfstein's gaze drifts back toward the bathroom, expecting Rena to come out any second.

The bar is even shittier on the inside. It's dark, and a heavy smell of stale smoke blankets the place. They probably don't allow smoking anymore officially, but she's sure this place gets smoked out every night into the wee hours. With its pinball machine and crumpled Yankees banners and pictures of cops and firefighters on the walls, it looks like a bad approximation of a working-class bar from a bad movie. The kind of place a Matt Dillon character would drink at when they were trying to make him look like a guy who plows driveways for a living. The bartender is a wretch. Skeezy, with bloodshot eyes and carrot-colored hair and NEVER FORGET tattooed on his neck. Pescarelli goes to him and orders a pitcher for the table, flashing his shield. The bartender pulls the pitcher and hands over three plastic cups and says it's on the house. Pescarelli's tip is lousy.

Still no Rena.

Pescarelli pours their beers.

Mo looks lit up with life. "What a morning," she says, lifting her cup and tapping it first against Wolfstein's and then against Pescarelli's. "Here's to it."

"I like you," Pescarelli says to Mo. "You've got a real touch of class about you."

Wolfstein gets up and goes back to the bathroom to check on Rena, taking her bag with her because she's not leaving it behind anywhere ever. She half-expects Rena to be gone, so she's not entirely shocked when she finds the little bathroom window open, its tattered blinds clanking against the high part of the glass, and Rena nowhere to be seen.

With Lucia on the run, Rena must be thinking she doesn't have time for the cops. That deep panic must've set in. Wolfstein understands, she does.

She just wants to help. She doesn't know how far Rena could possibly get, though. Cops are everywhere. Buses will be held up, no doubt. There's no car Rena can take. She has no idea where Lucia is.

Wolfstein considers going back to the booth but then decides to climb out the window to go look for Rena.

The window opens on a narrow parking lot that butts up against back ends of businesses on the main strip. Wolfstein scans the area, wondering if she'll see Rena trying to pick a lock or break a window on a car. She knows it won't be long before Pescarelli and Mo are on her trail, too.

At the end of the lot, Wolfstein looks right, which is where all the action they left in their wake is still unfolding. The bus in the distance, the plane, Crea, spinning cop lights, more ambulances, everything.

To the left is a quieter stretch of street running alongside the twin lake. She sees Rena, lurching close to a white Toyota Camry with its wheels up on the curb. Wolfstein calls out her name. Rena looks back.

"Where are you going?" Wolfstein says, as she closes in.

"I need to bury Adrienne," Rena says. "She needs a proper funeral. What we did, leaving her, it's not right. And I need to find Lucia. I can't believe I lost the number for the phone I bought her."

"My house is a crime scene. We don't have any leads on Lucia."

"I can't just sit and wait," Rena says, fighting with herself. "I've gotta do something. That's my daughter and my granddaughter. I've gotta make an effort. Adrienne should be taken care of. She needs her mother. And I've gotta look somewhere for Lucia. I'm all she's got now. I know she's tough—or she thinks she's tough—but the world will chew her up. She'll lose the money. She'll have nothing and no one."

"What do you want to do?"

"I want to go back," Rena says, her desperation intensifying. "I want to get my daughter. I want to give her a proper burial. What kind of mother am I, running away? I want to find Lucia. I want to raise her right."

"I'll help, however I can."

Rena suddenly notices something back behind a cluster of office build-ings and starts walking toward it, harried. Wolfstein follows.

They cut up a gravel driveway, through the yard of a law office, and come back out on Stage Road, at the far end of the block, away from the police station and O'Leary's. What Rena saw, Wolfstein now knows, is a chapel. A beautiful little Catholic chapel with white siding and a thatched roof. Sacred Heart, it's called. Like something in a little European town. Feels out of place on the same block as the police station and O'Leary's, a seedy funeral home across the street, some rooming houses next door, a staggered disarray of other buildings whose purpose seems to be in question.

"I need to pray," Rena says.

Wolfstein's been to a few churches or chapels or whatever. For weddings and funerals. And there was that deconsecrated church she and Mo did a scene in. There was also one night at a chapel in Vegas when she almost got hitched to some high-stakes gambler named Keoghan. She remembers his pastel blue sport coat and the heavy dose of shitty cologne he wore. He had the laugh of a villain, but he was sweet, and she was drunk enough to think that marriage was a swell idea. Luckily, Mo had been along for the ride and sober enough to talk her out of it.

Rena pushes through the red doors into the chapel. Wolfstein's right behind her. It's quiet inside. Light falling on the pews. Churchy smells. No sign of anyone. A bare altar. Cross up on the wall. Stained-glass windows. All the shit she expects. It's pretty, but stifling and unpleasant. She feels the weight of guilt and shame.

"I need to pray," Rena says again, and she falls to her knees in the aisle and crawls toward the altar.

She's fucking snapped, Wolfstein thinks. *And with good reason.*

"Rena, sweetie, get up," Wolfstein says.

"I'm sorry. I'm so sorry. Whatever I did, I'm so sorry." Rena is pleading with God. Her voice is full of rage and regret. She's expecting an answer.

The way the morning's going, Wolfstein half-expects God to pluck the roof off the joint and stick his hand inside and scoop Rena up like he's King Kong and she's Jessica Lange.

That doesn't happen, of course. Rena continues her sad crawl. It reminds Wolfstein of the time she saw Valerie Sugar, drunk or high, crawling up the driveway at Mac Dingle's house, begging for coke, begging for pleasure, begging for anything. People ignored Valerie. They let her pass out behind the back tire of a rented limo. Wolfstein guesses she should just ignore Rena now, let her cry the pain out, let her figure her own way through this tangled mess, come to terms with what happened to Adrienne and with Lucia taking off for parts unknown.

"Why?" Rena asks God. "Why would you let this happen to me? Haven't I always been good? Haven't I always tried? Why did you take my daughter from me? Why did you let her get killed like that, so horribly?" Rena's crying now, the words thundering out, spit-stringy. She really thinks she's talking to someone.

"I'm here," Wolfstein says. "It's just me. I'll help you through this."

Rena starts saying the Our Father like a priest trying to exorcise a demon from a possessed girl. She sounds like the priest but also seems jangly and loose-limbed, as if she's the one possessed. Wolfstein knows that's what trauma and grief can do. They're flooding in now, raining down on her, crashing against the rocks of her soul, if there's such a thing as a soul. Rena's head must be a hurricane of brutality: Adrienne being killed; hitting Enzio with that ashtray; Crea with his hammer and gun; Richie splayed like a snuffed candle in the back of that coroner's van; Lucia with her bare feet and big dumb picture of a world that could be less than mean; probably even going back to her husband on that stoop.

Wolfstein doesn't know the words to the Our Father. Not really. She starts saying it along with Rena anyhow, picking up the words as she goes. They're ingrained in the culture enough that it's not difficult to settle into the rhythm of the prayer. "I'll pray with you, it's okay," Wolfstein says, setting her bag down on the floor and pressing a hand against Rena's back.

They're at the base of the altar now, and Rena collapses there, head on the first step, crying harder, stammering.

Wolfstein thinks of prayers as words flung out into a void. She pictures children kneeling at their bedsides with their hands clasped together, women and men clutching the arms of dying spouses, ballplayers crossing themselves as they step to the plate, soldiers in peril, on and on like that, all these wild prayers rising like smoke over the world and dissipating after too long, unheard, unanswered, nothing but sounds that end nowhere in particular.

To Wolfstein, all of humanity is wrapped up in the emptiness of prayer. And, yet, what can she do but encourage Rena, be a friend. Her role is determined.

A priest—an actual priest in his black clerical clothes—emerges from a door beside the altar. He's young, fortyish, with oily skin and bald patches on his head. His shirt is dusted with dandruff. He's got deep grooves in his face, and he's short, maybe five-three. "Hello?" he says. "Are we okay?"

The way he says, "Are *we* okay?" really bothers the shit out of Wolfstein. *Obviously, we're not fucking okay here* is what she's thinking, but she doesn't say it like that. Priests, you've gotta sidestep around like a homeless nut with a shiv. Anything can set them off. In Wolfstein's experience, anyway. She'd put the percentage of normal priests she's met at about a third. And she saw plenty of them in Los Angeles, some doing meaningful work, many in the gutters and lurking, deranged and fever-eyed, at the edges of sin.

"We're not very okay, no," Wolfstein says.

"Can I help?"

Rena crawls toward him on her hands and knees, prostrates herself before him like a sick peasant, grips his shoes. "Father," she pleads. "Father, please."

"What is it? What's happened?"

"Will God forgive me? Please."

"Do you want to confess?"

"I'm the worst."

The priest turns to Wolfstein. "Maybe she needs a doctor?"

Wolfstein squats at Rena's side, strokes her back between the shoulder blades. She talks up to the priest: "My friend Rena here's had a rough day."

The priest takes a step back, crosses his arms, fixes his gaze on Rena. "My name is Father Hughes. Tell me how I can help you, okay? I'm here to help. God is listening to your prayers, I can assure you of that."

"God isn't listening," Rena says, seeming to look for herself in the glare of Father Hughes's shiny black shoes. Her voice catches.

Wolfstein's taken aback by Rena's words.

"He can't be," Rena continues. "If he was, I would feel helped. I don't feel helped. I'm nothing. I've got nothing. I believed all the wrong things and look where it's gotten me."

Father Hughes leans down now. He reaches out for Rena's hand. "God is with you. Whatever's happening, he's with you. Rena—that's your name? Such a pretty name. Trust me, okay?"

Rena nods.

"Rena, honey, get up," Wolfstein says.

Rena does stand, acting momentarily as if she's going to shake this off and get it together. She swipes at her cheeks, runs her hand against her mouth, straightens her back.

"There you go," Father Hughes says.

"I'm just so angry," Rena says in a whisper, looking woozy suddenly. She collapses against Father Hughes, hugging him now, eyes closed, begging forgiveness again, asking God to set things right.

And then she's silent, passed out or blacked out or delivered by her anger to some other realm of consciousness, her head on his shoulder. It reminds Wolfstein of those wild nights where she screwed herself to sleep.

"She's asleep?" Father Hughes asks over her shoulder.

"Fainted, I guess," Wolfstein says, tapping Rena on the shoulder. "Good thing she's so light."

"She must be exhausted."

"She's had a rough run." Wolfstein's having a hard time loosening Rena's grip; she's clutching the little priest the way a child clutches a stuffed bear.

"She's really squeezing me," Father Hughes says.

Finally, Wolfstein gets Father Hughes free and carries Rena over to an empty pew. She's on her back, out cold. Wolfstein asks Father Hughes if he has a car and he says he does, that it's parked in the back. Wolfstein says she'd hate to put him out any more than they already have but asks for a ride, not far, just to a quiet motel somewhere so they can collect themselves. He nods and says he'd be happy to help.

They carry Rena out to his dumpy Altima in the driveway and put her in the back seat. Wolfstein returns to the chapel for her bag and then sits next to Rena in the back, Rena's legs sprawled in her lap.

Father Hughes gets behind the wheel. He digs around in the glove compartment and finds a box of Marlboro Lights and a book of matches. "You don't mind if I smoke?" he asks Wolfstein.

"Of course I don't," Wolfstein says. "Can I bum one?"

"Sure thing," he says, passing one to her and then striking a match and leaning back to light it for her. He lights one for himself next and rolls down the window and takes a long drag.

Rena stirs, says something in her sleep.

Father Hughes jumps in his seat, spooked by the lady who fainted in his arms.

Wolfstein laughs. "Take it easy, Father," she says. "You'll be okay."

RENA

Rena is next to Vic in the back of the ambulance. They've got a mask on him, the paramedics. His shirt is ripped open, and they're talking to him even though he can't hear them. His eyes are closed. She's holding her rosary. There's blood, crawling like vines off the edge of the gurney.

She can't hear anything. She's thinking of the day Adrienne was born. She's seeing Vic, sitting in the hospital room, holding his newborn daughter, his collar open, that tumbleweed of chest hair puffing up from his neckline, that big, beautiful smile of his.

"She's gonna grow up to be famous, I can already tell," that's what Vic said to the nurse in the room with them.

And then she's at the house five days later. He's rocking Adrienne while Mama Ruggiero stands nearby, pacing, concerned that he'll drop her. Rena is watching from the couch, where she's all set up with pillows and blankets, tired, barely having slept since Adrienne was born.

In the ambulance, the sound of the siren spins in her head as they rush to the hospital. The sound of the tires squealing below her as they take a hard turn.

She's saying Vic's name. She's praying. She's trying to picture God, listening to her prayers. She wonders what other people see when they picture God. When she was a girl, she pictured a king, white beard, throne, flowing robe. Now she pictures a man on a street corner, warming his hands over a fire in a garbage can, like a lost member of some doo-wop group. Why a man? What if God is a woman or a cloud of smoke or something you can't even see? A voice emanating from a light. Matter. A vibration.

She wants Vic to open his eyes and open his mouth and to say her name. She wants to see him look at her with love, the way only he can. He's been good to her, hasn't he? He's been a good man, no matter what bad things he's done. The world pulses with violence. Violence made the world. The weak get trampled. Vic's figured out how to survive, that's all. He's been good. *Gentle* Vic. See, that's proof. They made that his name because he was tender, soft-voiced, meticulous. She leans over and kisses his hand now. Splatter of blood there. The raised softness of a vein. Liver spots like spilled coffee on a map.

She prays for an ordinary day. Watching the morning talk shows, listening to a ballgame, letting Vic's work seem far away, stirring gravy, making spedini, a hug in the kitchen, putting on a wash in the cellar, the quiet tremble of their old house.

When they arrive at the hospital, everything is so fast. They're out of the ambulance, hit with warm air from the whooshing doors of the ER.

And then Vic is on a chaise lounge at Gershwin's, and Rena is aware that this isn't the waking world, it's a dream or something like a dream, not quite living inside a memory, something more elastic than that. Vic is smiling. He's got on a striped Speedo. He's tan. His eyes are full of love. He's not Young Vic, and he's not Old Vic—he's somewhere in between—but he was never this age when they were at Gershwin's together.

She looks down at herself, at her legs. Is she the director of this dream, or whatever it is? Her legs are covered in fur. Not hair. Not like she hasn't shaved. Animal fur. Smooth, soft. She touches the fur and she's expecting silkiness, but she can't feel anything.

"I don't remember this," Vic says.

"Neither do I," she says.

He leans over and kisses her. The kiss has the feeling of fading away before it even starts. Their tangled mouths become fuzzy.

His face is snow now. She's a girl, in her puffy winter clothes. She's dipped her head into a snowbank on the sidewalk outside her house even though her mother is yelling from the front stoop for her to stop. Stoops. Something about stoops. Her father is next to her mother, reading a newspaper, smoking a cigar, not dressed for the weather. Her nose is buzzing from the cold. She looks down at her gloved hands. She plucks the glove from her right hand. That animal fur again. And now she has cat claws, not regular human nails, and she smiles because she's a girl and she's cold and she figures she must be some sort of miracle.

And then she's old, dying in some sad bed in hospice, tubes strung from her. She recognizes the room, though she's never been there. The future, maybe. Flowers are everywhere. The walls are flowers. The ceiling is a black hole. A nurse is puttering around, angry, saying something in a language that sounds like music. The fur on Rena's hands and legs is white now. She's shaking like old things shake. She feels thunder in her body, and rain. She thinks her bones must be made of rotting wood.

"Nurse, where is he?" she asks, and she's not sure who she's talking about, and the nurse's response is just someone holding down the keys on an out-of-tune piano.

The flowers begin to pour out of the walls like water. They cover the floor. They rise up the sides of her bed. The nurse drowns in them. She makes a crinkling sound, like a present being unwrapped on Christmas morning. The flowers cover Rena. They don't smell like flowers. They smell like an ashtray.

⌐

Rena wakes up with a start in a dark motel room, heavy shades drawn, TV tuned to the old movie channel. A painting of a waterfall like the one by Mo's mother hangs on the wall. Rena sits up and sees Wolfstein on the other bed, smoking a cigarette, crying.

Wolfstein looks over and notices that Rena's awake and dabs at her eyes with the heel of her free hand. "*Now, Voyager*," she says, pointing at the TV screen with her cigarette. "You ever see it? Bette Davis."

"Once," Rena says.

"Saved my life back in Los Angeles. I saw it three nights in a row when I was in a particularly bad place."

"Where are we?" Rena sits up, stretches, looks at her hands. They're shaking. Her knuckles are red.

"The beautiful James Motel on the outskirts of Monroe."

"How'd we get here?"

"The priest drove us."

"Oh my, I wasn't very nice to him, was I?"

"He's a priest. He can take it."

"I really lost it. I'm sorry."

"It's understandable."

Rena stands, stretching her arms above her head. "I should go," she says. "I need to go."

"Where?" Wolfstein asks.

"Adrienne. Lucia. I wish I had that number." She searches the floor of the bus in her mind, tries to remember the numbers she wrote. She feels around in her pocket for the phone. It hadn't even occurred to her that Lucia might've tried to call. Maybe she got scared right away, regretted taking off. She turns on the phone and there's nothing, no missed calls, though she's honestly not a hundred percent sure if the thing's even set up to work yet. She must've left the instructions in the package on the bus, too.

"One's gone for good, and the other's MIA. Rest up, Rena. I bet the cops find Lucia soon; she won't last out there on her own. As for Adrienne, it's horrible, but it'll be nothing but red tape right now. You can deal with it in a day or two."

Rena knows in her heart that Wolfstein's right. There's nothing to be done about Adrienne with the cops running the show. And what happens with Lucia's a wild card; chances are good she winds up sitting down on that briefcase on the side of the highway and trying to hitch a ride and getting picked up by a state trooper. Even without Rena's participation, word must be out on her. Or maybe she'll call after all.

"How on earth can I rest?" she asks Wolfstein.

"Can I tell you a story?" Wolfstein gets up and lowers the TV but leaves the picture on. A close shot of Bette Davis smoking fills the screen.

Rena stares at those heavy, beautiful eyes. She feels lost in them for a moment, yearns for eyes like that, for a different life where she could've been Bette Davis. "I don't think I have time for stories," she says to Wolfstein.

"The first movie I made was in New York. This was in '73. I was living in the shittiest motel you could imagine, not far from the Port Authority. We called it the Scouring Pad. Place made this joint look like the Waldorf. I was living with this gal from Iowa City. Cully was her name. She was thirty-five at the time, but she looked fifty. She had a pimp. I didn't want that life. I wanted to call my own shots."

Rena walks into the bathroom and turns on the water. She puts both faucets on high blast, collecting some water in her cupped hands, and then splashing it over her face as if to shake herself out of this nightmare. "I can't believe how I acted with that priest," she says to herself in the mirror.

"Anyhow," Wolfstein continues, coming up behind Rena in the doorway, "I was telling you about me and Cully at the Scouring Pad and my time on *Sweet Cupcakes*."

"*Sweet Cupcakes*? That was the name of the movie?"

"Right. It was lighthearted. A simple romp. We were getting our footing.

I played a maid. I was serving all these cupcakes to these upper-crust types. Dorothy Cumming was the lady of the house."

"Why are you telling me this?" Rena shuts the water and dries her face with a stiff towel. Wolfstein's hands are on her shoulders now, rubbing, kneading.

"Stay still," Wolfstein says. "You've gotta get rid of some of this tension."

The massage actually feels good, and it doesn't feel wrong to have Wolfstein's hands on her. She'd shriveled at Enzio's touch, but she'd totally forgotten what well-intentioned hands could feel like, how welcome mere contact could be. She closes her eyes and lets Wolfstein work.

"I was a masseuse for a few months," Wolfstein says.

"Of course you were," Rena says.

"You can just see me, right? Carrying around that massage table, karate-chopping some fat fuck's back?" Wolfstein's hands on her shoulder blades now, pushing hard against a knot. "I've never felt someone as tense as you."

Rena's not sure what to say. Under normal circumstances, she's stressed, tense as hell. Now, with all that's happened, with what she's seen, her body has felt like murder. Her muscles raw and burning. Her bones older than ever. Her head buzzing. Her jaw tight. She imagines the pain inside her as cancerous clouds.

"Let go of some of it," Wolfstein says, her voice a whisper in Rena's ear.

Rena leans her head back slightly and exhales. She feels lighter, looser.

"Why was I telling you about '73?" Wolfstein says. "Getting old is the pits. I had a story. It had real significance."

"You'll think of it."

The white shirt Rena's wearing clings to her. She can smell her own sweat. She wishes she had her deodorant. Wolfstein reaches up under the shirt and now she's working Rena's lower back, fingers pulsing against bare skin. She knuckles around Rena's bra strap.

"That feels good?" Wolfstein asks.

"Uh-huh," Rena says, almost cooing.

"I remember now."

"Remember what?"

"Where I was going with that story. There's the movie part of the story, and then there's the Cully part. On *Sweet Cupcakes*, I had trouble with this piece of shit, Frankie Mangello. He thought who he was. We only had one scene together, but I hated every second of it. Frankie was just a bum, mean as hell, big into drugs. He was from Brooklyn, like you. Bay Ridge. I hated to see him eat a slice of pizza because of his mustache. Mustaches and pizza don't mix, you ask me."

Rena crosses her arms over her chest.

Wolfstein continues: "Frankie comes to me one day after we're done and says, 'Wolfie, I've got a proposition for you.' 'No,' I says, without hesitation. I'm not getting into anything with this guy. I'm no dummy. To this day, I don't know what the proposition was. Well, he held a big grudge against me after that. This other afternoon, maybe a week later, I'm shooting my scene with him. He gets a little rough. The director tells him to cool it. I go nuts. I yell at him. We finish, but he's giving me this nasty look the whole time, and I'm miserable. A few hours later, no shit, he's walking on Ninth Avenue and an air conditioner falls out a seventh-floor window in an apartment building and nails him. He wound up in a coma. Died three days later. That's what you get, I guess."

Rena's trying to make sense of the story. She's scrunching her eyes together, waiting for Wolfstein to continue, to make sense of it for her. "That's the story?" Rena asks.

"Just part one," Wolfstein says. "I went home, and Cully was there. She wasn't feeling well. Had cramps. She was a sad case, like I said. But a true sweetheart. I told her I was upset, cried about Frankie. I wasn't upset that he'd been hit by the air conditioner; I was upset about how he'd treated me. I was upset about my life. I was thinking I'd made all these bad decisions already and that there was no turning back from them. Cully took me out for pancakes. She listened to me. I sat next to her in the booth at the diner and put my head on her shoulder. She told me it was okay to cry. She stroked my hair. She even fed me my pancakes, you believe that? It was really nice."Wolfstein stops rubbing and steps back over the threshold. "You feel a little better?"

Rena turns around. She crosses her arms tighter, hugging herself into a shiver. "The air conditioner killed Frankie, and Cully fed you pancakes? What's it mean?"

"It means friendship is the greatest romance. And it means men ruin everything, but sometimes air conditioners fall on their fucking heads when they're out walking."Wolfstein gives a big smile. "I want to get loaded. Don't you want to get loaded?"

"I don't think so."

"There's a liquor store across the street. I'm going and I'm getting vodka, and then I'm twisting your arm to have a drink with me. Why don't you take a shower?"

Rena doesn't say anything. She watches as Wolfstein goes over to a chair in the corner and leans over her bag and withdraws a hundred.

"I'll get a little something to nosh on, too." Wolfstein zips the bag and heads for the door.

"You're just leaving that here?" Rena asks.

"Keep an eye on it for me, would you?" Wolfstein pauses as she puts her hand up to turn the knob. "And don't run off on me again. Won't get us anywhere."

Rena nods.

"I've got the key,"Wolfstein says, holding up a flimsy-looking white card before tucking it in her pocket. And then she's gone out the door, singing under her breath.

Rena goes to the window and peels back the heavy curtain. She watches Wolfstein trot across the parking lot past a scatter of dented cars. This is a woman life can't take down. Rena admires that. She closes the curtain and sits on the bed, staring at Wolfstein's money. Maybe she should just take a shower and cool down.

She brings the bag into the bathroom with her and sets it on the toilet tank, making sure it's secure. She turns the shower on hot and waits for the bathroom to get steamy. She locks the door and gets undressed, folding her clothes neatly and putting them on the counter next to the sink. She puts her arms up over her head and stretches. She just stands in the steam, letting it rise up around her.

This isn't a very nice motel. She can tell from the threads of mold in the grout, the peeling paper on the walls, the brownish water stains on the ceiling. The mirror over the sink is cracked. The toilet seat is crooked, stray hairs curled in the nook between the seat and the tank. The garbage can on the floor is full. She wonders how long the hot water will last.

In the shower, she lets the water needle over her. She gets lost in the thrumming sound. Whatever else she can say about this room, about this motel, the water pressure's pretty good. It takes her out of herself for a minute. Her hair dangles into her mouth, and she sucks water from it. She wonders about Lucia again. She tries to picture her, adrift in the world. She sees what happened to Adrienne on a loop in her mind's eye. She doesn't know if she *is* anymore, if she can ever *be* again.

The hot water lasts and lasts. She can't believe it. She's thankful.

When she gets out, her fingers and toes are pruney. She towels off and tries not to see herself in the fogged-over mirror. It's warm in the bathroom, still full of steam. She can hear Wolfstein out in the room now, bottles clanking, the TV louder than before.

A knock on the door. "I hope you've got my bag in there," Wolfstein says on the other side.

"I do," Rena says, as she gets dressed. "Figured better safe than sorry."

"Gave me a little scare."

Rena puts her hair up in a towel and opens the door. The steam ghosts out. Wolfstein's standing by the TV with a bottle of vodka perched next to her on the desk, unwrapping one of those plastic-wrapped motel cups. "I thought maybe you put the shower on as a distraction and took off with my dough," Wolfstein says. "Just for a sec that thought went through my mind, I'll admit. I know your brain's a million places."

"I would never do that," Rena says. While the thought of leaving again did pass through her mind, she never would've entertained the idea of taking Wolfstein's money.

"How was the shower?"

"Hot."

"Good. I'm pouring you some vodka." She swipes her free hand away from the vodka and points to the bed, where a big bag of Utz potato chips and a couple of plastic bottles of Seagram's club soda are propped against the pillows. "I also got other refreshments."

"I'll just have a club soda."

"I'm strong-arming you into a little vodka. At least a splash. I don't want to drink alone." Wolfstein unwraps another cup and sets both on top of the TV. She half fills them with vodka and then retrieves the club soda and adds it to the mix.

Rena: "That's a splash?"

Wolfstein shrugs. She plucks up both cups with one hand, pinching them together between her thumb and pointer, and delivers one to Rena. She taps hers against Rena's and says, "Here's to it."

Rena sips a little. It's strong, burns the back of her throat. She can't remember if she's ever had so much as a sip of vodka. A girl she went to high school with, Jane Williams, liked vodka, kept a stash in her purse. She remembers that name, but she can't remember Jane's face or what color hair she had. She must not have been Italian. Williams could be anything. She remembers Bobby Murray chugging his vodka and how that led to Adrienne getting shot.

Wolfstein sits on the bed and slurps down some of her drink. A different movie is on TV. "I don't know this one," she says to Rena. "You know this one? That's Gloria Grahame. I like her so much. But I've never seen this one. Don't you love that? When it's a movie you've never seen with an actress you love?" She searches around for the remote, sloshing vodka on the bedspread, and clicks the info button. *The Big Heat* is what it says in the blue strip on the top of the screen.

Rena thinks how she's never had that feeling Wolfstein mentioned: a movie she's never seen with an actress or actor she loves lighting her up. She's never cared that much about movie stars, she guesses.

"Lee Marvin's in it, too," Wolfstein continues, plucking a couple of chips out of the Utz bag and chomping on them. "He's so young here. I met his first wife once. Betty. She was something else."

Rena sips the vodka again and tries to stay focused on the movie. She remembers the phone she bought at the bus station and finds it on the nightstand, hoping for a call from Lucia. It's on now, that's clear, but there aren't any missed calls that she can see. She dials her house number and lets it ring. She doesn't have an answering machine. She's not sure why she's doing it. She imagines the phone just ringing on the hook in the kitchen, that terribly sad sound filling the house. Thinking of her empty house sets something off. She feels tears on her cheeks before she even knows she's crying.

Wolfstein lowers the volume on the TV. "You okay?"

"It hits me in waves," Rena says, going into the bathroom for a tissue.

"You ever meditate?"

"I'm Catholic."

"You can be a Catholic and meditate. It's just about getting things straight. Facing your fear instead of walking away from it."

"You meditate?"

"I used to. A lot. Now, I just try to relax. That's what I've been doing these last couple of years. Relaxing. One thing I read along the way really stuck with me. We all have troubles, we all have heartaches and tragedies and traumas; that's what defines us. You can be a coward and still be the bravest person in the world because you do things anyhow. It's okay to be scared. Necessary, even."

Rena lets Wolfstein's words wash over her. What she's saying is pretty smart.

"That and 'drink up' are good pieces of advice," Wolfstein says. "Nothing can hurt you too bad if you just drink up." She tips back her cup and finishes her first drink, shaking it off when the vodka hits. She goes and pours herself another, no splash of soda this time.

Rena has nothing to lose. She downs her drink, and it seems to explode inside of her, firecracker snaps under her skin, a raw feeling in her throat, something wretched crawling in her stomach. She drops the cup and races to the bathroom, falling to her knees and puking into the toilet. She looks up at Wolfstein's bag on top of the tank and catches her breath.

Wolfstein's up and in the doorway again. "I used to know a guy, he was a writer, he'd say no story should have puking or crying. He wasn't any good. He wrote about college professors jerking off in their gym socks. Please, give me a little vomit, that's fine with me. Life is full of puke and tears, right?"

Rena unspools some toilet paper and dabs at the corners of her mouth.

"What's your fantasy?" Wolfstein asks.

"My what?"

"Your fantasy. Like, you and your husband on a bearskin rug in front of a fireplace?"

"I don't think like that." Rena sits up, her back against the bowl. She reaches behind her and hits the handle, flushing away what's there.

"I'll tell you mine. Just to distract you. I'm on an airplane, drinking champagne in first class. Marty Savage is my flight attendant. Paul Newman's the pilot. He's got a beard. You ever see that picture of Paul Newman in Venice with a beard? Jesus Christ. That's enough to make you believe that God's a sculptor with the softest hands and most everybody's fuckups, but with Paul Newman he really got it right."

"I've never seen it."

"Doesn't matter. Close your eyes and imagine. Any version of Paul

Newman will do. *Cool Hand Luke* Paul. *Verdict* Paul. *Nobody's Fool* Paul. It all works."

"I've never seen any of those."

"Jesus Christ, Rena. Just go with me here. Come on, close your eyes." Wolfstein sits on the floor just outside the doorway, careful with her legs, seeming to wince in pain a little as she settles her back against the doorjamb, even more careful with her vodka.

Rena closes her eyes. She doesn't see anything. It doesn't even seem like darkness there on the backs of her lids.

Wolfstein lets out a long sigh. "So, Marty Savage, he's neglecting the other passengers. He's just standing there, ready to pour me more champagne. He's got one of those little towels so he can wipe off the neck of the bottle after he pours. So hot. I'm sucking it down. This is the best champagne you ever heard of. It tastes like rainbows. Marty's sweating a little. He leans down and whispers, 'Meet you in the bathroom in two minutes?' And I just nod. When I get there, it's not just one of those little boxy airplane bathrooms. It's magnificent. Mirrors on all sides. It's small, but there's carpet on the floor and everything is new and clean. Marty comes in. He brings the champagne. I sit up on the sink and tell him to take off his clothes. He does. You know what's coming next, right? Paul Newman joins us in there. 'Who's flying the plane?' I ask. 'It's under control,' Paul says, and he gives me that smile. He comes over and kisses me on the neck. His beard smells like rosemary. We pass around the champagne."

"Stop," Rena says, opening her eyes, the feeling of needing to puke hitting her again.

"I'm getting carried away?"

Rena turns and throws up again.

"You poor thing," Wolfstein says.

"I'm sorry," Rena says.

"It's okay. You get the point. Me and Marty Savage and Paul Newman steaming up that little dream bathroom."

"I was enjoying it." Rena says it just to say it at first, but then she realizes it's true.

"You were?"

"I was, I think." Rena again rips off another square of toilet paper and scrunches it against her lips.

"You want me to finish?" Wolfstein asks.

Rena nods.

Wolfstein starts talking again, continuing the fantasy, talking about her and Paul Newman and this Marty Savage taking off what's left of one another's clothes and touching and kissing and seeing it reflected all to forever in the mirrors. The plane hits turbulence at one point. Another flight attendant squeezes into the bathroom, and it's sweet little Ginny McRae with her velvety lips and chirpy laugh. They're one body with eight hands. Everything smells like Paul Newman's rosemary beard. She seems to know when to hold off from going too far. She knows her audience.

Rena's not sure if it's just the act of listening or the fantasy itself or Wolfstein's sense of humor that's gripped her. Whatever it is, she feels a little better.

Wolfstein describes the climax with bravado: "Me and Paul are balling against the mirror, while Ginny and Marty watch. The plane crashes on a desert island. We're the only four survivors. We live happily ever after."

"Wow, that's something," Rena says.

"Right? I like imagining things. That's why I liked the movies so much." A beat. "Tell me yours."

"My what?"

"Your fantasy."

"I told you already: I don't think like that."

"Make one up. Have fun. It'll help clear your head."

"I don't think so."

"Just start somewhere."

Rena searches her memories. She thinks of Vic at Gershwin's. She thinks of Vic coming out of the shower, wearing a towel. She thinks of how they were before Adrienne was born. She thinks of the night Adrienne was conceived, those silk sheets, the chandelier in their bedroom turned down low. She thinks of a morning not long before Vic was killed—they weren't sleeping together much at this point—when they were in the cellar together and he came over while she was putting clothes in the wash and pushed down the pajama bottoms she was wearing. She felt so young. It was short, two minutes or less, a quick thrumming against the washing machine, and then Vic kissed her on each shoulder and pulled up his pants and buckled his belt and disappeared upstairs. She'd hummed while she put the wash in.

But these are just memories; none are fantasies.

She tries to remember what her desires were like before Vic, what excited her. She remembers loving the story "The Little Mermaid." She'd read some beautiful illustrated version as a girl, and it got her interested in mermaids. She read anything she could that had mermaids. She'd go to the beach in Coney Island and wonder if they were out there, swimming under the pier, lounging hidden behind rock jetties. She remembers that she used to day-dream about being a mermaid, about being naked in the water, glistening with scales, smooth all over, hung with seaweed. As she grew up, she forgot all about it. Much later, when she'd been married for a while, that Daryl Hannah movie came out. *Splash*. Tom Hanks was in it, too. Rena saw it alone at the Loew's Oriental. It made her remember. So, for a couple of weeks in her forties, her secret desire to be a mermaid returned.

"I'm a mermaid," Rena says now.

"That's good," Wolfstein says. "Mermaids are sexy. What happens? Where are you?"

"I'm just poking my head out of the water. The water is really cold. I can see all the stars in the sky. I'm not wearing anything. I have long hair and a long tail, and my skin is glittery."

"Perfect. See, you're doing great. And who comes swimming up? Gentle Vic? Maybe a young Al Pacino?"

Rena closes her eyes again and puts herself in the fantasy. She's seeing and feeling as if she's in the water, in this big expansive ocean, the stars peppered overhead. She's seeing it all. "No one. I'm here alone. It's quiet. It's perfect. The water feels so good."

"Okay," Wolfstein says. "It's your fantasy."

Rena sucks some water up into her mouth or imagines sucking it up into her mouth, and she feels her body under the water. She feels how free she is, how her body is not clobbered by worry or fear or anything. Then she starts to feel self-conscious. She's sitting on the floor of a bathroom in a sad motel, having just vomited twice. She opens her eyes.

"You lost it?" Wolfstein asks.

"I'm no good at this."

"The hell you're not. Being a mermaid was a good start."

A ringing echoes from the nightstand. At first, Rena assumes it's the room phone, and she wonders who might be calling. Maybe the front desk. But then she realizes it's the phone she bought at the bus station. She jumps up and makes a beeline for it. She fumbles it for a second, but then manages to snap it open and palm it up against her ear. "Hello?" she says into the air, at first thinking this itself must be some fantasy.

But then she hears the voice. "Grandma Rena, it's me," Lucia says. "I need you."

LUCIA

When Walt opens the door of his Brooklyn apartment, Lucia is surprised by how he looks. He's shockingly thin, with a wispy beard and bad teeth. His skin is almost gray, as if he's sick. He's a little bald on top, but he's got a ponytail, and it's held in place with one of those wiry twist ties typically used on bread bags. He's wearing an oversize T-shirt with the sleeves cut off. The shirt is white and features a black silhouette of a leggy pole dancer; next to that, in big bubbly script, it reads SUPPORT SINGLE MOMS. A tattoo on his upper arm seems to be of a rat riding a rocket. He's got on saggy brown cargo shorts, and she can see his white boxers puffing out of his waistline. "There's my Lucia," he says.

Lucia hesitates. She's immediately sorry she didn't tell her upstate cabbie, Justin, to wait a few minutes. The ride down had been nice, relaxing. Justin had been easy to talk to. She hadn't thought too much about a backup plan. She'd memorized the number for Grandma Rena's new phone just in case, but she didn't like to think she might have to call in desperation. Now, here she is, all the money in the world right there on her back, about to walk into the apartment of her sketchy-seeming old man.

"Hi," she says.

Walt pulls her in close for a hug. He smells of cigarettes and Vaseline. His shirt seems like it hasn't been washed in ages. She sees what looks like the crumbs of Cheez Doodles powdered across his belly. He releases her and then puts his hands on her shoulders and leans toward her. "Let me get a good look at you. You're a beauty, that's for sure. Mostly your mother, but I see a little of me in your features."

Lucia sees none of him in her. She absolutely can't imagine that this is her blood father. She'd at least hoped, after talking to him on the phone, that he was handsome in a dangerous way. She could see herself being the daughter of a man like that.

"You're not too impressed with me, I can tell," Walt says.

Lucia looks over her shoulder and retraces the way she came in: heavy wooden door, dingy staircase, the Laundromat downstairs in full swing.

Walt continues: "It's okay. I'm used to it. No one's ever really impressed with me. Come in. You need to hit the panic button and split, it's okay with me. No hard feelings." He smiles, and Lucia gets a better look at just how rotten his teeth are: stumpy, yellow, mangled, at least a few missing.

"I don't know," Lucia says.

"You're right to be cautious. That's using your head. You don't know me from Adam. I've got an idea." He disappears into the apartment.

Lucia looks inside. She sees a cream-colored couch littered with empty bags of Cheez Doodles and Styrofoam coffee cups, pulled up in front of a black-and-white TV with rabbit ears showing the news. Sealed cardboard boxes are stacked in the corner next to a doorway into the kitchen that's draped with a moldy, see-through shower curtain. Clothes are piled next to the couch. Walt's disappeared out of her sightline.

When he returns, he's holding a big kitchen knife. It's got a black handle and a sharp eight- or nine-inch blade.

Lucia takes a few steps back, headed for the stairs but not taking her eyes off Walt. She pauses at the top of the staircase.

"Whoa! It's for you!" Walt explains, holding the knife down at his side. "You just hold it. I want you to feel comfortable."

"You want me to feel comfortable holding a knife?"

"Sure. This way, I try anything, you can just stab me."

"I don't want to stab you. I've never stabbed anybody."

"It's just for protection. Think of it like mace. Come on, take it." He holds out the knife, handle first.

Lucia moves toward Walt and takes the knife, afraid for a moment that he'll tug it away from her. He doesn't. It's rusty and even sharper-seeming than she'd first thought. She holds it in front of her with both hands, as if she's never held a knife before.

"Hey, nice kicks," Walt says, pointing at her sneakers. "New?"

She gulps and nods.

"Come on in, sweetie. Welcome to my humble abode. 'Walt's Vault,' I call it. Where all the magic happens."

Lucia follows him inside and sits on the gross couch. She keeps the knife in her lap, pointing upward, and keeps the backpack on, forcing her to sit awkwardly.

Walt moves over by the window and turns a folding chair around, placing his legs on either side and using the back of the chair as an armrest. The window doesn't have curtains. It looks down on the street. Lucia has a clear view of the lingerie shop that Walt said on the phone is a front for a brothel. This stretch of Thirteenth Avenue is all storefronts, hunched buses, people walking with purpose out of banks and delis.

Lucia takes in the apartment. The walls are yellow from age and neglect and water damage. A clothespin is stuffed into a slot on the front of the TV in place of a missing knob. She imagines that he uses the clothespin somehow to change the channels. The rabbit ears are bent, and the picture on the screen is fuzzy. The boxes stacked by the doorway are sealed shut

with packing tape. Names are written on the sides of the boxes in Sharpie:
TOMMY G., DURANTE, CLAM MAN, CHUB, TONY, GILLY, SLAM BAM. The pile
of clothes on the floor next to the couch smells funky.

"Tell me all about Lucia," Walt says. "I never would've named you that,
by the way. I had any say in it, I would've pushed for Debbie or Cindy or
even Kelly."

"There's not much to tell," Lucia says.

"There's an inheritance, right?"

"It's not much."

"Not much is more than I got. You got a bank card or something?"

"I've got this knife."

Walt laughs. "That's good, that's good." He pauses. "You've got a little of
me in you, that's for sure."

Coming here was such a bad move. What does she want with a father
anyway? She doesn't need one. She's never needed one. What she was
looking for, she guesses, was the fantasy of a father. This gross creature in
front of her—like Gollum in that *Lord of the Rings* movie—he's nothing to
her, and he'll never be.

"Where do you go to school? What's your favorite color? You have a
boyfriend?" Walt puts his hands up. "See, I'm good at this old-man shit. You
want a Capri Sun? I got one in the fridge. I was saving it for later, but it's
yours if you want it."

"I'm good."

Lucia's wondering what to do now, where she can possibly go. Maybe
she'll call Grandma Rena, and maybe she won't. Maybe she'll just ride the
train from Brooklyn to the Bronx, back and forth. *Yeah, real smart, carrying
all this money around.* Maybe she'll go back to the Bronx and get an apartment near Yankee Stadium and put all the money in a safe deposit box at
some bank and then she can go to every home game and get Derek Jeter's
autograph again and again and again.

"I can take you to the whorehouse across the street," Walt says. "Introduce you to some of my pals."

"I'll pass," Lucia says, angling the knife in his direction.

"Looking at me, I bet you're wondering why your old lady ever threw a lay on me." He brushes his hand over the bald spot on the top of his head. "I had a full head of hair. My teeth weren't bad. I was in a metal band called Lapse of Sanity. We even played at L'Amour. La-Morz. You heard of that place? 'Rock Capital of Brooklyn.' We opened for White Lion once, that was our big accomplishment. Vito Bratta, he was the best guitarist ever, man. Your mother was deep into metal. And, Jesus Christ, was she hot. She'd wear this little Catholic schoolgirl skirt and a band T-shirt just like that GNR shirt you've got on. She had the hair. It was her secret world nobody really knew about." His eyes wander out the window. "I played guitar. I gave it up. The scene changed."

Lucia is trying to process this new information about Adrienne. She knew her mother had liked a few of those bands—Guns N' Roses, of course; Cinderella; Skid Row; Mötley Crüe—but she never knew there was a whole other her that sort of existed in that world, one that'd even go to shows. She tries to picture this trashy metal groupie version of Adrienne and can't.

Walt continues: "That was her shirt, huh? We saw Guns N' Roses at L'Amour in October '87. Ten bucks. What a night. We were kids."

"I should go," Lucia says.

"Where you gonna go? You're practically an orphan. I can take care of you. The money you got, however much, it can get us off and running. I've got places to invest, ways to double it, triple it, even. We could move out of this dive, me and you, get a nice joint. I'm not gonna be the kind of old man who rides your ass. No curfew, no lectures on drugs, you can smoke and drink and screw to your heart's content. You like to screw? You've got a little boyfriend, I bet."

Lucia stands, the knife at her side now.

"Come on, kid. You came here because you wanted a relationship, right? I'm offering you one."

"I don't know why I came here."

"I know I'm not the guy you wanted or expected, but I'll clean up my act, I swear. I've got a reason to finally. I've been looking for a reason." Walt's on his feet now, approaching her. He's close, just a couple of feet away. He reaches out and puts a hand on her shoulder and squeezes, touching the strap of her backpack longingly.

Lucia winces, pulls away.

Walt moves closer. "Give me a hug, huh? A nice hug, that's all I'm asking for."

With one hand, Lucia pushes him back. She raises the knife in the other and shows it to him, keeps him at a distance. "Don't touch me," she says.

"I gave you that knife," Walt says, retreating, putting his hands in the air to prove he's harmless. "I'm not stupid. I just wanted a little hug from my long-lost daughter, that's it. You want to listen to music? I've got all these old tapes where I'm playing along to the radio. Show you how good I was on guitar."

"Just don't touch me. I've gotta think."

"What's in the backpack?" Walt asks, putting his hands behind his head and clasping his fingers together. "You haven't taken it off the whole time. You got something in there you don't want to lose?"

"Shut up!"

He makes a move for her again, snapping both arms quickly in her direction, and she's honestly not sure if he's going for a hug or trying to rip the backpack off her shoulders.

She dodges him and raises the knife and thrusts it forward, stabbing him in the forearm. She lets her grip slacken on the handle and then drops the knife to the floor.

Walt falls back on his ass, his mouth open, staring up at her. He looks down at the slash. He takes off his shirt and wraps it around the wound, clutching his arm to his chest. "You fucking stabbed me, you little shit," he says.

"I told you not to touch me," she says.

"I didn't think you would. I'm bleeding. It really hurts. Can you call someone? Call Gilly. He'll bring his cousin over; she's a medic. His number's in the junk drawer over there." He thrusts his elbow toward the kitchen.

Lucia is breathing hard. She looks out the window, looks all over the apartment. She isn't sure what to do with her eyes or her hands or even her feet. She avoids Walt, who's whimpering now. Lucia sits on the couch and rocks back and forth. She knocks her knees together. *Just leave*, she thinks. *This isn't happening.*

Walt coughs. "I'm feeling a little light-headed. Just call Gilly. He'll know what to do."

Lucia stands again. She looks at her hands. They're shaking. She looks at Walt. It's a strange feeling to have stabbed someone. He won't die. It's just a cut on his arm. He shouldn't have given her the knife. He shouldn't have touched her. The panic she's experiencing has more to do with anger and fear than guilt.

She moves toward the kitchen, pushing back the moldy shower curtain. Walt's refrigerator is wide-open. A Capri Sun is on the top shelf next to an uncapped jar of mayonnaise. Takeout boxes are overturned on the bottom shelf. The sink is full of dirty dishes. An overflowing garbage can flowers up under a small window looking out at a brown brick wall. Lucia takes a few deep breaths. She wants a glass of water, but she's sure there are no clean glasses, and she's not sure she'd even be able to fit a glass under the faucet with the mess in the sink. Her mouth is dry. She doesn't touch anything. She opens the junk drawer under the counter next to the fridge and finds a yellow legal pad. Funny there's a junk drawer when the whole place is junk. She finds Gilly's number but doesn't make a move to call him. Instead, she takes out her phone and dials the number she has for Grandma Rena.

It rings five times, and she wonders if her grandmother lost the phone or doesn't even know how it works, or if maybe it's dead or turned off.

Then Grandma Rena is there on the other end, and Lucia is telling her that she needs her. Grandma Rena cries out of relief. Lucia doesn't say exactly what's happened, but she says there's trouble.

"Are you safe where you are?" Grandma Rena asks.

"I think so," Lucia says, and then she gives her the address.

"Stay put. We'll be there as soon as we can."

"Okay." Lucia ends the call, her head in her hands.

"Just fucking call Gilly," Walt says. "I've got no feeling in my arm. I can't believe you really stabbed me."

"Give me a second to think."

He moans again. "At least go down to the CVS on the corner and get me some gauze and peroxide and bandages."

She could do that, but she won't.

Walt moans. "I'm dying," he says.

She goes to the TV and uses the clothespin to change the channel. She's hoping for baseball. No such luck. She settles for a Mexican soap opera. A black line cycles up and down the screen, warping the picture. She turns up the volume.

"You're just like your fucking mother," Walt says.

It'll be at least an hour before Grandma Rena arrives, probably longer. Lucia wants Walt to stop talking, but he won't shut up. She goes over and picks up the knife, a little blot of blood on the tip. "I'll stab you again if I need to," she says to Walt.

"You'd do me like that?"

"Shut up."

She goes back to the couch and sits down, holding the knife against her knee. She has the thought that she might actually have to stab him again. She'll do it if she needs to, if he makes a move on her. But right now he's pretty still, except for his big mouth. He groans and calls out the names of his friends. She watches what's on TV, a woman in a black dress, holding flowers, wiping tears from her cheeks, giving a speech of some kind. It's comforting. Lucia's taken Spanish the last two years; she catches a word here and there.

"I wish your mother would've had an abortion," Walt says. "Then I wouldn't be dying of this stab wound."

"Just shut up," Lucia says. She hasn't prayed in forever, but she prays now for the time to pass, for Grandma Rena to show up soon and take her away from this. She taps her foot against the floor. She sings Mariah Carey's "It's Like That" under her breath.

WOLFSTEIN

Wolfstein calls a car service in nearby Central Valley and tells the guy she needs a ride into the city. He's reluctant at first, explaining he's been burned on a few big fares recently, but then he caves when she puts on the heavy-duty charm.

Rena's frantic, anxious. Lucia gave her almost nothing to go on. Just told her that she's in trouble. But Rena's also clearly excited. She keeps saying, "Lucia said she *needs* me."

The car service picks them up in front of the motel fifteen minutes later. They get in the back seat of this scratched Lincoln Town Car that smells of apple cinnamon air freshener, Wolfstein holding her bag in her lap, Rena giving the driver the address Lucia gave her, fiddling with the phone, seeming to expect another call.

The driver has hairy ears and wears a battered blue baseball cap with the logo torn off. His name is Dennis. He's got a city accent. He says he moved up to Tuxedo with his sister about ten years ago and then they moved to Monroe and then Central Valley. He complains about Kiryas Joel. He's got on a green tank top from a charity golf tournament. Swirls of hair dot his shoulders like frosting. He beeps at a van that's driving erratically as they get onto the Thruway headed south. He apologizes for losing his cool. He says he's tired of this place, tired of everywhere, tired of his sister, tired of driving, tired of being tired.

Wolfstein puts her bag on the seat between her and Rena and then sits forward, reaching out and rubbing Dennis's neck. "I'm Wolfstein, and this is Rena."

He laughs. "Well, Wolfstein, I'll fall asleep, you do that."

But she continues. "I'll keep you awake by talking. We want to get where we're going in one piece."

"I'll get you where you're going. You've got the magic touch, you know that? I'm already feeling looser."

Wolfstein keeps at it.

Rena's looking down at her lap. "Should I stop and get her something? As a peace offering, you know? She used to love stuffed bears." She's asking Wolfstein, but she's really just saying what she's thinking out loud.

"My bet is she's a little past that stuffed-bear phase," Wolfstein says. "I say let's just get there. This is a rescue mission, right?"

Rena's fidgeting, lacing her fingers together in her lap. "Yeah, of course. You're right. What the hell was I thinking?"

"It's okay," Wolfstein says. "Don't beat yourself up."

"You're a good egg," Dennis says to Wolfstein from the front. "You're good at making people feel better, huh? That's a rare talent. I've known you fifteen minutes, I already feel like a million bucks. You hitched?"

"I'm not, Dennis," Wolfstein says.

"You enjoy single life too much; I get it. Me too. I go to the bar when I want. I come home when I want. I drink what I want, eat what I want, watch the shows I want to watch. Guys I know who're married, their wives watch the Hallmark Channel nonstop. Give me some cop shows. *The Shield*, you ever hear of that one? My favorite show right there."

Wolfstein moves to Dennis's hairy shoulder blades. When she's done, he thanks her again. She claps her hands together and says it was her pleasure.

They're on the Tappan Zee Bridge. Wolfstein looks out at the light hitting the Hudson River. This bridge makes her nervous. It reminds her of going to and from Nyack with Aunt Karen. She was maybe nine or ten when it opened in 1955. She remembers seeing the river as full of possibilities, how it seemed so everlastingly big at this spot, so hopeful and beautiful. She remembers how she thought she could see history—actually *see* it—when she looked down at the water and the shore and the trees. Ghosts moving. Boats that weren't there. Smoke from fires. She also remembers worrying, more than she ever had on any other bridge she'd ever crossed, that this one would collapse with her on it and that she'd be in the river in a car, banging on the window, gasping for breath, and that her world would end that way, that her pain would disappear into the deep darkness.

"I hate this bridge," Dennis says, seemingly just to say something. "What a piece of shit. It's gonna fall apart one day soon. Mark my words."

"I believe you," Wolfstein says.

Dennis drums the steering wheel. He turns on the radio. "You ladies mind a little music?"

"Fine with us."

He scans the stations, settles on oldies. Bobby Vinton's "Roses Are Red" is on. Dennis sings along. "My mother loved this song. My mother and all her sisters. She had six sisters. They're all dead. My mother's dead. Girl I dated in high school, Sophie, she loved this one, too." A beat. He slams one hand against the side of his head, his palm flat against his ear. "I'm sorry. Here I go again."

Wolfstein's hand is on his shoulder again. "What's wrong with remembering a thing like that? Loosen up a little. You're fine."

"I just don't want to burden you with my bullshit. I hear a song, I start blubbering about my old lady. You're gonna think my backbone's made of matzo, that's what. Crumbles like *poof*." Another beat. "Who am I even?

I'm the driver. 'Drive, dummy,' that's what you gotta say to me. 'We don't want to hear about what your mother had for breakfast in 1958 or who you went to the dances at Cardinal Hayes with.'"

"You went to Cardinal Hayes?" Wolfstein asks

He nods. "Big time. You're not from the Bronx, are you?"

"Riverdale."

"No shit."

"It's true. You're from Concourse?"

"Mott Haven."

"Tell me"—Wolfstein nudges forward in her seat again—"you don't happen to smoke, Dennis sweetie, do you? I lost my pack somewhere along the way."

Dennis gives her a big smile in the rearview mirror. "Do I smoke? I was born smoking." He punches open the glove compartment and takes out a pack of Marlboro Reds and passes it back to Wolfstein. He pushes in the car lighter and waits for it. "I need one, too. How about your pal? She's quiet. She needs a smoke, maybe?"

Wolfstein holds up a cigarette. "Rena?"

Rena shakes her head. "Maybe I should get her a necklace. Just a little something."

Wolfstein hands Dennis a cigarette and pops one between her lips, keeping it there until Dennis gives her the stubby lighter. She lights hers, the cherry sticking to the coils, and then reaches into the front and lights Dennis's for him. He's grinning as he draws in on the cigarette, like this is the sexiest thing he's ever experienced. Soon, the car is full of smoke.

Rena zooms down her window.

"You were in Monroe; you know what the hubbub was there?" Dennis asks. "I heard a lot of sirens, caught snippets on my radio. Something about a bus."

"No idea," Wolfstein says.

"Well, what's in Brooklyn, you don't mind me asking?"

"Rena's from there."

"One's from the Bronx, one's from Brooklyn, so what're you doing up in the sticks?"

"We're having an affair, me and Rena here. Running around behind her husband's back. Had to get an out-of-the-way motel." Wolfstein's straight-faced.

Dennis's eyes are slits in the rearview mirror. He draws in deep on his cigarette. His body language changes, shoulders slumped, hands tighter on the wheel. "You're having fun with me."

Wolfstein reaches out and takes Rena's hand. It's cold. What she's said hasn't even registered on Rena's face. "Nope, sweetie," she says. "We're lovers, and we just rampaged that shitty little motel room."

"You two are 'lovers,' huh?" Dennis says, his eyes darting between them in the mirror, studying their expressions for proof it's a joke. "What a word."

"We sure are. Right, Rena?"

Rena's lost in thought, not even paying attention. "What? Sure. Right."

Dennis blows a line of smoke at the mirror. "Describe it to me. What happened back in that room."

"You want a play-by-play?" Wolfstein asks, smiling. She exhales her own cloud of smoke over Dennis's shoulder, and it dissipates in a puff against the windshield.

Rena coughs, shoos smoke away from her face, seems to shake into awareness. "What are we talking about? Where are we?"

"We're still on the Thruway south," Wolfstein explains. "Good old Dennis here wants us to talk about our time at the James Motel." She winks.

Dennis's face gets flush. "Don't get me wrong. I don't mean no disrespect. I just got the feeling you were having fun with me."

"I don't understand," Rena says, obviously oblivious, her mind full of Lucia. "What's going on?"

"You two are having a little love affair, huh?"

"What?" Rena seems confused, as if Dennis is talking in a language she doesn't quite understand.

Wolfstein reaches over the bag and elbows her in the arm. "We're in love. Really in the thick of it. Don't tell her husband, okay?"

"It's true," Rena says.

"Hot and heavy, that's what I told him."

"Good for you," Dennis says. "God bless. To each his own. I'm happy for anybody who has passion in their lives, cheating or no. Woman like you, I bet your old man's good for nothing. Chased you away."

"Something like that," Rena says. And, after a pause, her eyes drift to Wolfstein and she continues: "When she touches me, I feel alive in a way I haven't in a long time."

Wolfstein looks at Rena and can't tell if what she's saying is genuine or if she's suddenly playing along, too. She realizes, she guesses, that sometimes people say something they don't think they really mean but realize they actually do mean while in the act of saying it. Maybe her hands on Rena *mattered*. Rena, after all, hadn't been touched by loving hands in a long-ass time.

"That's lovely," Dennis says, tearing up. "Just lovely. I wish someone felt that way about me. You know, I can attest to the power of her touch. That little massage she gave me—wow. I felt electric. You were okay with that, right? I'm sorry if I was out of line."

"You were fine," Wolfstein says. "Rena's not the jealous type."

"I wish someone felt that way about me," he says again, and now he's crying harder, choking on it, trying to hold back but finally letting it come. He jerks the car over to the shoulder, jolting Wolfstein and Rena around in the back. He stubs out his cigarette in the ashtray and tries to compose himself. "Fucking stupidhead, that's all I am."

Wolfstein's cigarette had almost been knocked from her hand, but she's still holding onto it, and somehow the tip is two inches of trembling ash. "Don't take it so hard, sweetie."

"Matzo, that's what my backbone's made of."

Rena's sitting up straight, looking at the phone in her palm. "Can we get moving, please? I need to get to Lucia."

Dennis settles down a little, paws at his eyes with the heels of his hands. "Who's this Lucia?"

"Her granddaughter," Wolfstein explains.

"You should keep a kid out of whatever mess you're making." A beat. "Forget it. Who am I to talk? I'm the king of messes. I'm sorry. Forgive me. You don't need this out of a driver."

He puts the car in drive, and they roll back into the flow of traffic. Wolfstein smokes out the window, squishing the filter against the glass when she's done and letting it drop to the whooshing blacktop, a smudge of ashes left behind.

In the city, they hit congestion. Dennis has clammed up. It's just the radio, the heavy sound of the brakes, the Town Car's chassis squeaking occasionally, horns and sirens outside. They cross the Willis Avenue Bridge and get on the FDR. After that, it's the Brooklyn Bridge, where an ambulance missing its back doors almost stalls out in front of them. The bridge feels like a cage.

Truth is, it's been a long time, a very long time, since Wolfstein's gone into Brooklyn, let alone driven into it. Could be it's been more than thirty years. And, even then, was by subway. She had a friend, Nellie, who lived in Greenpoint back then. And she briefly dated a guy, Benny O'Quinn, who bartended in Red Hook and had tattoos on the backs of his hands that read RED MEAT and COLD BEER. That was a brief fling. Two weeks of tequila nights and late breakfasts at greasy spoons.

It sometimes hurts to think of herself as young, as flitting around with so much dark, beautiful energy, like a bird hitting windows. Her hands were young, her eyes, her legs (*this pain's getting worse*), her nails, her hair, everything younger. In the place those memories live, she sometimes sees flashes of faces she no longer has names for. She often wonders what's real and if there are places where dreams have mixed with memories, or even overtaken memories, to make something that never happened seem like it did. Like Hector Cruz from her third movie. He doesn't even seem like he could've been. They'd balled on a Greyhound bus, as in a dream.

Where they're going, Wolfstein's never been. Dyker Heights. They're on the BQE and then the Gowanus and then the Belt Parkway, the traffic moving tidily now. She's looking out at billboards and brick buildings, covered in graffiti. She's looking into open windows. She's looking out at the water, the Narrows, the Statue of Liberty. She thinks of that Lou Reed song, "Dirty Blvd": "Give me your hungry, your tired, your poor, I'll piss on 'em. That's what the Statue of Bigotry says." She'd met Lou once. He was wearing sunglasses and had a mullet. He was detached, not very friendly. He said he'd seen her movies. He called her the Actress, real snide, like she wasn't an actress at all.

They get off the Belt at Thirteenth Avenue.

Rena's bopping around in her seat now, checking the phone. Wolfstein's still hung up on what Rena said about feeling alive at her touch. Dennis has flung one arm over the back of the passenger seat. He's singing under his breath.

Wolfstein reaches into her bag on the sly and plucks out three hundred bucks. She reaches into the front seat, the bills folded in her hand, and she places them gently on top of the ashtray, hoping Dennis won't comment.

But he does. "What's that? It's too much."

"You went above and beyond," she says.

"I don't need no charity."

"It's not charity."

Dennis lets out a sigh.

"Plus, it could be I'm interested in buying more of your time," Wolfstein explains.

"Interested how?" Dennis asks.

"We run into the place we're going, you keep the car running."

They're driving up Thirteenth Avenue, Dennis constantly braking behind a city bus, groaning, double-parked cars everywhere, pedestrians dashing from sidewalk to sidewalk between cars. Rena's saying the address from Lucia out loud over and over, as if she'll lose it if she doesn't.

"I'll wait for you, sure," Dennis responds after a lag.

"Thanks. You're a pal." Wolfstein puts her hands on his shoulders again, but he bristles at her touch this time.

A couple of blocks later, Dennis pulls to a stop at the curb in front of a Laundromat with blinds lowered in the window to keep out the sun and a weathered, hand-painted blue sign that reads WASH DRY FOLD. He's parked at a hydrant with his blinkers on.

Rena says the address one last time.

"This is the place," Dennis announces.

No way Wolfstein's leaving her bag in the car. It was a mistake to leave it with Rena back there in the room even for a few minutes, testing fate. She's not a hundred percent on Dennis sticking around. She gets out, hauling the bag with her, the door screeching open, and Rena follows fast on her heels.

"You're gonna wait, right?" Wolfstein asks Dennis.

He nods without looking at her.

She slams the door.

Next to the Laundromat is a dollar store. Rena sees it and darts inside. Wolfstein's on her trail. The store is narrow, with overcrowded shelves, colorful towels hanging from racks, blow-up pool toys, weird little dancing dogs. Boxes are full of keychains and cheapo rings and those boogery things kids throw against walls to see how long they'll stick. Rena's on her tiptoes, searching the aisles.

"What are you doing?" Wolfstein says.

"I just want to get her a little something," Rena says.

A display case next to the counter is full of small stuffed animals. The woman behind the counter looks like a tragic fortune-teller. She's wearing a headscarf and a red blouse and has big hands. She's writing on a yellow legal pad. Her nametag reads MY NAME IS . . . MAD DOG, ASK ME ANYTHING.

Rena approaches the display and digs through the stuffed animals. She finds a brown bear with a pink tiara and little pink sewn-on heart in the middle of its chest and a crooked smile made of thick black stitching.

Rena puts it on the counter and asks Wolfstein to lend her money to pay for it.

"You're going with the bear anyhow, huh?" Wolfstein says, coughing up the dough.

Rena shrugs. "I think she'll like it. I'm her grandma. It's a grandma thing to get it."

"Your call."

"Excellent choice," Mad Dog says.

They walk back outside. Rena stands in front of a door marked with the numbers from the address Lucia gave her. Wolfstein's guessing her biggest hope right now is that Lucia is still there, that she hasn't bailed or had second thoughts, or—even worse—that she hasn't gotten into some new kind of trouble. She can also tell that Rena's deeply confused about whose place this is, about why Lucia would even be holed up in some scrubby second-floor Dyker Heights apartment. She's not asking those questions now, though; she's just clutching the little bear to her chest. Wolfstein understands why.

Just as Rena places her hand on the knob of the door leading to the apartment, Wolfstein puts the bag under her arm and touches Rena's cheek. "It'll be okay," she says.

Rena nods. "Thank you," she says.

Wolfstein looks back toward the street. Dennis is still sitting there in the Town Car at the hydrant. Rena opens the door, and they head up a staircase that smells of mildew. "It'll be okay," Wolfstein says again, this time to Rena's back.

RENA

When Lucia opens the door, Rena reaches out and embraces her grand-daughter. The girl's wearing an oversize backpack. She's pale, shaken. She takes the hug.

"I'm glad you've got new sneakers," Rena says. "You gave me such a scare. We need to stick together."

"I'm sorry," Lucia says.

Rena pulls back and presses the bear into Lucia's hand. "I got you this. I know you probably don't like stuffed animals anymore, but it reminded me of you when you were little. It's cute. Just a dumb little thing."

Lucia seems to be studying it. She thumbs the tiara, bites her lower lip, fights back tears. "I like it a lot."

"What is it? What's wrong?"

For a minute, it's almost as if Wolfstein isn't there—she's quiet behind Rena—but then she steps into the apartment past them, closing the door, and says, "I think I see the problem."

Rena looks over near the window and sees a man sprawled there, no shirt on, a bloody shirt wrapped around his arm. It reminds her of Enzio.

The man looks to be out cold, but then he opens his eyes and lets out a prolonged moan. "Rena?" he says. "Oh, Jesus Christ. What'd I do to deserve this day? I gave her the knife. I've always gotta be a smart guy."

Rena recognizes him then. "Is that—?"

"My father," Lucia cuts in.

"Walt Viscuso? What happened here, Lucia?"

"I found him and then . . ."

"And then the little turd knifed me," Walt says. "Look at me. I'm dying here, Rena. Call my pal Gilly. His cousin's a medic. We've been sitting here over an hour. I'm bleeding out. My vision's all blotchy."

"He gave me the knife to protect myself," Lucia says. "And then he acted like a creep. He just shouldn't have given me the knife. I would've just left. All he wanted was money."

Wolfstein chimes in: "Does anyone know you're here?"

"No. But he has friends. He talked about his friends. Maybe they'll just show up?"

"Just call Gilly," Walt says again. "We'll forget all about this."

Wolfstein goes over and leans over Walt and starts to unwrap the shirt. He protests, tries to push her hands away. She gets the shirt undone and shakes her head. "It's nothing. A little cut. He'll be fine."

"A little cut?" Walt says. "This is deep, sister."

"We've got a car downstairs," Wolfstein says to Rena and Lucia. "Let's go. Look at this place. No one cares about this guy. He can get up and call his pal."

"Okay," Rena says, without hesitation.

"I can't believe I stabbed him," Lucia says. She's holding the stuffed bear tight around the neck.

Rena walks over to Walt. The TV is on behind him, a news show in Spanish. She doesn't remember much about Walt, in all honesty. He wasn't someone Adrienne brought around. He was another secret she had. That long hair. The loud music he played. Rena couldn't believe it when she found out he was the guy who knocked Adrienne up. And Vic, he went absolutely bonkers. He wanted the guy's head on a stake by the Verrazano tollbooths. It was her and Richie—this before she knew of Richie's history with Adrienne—who talked Vic down and said the guy wouldn't be a problem, he'd stay out of the picture, the kid would be fine and better off. Vic would be her old man.

Early on, Rena had always imagined and hoped that Adrienne would wind up with a gentleman, someone who'd hold doors open for her and pull out chairs, someone who shaved every day and got his hair trimmed once a week. Of course, Adrienne had raged against her mother's hopes. Walt represented something vastly different. He was ugly. He was a nobody. Rena knew his parents a little back then. She wonders if they're still alive. They were terrible people. They drank and they partied, and the father had done some jail time for robbery, and word was he was always peeping on young girls. The mother was a diabetic with bleached-blond hair who wanted everything free.

"You were never worth anything," she says to Walt now.

"Oh, that's really nice, Rena," Walt responds through clenched teeth. "I'm sitting here, *wounded*, and you take the time to insult me. Thank you."

"I just wanted to see who he was," Lucia says. "I wanted to see if I was anything like him, if I could be his daughter."

"Protecting yourself was the right thing," Rena says.

"You've had a fucked-up couple of days, kid," Wolfstein says. "I mean, we all have, but you especially."

"Let's just go," Rena says.

"I have the money in this backpack," Lucia says.

"I don't care about the money. I care about you."

"Leave me a few bucks, kid," Walt says. "Come on. It's the least you can do. Medical bills and whatnot."

They leave the apartment, Wolfstein grabbing her money bag, Walt wailing on and on about Gilly and about feeling like he's going to pass out.

When they get outside, Dennis's Town Car is still there. People flooding in and out of the Laundromat pay them no mind. No one can hear Walt. Or they just don't care. They all get in the back of the Town Car, Lucia smooshed between Rena and Wolfstein, holding the bear now like she would've as a kid, cradling it against her neck, her pack in her lap.

"This is the famous Lucia, huh?" Dennis says, taking a look at Lucia in the rearview.

"Who's he?" Lucia asks.

"He's the driver," Wolfstein says.

"Nice to meet you, kid." He jolts them away from the curb, cutting off a flashy little sports car, and then looks over his shoulder: "So, where am I taking you ladies now?"

"My house," Rena says. And then to Wolfstein: "We'll be fine there, right?"

"For a little while, I bet. We're just people who have to answer some questions eventually, anyhow."

"I don't have any food at the house. We'll have to stop at Meats Supreme. Are you hungry, Lucia?"

Lucia nods.

Rena smiles. "Good. I'll get everything. I'm excited to be able to feed you. You like braciole? I'll make braciole and baked ziti and sausage and peppers. We can stop at the bakery and get some cookies, too. Rainbows, black and whites, linzer tarts. How's that sound?"

"That sounds so good," Lucia says, settling down a little, leaning close to Rena, almost like someone who desires to be embraced.

Dennis, in the mirror, looks confused. "What about what youse were talking about earlier? Your husband? You *were* messing with me."

"Just a little," Wolfstein says. "I was. Rena was just going along with it. Rena's a widow."

Dennis slaps the wheel and laughs. "Boy, you're a piece of work. You really are." He sings "Roses Are Red."

Lucia nudges closer. Rena puts an arm around her and says, "It's okay. Grandma's with you. There's no more trouble coming."

They get on the Belt again to head to Rena's neighborhood. When they exit, they're down by Ceasar's Bay Bazaar. The water's right there—Gravesend Bay—and Rena looks all around: the tennis courts, the promenade, the big lot by Toys "R" Us and Kohl's and Best Buy. She's not even sure what time it is, maybe late afternoon, judging by the sun. The light on the water is pretty. So is the Verrazano, powder blue against a darker blue sky, speckled with light and shadows. When the bridge was built, she remembers thinking it was the most important thing that had ever happened in the world.

Rena tells Dennis how to get to the store. They drive up Bay Parkway. Dennis makes a left at Eighty-Sixth Street and parks across from Meats Supreme. "I'll be right back," Rena says. "I'm just going to get a few things."

"I'll come with you," Lucia says, pulling on her backpack and setting the bear behind her on the rear dash.

In the store, they look over the cheeses and meats first. Rena fills a cart with everything she needs as she scans the shelves and coolers, insisting she doesn't have anything at home. Parmesan cheese, eggs, Italian bread, mozzarella, provolone, parsley, olive oil, flank steak, ground chuck, macaroni, bread crumbs, cans of crushed tomatoes, garlic, basil, ricotta, Italian sausage, bell peppers.

Wheeling the cart over the sawdust-covered floor, Rena points to a wall over by the fish counter. "There's Papa Vic," she says.

"Huh?" Lucia says.

"His picture."

They walk over and stand in front of it, as if taking in a painting at a museum. It's the one of Vic with Scorsese, De Niro, Pesci, and Sorvino—that's the other actor's name, she finally remembers. Two of Vic's henchmen, Steve Z. and Willy Zip, are on the edges of the shot, their arms crossed. Vic looks so proud and happy. He's smiling as big as she's ever seen him smile, and that's saying a lot. Sloppy, faded signatures are etched across the bottom part of the picture.

Lucia reaches out and taps her finger against the glass over Vic's face, leaving a smudgy print. "Cool," she says.

"I was thinking this should be mine," Rena says. "I have a lot of stuff, a lot of pictures of Papa Vic, whole albums, but I don't have anything like this."

"Take it."

"You know what? I think I will." Rena reaches up and plucks the picture off the wall. It's an old frame, hanging on a crooked nail with a piece of piano wire. The guys behind the fish counter don't see her. She zips opens Lucia's backpack and wedges it on top of the money, taking a couple of hundreds for the groceries while she's in there. Lucia watches over her shoulder as Rena deals with the zipper.

The spot on the wall is bare, a dusty outline where the picture was.

"I feel good about this," Rena says.

They walk up to one of the registers to check out. The registers aren't in view of where the picture was. No one here could've seen her. Nina is the clerk. Rena knows her from the store and church. It occurs to her then that word about what happened to Adrienne and Enzio could've reached here. She looks for some sign of sympathy or gossipy indulgence in Nina's face but sees only the blank stare of someone who can't wait to get off work.

"How're you doing, Nina?" Rena asks, small talk she probably wouldn't make if not for the picture.

"Every day gets harder," Nina says. "My husband, you know him? He crapped the bed last night. You believe this? 'Dan,' I says, 'this is how wars start.' He's fifty years old, not a hundred. What kind of guy craps the bed? I married wrong, and I married dumb."

Rena's reaction is a mix of a downturned grin and a confused sneer.

"Who's this?" Nina says, cocking her head at Lucia, quickly ringing up items.

"My granddaughter, Lucia."

"How grown up."

Lucia forces a smile.

"How're your grandkids?" Rena asks.

"Don't get me started. One's stupid as bricks. The other's ugly as sin. Takes after the father. He's a bum, a loafer. My daughter brings home the bacon."

Rena nods. Nina wouldn't normally bring up Adrienne, knowing they're on the outs, so that makes Rena think the news hasn't gotten here yet, or maybe it's just that no one around here cares enough to spread the news.

When they're all done, paid up, bags packed, Rena and Lucia head to the car, careful crossing the street with their arms full of groceries. Dennis pops the trunk. They get in. Wolfstein's sitting in the front now. "What's the good word?" Wolfstein says.

"I took it," Rena says.

"Took what?"

"Vic's picture."

Lucia has the backpack in her lap again. Rena unzips it and withdraws the picture and passes it up to Wolfstein.

"I'm proud of you," Wolfstein says. "Which one's Vic? Let me guess." Her finger passes over the obvious *nos*—Scorsese, the famous actors—and she seems to inherently know it's not the greasy, too-young henchmen, so she points to Vic.

"That's my Vic," Rena says.

"Handsome," Wolfstein says.

"He was, wasn't he?"

"Looks like a guy who could take care of things."

"That's . . . that's Vic Ruggiero," Dennis says, almost choking on his words. "You were married to Gentle Vic? What am I involved in here?"

"Can you take us over to Elegante on Avenue U?" Rena asks. "While we go get some cookies, Wolfstein can fill you in."

They drive to Elegante, her favorite bakery—and Vic's longtime favorite, too—between West Sixth and West Seventh. Vic grew up in a house right around here, on Lake Street, with his three brothers and two sisters. They're all dead, have been for a long time, mostly of natural causes, except for his brother Alfredo, who was poisoned with lye by his whackjob girlfriend in 1972 on the Feast of the Immaculate Conception. The Ruggiero house was always full of action: Vic's brooding mother, his piano-mad brother Pasquale, his father at the kitchen table with a bottle of vermouth.

Again, Lucia accompanies her, while Wolfstein starts talking to Dennis about the insanity of the last two days. They pass a newsstand on the way in and see the headlines. The *Post*'s is BRONX BLOODBATH. In the *Daily News*, it's SILVER BEACH SLAYING. Both feature pictures of Wolfstein's house, along with mugshots of Crea and Richie Schiavano and smaller pictures of Adrienne, Bobby, and Enzio. The picture of Adrienne, Rena's not sure where it's from. Maybe her driver's license. Rena steers Lucia away.

The bakery glows bright. The girl behind the glass counter wears a cap and speaks in broken English. She's from Italy—Calabria, Rena remembers—and she's got a sweet smile. Rena tells Lucia to pick out whatever she wants, and all her energy goes into deciding. When she says something looks good, Rena tells the girl to put it in a box. Rainbows, S cookies, pignolis, sesame biscuits, savoiardi. The girl sprinkles powdered sugar on top, weighs the box, and ties it with baker's twine. Rena gets a couple of black and whites and linzer tarts in a bag and then pays with what's left over in her pocket from Meats Supreme.

Back in the car, Dennis has clearly been rattled by Wolfstein's report. "What're you going to do?" he asks Rena, but he means it for all of them.

"We're going to have a nice dinner," Rena says. She wonders how much Wolfstein told him, if she told him about the money. Between Lucia's backpack and Wolfstein's nest egg, there's got to be close to a million dollars in the car, which is astounding. If anyone's coming for anything, it's the money. But that thread may be lost with Crea and Richie gone. It wouldn't be that hard to put two and two together. But who could know that they have it?

Anyhow, in Rena's current frame of mind, she can't help not caring about the dough. She's so glad to have Lucia back. That's what really matters. And she's grateful as hell for Wolfstein.

"You can come, if you want," she adds.

"To dinner?" Dennis says.

"Sure. I'm gonna cook up a storm. My greatest hits. Baked ziti, sausage and peppers, braciole. Cookies for dessert."

Dennis looks at Wolfstein. "That's okay with you?"

"You've been pretty good to us," Wolfstein says. "You don't have anywhere to be, hang on for a bit. Never quite know where you'll wind up with this crew."

They drive back to Rena's and park in the normally empty driveway. Rena looks over at Enzio's, at his freshly vacant driveway. If the cops have been there, and she's sure they have been, they're not treating it as a crime scene.

Her house is the same. She'd honestly wondered if she'd ever see it again. She certainly couldn't have imagined that this fiasco would end with her cooking at home for her granddaughter, a new pal, and a strange cabbie with hairy shoulders.

Dennis helps them carry in the groceries. Lucia remembers her bear on the rear dash. Wolfstein has her bag and the picture of Vic from Meats Supreme.

Rena checks the mail. A copy of *The Tablet*, her electric bill, her gas bill, some circulars, and a business card for a Detective Rotante from the 62nd Precinct with illegible scribble under his printed contact info. She's not sure what they know, how much they've pieced together, if they think she's just a mother they're delivering bad news to or what. Either way, this Rotante—or someone else—will be back.

The house is cool, quiet. They settle in the kitchen. The flowers Enzio brought her are wilted in their vase already. Rena drops the mail on the counter and puts the eggs and cheeses and meats in the fridge. Everything else she keeps out on the counter.

Wolfstein props the Vic photo on the counter by the stove, under the phone.

Lucia drops her backpack in the living room and looks at all the pictures on the wall. Rena joins her and watches as she takes them in: Rena and Vic at their twenty-fifth wedding anniversary dinner at Colangelo's on Stillwell; a picture of them embracing at Gershwin's on their first visit; Adrienne as a baby, wearing a silk bonnet; Adrienne's sixth-grade class picture, her hair in a ponytail, her eyes bright and happy.

"That's my mom?" Lucia asks, pointing to the baby and then to the sixth-grade girl.

"Who else?" Rena says.

"I never pictured her as a kid."

"She was a sweetheart. I have a million more albums. Pictures of me and Papa Vic, pictures of your mother's birthday parties, her Communion and Confirmation, her school plays, everything. We can look at them after dinner."

"Okay."

"I'd like to take you to Papa Vic's grave, too. We can spend an afternoon there, have a picnic, bring some bread and cheese."

"A picnic at the cemetery?"

"It'll be like having a meal with him. You can tell him all about yourself."

"Tell him how I stabbed my father."

"He'd understand."

Rena shows Lucia all around the house and asks if she remembers it at all.

"I've been here?" Lucia says.

"When you were little. I think you were three the last time. You were running all around. You bumped your head on the kitchen table and left in tears."

Lucia looks in Rena's bedroom, where nothing's changed since Vic. She looks in the room that was Adrienne's as a girl, the tired white walls and dusty light fixture, Adrienne's height measured in the doorway, stopping around age ten. Rena's always hung up on how quickly things end, but maybe she should be thinking more about the possibility of starting anew.

They go upstairs, which is where she'd lived with Vic when they were just married and her parents were still downstairs. The apartment's out of time. She doesn't go up there much. A bookcase in the living room is full of her photo albums. A crate of Adrienne's Cabbage Patch Kids is on the couch; Rena would sometimes, back when she and Adrienne were first on the outs pretty severely, hold them and remember how Adrienne had cared for those dolls as a girl. Vic's boxes are piled in a corner next to their little scuffed starter dinette set. More pictures on the walls: Vic in a tux on their wedding day; Rena as a bridesmaid for her cousin Vivian in Staten Island; her parents on their sixty-fifth anniversary, having pizza at Di Fara.

"What if someone comes for the money?" Lucia asks.

"I don't know," Rena says.

"I don't think we should let this driver guy know everything."

"I'm sure Wolfstein only told him some of it."

Wolfstein and Dennis are at the kitchen table downstairs, playing cards. Rena and Lucia find them in a heated game of Rummy 500. They have a scratchpad out, and Wolfstein's cleaning up. They're sharing some airplane bottles of vodka that Wolfstein must've found in the back of the liquor cabinet behind all the twenty-year-old bottles of sambuca and vermouth.

Lucia says she's tired and goes into the living room to take a nap, sleeping with the backpack and the bear huddled close to her. Wolfstein and Dennis continue their game, laughing and drinking.

Rena starts her gravy. She browns garlic in olive oil. She pours in the crushed tomatoes, careful not to let it sputter up at her. After that, a little salt and pepper and a few leaves of the fresh basil. She puts a pot of water on at a low boil. She starts on the braciole, laying out the flank steak and flattening it with a meat hammer. She remembers the steps as her mother taught them to her when she was a girl, when there was nothing better than being in the kitchen with her mother and her grandmother and her aunts. She thinks of all the recipes that are lost to time, but she's happy that some live in her and that maybe she can pass them on to Lucia. She sprinkles oil on the meat and then spoons on bread crumbs, cheese, garlic, salt, pepper, and parsley. She rolls the meat and ties it with some butcher's twine she finds in the top drawer next to the stove. She browns the meat and then deposits it in her big pot of bubbling gravy.

Wolfstein's sniffing the air. "That smells amazing," she says.

Rena is focused on her work. It feels good to get lost in making food. She always loved feeding Vic and his guys. She loved feeding Adrienne as a girl. Her hands feel raw and useful, bread crumbs and eggs clinging under her nails. The smells are strong and good.

"Can I use your phone?" Wolfstein asks, going to the rotary on the wall.

"Of course."

She dials a number. "Mo?" She pauses, laughing. "Yep, you bet. Get back to it. I'll call you later." She puts the handset on the hook.

"Is Mo okay?" Rena asks.

"She's got Pescarelli tied up in her mother's bed. They're loaded." A beat. "I was thinking, Rena, and no pressure here at all, but I was thinking we could go to Florida, if you want to get away from all this. I know you've got the house here, but I've got connections down there. My friend Ben Risk could set us up with a nice place. You've got what you got"—she winks, indicating she hasn't spilled about the money to Dennis—"and you and Lucia could really make a new life down there. Maybe our new pal here, Sweetie Pie Dennis, can drive us."

Dennis shrugs. "Why not?"

Rena looks down at the kitchen counter. It could work. If no one comes for them here, why not indeed? "I'll have to think about it. I've got to do something with Adrienne first. I'm all she has." In the rush of excitement over being reunited with Lucia, Rena's managed to push away thoughts of seeing Adrienne dead and damaged on a slab, of seeing her in a casket, of having to lower her into the ground.

"Of course."

Rena picks up the card from Detective Rotante. "A detective was here. He left this. Maybe I should call."

"He knows where to find you." Wolfstein snatches the card from her and pockets it.

"Are we tempting fate being at my place?"

"I don't think so. Maybe. Let's enjoy it. The food smells so good."

Rena starts the sausage and peppers. Another favorite of her mother's. She cooks the sausage in olive oil, the aroma of fennel filling the kitchen, and then slices some yellow and orange bell peppers over the pan. The peppers sizzle in the oil. A little salt and pepper follows. A heaping spoonful of the gravy. Stirring it with the wooden spoon. Simple.

"My mouth's watering over here," Dennis says.

Smoke rises up under the range hood. She clicks on the fan.

She puts in the ziti. When it's cooked, she empties it over a strainer, dumps it back in the pot with some gravy, an egg, ricotta, and mozzarella. Then she spreads that in a foil baking tray and puts it in the oven.

Everything is going now. It won't be too long before the meal is ready. She sits down at the table with Wolfstein and Dennis and says, "Deal me in."

They start a fresh game of Rummy 500. Wolfstein pushes one of the airplane bottles of vodka across the table to Rena. Rena, fanning her cards facedown, unscrews the cap and takes a little pull of the vodka. She doesn't feel like she'll be sick. She drinks a little more.

Playing and drinking passes the time. Everything Wolfstein says makes Dennis laugh. She's on fire. Rena's laughing, too.

Lucia comes back out about forty minutes later, claiming the good smells woke her up. If she had nightmares about any of what's happened, she doesn't say anything. She just joins them at the table and says she can't wait to eat some of this delicious food.

"It's almost ready," Rena says. She gets up and checks on everything. It's getting dark outside. She can see that through the window. A curtain is falling over the neighborhood. She hears sirens, whistles, car horns, tires peeling out.

Wolfstein and Lucia play War now, Wolfstein slapping down a triumphant king. Dennis gets up to use the bathroom and then comes shuffling back.

The clock tells Rena it's time for the ziti to come out, and the braciole has cooked long enough in the gravy. She gets plates from the cabinet over the sink, forks and utensils from the drawer closest to the fridge, napkins, glasses. She sets the table. Wolfstein offers to help, but Rena says she's got it. She collects the cards and tucks them into a slot in the wooden mail organizer hanging behind the front door.

Rena puts a pitcher of tap water on the table. Lucia sneaks a pull off one of the airplane bottles of vodka. Rena sees her and decides not to say anything. She dishes out the ziti and braciole and the sausage and peppers, spooning more gravy over everything. She passes around the bread.

The doorbell rings. Rena remembers that Dennis's car is in the driveway. She wonders if it's Detective Rotante. Or maybe it's just another real estate agent; they often come around at dinnertime, when they most expect to catch people at home, wanting to remind them that these days you can get a lot of dough for a house like this. Or maybe, God forbid, it's someone from Sonny Brancaccio's crew, putting out feelers.

"Ignore it," Rena says.

Lucia looks concerned. So does Dennis. Wolfstein reaches across the table and puts her hand on Rena's forearm.

Another ring, followed by some light pounding on the door. No voices that she can hear. After a couple of minutes of silence, whoever it is hasn't rung or knocked again, and Rena lets out a sigh of relief.

"Lucia, you want to do us the honor of saying grace?" Rena says, sitting down and wiping sweat away from her forehead with a napkin.

Dennis takes off his ball cap and chucks it on top of Wolfstein's bag on the empty chair in the corner.

Lucia hesitates and looks around, as if searching for something that could double as a prayer. "I'm thankful we're here," she says. "I hope this meal never ends."

"Amen," Wolfstein says.

Dennis says it, too.

Rena doesn't, but she smiles. "Don't forget to save room for cookies," she says. They sit around the dinner table, the tray of ziti on a crusty oven mitt in the center, the braciole on a green porcelain plate, extra gravy in a dish next to that, the sausage and peppers in her beautiful hand-painted Ricco Deruta bowl, everything still hot and perfect, and there's suddenly the music of living in Rena's old, sad house.

ACKNOWLEDGMENTS

I owe a great debt of gratitude to my agents, Nat Sobel and Judith Weber, and to everyone at Sobel Weber: Siobhan McBride; Sara Henry; Kristen Pini; and Adia Wright. Thank you all.

Tom Wickersham's input on an earlier version of the manuscript was invaluable. Thanks so much, Tom.

Thanks to my wonderful editor Katie McGuire, and to Claiborne Hancock, Jessica Case, Sabrina Plomitallo-González, and everyone at Pegasus Books.

Love and thanks to my French family: François Guérif; my translator Simon Baril; Oliver Gallmeister, Marie Moscoso, and everyone at Gallmeister; Jeanne Guyon; Laurent Chalumeau; Sébastien Bonifay and my new pals in Corsica; and to the all of the wonderful booksellers and readers I've met.

Thanks to Ion Mills, Geoffrey Mulligan, Clare Quinlivan, Claire Watts, Clare Holloway, Katherine Sunderland, and everyone at No Exit Press.

Thanks to Wolfgang Franßen and everyone at Polar Verlag in Germany.

I'm beyond thankful for the friendship and support of Megan Abbott, Jack Pendarvis, Ace Atkins, Jimmy Cajoleas, and Alex Andriesse. As Barry Hannah said, "Heaven is pals." I love you guys.

Thanks to the Farrells, Neubauers, Adlers, Clarkes, and Frawleys of Throggs Neck and Monroe, New York and to the Farrells and Orrs of San Francisco. Thanks especially to Uncle Bobby Farrell. I'm lucky as hell to have married into this family.

Thanks to my pals George Griffith, David Swider, Tom Franklin, Beth Ann Fennelly, and Tyler Keith.

Thanks to Richard and Lisa Howorth, Cody Morrison, Lyn Roberts, Bill Cusumano, Slade Lewis, Katelyn O'Brien, and everyone at Square Books.

Above all, thanks to my family: my wife, Katie Farrell Boyle; our kids, Eamon and Connolly Jean; and my mother, Geraldine Giannini. I love you all so much.

This book is dedicated to the memory of my grandparents, Joseph and Rosemary Giannini, who—I hope—would've gotten a kick out of it.

THE

A NOVEL

LONELY

WITNESS

WILLIAM

BOYLE

"With echoes of Lehane and Pelecanos, but with a rhythm and poignancy all its own."—Megan Abbott on *Gravesend*

When a young woman with a sordid past witnesses a murder, she finds herself fascinated by the killer and decides to track him down herself.

Amy lives a lonely life, helping the house-bound receive communion in the Gravesend neighborhood of Brooklyn. One of her regulars, Mrs. Epifanio, says she hasn't seen her usual caretaker, Diane, in a few days. Supposedly, Diane has the flu—or so Diane's son Vincent said when he first dropped by and vanished into Mrs. E's bedroom to do no-one-knows-what.

Amy's brief interaction with Vincent in the apartment that day sets off warning bells, so she assures Mrs. E that she'll find out what's really going on with both him and his mother. She tails Vincent through Brooklyn, eventually following him and a mysterious man out of a local dive bar. At first, the men are only talking as they walk, but then, almost before Amy can register what has happened, Vincent is dead.

For reasons she can't quite understand, Amy finds herself captivated by both the crime she witnessed and the murderer himself. She doesn't call the cops to report what she's seen. Instead, she collects the murder weapon from the sidewalk and soon finds herself on the trail of a killer.

Character-driven and evocative, *The Lonely Witness* brings Brooklyn to life in a way only a native can, and opens readers' eyes to the harsh realities of crime and punishment on the city streets.

GRAVESEND

A NOVEL

WILLIAM BOYLE

"With echoes of Lehane and Pelecanos, but with a rhythm and poignancy all its own." —Megan Abbott

In a masterful work of neo-noir, this novel expertly captures the desperation of Brooklyn neighbors who find themselves caught up in crimes of the past.

It's been sixteen years since "Ray Boy" Calabrese's actions led to the death of a young man. The victim's brother, Conway D'Innocenzio, is now a 29-year-old Brooklynite wasting away at a local Rite Aid, stuck in the past and drawn into a darker side of himself when he hears that Ray Boy's been released. But even with the perfect plan in place, Conway can't bring himself to take the ultimate revenge.

Meanwhile, failed actress Alessandra returns to her native Gravesend after the death of her mother, torn between a desperate need to escape immediately back to LA and the ease with which she sinks back into neighborhood life. Alessandra and Conway are walking eerily similar paths—staring down the rest of their lives, caring for their aging fathers, lost in the youths they squandered—and each must decide what comes next.

In the tradition of American noir authors like Dennis Lehane and James Ellroy, William Boyle's *Gravesend* brings the titular neighborhood to life in this story of revenge, desperation, and escape.